Monica Dickens, great-granddaughter of Charles Dickens, wrote over forty novels, autobiographical books and children's books. Her first book, *One Pair of Hands*, which arose out of her experiences as a cook and general servant, made her a best-seller at twenty-two, and is still in great demand. Her books reflect the varied aspects of a full and eventful life. Three years' wartime nursing led to *One Pair of Feet* and *The Happy Prisoner*. After a year in an aircraft factory she wrote *The Fancy*, and this was followed by *My Turn to Make the Tea*, about her job as a reporter on a local newspaper in the 1950s.

Marriage in America was fictionalized as *No More Meadows*, while *Kate and Emma* was the result of her involvement with the NSPCC. Her lifelong love of horses and all animals produced fourteen children's books, one of which became the successful Yorkshire TV series *Follyfoot*. *The Listeners* developed from her work with the Samaritans, and in 1974 she started the first Samaritan branch in America in Boston, Massachusetts, near Cape Cod, where she lived for thirty-three years with her husband, Commander Roy Stratton, US Navy, until his death in 1985. She then moved to a thatched cottage on the Berkshire Downs in England. She had two daughters. Penguin have published her autobiography, *An Open Book*, and many of her other works including, most recently, *Enchantment*, *Closed at Dusk* and *Scarred*. *One of the Family* was Monica Dickens's last novel.

Monica Dickens died in 1992. Among the many people who paid tribute to her on her death were John Mortimer: 'She was a wonderful person and a very funny writer, and they are in short supply'; Claire Tomalin: 'She had courage, energy, a forthright tongue and great warmth of character ... Her writing showed a breadth of understanding and an ability to create and sympathise with odd, marginal characters'; while Rosie Thomas described her books as providing 'a window into an adult world ... they told a straightforward tale dextrously and with a great deal of modest skill'.

MONICA DICKENS

ONE OF THE FAMILY

PENGUIN BOOKS

PENGUIN BOOKS

Published by the Penguin Group
Penguin Books Ltd, 27 Wrights Lane, London W8 5TZ, England
Penguin Books USA Inc., 375 Hudson Street, New York, New York 10014, USA
Penguin Books Australia Ltd, Ringwood, Victoria, Australia
Penguin Books Canada Ltd, 10 Alcorn Avenue, Toronto, Ontario, Canada M4V 3B2
Penguin Books (NZ) Ltd, 182–190 Wairau Road, Auckland 10, New Zealand

Penguin Books Ltd, Registered Offices: Harmondsworth, Middlesex, England

First published by Viking 1993
Published in Penguin Books 1994
1 3 5 7 9 10 8 6 4 2

Printed in England by Clays Ltd, St Ives plc

Chapter One

On an August evening in 1906, Leonard Morley walked home from work, the toes of his polished boots turned out in measured acknowledgement of this familiar pavement. His obliging, beardless face showed no sign that the vile, mysterious letter from the afternoon post was tormenting him from his trouser pocket.

The busy evening streets still held the heat of the day in dusty, used-up air that made him want to take off his high collar. Working men in open shirts and waistcoats had their sleeves and trouser bottoms rolled up. Even smart young City jokers, swinging off a bus opposite the Royal Oak, were in braces with jackets slung over a shoulder; but Leonard Morley, Assistant Manager of William Whiteley's great department store in Bayswater, could not remove his stuffy frock-coat, nor even carry his hat until the cross-roads.

'Rich man Whiteley is your boss,' sneered the horrible note in his pocket. 'He is filthy scum.'

Three girls from Millinery were chattering on the corner of Queen's Road and Westbourne Grove, pecking at each other like chickens, sliding their eyes about to see who was passing. When one of them chirped, 'Good night, sir!' Leonard was too preoccupied to respond. 'Good night, Mr Morley!' He turned his head and smiled, and the girls exploded in giggles as he put his stick to his hat brim in salute.

They would not have dared to hail William Whiteley, whose paternalism had a tyrannical Victorian edge. *Scum*? Never. *A vile pervert* . . . ? What a lying and slanderous attack on a great man.

Among the homeward crowds in Westbourne Grove, Leonard was greeted here and there by shopkeepers and local residents and by the well-dressed shoppers who were drawn to newly fashionable Bayswater by the wondrous Mecca of Whiteley's.

Two pouter-breasted ladies in soaring hats stopped him. 'You were absolutely right about the Chinese red divan, Mr Morley,' the older one confided.

Leonard lifted his topper and inclined his head slightly, but not far enough to seem servile in the street. 'Mrs Robbins. Miss Robbins.' Part of his art was remembering names.

'My mother is quite pleased with the divan,' the younger one condescended.

'You have made my whole evening complete, Miss Robbins.'

She believed it. In a job such as Leonard's, you were seldom suspected of having any life outside the store.

Small greengrocers and newsagents were still open, but most of the shops were rattling down shutters and padlocking iron bars across their doorways. At the five-way crossing, Bradleys had already drawn thick cream blinds over all their windows. Whiteley's plate glass was uncovered and lighted until midnight to show the inviting displays, but haughty Bradleys had not thought that passers-by might want to look at their etiolated mannequins and furs, or did not care.

Once across the wide road that was the boundary between Bayswater and North Kensington, Leonard took off his hat and ruffled up his straight sandy hair, sticky from the heat and the hat. Sportier gentlemen wore boaters in the high summer. Leonard kept to his silk top hat, which was ironed every other day by Whiteley's hatters.

He undid the buttons of his coat and waiscoat as he walked into the golden intensity of the sun along his own street, named Chepstow Villas by the Welsh property developer who had built these comfortable stucco dwellings a century earlier on the outskirts of what was then a village. He had given each its own small plot of ground, so that businessmen could live quite rurally here and drive to work in Westminster and the City. Houses begat houses. Roads became streets and were paved with tarry woodblocks. Before the end of the nineteenth century, trains and buses and the underground railway had drawn North Kensington into the sprawling metropolis.

Traces of the Welshman's rural retreat still lingered among old trees and quiet gardens. Thick-leaved, the limes and skewbald plane trees hung breathless over the pavement where Leonard walked. Front gardens were full of blossom. A bed of tall white nicotiana sent heady perfume over a wall. Tubs of scarlet geraniums . . . *Blood money!* He was jerked sickeningly back to the poisonous note.

He managed a smile and a greeting for the men walking towards him from the buses and trains at Notting Hill Gate, who stopped for a word. His friend Arthur French was just reaching the gate at No. 44 as Leonard came up Chepstow Villas from the other direction. 'Evening, French.' 'Evening, Morley.' Arthur was a policeman, not a copper on the beat nor a detective in a curly bowler hat, but an inspector, quite high up at the baronial fortress of New Scotland Yard.

'Great day, Morley.' Ebullient, talkative, Arthur French was never an inscrutable guardian of the Law. 'The court finally allowed us to exhume the body of Edwin Dryden. Yes, *that* Edwin Dryden. Husband of Theresa, who stated, "When I took him up his cup of tea, he never drank it." Why? *Because he was already dead.*'

'You'll be searching for poison?' Leonard loved the orderly parade of Whiteley's days, but he thrilled at once to the drama of domestic crime.

'Following my first instinct.' Arthur nodded eagerly, his creased troll face alight. 'Back to the churchyard. We built a shed round the grave and got the poor man away under a tarpaulin, but there were dozens of sightseers sprung up from nowhere. I had two of them taken in for questioning. Looked too familiar for my liking. How's the emporium? Have you caught that watch-lifter yet?'

'We will. One of your men was around the jewellery counters today. Big florid face like a toadstool with whiskers. Enough to scare off any thief.'

'An undercover man.' Arthur let out his brief bark of a laugh which could open his whole mobile face and then close it down into hard-jawed severity in a second; very disconcerting for a suspect being interviewed.

'Hardly.' In Jewellery this afternoon, Leonard's hand had slid into his coat pocket to close over the grey paper of the horrible note, as if the bolting, bloodshot eyes of the policeman could see through the material. He wanted to tell Arthur French about the dangerous letter, but shut his mouth on the impulse. William Whiteley was where his loyalty lay. He had got to make himself tell him first. It was Mr Whiteley's business.

Arthur put a hand on his front gate and vaulted lightly over. The puffed-out hair and sleeves of his new young wife could be seen behind the muslin at her front window. When Arthur's first wife had died three years ago, it was only the reputation of the Force that had kept him from blowing his head off. Now he was reborn.

Leonard went on past the red-brick convent school and across Denbigh Road – the nationalist Welshman again. Walking with his head thrown back to the splendour of the lowering sun, he did not see Dicky rush at him out of the open gate of No. 72, hurtling into his stomach.

'Pick up my hat, blast you!'

The boy swooped on the top hat and put it on his head, where it obliterated his eyes like a cylindrical black snuffer.

Gwen, Leonard's wife, had planted bright flowers in the urns at the bottom of the front steps. Otherwise the garden, supporting only a few indestructible plants and bushes under the plane trees and the spiky may, remained something she was going to do something about. Gwen was divinely indolent, while appearing to be quite busy. She could put on a bustling face and little trotting walk to get to nowhere in particular, or pass the back of a hand tensely across her brow, raising distracted floating wisps of hair, even while reclining, relaxed, on a sofa.

Leonard protected her too much, his older children said, but he had undertaken to do so twenty-eight years ago, when he had married this woman so blissfully unlike his mother, and it had continued to suit them both.

He followed Dicky into the outer hall, shut the heavy front door with a satisfying thud that shook the square solid house from attic to ice cellar – Master's home! – wiped his boots unnecessarily on the hotel-sized mat sunk into the floor and dropped his stick neatly among the umbrellas and parasols in the green majolica jar from Whiteley's Art Imports.

In the long inner hall, he automatically took out his watch to check it against the grandfather clock. A Whiteley's red and purple Persian carpet surrounded by highly polished russet linoleum in a trefoil motif led to a red stair-carpet in a different pattern, bordered by the thick-layered glossy cream paint that also smothered the banister posts and dados and window frames and held this house together like glue.

Whiteley's Masterpiece Prints climbed the high walls. The garlanded plaster ceiling was far above, with the chandelier chain too short, so that the hall was poorly lit in winter. The dark-brown doors were very tall, like giants' doors at the pantomime, with heavy embossed brass knobs which could work loose to foil a maid with a knee under a loaded tray outside the dining room.

In spite of Leonard's go-ahead younger sister Vera – 'Show your naked wood, for God's sake. The Queen is dead' – the wall tables were still draped with light velvet rugs under the vases of plumed pampas grass and magazines and variegated baskets for letters and gloves and cards.

Leonard went to hang up his formal braided frock-coat by the stairs. Dicky threw the top hat neatly up on to a peg and slid past his father under the coats and capes like a jungle animal towards the lavatory at the top of the kitchen steps.

6

'No,' Leonard said. 'That's the Gents.' Sacrosanct, like a smoking room.

'Aren't I a gent?'

'You use The Place upstairs.'

'That's for women and children.'

Leonard did not say, 'You are a child.' Dicky could behave like his ten years, or younger, when it suited him. Mostly, he thought of himself as one of the grown-ups, with equal freedoms.

Dicky was an afterthought – not even thought of, since Gwen had no idea that she could conceive a baby at forty. Madge was thirteen when her second brother was born in the big bed upstairs, and Austin almost sixteen. Dicky had turbulent golden hair, like his father's years ago before it thinned and dulled and flattened. His blue eyes were brighter than Leonard's had ever been.

If Leonard mused indulgently that Dicky was worth waiting for, Madge would knock him down with, 'You mean, Austin and I were substandard goods?'

'Just trial castings.'

You could say anything to Madge, because she was that rare kind of young woman who did not take herself seriously enough to put on sensitive airs or take offence. She had assumed without effort the *fin-de-siècle* independence of the New Woman, but without the strenuous oratory. She had cut her shining blonde hair this year above her ear lobes, which made her look even taller, her graceful neck longer. The short hair was not a defiant modern pose, but a genuine convenience for washing out the dirt and dust of her place of work.

Madge was an energetic volunteer at the Loudon Road

7

Settlement in the East End. While most of those who had discovered The Poor ranted about exploitation and inequality, and her rich cousin Bella up the road in Ladbroke Lodge talked earnestly about what needed to be done, Madge went ahead and did it.

Leonard had hoped to get a moment alone with his wife to tell her about the poisonous letter; but he was late home, because Mr Whiteley, who never watched the clock, had kept him talking, and now the gong called the family into the dining room.

Because Leonard and Gwen Morley had some natural good taste without worrying about what taste was, this square high-ceilinged room with embossed wallpaper and chocolate dados had never succumbed to late Victorian excesses. Since vulgarity was calming down, they were somewhat in style. The brown velvet curtains hung straight from the rail with no swags or swoops. The oak table bore only the necessities, grouped round the silver flower-boat that had been made for Leonard's father. Above, a wheel of small lights was skirted with a plain burgundy pleated silk.

'Young Will not here?' Leonard started to drink turtle soup with a vast spoon. Whiteley's, who imported turtles for their own exquisite clear soup, had just begun to stock this cheaper line, and he had brought home some tins to try.

Madge's friend and co-worker Will Morrison often came home with her for a good meal. 'He's sleeping at the Settlement dormitory now,' she said. 'It seems like a good idea. I might do that sometimes too.'

'Would that be proper, dear?'

'It doesn't matter. It's thought we could be a civilizing influence on the Stepney people.'

8

Leonard, Gwen, Dicky, Madge herself and Flora Bolt, fiddling at the sideboard, had a healthy laugh at the idea of revolutionary Madge civilizing anyone.

When the house-parlourmaid, big breathy Flora, had collected the plates, Gwen said, 'There's something not quite right about that soup.'

'It's mock, 'm,' Flora answered. 'Made of calf's head.'

'Will the customers buy tinned dishwater, Leonard?' Gwen asked, as if she had ever tasted that, or even had her hands in it.

'I told Mrs Roach she'd watered it down too much,' Flora said.

'Why did she?'

'Make it go farther, sir.'

'I brought enough home.'

'Not for downstairs.'

'My apologies.' Leonard sharpened the long thin knife and carved the gammon joint expertly at the table.

'Quite all right, sir,' Flora told him briskly. She had been with the Morleys about six years, since she had left her husband when she was twenty-five. Her policy had always been: you play fair with me, I'll play fair with you.

With the fruit, when Madge and Dicky had left the table and Flora Bolt had at last finished clattering and gone below, Leonard took the terrible letter out of his pocket, where it had weighed like lead all afternoon.

'Read this, Gwen.' The note was a thick black spiky scrawl, the handwriting probably disguised. Because the small grey envelope had been marked 'Private and Personal', one of the correspondence clerks had given it to Leonard for him to open.

9

Rich man Whiteley is your boss. He is filthy scum. He won't listen, but you can tell him he is a vile pervert and must pay for what he's done. Blood money! I demand it. Or else.

Gwen looked for her glasses in vain, read the note with her beautifully arched brows raised, then lowered them to read it through again.

'Oh dear.' She shuddered. She folded the harsh grey paper in its creases and gave it back to her husband. 'What is a pervert, Leo?'

'Well . . . it's a vicious slander. The whole thing.'

'What does W.W. say?'

'I haven't shown it to him. I've not had the heart. It's twenty years, Gwen, since those devastating fires at the stores, and four years since the laundries blaze. It's all over, the envy and hatred of local shopkeepers, and everything is going so well. The Chief's an old man, but he's still at the peak of success. He's probably the most respected man in London.'

'I'm sure.' Gwen laid her soft unblemished hand on Leonard's arm and searched her husband's face with fond, misty grey eyes. 'This is only a madman. A vicious madman.'

'I saw Arthur French on the way home, and almost told him about it. But the last thing W.W. would want is any sort of police investigation now. It's bad enough when there is shoplifting, or dishonest staff to be charged. He doesn't enjoy that as he used to.'

'Who could feel like this about him? The incendiarists – whoever they were?'

'After all this time? A disgruntled ex-employee, perhaps,

carrying an unhealthy grudge.'

'But why send this horrid thing to you?'

'To upset me, as well as the Chief.'

'But why *you*?'

'Because the Manager is away. Wait – whoever it is must know he is away. That's bad.'

'Has it upset you?'

Leonard nodded. It was hard for him to talk about emotions. The letter had also made him afraid, but he did not tell Gwen that.

'They shan't, on a beautiful evening.' She came behind him with her bare arms laid downwards along his upper arms and her imprisoned breast pressing into the back of his neck. 'Forget this stupid thing.'

'I can't. It's like a dead weight on my mind. What does it *mean*, Gwen?'

'Oh, pooh – nothing.' She had a wonderful way of banishing anything disagreeable. 'You're so hot, dear, are you ill? I'll get you some Arctic Pills.' Gwen Morley, the darling of the patent-medicine advertiser, had pills and powders for everything.

He turned his head to smile up at her. 'I'd rather take you on the river.'

'It's much too late. We'll get a cab and go to the Serpentine and stroll about in your linen hat and my girlish sailor, and people will think we are young lovers.'

Chapter Two

Leonard's older brother Hugo lived at Ladbroke Lodge, a hundred yards up the road from No. 72 Chepstow Villas, and a much grander establishment, four storeys high, with its own private gate into the desirable gardens of Ladbroke Square. It irked him that Leonard, a mere shopwalker when all was said and done, had been able to buy a key to the gardens.

Hugo, who was a financier, commanded a fair salary for amorphous duties on the board of two City companies. His wife Charlotte, born Carlotta Müller of Magdeburg, had money of her own, which compensated for the traces of Prussian speech that Hugo had gradually dislodged, along with the original version of her name. Charlotte believed in the worthy Victorian principle of: 'If you've got it, show it.' Beyond the great stone leopards, black and princely, which guarded the front steps, varnished double doors with enough brass on them to sprain a footman's elbow admitted you to a daunting hall, hung with bought trophies and tasselled weapons. Statues smirked in niches between barley-sugar pillars. Over the banister at the turn of the grand stair, a Kashmir shawl descended like a gold-encrusted waterfall.

If you were privileged to ascend the first wide flight and enter the drawing room, you would tread carefully over rugs upon rugs, all with fringes and one with a head and paws, splayed awkwardly before the marble fireplace. The high windows that surveyed Kensington Park Gardens at the front and lush Ladbroke Square at the back were rigged out in velvet and gold cords. Knick-knacks, photographs, shepherdesses, bon-bon dishes, snuffboxes – there was a forest of little tables, but nowhere to put down a teacup.

Reflected in one of the gilt mirrors, Edwin Deedes, Bella Morley's gentleman caller, still held his empty cup and saucer. Tea was over. Whisky had not been offered, although the decanter and siphon were on a side-table. Bella, her undissembling face heavy with boredom, uttered desultory criticisms of Lady Prout's ball earlier that week. She had not enjoyed herself, so it must be the Prouts' fault. Was Edwin going to Millie Scott's wedding?

'Yes, indeed.' Edwin gave a dissertation on his connection with Colonel Scott. 'Are you to go?'

'I might.' Bella looked at her mother, who said, 'We are going.'

Would Bella like to come to a private view of the theatrical costumes exhibition?

'No, thank you,' Bella said, and her mother remarked to the air, 'We had an invitation.'

'I could fetch you, my dear Bella. It would be jolly.'

Bella shook her head. Edwin Deedes, with a touch of dye on his side-whiskers and elasticated around the paunch, was at least fifteen years older than her, and out of whatever running there was.

Mrs Morley stood up and held out a fatly ringed hand. 'I must go up and change for dinner.' Although Edwin Deedes was adequate, if all else failed, to escort her daughter to minor functions like charity concerts, he need not expect to get his legs under Charlotte's table at will.

As Deedes showed a tendency to linger, she swept him towards the door with a muttered, '*Wer gehen soll, der geht,*' to which he bowed politely, not knowing that it meant 'If you're going, go'.

In the front hall, poor Edwin was asked by the butler, 'Not staying for dinner, sir?'

'I have another appointment.'

Edwin took his Homburg from the man and hurried out, as if he were late.

At No. 72 Chepstow Villas, serving dishes were put on the table, as they had always been. At Ladbroke Lodge, dinner was more elegantly handed round, *à la russe*. The butler, Hurd, was assisted by the parlourmaid Crocker. Dinner, even with no guests, which was fairly rare since Hugo liked to entertain and Charlotte liked to show off her house, was a long-drawn-out affair of unnecessary ritual and too many courses.

Bella fidgeted with the glass and silver and asked herself, as she had ever since she could remember, What am I doing here? Her mother ate immensely, after greeting what was on her plate with an upper lip raised suspiciously towards the fleshy parrot curve of her nose. In the intervals, speaking rather affectedly as she did about even very minor royalty, she told an involved story about a Middle European countess who had married someone called Prince Albert von Hoch Eisenberg und zu Auber. Hugo Morley, florid and breathing stuffily in his tight dinner clothes, made some statements on current affairs, authoritatively, which was how he stated everything, whether he knew anything about it or not.

He had to bring in the 'shrieking sisterhood' to rattle Bella. '*I* say, "Keep hysteria out of politics",' he boasted, as if no one had ever said this before.

'Politics is not the point now, Father. It's not just about the vote.'

'Then what is it about, pray?' He ate a potato without looking at her.

'Well everything. It's about women's education and property, and –'

Her mother frowned and tapped the back of a knife against her wine glass.

'And opportunity, and –'

'And neurosis. The female disease.' Her father cut meat with civilized savagery. 'They should be put away.'

'Hundreds of women are in prison.' Bella stared at him across the table. 'I'm not a fool. Talk to me seriously – please.'

'Why don't you join 'em?' This was his idea of a joke.

Charlotte laughed nervously, and said, 'Give up, Bella. Let us talk of something more wholesome.'

But Bella would never give up wanting her father to think her sensible and clever. He was proud of her elder brother Thomas. He had educated him and engineered his start in business and made over a handsome sum on his marriage. Did he not even *want* to be proud of Bella?

'I'm going to march in a procession next week,' she muttered defiantly.

'Why?' he said in his distant voice.

'Because petitions only end up in ministers' waste-paper baskets.'

'So they should.'

'Well, I'm going. They might let me carry a banner.'

Bella's mother said, 'I forbid it, child.'

'I'm twenty-three, for that matter.'

But Charlotte had found a new worry. 'What would you *wear?*'

After the raspberry *bavaroise*, Bella pushed back her chair and asked permission to leave.

'You're too restless.' Charlotte's face often wore a frown for her daughter under the padded swoop of grey hair that reared above her forehead like a breaking wave. 'Stay and have some nuts. Whiteley's has got the first hazels over from France.'

She leaned the vast slope of her bosom over the table to disparage the nuts in their fluted silver bowl, because France was suspect, since the war with Prussia, and Whiteley's too, since her brother-in-law Leonard worked there and brought down the tone of the family. 'They may be all right.'

'They gripe me.'

Bella's mother tilted her large head slightly towards the butler, but he never appeared to be interested in anything but his duties. If you addressed him during a meal, his stiff pose and detached reptilian face would be disturbed by a slight start, to show he had not been listening.

Bella got up clumsily, dropping her napkin on the floor, and worse, bent to pick it up, as if there were no servants in the room. 'I'm going to 72.'

'You spend too much time there,' her mother said.

'I'm not really going.' Bella lied easily from years of practice. 'I just said that to annoy you.'

'Where are you going, then, if one may ask?'

'To see Beatrice.' Bella named a local nincompoop on Campden Hill who was approved of.

'Her mother lent me a book about Elizabeth of Bohemia,' Charlotte said. 'You can return it.'

'Have you finished it already?'

'You can say I have.' Charlotte got along better with magazines than with books. 'It's in the morning room. And I wish you to come home before dark,' she added, as if Bella were thirteen.

The butler narrowed his eyes at Bella as she passed, and she had a muttered word at the door with the parlourmaid Crocker, who remained prim and official, although they were supposed to be friends. Bella took the Queen Elizabeth book upstairs, left it in a drawer in her bedroom and went out.

With a hand on the flat head of a princely leopard for luck, she turned right from the wide bottom step. Instead of going straight across to Chepstow Villas, in case her mother or one of her paid spies was watching, she turned right at the corner past the Ladbroke Square railings, then crossed Kensington Park Road further up and ducked back to her cousin Madge's house.

Madge opened the door. Bella could never answer her own front door, even if it was someone special like Gerald Lazenby, for whom she would like to fling open the door, flushed and welcoming. But when the big brass knocker descended, echoing off the hollow pillars, and she ran down the stairs, the butler would manifest himself silently into the hall. 'Are you dissatisfied with the service, Miss Bella?'

Madge pulled her into the welcoming, familiar hall, smelling of Ronuk polish and dinner, and took her up the stairs.

'Let's go up to my room. Mama and Daddy have gone out. I'm so glad you've come.'

From the top of the stairs, Dicky shouted, 'Bella! Come and see my construction – quick!'

No wonder Bella spent as much time as she did at No. 72. She was always welcome, sure of the love and approval she had desperately sought and never found from her preoccupied, pretentious mother and the cold, critical father who had made her childhood wretched and forced her to rely on lies and fantasy.

Ladbroke Lodge was chill and uncomfortable and oppressive. No. 72 Chepstow Villas was warm and full of life and laughter.

'I'm sorry about this toffee dress.' Bella used a word from their childhood, when they had made fun of 'toffs'. Charlotte had made Bella put on the accordion pleated silk to receive Edwin Deedes, who was nobody, but at least an unmarried male nobody.

'Oh rot, anything will do here,' Madge said, as if her cousin were in rags. Madge wore a rather grubby skirt, drooping at the back, and an old shirtwaist blouse with unpressed tucks and rolled-up sleeves. Dicky, his blithe face unwashed, was in pyjamas a size too small.

He dragged Bella off to see a complicated structure of wood and string taking up one corner of the disordered front room that was still called the nursery. As Bella began dutifully to try to understand what it was, Dicky became tired of that and demanded to play a game.

'No,' Madge said, 'Bella came to see me. You're supposed to be in bed anyway.'

'Not till we've played a game, kind, lovely Madge.'

Dicky, child king, thirteen years younger than his sister, got away with murder, but was none the less charming for it.

He chose Ludo, because it took a long time. He was very competitive, like the whole family. When Bella dropped the dice and Madge thought she was cheating against herself by misreading it under the table, she said, 'No – don't let him win.'

Bella, who was actually hoping to cheat in favour of herself, pleaded, 'He's only ten,' to sound indulgent.

'He's got to take his chances like the rest of us.'

Dicky won anyway, which got him sent off to the narrow bedroom between the nursery and his parents' room, where the bed just fitted from wall to wall on a level with the window ledge. In her bed-sitting room at the back, which used to be the night nursery, Madge made tea on her spirit stove, and she and Bella shouted back at Dicky when he called to them that a man with a wooden leg was being chased on the pavement, or the flickering gas lamp outside was going to explode, until he finally fell asleep from one moment to the next.

After they had looked in on the beautiful sleeping boy, Madge said fondly, 'One day, I'll have some of them.'

'Not girls?'

'Oh yes, some of those too.'

'Shall you marry Will?'

'Heavens no, we're much too good friends.'

'Who, then?'

'I'll find someone.' Madge was superbly confident. If she went shopping, she found the right dress at once. People were always at home if she called. The sun shone on her birthday. Men came to her because she did not look for them.

'Madge. Have you and Will ever . . . ?'

'No, silly.'

'You would tell me if you did? What it's like, I mean.'

'You'd be better off finding out for yourself.'

'When I marry . . .' Bella hoped she meant that. 'If I do. It's all right to be a single woman nowadays. Especially if you're doing something worthwhile.' She still nursed the fantasy that she would be a pioneer woman at a university and have a significant career.

'Like saving the world?' Madge smiled.

'I hope so.' Bella sat on her cousin's bed with her shoes off and stroked her bony ankles and feet, which felt more graceful than she thought they looked. 'Medicine . . . science. I was good at that at school, in any case. I might have an important role to play, if I could just get the chance.'

'You're twenty-three and you haven't done anything yet,' Madge said bluntly. She and Bella were always honest with each other.

'Where does one start? So many people are so dreadfully poor and needy while so many other people are disgustingly rich. That's too vast a problem to solve.'

'Only if nobody tries. Come to the Settlement with me and you'll see where to start – just helping a few people in small ways.'

'What could *I* do, in any case?'

'You could teach, work with the children. Play the piano. Serve lunch to the cripples. Help to feed them. Some of them can't use their hands. They put their faces into the bowl like little dogs.'

'Thank you very much.' Bella grimaced.

'There's this little girl – Angel we call her. She had been curled up in the corner of a dark room, never went out, because her mother didn't want anyone to see her. We've had her six months now, and the change! She used to grunt. Now she laughs and tries to sing. Will and I took her to Victoria Park last week. It was such a joy to watch her rolling about on the grass.'

'One child out of thousands,' Bella said, but with less conviction than before.

'I know we can't help everybody, but, oh, Bella, when something works, it's so wonderful! Come with me. Come tomorrow.' Madge leaned forward, searching her cousin's face to see if this was the right time to try to ginger Bella up again. Her short fair hair swung forward on her peachy cheeks.

Bella put up a hand to her own dull brown nest and teased out the sides with her fourth finger. 'I can't tomorrow. I've got too much to do.'

'Ladies' luncheon?' Madge shook back her hair and bared her white even teeth. 'Shopping? The poor will have to wait. You're always spouting theories, but you never *do* anything.'

Bella, who had dropped back against the pillows under the abuse, sat up to attack with some spirit. 'Well, you're a fake. *You* only go to your precious Settlement because you like it there.'

'True. Sacrifice isn't required.'

'And because Will is there.'

'True again.'

Bella fell back, irritated. After all these years of being

confidante cousins, she had not found a way to wipe the easy smile off Madge's face.

She saw her own reflection in the mirror at the foot of the bed: round puzzled brown eyes under heavy brows, strong nose and lips, short neck carrying square chin. 'Handsome' was a compliment she did not care for.

'Why can't I be pretty instead of you,' she asked Madge, 'since you don't seem to care whether you're pretty or not? Why can't I even be tall? Dumpy women are out of style.'

'You're petite,' Madge said hopefully. She got up and sat on the bed by Bella's large knees.

'You're a liar,' Bella said.

'What are you two laughing at?' Dicky appeared in the doorway, ruffled, blurred, half blind with sleep. 'You woke me up.'

Chapter Three

If Leonard Morley and his daughter left home at the same time in the morning, he often made a detour for the pleasure of her company up to Notting Hill Gate, then doubled back down Pembridge Villas to Westbourne Grove.

They walked fast up Kensington Park Road, both with the same long legs, both eager to get to work.

'Bella accuses me of only going to the Settlement because I enjoy it,' Madge told her father.

'Quite right. Like me and Whiteley's. Like W.W. himself. He'd rather be there than anywhere else. Unlike my discontented Chief Buyer, Henry Beale, who would rather be almost anywhere else, except on pay day.'

'I met him at the Cecil Hotel.' William Whiteley held an annual banquet for senior staff and business colleagues, and Madge had gone last year instead of Gwen. 'He said he was the Chief's favourite. He drank too much and had bad breath and told me – I swear he winked – that his wife is suspicious of him and the female staff.'

'She needn't be, poor woman. He's not as popular as he thinks he is.'

'Even with W.W.?'

'He butters the old man up because he's after promotion, but he's malicious behind his back. My God!' Leonard stopped dead outside the bullet-shaped window of Funeral

Furnishings, where Kensington Park Road curved sharply round into Pembridge Villas.

'My God, what?'

'A sudden nightmare thought.' But the idea of Henry Beale, pompous taskmaster and secret buttock-stroker, sending the poisonous letter, now locked in a drawer in Leonard's study, was insane. 'I must be going mad.'

'Oh, is that all? Bye, Dad!' Madge was striding across the busy street with her sunlit head up, dodging among the motor cars, buses, horse-vans and the bicycles of delivery boys towards the tube station.

Madge's Aunt Charlotte, who supposed you could throw money at the poor and leave them alone to pick it up, accused the organizers of the Settlement of self-interest.

'You are mollycoddling the masses,' she told Madge, 'to try to ward off revolution.'

But there was nothing either coddled or revolutionary about the East Enders who came to the Loudon Street Settlement looking for learning, for relief, for some shred of beauty, for new hope.

Other enterprises had been started by church groups or political reformers, and had continued to do good work while force-feeding salvation or socialism. The Loudon Street Settlement was organized as a democratic fellowship, with beneficiaries on the committee along with benefactors, and no strings attached.

The meeting hall and the classrooms and the kitchens and dormitory had been adapted from disused factory buildings, round a large sooty courtyard where games were played and races run and vegetables grown in old cisterns and bath-tubs. It was a dirty, scrappy jumble of a place, with a man's club and a children's playroom and books from the Literary Institute and classes which varied according to what was wanted, as well as teaching the basics of reading and writing. There were always men up ladders painting and hammering, and women preparing food in great steam coppers, and often some music to liven this tiny corner of the sad sordid warren of East London.

Madge's friend Will Morrison was a law student who had taken time off from his studies and did not see how he could ever go back to them, since there was so much to do here. He was an intense young idealist with fiery eyes and a red beard. Madge's mother, Gwen, said he looked like an uncarnivorous fox. Madge had learned something from him of how to keep the dream in spite of the hopeless mass of need. Will had learned something from her about realistic commonsense.

She pulled on the unbleached smock which all the women volunteers wore to disguise too decorative clothes and joined Will in the adult reading class, where he was the professor and she moved about among the battered benches giving individual help to students like laundrywoman Bridget, who was infatuated with words but could not turn them into sense, and frowning young Ted Barrett, who might go on to industrial school when he could read and write.

Madge knew Will so thoroughly that she could see through the tricks and dramatics that he used to inspire the shabby group, walking up and down, waving his arms about and exploding into poetry to drive the beauty of the English language into inarticulate men and women who were labouring over a single sentence. Three of the men who were on night shift at the dockyard were asleep. Sometimes Madge felt that perhaps she might love Will after all. She admired him, and they were very close; but there was no time for sentiment, and their equality was not a basis for love between a man and a woman, as Madge understood it.

At a trestle table together in the hall, they had soup and bread made by the domestic class. The grubby little girl Angel sat on Madge's knee to have soup fed into her. When her threshing limbs tipped over the bowl and knocked away the spoon, she turned her smashed-looking face up to Madge with a crow of laughter.

The invalid children, 'the cripples' as they were called, in their special chairs and little carts, made as much noise as anyone. Mr Firbright, the Settlement Director, banged out tunes on the propped-up piano, with a chorus around him eating hunks of bread and singing.

Madge wanted to stay with the children, but Will told her, in his quick, breathless way, in a scurry of words, 'Go and help Jack Haynes, Maddy. He's upset about something. I tried to talk to him last night, but he wouldn't.'

Jack was on his way out to the yard to take a boys' group in physical drill. He was a broad, strong fellow with bristly black hair, who had drifted here one night when he could no longer try to sleep in the Salvation Army penny sit-up, or on his feet, leaning on a rope in the doss-house. He had been wary, sullen, afraid that his cot in the dormitory was a trap. In his twenties, he was cut off from his fellow men. He had been almost completely deaf since a childhood illness. The Settlement was now his home. He was learning carpentry, and the Director gave him a little money for helping with the boys.

Madge found him ambling down an airless underground passage that led to the hot square of the courtyard. She touched his arm and he turned and gave her his bulldog smile.

'Can I come and help?' She made signs that they had invented between them.

Jack had heard and spoken and begun to read and write as a child, before he lost the sounds of the world. His speech was rough and flat and often too loud, but fairly understandable when you knew him well.

In her loose smock, Madge stood with him at the front of the disorderly group in the yard, and kicked off her hard-heeled shoes to show the exercises. The group soon broke up, hooting, into a scuffle with a ball. Jack shrugged his shoulders and started to go off, but Madge stood in front of him, the cinders of the yard prickling through her stockings.

'What's the matter?' If she faced him and spoke loud and slow with an expressive face, he could partly hear and partly guess at what her mouth was saying.

Jack looked away from her. 'Ou'sidc.' He jerked his head beyond the high wall at the end of the yard. He clasped his hands together in the sign for 'friends' they had invented.

'What friends, Jack?'

He shook his head and looked sly. He tried to leave her, but she grabbed the sleeve of his patched shirt and made him stay with her in a corner of the yard. Using a mixture of miming and Jack's distorted speech, Madge understood that cronies from his old lawless days were after him.

After he had lost his hearing, his mother had put him into the overcrowded Old Kent Road asylum where he had

27

learned a few hand signs; but they had pushed him out at thirteen to be abused as a sweatshop apprentice, until he had disappeared into the streets. Madge knew that a gang of robbers had found him useful as a lookout, because the police thought he was only a mental defective.

'Friends.' Jack made the hand sign again and grinned unhappily.

'No, Jack, you've got too much to lose.'

He looked blank. You were never sure whether he did not understand, or was pretending. Profound deafness was Jack's handicap. He also used it as an escape.

'Money.' He made the sign with his forefinger in his palm.

'Keep working here, and soon you'll have a job. You'll be paid money.'

His eyes wandered off to some dream of his old street life where there was nothing as stable as work or wages.

'Don't be a fool,' Madge said clearly.

'Me a few?' Jack repeated. He put his hand in his pocket and gave her two coppers before he ran off among the shrieking boys, kicking the ball away from them. 'Oi! Oi, Jack!'

'Oi!' he shouted, and was gone through the iron gate out on to the streets.

'How was Jack?' Will asked later before Madge went home.

'Wavering. Sometimes I feel he's like a wild animal that's been tamed but could break out at any time. In the end, we may lose him.'

'No,' Will said. 'He's come so far. Hold on, Maddy. We never give up.'

'But if it's hopeless . . .'

'Nothing's hopeless.' His eyes blazed into hers. He kissed her with warm red lips within his rough beard and held her very tightly.

'Come back with me to 72. My parents are asking for you.'

'I can't.' He loosened his grip. 'I've too much to do.' He pulled away, looking fiercely preoccupied.

Madge let him go, and went to Chelsea on the way home to enjoy inconsequential conversation and jokes with her youngest aunt, Vera, who was never serious about anything.

In the comfortably furnished upstairs consulting room, the woman's face was prettily flushed, her large eyes bright and anxious.

'The palpitations . . .' She put up a hand to her neck, where the pulse beat rapidly. 'I'm so afraid they're starting again. I'm losing my breath, I –'

'Calm down, my dear.' The man moved across quickly to sit beside her. 'It's all right. Just let me loosen your collar, so that you can breathe more easily.' He opened the fastenings at the top of her dress, and kept his hand on the white fluttering skin. 'There, it's all right, try to breathe slowly.'

With his hand on the naked swell of her breast, stroking, soothing, his voice murmuring close to the soft perfume of her cheek, he held her against him, and gradually her breathing turned to sighs of pleasure.

He congratulated himself. This was how to deal with hysterical women. Especially the pretty ones.

After lunch on that Saturday, with Leonard not yet home

from Whiteley's, although the store was closed at one, Gwen Morley was sitting with her feet up by her open drawing room window, listening to her cousin's son, who had a broken heart.

A lot of people brought their troubles to Gwen. As a rather dreamy and inactive woman, she was often to be found at home, doing nothing more preoccupying than reading a novel or sighing over the household accounts. She was kind-hearted, too kind ever to be 'out' to anybody, and too curious. Her gently smiling face invited confidences, and she did not fortify her peaceful sympathy by doing something positive, like writing a letter of reference, which might force a vacillating soul to action.

The sad young man was interrupted by Dicky, bounding down the length of the room to tell his mother that he was off down the Lane with Flora, who was going to buy greens at the market.

'All right, darling.' His mother kissed his firm shining cheek. 'Be back in time for your supper and bath before the family comes for the birthday dinner.'

'Whose birthday?'

'Aunt Teddie's.'

The boy made a vomiting sound and dashed out. Gwen stood on the small balcony to watch him run ahead of Flora Bolt in her plain market hat.

'What's "down the Lane"?' the young man asked morosely behind her.

'The Portobello Road.' She pointed towards the narrow street that ran along the side of the house. 'That's what they call it, the friends Dicky plays with down there.'

'Don't you worry about him running free in the street like that, Mrs Morley?'

'No, why should I? The Portobello Road is his village.' She sat gracefully down again with her small slender feet on a tapestry stool. 'Now Eric, my dear, go on telling me what Penelope said in her last letter.'

The young man was very pale and anguished. Gwen thought she might suggest a strychnine tonic.

The Lane was once a country road that led to a farm called Portobello, after an eighteenth-century naval victory in the Caribbean. It eventually grew into a busy winding street of houses and small shops that did a useful trade in every kind of food and household goods the neighbourhood demanded. People who thought in pennies shopped here, but so did many of those who thought in guineas and came from the middle-class colonies of crescents and villas at the respectable end of the Lane.

Every week costermongers and street traders set up their stalls in the Portobello Road, selling cut-price food and old iron and cheap clothes and bags of cloth remnants and china and knick-knacks and medals and jewellery whose origins nobody except the police worried much about. On Saturday, market day, with the fruit and vegetable barrows, and the shop goods spilling out on the pavement, and the jugglers and barrel organs among the noisy crowds, the narrow Lane was impassable to anything on wheels wider than a bicycle.

Dicky's friends Tiger and Noah were waiting for him at the first corner by the Lord Nelson. They could have come up to his house, but they preferred to keep clear of Chepstow Villas.

Noah had a thatch of dusty hair and Tiger had a shaved

head this summer, with the white marks of ringworm. They were both like monkeys, quick and daring, and a great joy to Dicky as a free-spirited change from the friends with whom he went to school.

Flora kept them close to her as long as possible by promising them pennies for liquorice strips. Further down towards the raffish end of the market, they found Flora's stepbrother Ben with one of his pals at an intriguing stall of jumbled treasures. He smoked a black cigar and wore a white scarf in the neck of his flash jacket and sharp side-whiskers under a yellow boater. He was a thrilling and powerful personage, for whom Noah and Tiger, and even occasionally Dicky, had worked as runners between the various curio stalls, checking prices and watching for known crafty characters, or the plain-clothes police who might be watching those.

After Flora had handed out the pennies to stop their clamour, the three boys left her gossiping with Ben and ran on, dodging among the crowds, beyond the market to where the Portobello Road meandered into the miasmal slums of Notting Dale.

Noah and Tiger were barefoot, in skimpy breeches. Dicky, in square flannel shorts to the knee, had taken off his stockings and boots and stuffed them under a crate at the back of Ben's stall. They ducked down an alley to peer through the gate of the little graveyard where slanted and toppling tombstones jostled each other like pebbles on a beach. Sucking the liquorice, with noses through the wrought iron, they imagined the rotting stench of local legend.

'Cor, smell them stiffs!'

Their eyes bulged to spot a spectre.

'I'd go in there,' Dicky boasted, because the high gate was padlocked.

Arm in arm, they swaggered through backstreets like a gang, playing games of chasing and hiding, and seeing how far they could get over backyard walls and outhouse roofs without being spotted and yelled at. Outside a public house, they watched two policemen lift an intoxicated man off the cobbles and take him away strapped on a cart. Noah and Tiger ran behind, jeering. Dicky did not. They were getting dangerously near the outskirts of the Potteries, the foul old brickfields where pigs were still penned in bogs outside some of the hovels, and blood and offal, Flora said, were boiled up in coppers to make rancid fat. Whose blood? A child might disappear in Pottery Lane.

'Bit early for drunks,' Dicky said knowledgeably when his friends came back looking for him. Later, after he was in bed, he might wake to hear from his front window the Saturday carousers come caterwauling down the Lane from the Sun in Splendour with howls of song and hawking coughs.

Thinking of his safe bedroom reminded him: 'I've got to go home.'

The boys punched each other and parted. When Dicky reached for his boots under the canvas back of the curio stall, Ben's pal was arguing over a vase with an angry buyer, and Ben and Flora were gone.

Chapter Four

Being a confident and adventurous character herself, Flora did not worry about Dicky. The nipper would turn up at home all right, with new tears in his clothes and new scrapes on his knees. When her stepbrother Ben vanished into the market crowds, she took a quick side-trip down Talbot Road to see her mother, stopping at the draper's to buy a length of tartan ribbon for her sister's hair, and getting the farthing change in a paper of pins.

This younger sister Violet was the shining light of No. 7 Talbot Close. She wore a self-conscious waterfall of long thick wavy hair down her back, and attended the church school and the Girls' Friendly Society. She was her mother's last focus of hope. The first son had disappeared to sea. The second son, a wall-eyed night watchman, came home to eat and sleep at the wrong times and kick the cats. Flora was in service, but she had married a drunken bigamist when all was said and done.

After Flora's father had died while serving a sentence for robbery with violence, her mother had married a sullen man who had returned from the Boer war with nerves, and never lost them for fear of being reclaimed by the Army. Daddy Watts, as he was known, spent a lot of time in the bed in the corner of the kitchen, where he could monitor everyone in the house.

'Get up and get a job,' his wife said automatically every day, like, 'Good morning.'

'A man in my condition?'

Daddy Watts was a fence, working with his son Ben and selling to market traders all over London. The room that had been Flora's narrow bedroom was always crammed with 'supplies', which came in after dark from the alley behind. Flora now lived in the narrow back-basement room off the scullery at No. 72 Chepstow Villas. Before that, she had lodged with her husband Bill, known as 'Bull' Bolt, until he kicked her out in a drunken rage. Sometimes he came here looking for her. If he ever came bothering her at Chepstow Villas, she would kill him.

'Seen Bolt about?' Flora asked her mother.

'Bolt, she says.' Her stepfather took out his short crusted pipe to spit over the side of the bed in the rough direction of a cracked chamber-pot on the floor.

'Only once, on the bus,' her mother said. 'He was in a fight with a man who wanted to go the other way.'

Bull was a 'cad', a conductor on the horse-buses who padded out his lean wages by cramming too many passengers on board and pocketing some of the fares.

'That's my man.' Flora had a permanent scar under her frizzy fringe from Bull Bolt, but there was still a tug of fascination.

'Sit down, girl, and tell me about the family.' Her mother tipped a battered tabby cat off a chair. She craved news from the higher levels, as long as it wasn't all good. 'Poor things,' she added hopefully.

'Poor things, Ma?'

'With all the responsibility of property and wealth.'

'Wealth? She'd like to hear that, Madam would, when she's paying the tradesmen's bills.'

'Ruined?'

'Rubbish.' Flora gave her great ho-ho laugh and went to the door. 'I've got to get back to lay the dinner table. I only popped in to give Vi the bit of ribbon.'

'Which is too short,' Violet said smugly.

'I'll make *you* too short.' Flora showed a fist.

'Bows are bigger now,' Violet said in her Girls' Friendly, vicar's pet voice.

'Well, yours won't be. I'm off.'

'You'd think she'd stay to help us here,' Daddy Watts crabbed from the bed.

'She came, didn't she?' Flora's mother rounded on him with a twist to her bluish mouth.

'Might as well not have.' Daddy Watts wore a kerchief round his head, slantwise, so that he could leer at you with one eye open and one half closed.

Why do I bother? Poor batty Ma. We were better off after my dad was put away. Why do women go on hitching theirselves up? Flora raged up the slope of Kensington Park Road to get back to No. 72 before Winnie Stokes, the outside parlourmaid, arrived to help with the dinner.

Dicky, who was not staying up for late dinner, wanted to have his supper in the kitchen, where there was a lot going on, which was why the cook, Mrs Roach, said No. She and her niece Tat, who worked here as housemaid and kitchen-maid, were getting together a five-course meal for fifteen. Cream soup, scalloped brill, roast turkey, Queen's pudding (for Aunt Teddie's birthday), mushrooms *au gratin*. Flora and Winnie Stokes were in and out with huge trays. Mrs Salter the charlady, who had come in to help with the washing-up, was in the basket chair by the window with a cup of hot lemonade to flush her kidneys. Dicky, grubby from the Lane, sat down at a corner of the big cluttered table and wanted bacon and fried bread. 'And mushrooms,' when he saw them in a bowl.

'Upstairs, Dicky darling.' Mrs Roach was slow-moving and not rattled, but she was breathing hard and had tied a cloth round her forehead to catch the perspiration. 'I've got cutlets cooked for you.'

'Let me stay and chop celery.' Cook took the knife away from him.

Tat, said to have been christened Tatiana because her mother had devoured romances of the Russian aristocracy, carried a tray up to the nursery. Dicky ate the breaded cutlets and fried potatoes with his fingers, wiping them on the rough side of the oilcloth table-cover.

Tat had run his bath water. He played childishly with boats until his older brother Austin arrived with his wife Elizabeth and came to hurry him up. Nostalgic for No. 72, Austin sat on his old bed, now Dicky's, to see the well-remembered view of the Chepstow Villas street through the plane-tree leaves, then slid down with him on the banisters.

It was raining when Aunt Teddie arrived with her sixteen-year-old twins for her birthday party. Her husband Ralph Wynn held up an umbrella as she came from the car in her brown lace and taffeta dress, but rain or wind was a malevolent personal affront, directed at her personally.

'You should have one of those glass arcade roofs over the front path and steps' was her greeting, as her brother Leonard came affably to greet her in the hall.

'They're ugly. The porch is dry anyway.'

'By the time one *gets* there.'

Edwina, always known as Teddie, carried negativism about with her like an armour against being suspected of enjoying life. Her barrister husband Ralph, who had originally fallen for what he thought was a girlish romantic melancholy, paid little attention to her persistent gloom, and got on with his own pleasures. Teddie, self-centred like most people who are discontented with themselves, took no interest in Ralph's divertissements.

Teddie's elder brother Hugo and his wife Charlotte were at the Albert Hall for a farewell performance by the prima donna Madame Patti.

'And what is my birthday to *that*, pray?'

'But, *we're here*, Aunt Teddie, dear.' Hugo's daughter Bella kissed her stiff aunt, which was like embracing a post. 'So don't feel insulted.' Bella had come with her brother Thomas and his wife. She quite liked this gruesome aunt, because no one else did. And she was no threat.

Aunt Vera, youngest of the generation of Hugo, Leonard and Teddie, was a little threatening to Bella, because she was smart and witty and go-ahead. She wore *nouveaux* colours and swung long Bohemian beads and drank whisky and smoked cigarettes and did not care what people thought.

Brought up with her mother's motto of *Was würden die Leute sagen* (What would people say?), Bella both craved and resented others' freedom.

Vera's husband Charles Pope was a gnome of a man with a giggle. Their two daughters were Henrietta of the sparky violet eyes and more serious-minded Helen, who saw herself as the intellectual of this bourgeois family.

Aunt Teddie's gifts were piled on the piano in the draw-

38

ing room and presented by Dicky, who enjoyed anyone else's birthday almost as much as his own. 'What's this, what's this, a beautiful scarf! Here, put it on. Look, a photograph frame, Aunt Teddie, do look, it's for you! A clock with a musical alarm – listen, it works like this.'

He had no childish jealousy, since he sunnily owned the world.

Teddie had her own version of appreciation: 'You shouldn't have.' 'That's much too grand for me.' 'I couldn't wear that colour, Vera.' 'Oh dear, did you forget I can't eat hard centres?'

'How *is* your dyspepsia, my dear?'

Gwen and Vera, with the normal hypochondria of their times, seized on the symptoms and enjoyed a conversation with Teddie about medicines, and who swore by what. Bile beans before or after meals, or during? Clarke's Blood Mix versus Steel-drops. Vera had discovered a sensational new laxative.

'It goes straight through you.'

'Don't be coarse, Vera. The young might hear you.'

'Try it, my dear. "Clean inside and out." They show a picture of Circe stepping into a woodland pool.'

There was always some new nostrum advertised, one of the miracle remedies in which they loved to believe. Pharmaceutical chemists did a better trade than doctors, who had less to offer.

Poor little Sophie Wynn, Ralph and Teddie's daughter, who was guiltily familiar with purgatives, which she took when she was punishing herself for eating rich food, listened to the talk, biting the sore skin at the corner of a nail, and watched her elders' faces from under her hair.

39

At sixteen, she was getting round-shouldered from trying to conceal her developing bosom. She did not want to grow up, and yet she did not want her critical mother to treat her like a child. She did not know what she wanted.

The men, who were also interested in magic potions, but more privately, talked about Ralph's new Lancia and Hugo's Mercedes Benz, the first motors in the family.

Vera's daughters Helen and Henrietta were bored. Helen's present to her aunt had been picked up by Dicky with an approving whistle, but Teddie had not looked at it yet, because it was a book.

It was an 1872 gold-embossed edition of an early novel by their late patriarch Ernest Austin Morley, father of Hugo, Leonard, Teddie and Vera and grandfather of Helen, who revered his memory.

Sir Ernest Morley had been a successful merchant with a chain of small household shops in the Thames Valley towns. In his forties, he unexpectedly wrote a novel about a prostitute which, astonishing to him, was published and – even more astonishing – became very popular at W.H. Smith's and Mudie's libraries.

His success surprised him less as he wrote on, eventually selling his business to give all his time to what he thought of as his 'story-telling'. He wrote mostly about ordinary men and women, and in an age of superheroes, when novelists were dizzyingly preoccupied with magical and exotically religious themes, he involved his readers in real-life dramas that just might have happened to them. Once released, his stored-up feeling for England and its people poured out in scenes that somehow seemed more real than reality. 'Life as it ought to be' was how *Harper's Monthly* announced their

E.A. Morley serializations. No preaching or moralizing. Good and bad brought to life so humanly that an enchanted reader could believe: Yes, we are all fascinating creatures of infinite potential. Even me!

He was 'The People's Story-teller'. Queen Victoria made him a knight and invited him and Lady Morley to tea. After his death in 1896, in the middle of *Narrow Boats*, a tale of rumbustious life on the river barges, his books continued to be read, and admirers continued to make pilgrimages to his home in Goring-on-Thames, where they were patronized by Adelaide Morley, his stout widow.

The rest of the family more or less took him for granted, as families of great men do. His granddaughter Helen Pope did not, because she was 'a writer', with the first chapters of a novel on a shelf under her dressing-table skirt, like Jane Austen. Secretly she felt that if genealogists were right, and exceptional talent was passed only to one person, then she was that person. One day she would complete the unfinished *Narrow Boats* for her grandfather.

Dicky had already read snatches of the novels. He followed the birthday girl about the drawing room, holding the book open and nagging, 'Look, Aunt Teddie, please look! It's beautifully illustrated. Look, here's the bit where the lady throws herself off the bridge! "Long after the slender body had slipped below the surface of the river, the petals of the horse-chestnut blossoms fell softly, like a fragrant white shroud."'

'Do you allow this child to read morbid scenes, Gwen?'

'Well, it *is* by his grandfather.'

'Oh, is it?' Teddie peered. She had not been listening to what Dicky and Helen had told her.

41

'Haven't you read it?' Dicky asked.

'Of course, child.'

'What's it about then?' The boy was not rude, but his sense of fair play would not allow a grown-up to cheat.

'Don't torment me.'

'Buck up, Teddie.' This was the only attention she got from her husband, who was trying to flirt with his niece Henrietta.

Leonard Morley echoed, 'Buck up, old girl! You're only forty-six and life looks wonderful.' He was happy at home here with the clan, being the centre of the family.

'It may do to you.' His sister turned her shadowed eyes to him heavily. 'Playing at Shops all day at Whiteley's, without a care in the world.'

Leonard caught Gwen's eye. She waved across the room. She had forgotten about the frightening anonymous note. *Blood money!* Leonard could not forget.

Flora Bolt sounded the brass gong in the hall. When it was only family, she did not send in Winnie Stokes to announce, 'Dinner is served', in her superior accent. They all moved into the dining room, and Dicky went unwillingly up to bed.

'And tomorrow some of these buggers will be back for Sunday lunch,' short, squat Tatiana grumbled, stout legs planted on the scullery duckboard, up to the elbows in green jelly foam. 'Hardly worth putting them plates away, Mrs Salter.'

'We don't use the best china for Sunday lunch.' Flora thumped her fist on the top of Tat's low-level head as she passed on her way to her room behind the scullery. 'As you should know as well as anyone. As you would know too, if your upbringing had been different. The Morleys like to be together. If more families were like this lot, the world would not be sliding to hell on a tin tray.'

'Auntie!' the girl called through to the kitchen. Hints about Tat's dead mother and unknown father were not fair.

But the cook, who had poor blood, had gone to her room, and by the time Tatiana got there, she would be sprawled diagonally across their shared double bed.

After he had been woken by the carriage wheels and the horses and the explosive engine of Uncle Ralph's new motor, Dicky lay not sleeping, and he heard his parents and Madge come up to their rooms, and then heard the Saturday drunks roaring down from the Sun in Splendour at the top of Portobello Road.

Howling for his blood? He knew that one night he would hear them stop by the corner and growl and spit about what they would do to him. He knew that one of them would be the terrible Bill Bolt, the man Flora called 'The Bull', 'strong as an ox and cruel as the horned devil. If he ever come looking for me 'ere . . .'

If he did, he would look for Dicky first. *Is he here?* He lifted his head to try to look through the plane-tree leaves and detect the bellow of the horned man among the blurred curses. His body was tense with fear. He nerved himself to courage. Even when the mob had crossed Chepstow Villas, fighting, and were fading down the Lane, he still lay stiffly with his fists clenched by his sides. Had his hero brother, deep-voiced, grown-up Austin once lain like this and listened when he was a boy in this same room? Dicky could never ask him. Had Austin called out? Dicky would never call, though Madge and his mother and father would all come running to comfort him. He lay, still listening to the distant sounds of battle, his eyes on the ghostly dripping leaves in the mist round the gaslight. He would not be the baby of the family.

Chapter Five

The upstairs room again. Standing close to the tall, smiling man, the woman raised her large bright eyes trustingly to his face.

'How are the palpitations?' he asked her.

'I feel a great deal better. You helped me so much last time I was here.'

'I'm glad. And how can I help you now?'

'Oh, my dear . . .' She put a hand tenderly on his arm. 'I think you know.'

'Wait a minute. No, look here –' He backed away from her. 'You must understand. The last time, I was merely trying to help your breathing.' This should teach him to keep his hands off hysterical women.

'Oh,' she persisted, 'but I do understand.'

As she came towards him, the man took another step backwards and knocked a lamp off a small table. 'Please,' he said. 'Sit down. I shall prescribe you something to calm your nerves.'

After she had gone, he bent to pick up the broken pieces of the glass lamp, and wondered whether he should send her a bill for it.

Some people disliked going back to work after the weekend.

'Monday is the invention of the devil,' Henry Beale, the Chief Buyer, maintained.

Leonard loved Mondays. Whiteley's was his heart's delight. He had been fascinated with stores and selling since he used to do the rounds of his father's shops as a child. When this methodical, secretive man had unexpectedly sold his places of business and retired to a writing-table in the window of the house on Goring's High Street, the child Leonard had mourned for merchandise, and recaptured it as soon as he was old enough to get a sales assistant job. Had his father been proud that he had risen to the top in a much grander field than Streatley or Wallingford or Pangbourne? Who could know? Ernest Austin Morley did not hand out praise. His elder son Hugo had inherited that from him, as his younger son had inherited retailing.

When success came to E.A. Morley – his novelist's title – and he built a large white house in the hills above Goring with a vast leather-topped desk and a view of his own sloping lawns instead of the busy village street, he was too absorbed in his 'story-telling' to be more than vaguely aware of his children growing up and pursuing their own ends.

On a Monday in September, Leonard went in to Whiteley's early, as usual, and took a tour of all the departments, setting up for business before the store opened. This was a chance to exchange a few words with the dozens of different buyers and to make a note of their grumbles, which was more gratifying to them than just being listened to, however attentively. He wished everyone good morning, using their names, with a special word for a nervous new employee, and a young widow in Children's Footwear, and the mother of a sick child in Embroidery, and grizzled, boatered Mr Raish at the fish counter, who had just won a long-service award.

Leonard passed through all the departments on the ground and upper floors of the extensive store which had started nearly fifty years earlier as one modest drapery shop. One by one, William Whiteley had bought up more than twenty separate shops in Westbourne Grove, added others in Queen's Road, often in defiance of cautious local authorities, and connected them up as departments of one giant emporium.

Leonard paced happily through the hundred and sixty little kingdoms: Boots, Gents Outfitting, Sporting Goods, Pets, Bicycles, Toys, Layettes, Costumes, Gowns and Mantles, Furs, Millinery, Curtains, Towels, Whitewear, Foreign Silks, Wickerwork, Pianos, Art Goods, Stationery, Books, and so on. The famous marble food halls, whose coming had angered local provision shops, were fragrant with the smells of baking and fresh meat and fruit and vegetables from Whiteley's own farms, and pungent spices and peppery salami and festooned German sausages. Aprons were starched and bleached, straw hats jauntily but not insolently angled. The butcher with the hussar moustache was cutting chops. A good-looking young lady was setting up a table to demonstrate a new household gadget.

'Shall I buy one for my kitchen?' Leonard stopped to find out about it.

'Ask your wife, Mr Morley.'

'I will.' Gwen hardly ever went into the kitchen, and Mrs Roach would not use things like electric coffee grinders or patent mixers.

It was opening time by now, and an early arrival, Sir Rawdon Filey, still charged up with last night's wine, waylaid Leonard by the lift with an imperious demand to

47

'send a man' to Sussex about new lighting fixtures for the Castle.

'I will look into it, Sir Rawdon.' The Filey account already bore a large sum outstanding.

'I mean *today*, Morley.' Sir Rawdon looked as if he had not been to bed.

Upstairs, Assistant Manager Morley, steward of all this while the General Manager was on sick leave, called in at the counting house and paid a social visit to the funeral offices and the domestic agency and the refreshment room, which were not his business. Before long, when the store came to full teeming life, he would return downstairs on the first of his slower, more comprehensive tours among the customers.

The whole place never ceased to amaze and enthral him. Nearly fifty years ago, a young Yorkshireman with ten pounds in his pocket, inspired by the dazzling displays of the Great Exhibition in Hyde Park, had dreamed of a vast emporium of the world's trade. Now he had it. The biggest store in London, the biggest store in the whole of England, that could supply anything for anybody. Rich customers had migrated from Shoolbreds and Heal's and Maples in the Tottenham Court Road to patronize hitherto unfashionable Westbourne Grove, now at the hub of commerce. William Whiteley, 'The Universal Provider', exported luxury goods to princes and rajahs, lit up Nelson's monument on Trafalgar Day, and monopolized huge contracts for catering at great events, like the wedding of Prince George and Princess May of Teck.

Leonard looked in to the Chief's office to tell him about Sir Rawdon's expansive order.

'Hm. Does he know that we can't extend him any more credit?'

'He has been advised of that, sir.'

'Advise him again woonce mower.' The Universal Provider had never quite cast off his Yorkshire speech.

A sales assistant from Trunks came breathlessly up the stairs. Mr Morley was summoned below by Mrs Forrester.

Mrs Vernon Forrester was one of the grand old ladies in antique furs who had never come to terms with Whiteley's innovation of fixed, clearly marked prices. In her day, you were not expected to pay the asking price. You bargained. She was refusing to pay ten guineas for a tropical trunk in which her nephew would convey his effects to Singapore.

'You're not the Manager. Send me the Manager.'

'He's away, madam. I am here in his place.'

'Do I know you?'

'Certainly, madam. I helped you with your granddaughter's bridal gift.'

'Oh, so you did. What was it?'

'The beautiful candelabra. A fine choice.'

'It cost enough.'

'A generous grandmother.' Leonard bowed. It was his role: the small deferential bow, the smooth modulated voice, part of giving customers what they wanted. It did not bother him to bow when necessary, although he drew the line at rubbing his hands.

Because of his job, customers assumed that he was not as good as them. No doubt they were right. 'Who are the Morleys anyway?' Charlotte had been heard to say when out of temper with Hugo or Leonard or Vera. 'Your father

49

was only a purveyor of brooms and buttons, who just happened to have some luck as a scribbler.'

Leonard went upstairs to his office. In the corridor, he gave his usual carefully polite greeting to Henry Beale, who slapped him offensively on the back with a falsely hearty 'Top of the morning to you, Morley!'

The post had not been sorted. The clerks would be going through the letters, but in the middle of Leonard's desk was another detestable small square envelope marked 'Private and Personal'.

He opened it with reluctance, using the paper knife carefully, with a vague idea of preserving evidence, and unfolded the cheap grey paper.

The same ugly scrawl. The message was uglier.

Why no money? The frigging swine knows where I am and who I am, and I'll tell the whole sodding world. If I don't kill him first. Sod you, arse-licker.

Damnation! thought Leonard. That's spoiled my Monday.

'Arnold!' He put the letter in the envelope and took it to his clerk. 'Do you know anything about this?'

'No, Mr Morley. It didn't come through the post.'

'I can see that.'

In his office, Leonard read the letter again. He wanted to tear up the filthy thing, but it had said 'If I don't kill him ...'

I must tell the old man about this.

How can I tell him? The Chief was purring along on such an even keel. He used to be impatient and fiery, imposing fines for small misdemeanours, dismissing a staff member without notice or a reference. At seventy-four, he had become slower and mellower. He still dealt with top customers and royals and knew everything that was going on, but he now left the unpleasant things to his senior staff.

Leonard must handle this. What to do? The police? Arthur French? William Whiteley did not think highly of Scotland Yard, since they had never solved the mystery of those vengeful fires in the Eighties, even though the last had killed three people.

Frank or William, Mr Whiteley's sons? They were not in positions of responsibility yet, and Leonard could not go behind the old man's back. He looked at the print of the founder's portrait, which was on the wall of every office. Impressive facial hair, the beard in two bushy parts on either side of his strong chin, less a beard than a pair of whiskers framing the determined face like a judge's wig with squared-off ends. His mouth smiled tightly, and his keen protuberant eyes assessed you all round the room from under their heavy brows.

He could relax on occasions, like the staff outing to the seaside. The young women in their striped beach clothes liked to see him 'unbuttoned', and would chat more freely and even tease him a little, as if he were a younger man. Whiteley's gossip had it that he'd been a bit of a dog in his day. But the next morning, the girls in their black and white uniforms would tidy their counters quickly and stand alert, however tired they were, if the Chief came stomping down the aisle, short and square and moral.

He was a fine employer. Not a friend. Leonard would never know him, but he trusted him and felt that he himself was trusted.

Damn it, the man is not a child. He'll give a snort at this ludicrous note and tell me to calm down.

Leonard was going to wait until Mr Whiteley returned from his afternoon tea, heavy Yorkshire-style refreshment in the restaurant. He remembered his father in his seventies, getting edgy before a meal. But the Chief summoned him to discuss plans for the lending library on which they had been working.

'My sons don't want me to go ahead with it,' he grumbled. 'They say I take on too much. How do they think this store has reached the top and stayed there?'

'By giving customers what they want, sir.' It was one of the standard answers.

'Correct. And customers want a lending library, here where they shop, and I'm determined they shall have it. To educate and entertain. It's a duty, Morley. It's argued that it will make a loss. I must take that risk.'

'Add conscience to capital.' Another of the Whiteley principles.

'That's *it*.' The old man banged the palm of his hand on the floor plan of the library, which was on his desk. With the eagerness and perception of a younger self, he discussed details that were new but crystal clear to him.

Why had Leonard been vacillating about the note? This man could cope with anything. When the Chief dismissed him, he took a breath and said, 'If I could just have a moment more of your time, sir?'

'Don't be long about it.' His interest in Leonard was over. He was ready to go on to the next thing.

Leonard came close to the desk. 'I have had two strange notes.' He cleared his throat. 'I felt I should show you the latest one.'

Mr Whiteley unfolded the note and scowled at it. He grunted once, but gave no sign of emotion. Then he folded the paper and looked up under the awning of his brows. His face was blank, except for the small, unamused tight smile that was always there. Leonard waited. They had been talking compatibly before. Now, whatever he said would be wrong.

At last the old man said, 'Ah've 'ud a few of these. They mean nothing. Where's the first note?'

'In my desk at home.'

'Tear it up.' Mr Whiteley tore the grey paper into very small pieces and handed them back to Leonard. 'It's yours,' he said contemptuously. 'Why bother *me*?'

Leonard felt condemned and humiliated. Stunned, sick with anger, he left the office without a word. He stood with his back to the Chief's door, holding the scraps of paper in his fist, not knowing what to do next.

A ledger clerk came down the corridor with a basket of papers, and Leonard moved on.

The first letter had come from outside. It had been postmarked Hammersmith. This one had been brought in early this morning and placed on his desk. By someone from outside? His nameplate was on the office door, but they would have to find their way up here. It must be an ex-employee, trying to make trouble. He knows who I am, Leonard thought. He went back over people who had lost their jobs. Some had resigned for various reasons, but not many had been sacked, now that the old man was readier to give offenders a second chance.

Suppose it was someone in the store? Leonard thought again of Henry Beale and the resentment that simmered sourly in him beneath his pompous manner. When the General Manager had had to take sick leave and a lot of his duties had fallen on Leonard Morley, Beale had made his feelings obvious. He felt he should have more responsibility. The old man didn't know what he was doing any more. He should be forced out. 'What *I* could tell you about Mr William Whiteley, if I chose . . .' sucking wet lips, his eyes venomous.

Did he already suspect what might be the truth – that because of his drinking and his heavy hand on staff, he might himself, one day, be on the way out?

If Beale, for some twisted purpose of his own spiteful mind, were tormenting the old man, that would be truly evil. But it would be better to know, and see justice done. The man had gone out on business this afternoon. Leonard knew that. Obsessed with an unreasoning desire to find him the culprit, he hurried round a corner and up a short flight of stairs to Henry Beale's office.

The door was not locked. Leonard went quickly inside.

The Chief Buyer's office was self-important, like its owner. The roll-top of the desk and the stuffed leather chair seemed to bulge more fatly than anyone else's. A framed notice exhorted anyone who came in that 'Only Excellence Will Do'. The portrait of William Whiteley was not above the desk, but in a corner. Where other office walls carried cheerful pictures of families and staff outings, Henry Beale's displayed himself, chin up in pompous business groups, or shaking the hand of some unknown notable.

He did have good contacts, that was true. He knew many of the leading manufacturers and wholesalers. Most

54

of the time, he performed well. That was why W.W. still employed him.

The lid of the desk was locked. Because it concealed more of that cheap grey paper shredded in Leonard's pocket? Was this where the man furtively wrote the brief obscenities? With no idea of what he might be looking for, Leonard opened the tall cupboard and looked at the neat shelves of files and ledgers. The lower drawers of the desk were not locked. Breathlessly, he pulled them open one by one, riffling through harmless papers, hoping to find something incriminating. At least a bottle of spirits concealed.

He was actually kneeling on the floor when the office door opened and Henry Beale stood there.

'Looking for something, Morley?'

'Oh, Beale . . .' he tried to sound calm. 'I thought you were out.'

'So I see.'

'I dropped my fountain-pen somewhere.' Leonard Morley, Acting Manager of London's greatest store, grown man of fifty, was panicking like a boy caught in the larder. 'It might have fallen into a half-open drawer.'

Could he somehow juggle the pen out of his breast pocket and into the bottom drawer? Henry Beale stood and looked down at him. Leonard scrambled absurdly to his feet, resisting the degrading impulse to dust off the knees of his trousers. 'Excuse me.'

'Not at all.' Beale came in and put his attaché case down on the table. 'I was hoping to talk to you anyway.'

'Yes?' Leo felt at a terrible disadvantage. His rage was cold within him, and turned to shame. How could he have got himself into this situation? How could he have been such an almighty fathead?

'Some rather good news,' Beale said loftily. 'You were aware that Dexter Crystal had decided that, to keep their prices up, they would trade with only one outlet?'

Oh God, here it came. The man he wanted to trample underfoot had brought off a spectacular coup.

'You've guessed it, Morley, my good sir.' Puffing out his veined cheeks, Beale opened the briefcase and fussed officiously with its contents, as if they were the State budget. 'We are to be that outlet.'

Leonard got himself out of the office as best he might, taking a last chance to save his face by putting it back round the door after his body was outside to say, 'If you do find my fountain-pen, please let me know.'

Why did I smile and say please? I could cheerfully strangle the man, for no better reason than not having to face him tomorrow. To calm himself down before the end of what had degenerated into such an upsetting Monday, Leonard took a last patrol among the late shoppers.

All the glass entrance doors were wide open to the warm afternoon, and the throngs on the pavement were part of the crowds that flowed in and out of the store. Standing on the second step of the main staircase, he tried to observe this with his usual satisfaction, but William Whiteley and Henry Beale and the poisonous letter had so unsettled him that he felt active dislike for the bulky wanderers who blocked doorways and aisles three abreast, the high-pitched women who treated the tired assistants like serfs, the affected maidens with small high Grecian bosoms, the competitive hats, the spoiled children, the gloved hands

56

that picked up articles labelled 'Please Do Not Touch'.

When a tall, well-dressed man knocked into him on his way up the stairs, the Assistant Manager forgot his professional courtesy enough to wince and put out a defensive elbow.

'I say,' the man said with a charming smile, 'I'm most desperately sorry.'

Leonard nodded, unable to answer, 'Not at all, sir,' and apologize for standing there.

'Perhaps you can save me time. It's getting rather late.' The man rattled on about wanting to find a glass lamp to replace a broken one in his office, that would be more like a drawing-room lamp in what was really not exactly an office, yet not a drawing room either. Which department would the Assistant Manager suggest, and would he guide him there to save time? Standing two stairs above Leonard, who had to look up at him, he said, 'I'm quite a regular customer. My name is Taylor. Tobias Taylor.'

'I'm sorry, Mr Taylor,' Leonard said ungraciously. He did not feel in any condition to deal with what might be a demanding patron. 'I must keep an appointment.'

'But surely –'

'Mr Jenkins will assist you.' Leonard spotted one of the floorwalkers among the crowd and clicked his fingers. 'Jenkins, forward!'

The customer shrugged his elegant fawn linen shoulders and went off with Jenkins, looking back once at Leonard with a raised eyebrow.

At home, Gwen was sitting on the drawing-room balcony with the gramophone playing. People walking along this side of Chepstow Villas looked up and smiled at the music. Leonard had put the shredded note back into its envelope. Out on the balcony, he dropped the pieces into an empty flowerpot.

'Another of those dreadful letters?'

He shrugged. He could not possibly show the filthy thing to Gwen. He did not even want to tell her about it, nor about the anger and humiliation that had come in its wake.

'Why can't I read it? I shall piece it together.'

Leonard bent and lit a match inside the flowerpot.

'Oh good,' Gwen said incuriously. 'Like in *Peril at Sunrise* where Astoria burns her only love letter from Sebastian because it could send him to prison.'

Flora stepped out over the low windowsill with the Master's whisky and soda, and saw the dying little flame. 'Burning the evidence, eh?'

'Something like that.'

'A friend of mine burned a pound note once,' Flora said, 'to show how little he cared.'

'For you or the money?' Gwen asked.

Unlike many wives – some within this family – she did not bother Leonard about what he had burned and why. She seemed to have lost interest.

Chapter Six

'Didn't you want to come to dinner, Uncle Leonard?'

In the first-floor drawing room at Ladbroke Lodge, Bella, in a harsh yellow dress, saw that he was out of sorts. Leonard saw that she had been crying.

'Of course I did, Bella.' He bent to kiss her. It was not like embracing his daughter Madge, who responded. Bella slightly stiffened back into herself if touched. 'It's just that I've had a rather unpleasant day.'

'Oh, so have I.' Bella pulled down her mouth.

'Poor girl, what happened?' Unlike his niece, Leonard was willing to pursue an offer of someone else's trouble.

'You wouldn't care to know.' Bella glanced at her father, posing in the long window with his sherry glass and graceful sister-in-law Gwen, so that he could be seen from the street to be entertaining a pretty woman.

'I would, Bella.' Leonard knew about Bella's disastrous relationship with her father, to whom she still longed to be close, even though he had been thwarting and denigrating her since she was an ugly duckling child.

'I was stupid enough to bring up the subject of university again. I went to see Gordie – my old governess, you remember? She told me that Leeds was taking more women, and she made me promise not to give up.' She bit her lower lip. 'I'm sorry. It's too boring.' Bella could invite you to be bored before she started talking.

So could Hugo's guest, an American businessman who was a devotee of the works of E.A. Morley. Hugo enjoyed being courted as the eldest son of the famous novelist, especially by someone who might be financially useful.

Mr Lloyd Loomis held forth on the plots and characters of Ernest Morley's books, as if the family had never read them.

'This is a stunning experience for me.' He beamed and bowed down the table to Hugo. 'I can't believe I'm really in this lovely home, in this beautiful room with so many of the great man's actual descendants. You knew him,' he told Hugo, with a tremor in his voice. 'You spoke with him. What wouldn't I have given for five minutes with the creator of Theodora Masters, paradigm heroine of that inspiring story of passion and crime: *Clamour of the Streets*?'

'Yes, we know,' his hostess said a little tartly. Charlotte thought that Hugo, majestic at the end of the table with his hands on the scrolled ends of his chair arms, as if enthroned, was lapping it up too smugly. She was glad of the fame of Ernest Morley, but after all, who *was* he, before he became somebody?

Thomas, the eldest son, summoned to dinner to talk banking with Mr Loomis, was polite but restless. He kept pulling out his watch. He had a late appointment at the Carlton Club. Tom Morley was too busy and pressured by work to stay long anywhere. Lord Rourke, invited to dinner to treat Loomis to a title, was having trouble with lamb fibres in his new teeth.

Leonard, still not himself, added little to the conversation. Lloyd Loomis, fork in hand, mousse *au chocolat* untasted, told him, 'Of course, you admired your father enough to follow in his business footsteps. That's hero worship, I guess. May we hope that you will also write about your experiences with the public, as Sir Ernest so tellingly did in *Barclay and Son?*'

Leonard said, 'No,' and accepted more mousse from the parlourmaid. When he was emotionally off colour, he was usually hungry.

Bella, who had studied her grandfather's books at boarding school and was as knowledgeable about them as anyone else, would have welcomed the American devotee as a chance to show this off. As her tearful eyes recovered in the candlelight and her flushed nose paled, she looked quite animated and confident, waiting for Loomis to stop pontificating about the ingenious symbolism of the racecourse crowds in *The Gambler* and eat his mousse, so that she could inform him that E.A.M. would not have bothered with symbolism when he was pursuing a fast-moving narrative of his hero-adventurer in peril of his life at Epsom.

When Mr Loomis lowered his fork, she leaned forward to tell him, 'Excuse me, but I think my grandfather would not recognize your rather complicated view of his writing. The great strength of his story-telling style is in its simplicity, you know.'

'That's very innaresting.' Mr Loomis swallowed and drew breath. 'I don't happen to agree, but I'll be glad to debate that with you.'

'Oh, good.' Bella's round brown eyes, her best feature, shone with an eagerness she did not usually risk.

But if this Monday was not Leonard's day it wasn't Bella's either. When, to emphasize a point made by Lloyd Loomis's flatteringly serious attention, she reached out to include the head of the family with, 'Isn't that right, Father?', Hugo replied with a crushing, 'Why are you dominating the conversation about a subject of which you know almost nothing?'

The table was struck into silence. Bella gasped, jumped up with her hands to her mouth and ran from the room.

Charlotte made her Queen Victoria face. Gwen, next to Hugo, laid a reproving hand on his stiff arm. His Lordship had a quiet little choke. Mr Loomis stared, chewing at the mousse as if it were steak. Thomas said, 'Look here, Father, that's a bit much, even for you,' and pulled out his watch again.

Leonard was so furious that he excused himself abruptly to Charlotte and followed Bella out of the room. He could not find her. A maid told him that Miss Bella had gone banging hysterically down the back stairs in her mustard dress and out into the gardens of Ladbroke Square.

He did not like to follow her out there. Curtains were not yet drawn. There was still enough light for him to be seen from houses round the square chasing a young girl into the bushes.

In the drawing room, Gwen rescued him to go home as soon as the gentlemen came up from their port. He was still so angry that, although he thought the American was a crashing bore and probably a fake as well, he told him, in Hugo's hearing, 'I'll be visiting Goring next weekend, Loomis. Since you're such an admirer of my late father's work, would you care to come and see his house?'

'*Would I?*' By God, Lloyd Loomis was telling himself, I'm in the big time here!

The man would be tedious for a whole afternoon, but to

Leonard, it was worth it to get back at Hugo. His brother's eyes protruded, as they did when he was puffed out with umbrage. Lloyd Loomis was *his* discovery, and *he* was the head of the family of E.A. Morley.

The following Sunday, it was Aunt Teddie's turn to have a rotten day. Her mother Adelaide, Sir Ernest's widow, had become increasingly demanding of her four middle-aged children, as she waddled through her seventies. Hugo was too selfish to respond enough, Leonard was too busy and Vera too nonchalant. Poor old Teddie, who used to be Mama's girl, was now too often Mama's martyr.

They all loved the river. Several of the family were taking the train to Goring station to visit the grandmother and take punts out on the quiet, tree-laden reach of the Thames above the bridge.

They met Lloyd Loomis, as arranged, in the murky vaulted splendour of Paddington Station: Leonard and Gwen and Madge and young Dicky, in white flannels with snake belt, and small boater on the back of his gold curls; their elder son Austin and his wife Elizabeth and little daughter Laura in a sailor dress; cousin Helen Pope, dispatched as a substitute for her mother Vera, who had something better to do.

Madge had tried to get her cousin Bella to come. Lloyd Loomis was a new man for her, even if he was as tedious as her father had warned. But Bella was taken up with a young hero named Gerald Lazenby, whom she fancied might call on her or telephone today. In any case, she did not want to re-encounter the American, in front of whom she had been so humiliated.

Mr Loomis, too smart for the occasion in a pale grey suit, a mulberry cummerbund, polished boots and a stiff new *faux*-panama hat he believed was essential for the river, was a little nonplussed by the small crowd waiting for him on platform number six.

'Is it a special day – an anniversary? I have brought my humble esteem for Lady Morley, but should I have purchased a birthday gift?'

'No, this is just a family that likes to go everywhere in droves,' Gwen said.

'You mustn't mind us,' Dicky told the American, with the friendly confidence he showed to strangers. 'Look, there's more coming! Well, it's only my aunt.'

Teddie was behind time, as usual, having risen late. She had once confided to her niece Bella that getting up in the morning was 'like crawling out of my own grave'.

'My sister, Edwina Wynn.' Leonard wished she had not worn her mud-coloured jersey coat on this good September day, but Loomis would not notice. He was in a rapture about meeting yet one more direct descendant of the great man. 'And with the gift of words also, for sure?'

'Not I.' Teddie gave him her dead-fish handshake. 'It's all I can do to write a letter these days. This is my daughter Sophie, one of my twins. She's cleverer than me.' A doctor had told Teddie that the child might start eating properly if she was given enough praise. 'Come and shake hands, Sophie, like a rational being. Don't skulk like that.'

Nostalgic pleasure began for Leonard with the first sight of the river at Reading, and intensified as they walked out into the soft sleepy air under the fretted wooden canopy of Goring Station. It was officially Goring-and-Streatley, but not in this family. Picturesque Streatley on the other side of the river, mostly owned by a brewing family, was as foreign as if there were no ha'penny toll-bridge between the two villages.

As a child, Leonard would have crossed the railway line towards the brick house on the High Street, from where he could run down to the towpath, or the seductive backwater under the rotting piles at the end of the old wooden bridge. Now the troupe of Morleys turned the other way up the chalky private road to the house in a fold of the hills to which the People's Story-teller had retreated from the advance of trippers, and Pre-Raphaelite ladies painting Streatley Mill.

Heron's Nest, named after the mysterious house on the marsh in E.A.M.'s sensational novel *The Caged Bird*, which feminist readers had claimed could only have been written by a woman, was hidden round a sharp bend. Intruders could not stare at the low white house from a safe distance. They must approach and have bristly yapping dogs set on them.

There was only one dog left now, old and mangy, and as fat and uncertain on its pins as its mistress. Young Helen crouched at once by the basket to pet it, but when Lloyd Loomis dutifully stretched out his hand, it growled and showed a few rotting teeth.

'Leave Maxwell alone,' Adelaide Morley said sharply. There had always been a canine Maxwell since the hero of her husband's lucky first book.

'Mother, this is Mr Loomis, from Pennsylvania,' Leonard said. 'He's a buff.' He winked at her. They knew about buffs.

'*Lady* Morley – this is such a great honour.' Loomis was

working himself up into an oration of homage, which she brushed aside with an imperious hand, nearly knocking the spectacles off his obeisant face.

'Who is this?' Suspicion glinted in her large hooded eyes.

'He's a friend of Hugo's.'

'Where *is* Hugo?' The matriarch was always more concerned with who had not come than who had.

Helen was here, being nice to the unsavoury dog, her hair tied back from her narrow intense face as if she were still a green girl, but she was asked, 'Where is your mother?' When Sophie bent to be embraced by the suffocation of rosewater and scarves and podgy old flesh, her grandmother said, 'You're skinnier than ever, child. Where is Greg?'

'Grandmother, we don't go everywhere together, just because we're twins.'

'My mother was a twin, as you must have been told, and she had to.'

'That was in the Dark Ages, Gran,' Dicky butted in.

'You rogue.' Adelaide was no more immune to Dicky than anyone else. 'Where is Bella?' She looked around. 'Twisted her ankle on the front step, like last time?'

Leonard did not remind her, 'Because *you* were leaning on her.' He invented: 'She sent you her love and I shall tell her you sent yours.'

He was always dutifully polite, but he was sick of Bella being automatically cast in the fool's role, and still angry with his brother Hugo for his cruelty. Mr Whiteley had been difficult all week, driving his staff unreasonably, and Leonard was edgy, dreading another threatening letter which he would have to keep secret. He was in no mood to put up with nonsense from the old lady.

66

He fetched her two ivory-handled canes and pulled her up from her great velvet chair, whose footstool had been stitched by Teddie at seventeen, when she should have been out enjoying herself.

'Oh,' she groaned. 'Argh – my rheumatics!'

'I thought they were better, poor Mama.'

'I am tormented with ten thousand hells.'

'Is Lady Morley sick?' Lloyd Loomis put on a deep, concerned voice. 'Am I out of line in hoping for a tour of the memorabilia?'

'No, not at all.' Leonard ambushed his mother by adding smoothly, 'My mother always insists on being the one to show my father's study.'

'The *sanctum sanctorum*,' breathed Loomis, as many others had before him.

Beyond the heavy oak door, soundproof, since E.A. Morley's children had been still quite young when he moved here, the large panelled room was intact. Sir Ernest had been halfway through Chapter Ten of *Narrow Boats* when his life-blood suddenly gushed out of him and he was gone. The desk and carpet had of course been cleaned, but there it all was.

In the bay window, the solid expanse of tooled leather desk-top looked out to the famous vista of garden and meadow slope and woods, on which the poor sportsman Anselm, crippled by a steeplechase fall, had brooded so bitterly in *Village World*, before he caused the high stone wall to be built, cutting off the mocking view from his wheeled chair.

Here was the writer's chair with the carved arms and back in which photographers had liked to pose him, the bookshelves from floor to ceiling stacked with his collection of classic novels, large reproductions of *The Day of Reckoning* and *Her Mother's Voice* and other pictures which told a story, the pens, the blotter, the spectacle cases ranged as neatly as tinned fish, the Literary Machine – a tall reading-stand given to him by the E.A. Morley Admirers Association – all the paraphernalia of this famous man whose growing children had hardly known him.

Lloyd Loomis continued to make a frothing ass of himself. Adelaide Morley, even stouter standing up, watched him closely under deep-mauve lids to see he did not pocket anything.

She was proud of her late husband, but she had known him for years as Ernest Austin Morley of Thames Valley Stores, who drove his own dog-cart and liked a cut of boiled gammon with turnips on Sundays. Apart from her title and the money which still came in, she took Ernest's fame calmly, and had little patience with zealots like this American.

Adelaide had various ways of disciplining people. Today, she chose exclusion. At lunch, she was exaggeratedly maternal, a spread hen gathering her brood close to her, to make Loomis feel an outsider. She was even quite solicitous of Margaret Biddle, her companion. 'Poor dear Margaret is so anxious about her father's illness. Pour Margaret some wine, Austin.'

Loomis had trouble with the trout bones. He put up a brave show of, 'So inspiring to see the congeniality of *Sir* Ernest passed on to his family.' When Madge was helping the elderly maids with the plates, Adelaide muttered to her audibly, 'Take him away.'

As the family set off for the boathouse, its matriarch dropped the tribal performance in favour of another.

'Oh no, Edwina.' She caught Teddie changing into soft shoes. 'You can't leave me alone like this.'

'Like what?' someone asked. Dicky was already running ahead down the drive in his billowy white shirt, and the others were gathering up wraps and tea baskets.

'You can see I'm not well.' The old lady had consumed lunch as usual. Leonard and Gwen and the younger ones pretended not to hear. Teddie tied her laces and turned back to her mother like an automaton. 'Take me to bed, Edwina.' Adelaide raised deep tragic eyes. 'I shan't get up again today.'

At the boathouse by Goring bridge, Lloyd Loomis, who now felt not only *de trop* but guilty about imposing on a sick woman, was taken aback by the narrowness and instability of the punts. His shiny boots were quite unsuitable, too hard and slippery.

Arranging themselves in two punts, joking with their friend the boatman, Gwen with her dotted muslin and ruched parasol in her perfect setting among the low cushions, the family, close-knit in this traditional pleasure, were relieved to see Mr Loomis set off for the station to take a train back to London.

That evening, when Leonard and Austin walked back to Heron's Nest to fetch Aunt Teddie, they found her downcast, and experiencing nervous tremors. Adelaide had told her that she was releasing her companion to visit her sick father. Teddie must stay here with her, as she had so often been obliged to do before.

'It's the dressmaker's day tomorrow, and then Ralph was

taking me to the Egyptian exhibition at the British Museum.'

'Come on, old dear.' Leonard patted her slumped shoulder. 'Come with us. Mother is perfectly all right here with the maids, and she can get the doctor to come if she's really not well.'

'But I'm always afraid she'll have a heart attack, and it will be my fault. Will one of you take Sophie home and explain to Ralph? Not that he'll mind.'

'Oh Lord,' Austin fumed, as they went back to the station. 'Why does Grandmother make a martyr of that poor woman?'

'She knows she can't get away with it with the rest of us.'

'Why does Aunt Teddie let her?'

'Why does a fish swim?' From the hill, Leonard savoured a last streak of light on the swift flat stream above the weir. 'It's all she knows.'

Chapter Seven

September and the river were past, and a windy October had almost blown itself out. There had been no more sinister grey envelopes on Leonard's desk, thank God. No more lunatic malevolence to upset the busy equilibrium of his days.

Mr Whiteley had dropped the terse, wary manner that had marred their relationship for a time. The Managing Director was convalescing abroad from his heart attack, so Leonard was still pretty much in charge. Henry Beale tried some mean little games of going direct to William Whiteley, leaving Leonard in the dark about important business, but W.W. was too sharp not to catch on. If Beale came to him with 'confidential' information, the Chief would summon Leonard in to hear it.

Once he said sharply to Leonard, 'You wonder why I keep Mr Beale on, don't you?'

'No, sir, I, er –' Mr Whiteley was God. Under his keen protuberant gaze, you did not doubt him.

'He's valuable in his position. He knows his job thoroughly, and I know him . . . thoroughly.' He was too discreet to specify items like stimulants or roving hands. 'He knows that I know, which ensures me control.'

The old Chief was very much in control, and business was thriving. On the first floor, alterations for the new lending library were under way behind a canvas screen boldly stencilled: 'The Universal Provider will soon provide you with your Literary Choice of Buying or Borrowing.' New stock was coming in to all departments. Gowns and Mantles had its own French designer. The Belgian patisserie was open. Big advertisements were splashed in all the newspapers. More assistants were being taken on. The Christmas catalogue had forty-four pages. Van deliveries spread north and south of London. Extra motor omnibuses were running on the Westbourne Grove route. A German band played every day on the Queen's Road corner. It seemed the whole world was at Whiteley's.

Leonard was quite often recognized on social occasions. 'Oh – fancy. Well, good evening to you, Mr Morley. How nice to see you – off-stage, as it were.'

'Enchanted, madame.' Leonard's versatile small bow was gentlemanly. His 'madame' was very different from his 'madam' for customers.

In the aftermath of a charity musicale, to which he had taken Gwen and Madge, they were moving down to the foyer of the hotel when a tall, well-made man with a sophisticated air about him said, 'Good evening, sir. We talked briefly a month or so ago.'

'Indeed?' That amused, unhurried voice was vaguely familiar. 'Where was that?' Leonard asked politely.

'At your place of business. In Whiteley's, to be exact.'

Gwen and Madge, descending shallow steps with their trains over their arms, stopped and looked round inquiringly.

'I clumsily knocked into you on a fruitless quest for a lamp. I apologize again.'

'No, no.' Oh heavens, it was the Whiteley's customer on

72

the stairs with whom Leonard had lost his professional civility because of the rage still simmering over the anonymous note, and W.W., and Henry Beale. 'It's for me to apologize. I'm afraid I was less than helpful, Mr –'

'Taylor. Tobias Taylor.'

Leonard remembered: engaging, humorous face, dark brilliant eyes, thick, well-groomed wave of hair.

'I hope it didn't put you against the store, Mr Taylor.'

'Why? What happened?' Madge was intrigued.

'I'm afraid this gentleman caught me at the end of a rather bad day.' Because Leonard had drunk a fair amount of wine, he had the bravado to add, 'A little matter of a hostile madman.'

'Oh? Trouble at the ironworks, Mr Morley? "The distant rumble of revolution's rough wheels"?' Tobias Taylor raised an eyebrow. This bright spark had learned not only Leonard's name, but his parentage, and knew something of E.A. Morley's 1880 factory novel.

The bright spark was introduced to Gwen and Madge. He joked about the fat tenor's passionately trembling high notes and made them laugh and toss their heads a little, Madge's hair swinging free and shining, Gwen's sweetly crowned with delicate flowers from Whiteley's Floral Arrangements.

'I hope we may meet again.' Mr Taylor seemed delighted with them. 'May I give you my card?' He bowed, keeping his eyes on their faces, and moved away to join someone among the crowd.

'Who was *that*?' Gwen asked as they waited under the hotel portico for Mr Beggs, the livery man who drove them in a hired brougham.

Leonard read the card. 'Tobias Taylor Esq., 42 Egerton Terrace, South Kensington.'

'A good enough address,' Gwen purred. 'I liked him, didn't you, Madge?'

'Yes, I did.' Madge, not self-conscious or threatened by men, never pretended to belittle them.

'I thought him attractive. Would he do for you, I wonder?' Madge was twenty-three. Gwen did not think that she would ever marry Will Morrison, or the other way round.

'He's probably got a wife and several mistresses, Mother.' Madge had seen the woman in feathers and furs who had beckoned to him.

Gwen put Mr Taylor's card into her sequinned bag. 'Should I have given him my card, Leo? I can never remember what's correct.'

'Thank goodness,' Madge said. 'That's why I like you, Mama.'

'Perhaps we should have invited him to Sunday luncheon today,' Gwen mused.

'Now that would *not* have been correct, since you want to know.' Leonard's professionalism made him aware of conventional etiquette. 'It would be too early in the acquaintance. If it *is* going to be an acquaintance, which I doubt. A man like that has too many irons in the fire.'

'What a pity. He could have met some of the family.'

'Lucky fellow.' Madge came into the large front bedroom in a scarlet wrapper and bare feet, which Leonard was not sure she should do while they were still in bed, although he liked the sight of her, with the red girdle embracing her supple waist. 'But he could have been even luckier and met Jack. Will is bringing him today.'

'Who is Jack?'

'Mama, I told you. Jack Haynes, from the Settlement.'

'The dumb one?'

'Not dumb, I told you. Deaf.'

'Oh dear.' Gwen had noticed the time, and was out of bed in her long cotton nightdress, collecting pieces of clothing, opening drawers, swaying about like a slender young bride among the dresses in the wardrobe.

'It won't be "Oh dear". It will be delightful. Jack needs to get out into life. His deafness used to turn him in on himself, but the Settlement is teaching him to look outwards. He's hungry for new experience. He needs to be fed on life and people – real people, not the riff-raff who used to take advantage of him.'

'It's very interesting, dear, but not when I haven't got my clothes on.' Gwen had gathered up an armful of garments and was on her way to the bathroom. 'We'll be late for church.'

After the service, and a mercifully short sermon, which was why they made St Peter's their parish church rather than the grander St John's, patronized by Hugo and Charlotte, some of the men of the family turned up at No. 72 for Sunday morning stump cricket in the backyard. This was a game devised by Leonard and his eldest son when Austin had started to play squash at school. Gwen had always wanted to have the paved yard dug up and planted with a tiny lawn and flower beds, but the Sunday cricketers would not have it.

The wicket was on a weighted stand in front of the open shed at the back of the house, which made the wicketkeeper's job easy. If he missed what the batsman missed, the ball could only thud around the shed breaking flower-pots. It could not go anywhere, unless the house door was open, in which case he chased the ball down the basement passage to the kitchen.

The bowler hurled an old tennis ball from the central grating and, without running, you scored off the walls which surrounded the backyard of No. 72. Two runs off the neighbours' garden wall, four off the high brown brick wall of the Portobello Bakery, five if the ball landed in one of Gwen's flower tubs, and six if you could clear the roof of the stable block in the mews.

Austin had been twelve when the game started in 1890, therefore boys of that age could join the men. Not fair, said the girls, whether they wanted to play or not. This year, the age had been lowered to ten, so that Dicky could play. Not fair, said the girls, and the older boys.

This morning, besides Austin, as enthusiastic and noisy as he had been at twelve, Hugo's son Tom was here and Teddie's son Greg, home for half-term. Leonard's police-man friend Arthur French came from farther down Chep-stow Villas almost every Sunday. His new wife watched from one of the back windows and waved, or clutched her hands to her mouth if someone slipped and fell or got hit by the ball, which could easily happen in the small enclosed space. When Arthur dropped an easy catch, she raised the window to lean out and join the jocular abuse with a shrill call: 'He can't catch criminals either!'

Will Morrison did not turn up in time to play, being a duffer at games, and although Madge had said the cricket would be enjoyable to Jack Haynes, who was strong and athletic for a boy brought up in the slums, Will thought she was wrong, knowing this tribal family.

They arrived at the same time as Hugo and Charlotte, who graciously directed them to the tradesmen's entrance. Madge ran down the front steps to rescue them, and introduced Jack with some rather wild gestures. 'My *aunt*. My un-*cool*.'

Jack nodded stolidly. Will had told him that the family was too large to worry about who was who.

'Why is Madge waving her hands about?' Charlotte demanded.

Jack, who could catch some of her words because she spoke clearly with a vigorous Germanic mouth, grinned and pointed to his ears.

'Ach! This person is deaf and dumb, Hugo.' She shouted at her husband to prove her point. 'I will say one thing, Gwen, you never know whom you may meet here.'

In the house, Charlotte leaned over the prow of her bosom to kiss her sister-in-law on both cheeks, which was fashionable this year, although difficult under their large church-going hats. Hugo went out to see the end of the cricket. With his son Tom, he had joined in when he was younger, but not since he had grown into a prosperous shape.

Leonard called out, 'Last over! Will you go and get the beer for us, Hugo? Flora will give you the jugs.'

'Not I,' his brother protested. 'Get your own beer.'

They packed up the game with a friendly dispute about who had won and took the big earthenware jugs to the public house down the Portobello Road for the ritual drawing of the Sunday beer.

*

On Sundays when it was cold luncheon, Flora and Tat put all the food on to the table and everyone helped themselves. Seeing how they enjoyed it and how much they ate, it had to be wondered why they bothered with the whole slow palaver of formally served meals on other days.

Little orphan Tat, who was a bit of a rebel because of being cheated out of a mother and father, had wondered this and been jumped on by Flora; for if the old order of things was ever swept away, what would you have left?

The order of Sundays at No. 72 stayed the same until the weather was too cold for the gentlemen's silly bat-and-ball game out at the back. This Sunday was a bit different because of the chimpanzee that Madge had taken out of the jungle to do good to. She might have done more good by showing him off to the Morleys when Mr Hugo and *Her* weren't there.

She, in that shiny coal-scuttle hat and buttons as large as plates on her busty jacket, had obviously thought he would lunch in the kitchen. No doubt this Jack would have been happier there. Upstairs was too polite. Some people ignored him, some tried too hard, leaning forward with exaggerated speech, pushing out their lips like Hottentots. Not easy with a mouth full of food. Flora thought he would rather be ignored. To answer, he had to put down knife and fork, his keys to heaven, to manage his rough speech and make the mumbo-jumbo signs with his hands.

Good little Dicky, nature's naughty saint who might have simply stared or giggled, took it on himself to teach the poor fellow everybody's name. When he found out that the ape could read a bit, he was tearing pages out of a notebook and writing names down.

'Bel-la. Horse-tin.' His baby name for his older brother. 'In-spec-tor French. Greg, my cou-sin.'

Dicky pointed. Cloth ears gave a grin and duck of the head, like a Punch-and-Judy puppet. The boy Greg grunted. He led his own life, Greg did, and wasted no words.

Nor did Jack, having so few of them. He leaned across Mr Will to tell Madge loudly, 'Lot food. You rich.'

She laughed and shook her head. The table had been shocked into staring silence, so Dicky tugged at the sleeve of the deaf man's awkward charity jacket and fed him another name.

'That's Lizzie. Horse-tin's wife.' Poor girlie, she could hardly reach the table. She carried her babies all to the front.

'Li-shee.'

'Don't call Elizabeth that,' Dicky's Aunt Charlotte ordered from under the black scuttle hat. 'Only servants are called Lizzie.'

Flora, bringing more bread, said, 'I beg to differ, Mrs Hugo. My Irish cousin was in service where the daughter was Lizzie, so they had to change the scullerymaid's name to Betty.'

Flora's own madam, at the end of the table in just the right sort of dove-wing November hat that put Mrs Hugo's to ridicule, said with interest, 'I didn't know you had an Irish cousin, Flora.'

'We don't talk about her much.'

'You talk about everything else,' snapped Mrs Hugo, a snob with her own staff, who despised her and robbed her blind. Madge and Bella sometimes tried to bring the old

79

girl into the twentieth century, but Flora thought it was too late. If she did ever think to treat her servants like members of the human race, they'd be dead suspicious. That crooked butler and the parlourmaid Crocker and them, they'd think *She* had found a new way of cutting wages and lengthening hours.

No one liked change really, whatever Madge and her East End lot believed. Even poor Bella might take fright if her parents suddenly started being nice to her. She had got used to being happier at No. 72 than she was at Ladbroke Lodge.

All this Flora saw. She did not miss much. Her step-brother Ben wanted her to be something better than a skivvy – 'Oh, yes, such as a criminal, working for you?' – but she would miss the drama of it, the free sideshow.

She saw that Bella was out to show her parents how good she was with the deaf specimen. She was usually shy with a strange man, but Jack didn't count. She smiled and talked into his face, like Madge had shown her, and he repeated her name loudly, 'Bey-ya.' Look! They had made friends.

But as everyone got up from the table and Jack put out a hand to pocket another apple, Flora heard Madge mutter to Bella, 'You're trying too hard. Don't *patronize* him.'

'I'm afraid it's you who are patronizing, Maddy,' Mr Will said when Bella had put out her tongue at Madge and taken Jack off to the piano, and Madge and Will had gone into the study for a cigarette. 'I know you want to give him a chance, but don't lose sight of reality.'

'Jack is my friend,' Madge said. 'Everyone brings their friends to No. 72.'

The door was open and Flora, hurrying to finish clearing

the table because it was her free afternoon, could hear them.

'All right, but don't get too *involved*,' he said, stern as a judge.

Madge laughed. 'That comes well from you. The Settlement is your life.'

'That's different. Our duty is not to damage in any way the people who need our help.'

'Oh – so sanctimonious.'

'No, Maddy, I'm right. I know you've done a lot for Jack, and he relies on you. But that's just the point. Watch that it doesn't become anything more than that.'

'You're jealous!' Good old Madge laughed again, which must have been hurtful to the poor gingery young man, because jealous was what he was, even if he didn't know it.

'Madge, come in here!' Bella called across the hall. 'Jack can get the rhythm when I use the loud pedal. Come and hear us sing!'

With her elbows out, Flora got her arms braced to the weight of the loaded tray and waddled down the hall to the back stairs with her hips steady and her feet out, as you had to do with half a ton of silverware and china. When she went out, later, she stopped in for a talk and a laugh with one or two old friends in Notting Dale and took a bottle of lemonade to her grandmother, who was in the last-call ward at St Charles's Hospital.

At No. 7 Talbot Close, Daddy Watts was asleep with his calico kerchief over both eyes after a Sunday pork dinner, so Flora and her mother drank tea and made toast by the fire in the front room, where her mother slept on the settee so as to hear her husband in the night.

'If I was you, I'd let him yell himself blue.'

'You're hard, Flo. That's why you've lost one man and not likely to get another.'

'I didn't lose Bull. I didn't want him. Better off without.'

'I don't know.'

'Six of one and half a dozen of the other.'

Like many of the women they knew, they needed men and suffered from them.

Violet was out singing in the choir at a special church service for the Girls' Friendly Society.

'Bad luck for the Friendlies,' Flora said. Vi's voice was high, but not what you'd call pure.

'She wants you to go and see that Mr Slowpoke for her. She promised to write a letter for him.'

'Why doesn't she keep her own promises?'

'Flo, she's at *church*.' Mrs Watts, like most of her neighbours, never went to church, but revered the idea of it, and was a stickler for the trappings. Vi's christening, Flora's wedding to Mr Bolt, the funeral of the stillborn baby after Violet, the last gasp of her womb, had all been grand occasions.

Slowpoke, whose name was Koslawpek, lived in a room papered all round with used postage stamps in a block of streets beyond Convent Gardens known as Jews' Island, where refugees from pogroms in Russia and Poland had settled. Although they had infiltrated the shops and market trading, many of them still could not read or write English. After Flora had made the best job she could of two business letters for him, she refused the tuppence he usually paid her sister, and went up the broken iron steps from his basement area.

The lamp-lighter came round later here, because there were no tips. The streets were already dark. Flora intended to go to some friends at Westbourne Park, who always played cards on Sundays. In All Saints Road, she passed a public house which was not open, but there was light in an uncurtained downstairs window. Inside, a man sat sideways at a table, a man with cropped hair and jutting jaw dented with the cleft of an old wound.

Her heart lurched. She stood for an instant paralysed with fear and sickness. Bull Bolt, her husband, lawful or not, she did not know, since no one was sure whether his first wife was alive or dead. Her face was quite close to the lighted window. For a moment they stared at each other, then his mouth opened square and black.

'Flor-*rer!*' He banged on the frame of the window, fit to break it.

She turned away, stumbled off the kerb and across the street and ran in a funk, not to Westbourne Park but back through the network of small streets towards Chepstow Villas, her home, her safe place.

Mrs Roach and Tat would not understand, but Madge was there, and she left the book she was reading to take Flora up to her room, out of breath, gasping, sobbing, shaking with fear, and something else she hated.

'Save me.'

'He won't come here. He can't hurt you.' Madge hugged her, tall and strong, and Flora was conscious of her own smell of sweat.

'I know. But it's me. A bit of me still – still – oh, Madge, it's disgusting.'

'No, it's not,' Madge said sensibly. 'It's sex.'

None of Flora's women friends down Notting Dale would have said that. They were crude enough, but they made out to be fearfully proper. Madge was the real friend.

She calmed Flora and joked with her and asked, 'What shall we do with the mad bull?'

'Nothing, I suppose.' Flora went to the window. Beyond the back of the house, rows and rows of roofs and chimney-pots piled away one upon the other into the smoky darkness. Somewhere in the streets below, *he* was there.

'We'll have to find you a new man,' Madge said.

'I don't want a new man. I'm done with men. But Madge . . .' Flora said with her back turned. 'Would you kill me if I ever went back to Bull?'

'No point.' Madge laughed and came to draw the curtains. 'He'd do that for me, I expect.'

'Madge, would it be all right –'

'Don't ask me to judge what's wrong and what's right. You know how I feel about that.'

'Would it be all right for me to have a wash in the bath before *they* come up?'

Chapter Eight

On Saturdays when there was no rain, or wind funnelling through the streets from the heights of north London, it was often Gwen Morley's pleasure to go shopping down Portobello Road. This November morning she was accompanied by her son Dicky and five-year-old granddaughter Laura, brought over for a treat by Austin, from Addison Road.

Gwen's Portobello Road was a different thing from the Lane of Dicky's adventures, and she had never penetrated into the meaner streets and the forbidden stews of Pottery Lane. She did not buy at the market stalls, but she knew many of the small shopkeepers and enjoyed a leisurely gossiping progress from dairy to butcher to ironmonger, inquiring after babies and ancient parents and stopping to chat in the street with housewives like herself, as if it were a village.

Dicky was greeted, discreetly because of his mother, by a different population of cunning, grubby boys and stallholders who knew him as an occasional lookout for Flora's stepbrother. He saw Noah outside the fried-fish-shop and winked at him, to disassociate himself from his proper Norfolk suit and tam-o'-shanter, but he had to stay close to Gwen and Laura, and carry the shopping basket.

They visited the grocer, where the children were allowed to take a handful of sultanas out of the sack in the back room, and bought lamb cutlets from the straw-hatted butcher and some kidneys for Mrs Roach to devil for Sunday breakfast. Although milk churns came round to No. 72 in the painted cart like a chariot, the children wanted to go to the Alderney Dairy, where podgy Miss Evans let Laura work the iron cow for customers. You put in a penny and the spout poured milk into your jug. On the way home, Gwen bought candles at the oil-shop, in case Kensington's temperamental electricity faded out again, before Dicky steered them towards the sweetshop.

'Dr Buckmaster said you were having too many sugary things.'

'It isn't for me, it's for Laura.'

He did not expect to be believed, and both children were allowed to take the little hammer and tap off triangular pieces of Palm toffee from a big block. Gwen bought Curiously Strong peppermints for herself, and the three of them took off their gloves and strolled home sucking and chewing, to deliver the cutlets for the Master's lunch. With Dicky scouting ahead, the basket bumping awkwardly against his knickerbockers, and Laura's sticky hand in hers, Gwen thought happily: This is what they mean by being fulfilled. The magazines she read told her she should be that, as a wife and mother. Her daughter Madge thought it jolly bad luck that she had never had a chance to *do* anything; but this was enough. Gwen forgot her world of servants and nannies, and exchanged a complicit smile with a fat breathless woman with a baby and two dirty toddlers: This is what we do.

Back at No. 72, with the purchases sent down to the kitchen and Mrs Roach's complaints about the size of the kidneys appeased, Gwen kept the children in the drawing room with her, so that it would look nice and domestic for Leonard when he came home. He loved his wife when she was feathery and frivolous, but also when she was cosily maternal. Just as he loved her to be dependent on him – 'Oh Leo, you do that, I'll never understand it' – but also to sympathize when he was low – 'Don't worry, darling. Gwen will make it all right.' People like her daughter, and her sister-in-law Vera who was here and there like a dragon-fly, thought she did nothing, but she was quite busy being what was expected of her.

Laura, who loved any game involving money, played with the old tin hussar who shot pennies into the gaping thick-lipped mouth of the blackamoor, once Leonard's father's toy. Dicky got the puff billiards from the bottom cupboard of the tallboy, and he and Gwen sat on the hearthrug by the fire to play.

The front-door bell rang. Had Leonard's latchkey come off his watch chain?

'I'll go!' Dicky said, but his mother was still puffing at the ball from her side, so he had to go on squeezing the bulb of his blower, or she might score. They were both frantic with laughter when Flora opened the door and said, 'Mr Taylor is here.'

Mr Taylor? Oh heavens, the intriguing man at the musicale who had looked with such speculative pleasure at her and Madge. Before Gwen could say, 'Show him in,' he *was* in, walking past Flora at the open door.

With no time to get up, Gwen sat back on her heels and held up an arm, seeing it rise pale and elegant from the fallen-back wide sleeve.

'*Mrs Morley*.' He took her hand. 'May I?' He tightened his hold to pull her to her feet, then changed his mind and loosed it to sit quickly down on the rug, as if he were not a stranger. Gwen was surprised at him, but not offended. He took a puffer bulb out of the box. 'May I play?'

Dicky thought he was topping, and Laura left the penny hussar and came to join in.

Dicky pushed her away. Laura squared her mouth ready to cry.

'She's too young. She can't puff.'

'She can with me.' Mr Taylor put his hand over the little girl's and squeezed for her, to make a high score, and win. Gwen had the feeling that he invariably won at games, like Dicky, who shouted, 'Fluke! Play again and I'll beat you.'

'No.' Gwen was getting up from the floor gracefully. 'We are going to have a glass of Madeira. Please fetch the tray.'

Oh, pooh, Dicky thought as he brought in the decanter and small glasses from the dining room. They're going to sit on furniture and be grown-up. He went upstairs. Laura asked Mr Taylor, 'Have you got any pennies? I want to fill Sambo up before I empty him,' and went back to the hussar.

Bella had a throat. This was the first of the many colds she expected to have this winter. Her mother was out in her big fur hat, lunching with a friend who had once been lady-in-waiting to a minor Austro-Hungarian princess, and her father took no heed of any colds except his own, beyond telling Bella to stop clearing her throat in that exasperating way. When she had been deprived of her governess and sent north to a Spartan boarding school, she had ended up

88

in the cottage hospital with pneumonia, because her father had not believed that she was ill enough to be brought home.

Now she went where she always went in need: to No. 72. When she entered the drawing room with her face flushed and swollen and her throat on fire, it was embarrassing to find a strange man sitting with her aunt Gwen by the fire on one of the chintz chairs that were less elegant than the furniture at Ladbroke Lodge but more comfortable.

'Oh, I'm sorry.' She felt clumsy. 'I didn't know you –'

'Don't be silly, Bella. Come in and shut the door, you're making a draught. My niece, Bella Morley. This is Mr Taylor.'

'How are you, Miss Morley?'

A rather stylish man in his thirties, clean-shaven, good-looking, though not as handsome as golden-bearded Gerald Lazenby, Bella's touchstone of the moment. Mr Taylor was tall enough to have to bend slightly towards Bella as he took her hand, which luckily was still gloved. She had an ugly chilblain on it already, hardly fair in November.

'I'm quite well, thank you,' she fibbed.

'Are you *sure*?' He made two caressing syllables of it. His eyes were dark brown with amber flecks, concerned for her.

'Yes, thank you.'

'I think you are not,' Mr Taylor said kindly, and Aunt Gwen added, 'You sound dreadful, dear. You shouldn't have come out.'

'My mother is not at home and I have no medicine. I wanted to ask you for some of your Mindeterer's spirit.'

'Of course.'

Gwen reached towards the bell, but Mr Taylor raised an

89

eyebrow and asked, 'You put your faith in Professor Mindeterer, then?'

'We do, yes.'

'It makes your eyes water and the top of your head blow
off steam, so you seriously believe it's clearing the passages?'
Was he mocking them?

'It helps me,' Bella said huskily, and Aunt Gwen, who
swore by Mindeterer's, said hopefully, 'We like the advertisements.'

'I see.' Mr Taylor's voice had sharpened from being soft
and sympathetic to a more authoritative tone. 'If you have
faith in it, it will do you good?' His upward inflection
carried a hint of a regional accent.

'What else would you suggest?'

Aunt Gwen was in danger of laughing lazily at him, but
he anticipated her, and laughed himself. His teeth were
almost as white and strong as Gerald Lazenby's, but less
prominent. 'It would be pree-sumptuous of me to tell your
niece what to do.'

'Do you *know*?' Aunt Gwen narrowed her grey eyes and
curved up her closed mouth like a cat.

'If it was up to me, I had rather see her simply take eight
or ten drops of camphor on a lump of sugar every two
hours.'

'That sounds too harmless.' Gwen preferred remedies
that scoured and burned and tasted drastic.

'I always get such dreadfully heavy colds, you see.'
Bella's throat felt as if it had swallowed a horsehair
bolster.

'Every winter?'

'Yes,' she said thickly. 'This is just the first.'

'Then let it be the last.'

He touched her arm lightly, felt that it was hot and moved his fingers down to hold her wrist.

'Do you know how to take her pulse?'

'Well . . .' Mr Taylor gave Gwen his charming tilted smile. 'I am by way of being a medical man.'

'A doctor!' Aunt Gwen and Bella were impressed. Because there was so much illness, real or imagined, doctors were held in some esteem, even though they were often at best no help and at worst dangerously wrong.

When the master of the house came in and Laura rushed to jump up and greet him, Gwen told him at once, 'Mr Taylor is a doctor, Leonard.'

'Of a kind. I hope you don't object to my calling on you, Mr Morley. I believe it's correct for the lady to call first.'

'I never can remember,' Gwen murmured.

'But I was afraid I might not see your delightful family again, and so . . .'

'How did you know our address?'

'Discreet inquiries.' Mr Taylor smiled broadly at Leonard and clapped him on the arm as if they were already friends. 'How are the ironworks, Mr Morley?'

'Very fine indeed, sir, very fine. May I interest you in any wrought-iron lamps today?' The Assistant Manager caricatured his 'Our Mr Morley' manner.

Flora Bolt came in and made questioning faces under her parlourmaid cap at Gwen, who said, 'You will join us for luncheon, of course, Mr Taylor?'

'You're too kind. I have an appointment. I hope I haven't held you up?'

'Not at all. Bella? We can stretch the cutlets, I'm sure.' She spread her arms vaguely.

'I couldn't eat anything. I think I'll go home and lie down and – and . . .' She looked at Mr Taylor. 'And try the camphor.'

'May I go and look for a taxicab?'

'So kind of you, Dr Taylor, but Bella only lives a few yards up the road, in Kensington Park Gardens.'

'In that case, I'll be happy to accompany Miss Morley.'

Although Bella liked No. 72 Chepstow Villas – square, unpretentious, welcoming – better than four-storey Ladbroke Lodge with its high haughty windows and imposing entrance, she quite enjoyed its effect on someone who brought her home for the first time.

'Very impressive,' Mr Taylor said dutifully. Bella ran her hand over the head of the left-hand black leopard, before he followed her up the wide marble steps.

She did not have a latchkey, as Madge did. Her mother liked to know at what time she came home, and saw nothing wrong in keeping one of the servants up to let her in. The butler Hurd opened the front door and raised his circumflex eyebrows to see Miss Bella in such personable male company. Wait until he sees Gerald Lazenby when he calls for me soon with a formal request to be a guest at Heckworth House for the Lord Lieutenant's Yuletide ball, thought Bella.

'I'll say goodbye.' Tobias Taylor stood on the front step as Bella went past Hurd into the hall.

'Won't you come in?'

'I should be off. Well . . .' He was looking round the rather splendid hall with interest. 'Just for a moment, then, just to make sure you are going to be all right.'

'Come and meet my father.' Dr Taylor and Hugo Morley might impress each other.

'He is in the dining room, Miss Bella,' the butler said. 'He did not wait for you.'

'Is he angry?' No, Bella, no. Don't demean yourself to this supercilious servant. Don't let Mr Taylor see you are afraid. 'I mean,' she covered it up before Hurd could anwer. 'He won't mind if we disturb him?'

Hurd opened the dining room door. 'You're late,' Hugo Morley said at once. 'Meals start on time in this house, in case you hadn't noticed.'

Bella was glad that Mr Taylor did not retreat at this welcome, but stepped quite boldly into the room.

'Father, this is Mr – Dr Taylor. He was visiting Aunt Gwen, and he walked me home.'

'Good afternoon, doctor.' Bella's father stood up, still holding his napkin, to show that he was going to sit down to eat again in a moment.

The men shook hands, and Hugo asked whether the doctor was in practice in London.

'Since fairly recently. I have been working and studying abroad.'

Bella was intrigued, but her father was clearly more interested in his cooling fricassee than in Tobias Taylor, who apologized for his interruption and stood back.

Hugo Morley grunted and sat down. 'Sit at the table, Bella. You'll have to miss the soup.'

'I don't want any lunch today, Father.' He accepted that without comment other than an instruction to Hurd about the sweet which kept the butler in the dining room, so that Bella was able to let Dr Taylor out herself.

He turned back to her on the top step, looking protect-ively down on her, which was nice from a tall man. 'Camphor,' he said. 'White sugar. Bed rest.'

Briefly, she thought his eyes disrobed her into a night-dress. She shut the heavy door quickly and listened behind it to his brisk footsteps going away, and then the sound of hoofs and wheels and his assured voice calling, 'Cabbie!'

Dr Taylor, eh? Well, why not, if it pleased them? If Toby had not been so unfairly dismissed from the school of medicine, he would own that title by right. 'It is an offence for anyone falsely to assume a title or description implying him to be a legally qualified medical practitioner.' But he had never called himself Dr Taylor. The Morleys had done that.

Nice family, the Morleys. Ordinary, middle middle class, comfortable, contented, the famous ancestor a flash in the pan. Miss Bella a misfit, for some reason which he might or might not discover. Her father, a bit *nouveau*, but *riche* as well, trying to be a tyrant, but perhaps no worse than thousands of other self-important fathers, whose daughters accepted a certain fear of them as a fact of life.

Among the London people known to Tobias Taylor, both socially and as patients, he had several contacts of some note or glitter, and others at the more questionable end of the scale. He did not often get to know stable bourgeois folk like the Morleys. He had never been part of a family. How would he see them again? Mrs Morley had spoken of a large clan. They might not need him. He must offer them something attractive.

*

94

'If your throat was bad enough to put you off your food,' Bella's mother wanted to know, 'why did you go out into the cold?'

'I wanted to get some medicine from Aunt Gwen.'

'Madge could have brought it round, or one of the maids.'

'Yes.' From her bed, Bella watched her mother cruise about the room, touching things as if she were taking an inventory, closing an open book, reading a half-written letter on the desk. Charlotte did not go into the subject of Dr Taylor, but she had received a full report.

'With me not at home, was it appropriate to bring a strange man to interrupt your father's luncheon?'

'He is a friend of Aunt Gwen and Uncle Leonard's.'

'It's the first I've heard of him. Who are his people? Your father thought him a bit of a bounder.'

'Oh, *Mother*.' Bella had been reading comfortably against the pillows in a warm flannel nightgown. Now she shifted about, restless and scratchy. The book dropped to the floor. 'Father grumbles at me for not knowing any young men. When I do bring someone home, he's got to find fault.'

'Don't speak against your father.' This was one of Charlotte's sayings, to ward off divided loyalty and comply with the duties of wife and mother. She was not cruel, as Hugo was. She was actually a fairly kind woman underneath the Victorian Teutonic snobbery, but too limited and cowardly to open any doors on truth.

Bella looked so ugly, poor child, slipped awkwardly down in the bed with her hair all tangles and her big nose red and swollen. 'If I was to have only one daughter,' Hugo had recently asked the Almighty, 'why this?' And Charlotte had not even murmured, 'Hugo – please,' and glanced at the butler to see if he had heard. She had felt herself sitting there like a stuffed parrot. She had missed her opportunity. She was an accomplice by default, in something that was savagery. *Because Bella had been there in the room.*

Remembering this with shame, she made an attempt to please her daughter by asking, 'If you haven't heard about the Yuletide ball yet, would you like me to get in touch with Mrs Lazenby?'

'No.' Bella scowled.

'Why not? I could –'

'Because I have heard.'

'From Gerald?'

'It's all arranged.'

'Splendid, dear.' Bella knew that her mother knew she was lying. 'We'll have to think about the chartreuse taffeta.'

Lies were easier than truth. Why didn't everyone use them more often to deflect hurt? If you were caught out, you told another lie, and then another, if necessary, until the whole thing had become so complicated that your tormentors were as confused as you were.

'In any case,' Bella said later to Sybil Crocker, the parlourmaid, 'they don't always believe me when I *am* telling the truth.'

Charlotte and Hugo had gone out. Bella had not ordered any supper sent up, but when she woke after a sleep, she felt better. She had been tapping out ten drops of camphor every hour, to double the recommended two hourly dose. There, see – it had worked. Who *was* this Tobias Taylor?

'Let it be the last,' he had instructed her, as if you could control extrinsic, omnipotent things like colds and chills. The family doctor, Dr Buckmaster, 'Little Bucky', as he was proprietarily called, although he was of medium height, talked of illness as an attacker. 'The enemy is storming the gates,' he liked to say lugubriously. Bacteria were 'foreign hordes' against which you were powerless. What was this Taylor person talking about?

Now that her throat was less sore, Bella was hungry. She could have rung the bell, but she was lonely, too, so she swung her sturdy legs down off the high bed, put on a dressing gown and slippers and went down to the servants' sitting room.

Sybil Crocker was her friend. Observing how Madge had made a friend of Flora Bolt, she saw that it could be done, especially with a parlourmaid who was more refined than slap-bang Flora. Sybil was an enigma, but Bella thought she was her friend. She wanted her to be. To that end, she sometimes made the mistake of spilling out confidences to the maid's untrustworthy ear.

Crocker fancied herself a 'lady domestic', of which there were known to be some below stairs, women of fairly good class who had fallen on hard times. If she wanted to maintain the fiction of having had to leave her neat suburban villa in Richmond when her husband had died young and left her nothing but his widowed mother, that was acceptable to Bella, who understood the need for fictions.

The butler and the cook and the housemaid and the scullerymaid, and probably the chauffeur, too, subscribed to the tale as one of the legends that coloured downstairs life, like the background of Hurd the butler, whose indistinct past was respected. It was known that he had held some grander posts and knew of scandals in high places, which he could reveal if he chose. He did not talk much of his family, although there were hints of a mysterious relative in the badlands west of Clarendon Road, revered as a witch doctor, it was said, in Pottery Lane.

'In any case . . .' While the fat cook nodded off in her armchair, Bella ate bread and butter at the sitting-room table, which looked up through a barred window to the back garden and the railings of Ladbroke Square. 'I do believe that I am invited to the Lazenbys' at Heckworth. Gerald has said as much. It's just that he's been so busy with his cubbing and all that, he's forgotten to confirm it.'

'Well, men are like that,' the housemaid said.

'Mine was not,' Sybil Crocker reminded her sharply. 'But then, of course, he was a gentleman.'

'So is Gerald.' Bella fired up with her mouth full, and coughed out breadcrumbs.

'In love with him, eh?' Crocker asked casually.

'Oh yes, I think so.' Bella knew she should not gush, but it was so nice to be able to let go in the fuggy air of roasted meat and the red hot fire and Hurd's cigar, stolen from upstairs. So nice to let her tight, nervous self feel swoony about Gerald, who had made a surprise dive to kiss her, sitting out on the stairs at the Hamilton House ball. The kiss had landed on the corner of her mouth, wet and bristly. He had grabbed at her front in a way that had made her stand up quickly and run down the stairs, her whole body suddenly feeling naked, exposed, the blush scorching up her face to set the roots of her hair on fire.

'That's right.' Crocker was quite encouraging. 'It's natural for a young healthy girl like you.'

'Oh, wait till you see him, Sybil. He's a real dazzler.'

'I'm sure. So you shall go to the ball, Cinderella, and dance with the prince, and get spliced, and keep us a pew at the back for the wedding.'

'Oh, stop.' Bella blushed. 'Stop teasing.'

'No, we wouldn't do that, Miss Bella.' Leaning back in his chair, the butler watched her with cold eyes under the curiously dark brows which did not match his pale streaky hair. 'We'd all like to see you wed.'

'Oh, I don't care if I never marry,' Bella protested, as always, in case she never did.

'Now you sound like your cousin Madge.' Crocker pinched her cut-back mauve nostrils and pulled down her mouth.

'What's wrong with her?'

'Well dear, you two are close enough. I should have thought you would be aware.'

'Aware of what?' Bella could not help asking, although she knew she should not gossip with these people, only half known, for all they shared her life in this house.

'Why did she cut her hair then?'

The parlourmaid slid a glance at the butler. He took out the cigar, tapped off a perfect fat cylinder of ash and replaced it in his fleshy mouth as if he were going to swallow it.

Bella pushed back her chair. 'Because she likes it short. It looks just right on her.' For no reason, Bella felt trapped. 'It's easier to manage,' she gabbled huskily. 'And she's a – she's a new kind of woman, you know. She's progressive.'

'Progressed a bit too far, you might say.' Crocker had

resumed her aloof look, eyes focused on the picture rail.

'There's nothing wrong with being a new feminist.' Bella liked to think she was one herself, if only on the fringe.

'There's another name for it.' The maid spat out a word which was not familiar to Bella.

'What do you mean, Sybil?'

'You've not heard of it? You're a bit behind with the latest topics, upstairs.'

The butler guffawed. The housemaid grinned and wagged her head.

'Women and women.' The cook opened her pig eyes to whisper it.

Bella had heard hints about such a perversion. It was one of the more desperate accusations aimed at the suffragists.

'That's disgusting.' Bella stood up. 'Madge has her friend Will Morrison, in any case.'

Why argue it at their level? Madge did not need Bella to stand up for her. She tightened the sash of her dressing gown and made for the door, while the servants watched her.

Chapter Nine

At the Loudon Street Settlement, Madge's job was mostly teaching the crowds of children, many of whom came from the workhouse and had never been to school. Tiny crippled Angel, jerking helplessly in her wooden cart, was brought in by a ten-year-old sister who sometimes forgot to bring her and sometimes forgot to collect her. Madge had not seen her for weeks when the low cart was pulled in one raw December morning. She hurried to wrap the shivering child in a blanket.

'She hasn't enough clothes on. Don't you . . . ?' But the silent sister had already disappeared.

Angel's crumpled face was pale, except where it was blue and bruised under the dirt. But she tried to hold up sticks of arms, and settled on to the lap of Madge's cotton smock like an old man in his fireside chair. Madge gave her some warm gruel from a jug, and the child coughed most of it back. She was listless and breathing badly, but it might be days before one of the volunteer doctors turned up.

Madge tried to rouse her by talking about the Christmas party. One of her helpers, a slovenly girl training to be a nursemaid, said knowledgeably, 'That won't live till Christmas, that won't.'

Madge was sad today, and Will was expressively angry. His face and body were made for it, with his curly red beard and smouldering eyes and his short wiry physique –

shorter than Madge's – which could seem taller when he held himself erect and tense.

He was angry with Jack Haynes, who was restless and moody, bored with his job as apprentice to a cabinet-maker. He had deliberately broken a tool in the workshop, and he had been seen by a policeman down under Blackfriars Bridge with some of his old gang.

In the dusty attic room which served as an office, Will was haranguing him clearly and loudly. 'You must *work*.' He swung an imaginary hammer. 'Your big chance. You *must* succeed now or you're lost!'

Jack stood woodenly, head bowed under the low ceiling, thick arms hanging away from his sides, face obtuse. You could not always tell what he was thinking, nor whether he had understood.

'After all we've done for you,' Will was driven to say. 'Do something for us!'

'But it's *his* choice, isn't it?' Madge murmured, looking away from Jack. 'You taught me your philosophy of help, Will. "No strings attached." Now you sound like a social reformer, worse than Mrs Humphry Ward.'

Will ignored her. 'What about it, Jack?' He was trying to do one of his electrifying tricks, but how could this poor bear of a young fellow commit himself to effort when he probably was not even sure what was being asked of him?

Madge stepped forward to face Jack, so that he could hear and see what she told him.

'*I* believe in you.'

Jack's jaw dropped and spread into its caricature of a grin. 'Maddy.' Will was angry with both of them now. 'I've told you,' he said quietly. 'Don't always make it so *personal*.'

Madge turned to answer him, and Jack's grin shut like a closed umbrella. 'You talkin' about me?'

You had to be so careful with him. How could deaf people *not* be suspicious? They never knew more than one per cent of what was going on.

Will had not liked it that she had taken Jack to No. 72 Chepstow Villas again, to experience the family – Gwen's kindness, people in and out of the house, Dicky's silly infectious jokes, Mrs Roach's chocolate cake, a surrounding of talk, as well as signs and gestures.

'Hand signs aren't language,' Madge had said. 'Language is a living thing, not just a convenience. Jack does very well, but he has no emotional words, like laugh, joy, sorrow, love.'

'I know what he needs.' Will liked to be the instructor. 'But not at your house.'

'I can't take him there just once and then not again. He would think he hadn't been liked.'

'I wonder,' Will had said, 'whether you credit him with too much sensibility?'

Now in the low-raftered office, when Jack had rubbed up his bristly black hair and gone away, Madge wanted to put her arms round Will and hold him to his dream. When she had first started to work with him at the Settlement, she had wanted him to be more practical. Now she wanted to hold on to his idealism. She knew that he was resisting pressure from his father to go back to his law studies. He was only occasionally sleeping in the dormitory these nights, but he was here every long day, disappointed with helpers who claimed exhaustion, but not able to see it in himself.

'You're tired, Will,' Madge said tenderly.

'Don't make excuses for me. If you don't agree with a woman, she always thinks there's something wrong with you.'

'I worry about you because we're so close. I love you as my best friend.'

She wished she could say just, 'I love you,' because she thought she did. The further they moved apart, the more she wanted him.

By the laws of etiquette, it was now Gwen's turn to call on Tobias Taylor; but before she got round to doing that, he came to Chepstow Villas again with an invitation to see *Peter Pan* with Gerald du Maurier and Nina Boucicault at the Duke of York's Theatre.

Looking very smart in one of the new dinner jackets with a brocade tie and waistcoat, he came in a hired motor car to fetch Leonard and Gwen and Madge and Dicky and Laura. He had invited Laura's parents too, but Elizabeth was very near her time, and Austin wanted to stay at home with her.

Tobias Taylor – 'My friends call me Toby, so please will you?' – was very good company for the children as well as the grown-ups. Most bachelors – if that is what he was – were irritated by children, or ignored them, but this Uncle Toby, as they began to call him, sat with Laura and Dicky on the little seats facing backwards, and went out of his way to make this a special evening for them. He told them some fascinating facts and fantasies about Peter Pan, and invented stories with them about people and places they passed on the way to the theatre.

Neither child was shy, and they responded noisily.

Leonard leaned forward to replace the plug in the speaking tube, so that the driver would not be distracted.

'Bee-chums peelz!' Dicky was reading out signs in a German accent, like his aunt Charlotte's brother. 'My mother takes those.'

'They can't do her any harm.' Dr Taylor smiled at Gwen. 'They're made mostly of ginger and soap.'

'Ginger soap!' Dicky made a face as if his mouth was full of lather. 'You shan't make me take any of those, Mama.'

'A good little Beecham's' was one of Gwen's favourite cure-alls. 'What would you prescribe for indigestion, then, Dr Taylor?'

'Please call me Toby. We're having a gay night out.'

'To-by.' Gwen drew out his name uncertainly. She was not used to making friends so quickly.

'Probably something herbal. I'm by way of being a naturopathic physician, you see.'

'I see,' said Gwen, who didn't.

'I'm glad,' put in Madge, who was looking lovely, Leonard thought, in a white undecorated dress, with her short hair burnished like the gold of her necklace. 'There are too many humbug patent medicines, and I'm quite afraid of all these new chemicals.'

'You should be.' Toby's eyes admired her. 'A motor can't run if there's grit in the petrol. Nor can the bew-tee-ful body machine if it's full of foreign substances.'

'Tell me something funny,' Dicky clamoured, to get his attention back.

The seats in the front row of the dress circle were perfect for the children. Toby kept them keyed up with excitement until the curtain went up and they, like every other child in the house, every grown-up, surrendered to the old magic.

Gwen, who was always carried away at the theatre, was in love with Gerald du Maurier, especially as Mr Darling. 'He doesn't really act,' she dreamed in the car. 'He just is himself.'

'Not really,' Leonard said. 'He isn't at all like that. I've met him in the store with his wife, and he seemed quite spoiled and impatient.'

'I'm in love, too,' Laura said sleepily. 'With Peter Pan.'

'Silly,' Dicky jeered. 'It was a woman.'

'Wasn't.'

'Was.'

'Wasn't ...' Laura fell asleep with her head against Toby. He put his arm round her and asked Madge, 'Who are you in love with?'

'Nobody.' She had told her father about her disagreement with Will Morrison. She told him a lot of things, though not, Leonard suspected, much about her inner self.

'What about you, To-by?' Madge asked, bold in the warm, leather-smelling box of the car. 'Is your wife still abroad?'

'My *wife* – why?'

'All men of your kind of age are married, more or less. It makes it hard for us, in our early twenties.'

Straightforward Madge did not often flirt. But when she did, it was very direct. Leonard thought she was too bold, and looked to see whether Tobias Taylor thought so, too. It was dark in the back of the car, but the light from a passing street lamp showed his handsome face unruffled.

*

After the successful theatre outing, Toby Taylor continued to see quite a lot of the Morleys. Gwen and Leonard visited the house in Egerton Terrace, South Kensington, where he saw patients on the first floor and lived in comfortable rooms above, graced with quite good furniture and pictures, some of beautiful women.

'My weakness,' he explained to Leonard.

'The weakness of us all.' Leonard smirked, as if he were a gay dog. He liked it that Toby treated him as a contemporary, and did not call him sir.

The naturopathic doctor came again to Chepstow Villas and met more of the family, making a clever score of twenty-three in the season's last stump cricket match on a mild December Sunday. He brought flowers to Gwen, talked about Society with Charlotte, went with them to the pantomime, joked freely about miracle cures with Leonard's younger sister Vera and made up a running jest with her about a man whose electropathic massage belt lit him up like a glow-worm on embarrassing occasions. He was pleasant and polite to Aunt Teddie, paying attention to her boring, negative conversation from which most people slithered away.

Edwina Wynn – significant that they defeminize her name to Teddie – is lonely, Toby thought. The family is tired of her. Her husband Ralph ignores her, even when he's there. The young twin son has escaped into a sturdier world of his own. The skinny daughter Sophie is beyond her reach. She seems to suffer from persistent melancholia. One in every big family.

Toby saw quite a few pessimistic and discouraged women like Edwina Wynn at his clinic, which, when he started to practise here six years ago, he had risked calling The Clinique to attract a good class of paying patients.

Miss Grover, who came to him weekly, had never really recovered from the death of her adored mother. Adored? The old lady had been a tyrant, keeping at home her spinster daughter who was now unable to use her freedom to start a better way of life.

Miss Grover had been to many doctors for her 'nerves' and chronic dyspepsia, which affected her whole digestive tract from her swallowing mechanism to the peristaltic functions of her colon. When she first came to Tobias Taylor, humanistic naturopath, she had been so scoured with fierce aperients and high colonic lavage that it was a wonder she had any intestines left at all.

Toby was treating her with an aromatic tea mixture specifically prepared by the herbalist in Wales who supplied him with pills and draughts and salves, and a healthier diet than the overdone meats and heavy puddings favoured by the old cook at her mother's house in Marylebone.

His first triumph with Irene Grover had been to persuade her to retire the suet-pudding cook in favour of a younger woman who understood about vegetables and salads and would cheerfully brew the herbal tea, instead of throwing it away and substituting Mazawatee. His next would be to encourage her to sell the gloomy steep-roofed house and buy a small villa in the suburbs where she could keep the dog she had always wanted, but still thought of as taboo, as if her monstrous mother were still alive.

To exercise her insides and get in training for the dog, she had to walk every day with head up and shoulders back and report to Toby something interesting that she noticed, and smile at a minimum of three people whom she passed in the street.

'I walked all the way here,' she announced when Mrs Drew, the housekeeper, showed her in to the consulting room, 'although I was very tired. I saw a gentleman fall down in the street,' she droned, as if reciting a school lesson. 'He was having some kind of fit. No, I didn't stop to help him. There were others more competent. What use would I be?'

She sat on the edge of one of the comfortable cane and chintz armchairs that Toby had bought at Whiteley's, and sighed and admitted that although she had felt too enervated to do more than cross to the other side of the street when the well-dressed, respectable man fell down foaming and making dreadful braying sounds, not having stopped had made her feel worse.

'Could you have done anything, do you think?'

'Yes. A young man had stopped and bent over him. He looked up and called to me to get help. I turned the corner.'

'Why?'

'I couldn't help it. You know what I'm like, Mr Taylor.'

'I know you can do more than you think.'

Miss Grover shook her head, sad under the bird's-wing hat that had at last replaced the funeral bonnet.

'But I should have,' she whispered, looking at her boots.

'There's no should or ought. The word is *could*, remember?'

'Thank you for giving me so much of your time,' Miss Grover said when he went over to the bell pull, tapestried for him by a patient.

'I never want to hurry our appointments.'

'But there's other people.'

'None more important than you.'

'I see them in the waiting room. They stare when I go out.'

'Because they are thinking, "There goes a good advertisement for Mr Taylor. Look how she comes out smiling."'

Her unpractised face moved into its difficult smile and she went out with Mrs Drew.

'Head!' he said, and she jerked it up manfully as she went through the door.

Young Mrs Ackerley and her husband had been to Italy in October. 'Just as you told us to do, Mr Taylor.'

'I didn't exactly tell you, did I? I suggested that it might be just the change you needed.'

Patients heard what they wanted to hear. He did not give orders, nor lay down hard and fast opinions, like some of the godlike doctors whom they had trusted and feared. But when patients had made up their own minds about what they wanted to do, they often liked to think it was what Toby had told them.

'Well,' said young Mrs Ackerley, pouting prettily against the veil of her hat, 'it's wather the same thing.' Since her ugly skin condition had improved, she had begun to practise some flirtatious little tricks, like fluttering eyelashes, and cheek pulled in to make a dimple, and smudging her Rs.

'The veil?' Toby asked.

It had taken two visits and the best part of a third to get her to raise the veil. He had had to peer through it at the skin rash which had been rubbed raw by a specialist's revolutionary new corrosive ointment.

She lifted it daintily over the brim of her hat, and sat slightly sideways, with her elbow on the arm of the chair and her small pale hand under her chin, as if Toby were going to paint her portrait.

'Bew-tee-ful,' he breathed. This was not strictly true, except in comparison with how she had first come to him. 'Beautiful, isn't she, Mr Ackerley?'

Her young husband, who always came to The Clinique with her, because he did not let her go anywhere alone, sat silent in the other chair and sucked the ivory knob of his cane.

He had never said much in the year it had taken to heal the ravages of the drastic treatment, which had promised a new skin for old, and to allow the herbal salves to do their work.

Mrs Ackerley only needed to come to The Clinique now for fresh supplies of her mallow-root gel and the beech-tar paste with which she masked her face like a religious ritual during the relaxation siesta after her special diet lunch.

'I continue to follow your regimen strictly, Mr Taylor.' She produced the dimple. 'It has been my miracle.' She fondled the jar of ointment supplied by Toby's herbalist. 'My mysterious miracle, whose secret you will never tell.'

He smiled at her enigmatically, and she said, 'It's only herbs, isn't it? Dandelion and thistle seed, like a witch's brew. Why are herbs always tied up with myths and magic?'

'Because many of them can be toxic. The myths were woven centuries ago to keep the ignorant from poisoning themselves and other people with home-made remedies.'

'*I* wouldn't.' Young Mrs Ackerley pulled down her veil

so as to give him an innocent siren's eye from behind it. His eyes responded suitably. Did she ever practise these puny wiles on her blank husband? Would he even notice?

'Every healer has had some disastrous followers,' Toby said. 'Look at Dr Mesmer and the harm that was done in his name.'

'Magnetism. My gwandfather was very taken with that. He used to make hotel staff move his bed all over the room until he could be sure it faced north-east. Or was it west? Should we move our bed, do you think, William?'

Her husband lifted his mouth from the cane to grin his wet lips at her quite lasciviously. A good sign. Toby thought that the improvement in young Mrs Ackerley's skin was due not only to his salves, but to the confidence they – and he – had given her to behave like a woman.

In gratitude for her miracle, she had brought him a small parcel wrapped in green paper. 'I bwought you a little something from Italy.' It was a tiny alabaster model of a birdbath, complete with four doves on the edge.

Toby was careful to include them both in his graceful thanks. Mrs Ackerley bridled a little. Mr Ackerley continued to suck the knob of his cane. If I was to push his head down, Toby thought, I'd knock out his front teeth.

After them, he saw a man with a floating liver who had been bled and purged and prodded and lectured by doctors who could not help him until he stopped drinking, but who would not stop drinking if he could not be helped. Either more or less intoxicated, he would reel into The Clinique to talk about death. Toby did not talk to him about life. He gave him a strong whisky and water.

It was a relief, at the end of the afternoon, to take off his stiff collar and jacket and stop being courteous and charming. To address discreet Mrs Drew as Neelie, and shout at her down the stairs to hurry up with his coffee and cakes.

As his practice had grown, by word of mouth, since he was not registered as an acceptable referral for professional medical men, he was seeing several patients a day, often productively, sometimes not, and constantly learning from his failures and successes.

He knew that, had things been different, he would have been a wonderful doctor, a leading man in his field, fetched to Buckingham Palace in a carriage with footmen. His ambition had been thwarted, but as this pleasant humanistic, naturopathic practice prospered, he began to see that being expelled from the London medical school could have been a stroke of luck.

After all, hadn't he been pushed out because he was too clever? After two years of study, he had felt himself to be more effective than some of the dry-as-dust prehistoric professors who had been teaching the same principles and practices since the middle of the nineteenth century. He rebelled against the limitations imposed, even on senior students. When no one was looking, he behaved like a doctor. Patients on the wards liked him. He answered their questions and they talked to him, timid sick people who were afraid to open their mouths before one of the whiskery great men. Toby Taylor had been evicted from the hospital because he did too much and told too much. That unfortunate business with the nurse – that was just another weapon they used against him.

Luckily – Toby believed his life was full of luck – this had happened after the death of his father, who would have been savagely furious. The old man had been an irascible physician in Swansea. He hated being called out at night – it interfered with his drinking – and he did not like his patients, so he had moved into research, and muddling about in the confused waters of local health programmes.

His wife, whom he considered inferior and had always dominated, had been too unsure of herself to give Toby enough childhood security. He and she were close, because they were both victims, and they had shared some love and innocent good times together, but Toby stayed away from home as much as he could, to avoid drunken rages or black glooms, and the fleshy vulgar women his father began to bring home, to torment his already unbalanced wife. As soon as he could, Toby had lied and charmed his way into a place at the London medical school, to escape the drinking and the scenes and the women, one of whom had initiated him expertly at the age of fifteen.

When Toby went back to Glamorgan after his father's death, he found his widowed mother stranger than she had already been when he left home, and wandering dazedly down the road to insanity. He had taken a job as a hospital attendant in Swansea, which had taught him a lot of practical, down-to-earth things medical students never learned, and had managed, with help from a local old totty, to take care of his mother. It was during this time that he had made friends with Glyn, the gentle genius herbalist who had taught him some basics of his craft and now supplied The Clinique with nature remedies.

The kitchen manager at the hospital, where Toby was at that time on the Almoner's staff, went to London to work with a faddist physician who believed food to be the cause and cure of all illnesses. Toby followed her, was soon the faddist's assistant, and added some knowledge of diet to his repertoire.

His mother could not live alone, so he had her certified and moved to an institution within reach of London. On his visits there, he talked with one of the few genuine psychologists on the staff of this huge pinnacled institution called The Keep, an idealist who gave time to studying the individual, rather than classifying diseases of the currently voguish central nervous system. He encouraged Toby to read Sigmund Freud, and taught him something about the psychology of human behaviour.

Picking up smatterings from everywhere seemed to Toby to be far more valuable than giving your life in depth to the pursuit of only one kind of knowledge. By his late twenties, he had begun to see how he could present himself as a man of healing.

Six years ago, he had started his naturalist practice with few misgivings and a sincere desire to help his fellow man. If he made money along the way, that would only strengthen his dedication. Believing in luck was really a belief in yourself and your ability to grasp opportunity. His patients, men as well as women, wanted to believe in him. He was handsome and engaging and clever and attentive, unlike any doctor they had known. Charm was an important tool of his trade. He gave people what they wanted. Doctors gave them pills, and assaulted them with treatments that were often humiliating or painful. Toby's gift was to make them feel better about themselves. He prospered.

That successful old charlatan Mesmer, who had the

gullible moving their beds about all over Europe – he knew about charm. He resurrected the word *charisma*. His magnetism had not all been the kind displayed by a compass. Trading on old daydreams and extravaganzas of long ago, he added the mysteries of planets and loadstones to ordinary nervous excitement. At healing ceremonies, he wore a sweeping lilac gown and held a wand over female supplicants, while young male assistants massaged spines and induced 'magnetic fluid' by applying fingertip pressure to breasts . . .

But the old Teutonic mountebank had discovered some truths. He knew that 'one man's energy affects another's sensibility'. That spoke very clearly to Toby.

Although somewhat drained of charm and energy at the end of a busy day, he had restored both with tea and whisky by the time Mrs Marie-May Lacoste came in on her way to the theatre.

Glorious Marie-May was in the second act of a Beerbohm Tree drama, so she sometimes came to Egerton Terrace for an early light meal, or after the performance for a late supper. Sometimes Toby went to the theatre and hung about in the dressing room before taking his mistress with the frosty fair hair out to supper. Although she was married, after a fashion, it was always to a restaurant and at a table where they would be seen. Marie-May, on the ascent in her stage career, needed to be seen in the cobwebby gowns which, with her astonishing cloud of hair, made her seem to float. Toby Taylor, on the ascent as a practitioner, needed to be seen with her.

It was a useful as well as an exciting affair, although lately it had acquired a *frisson* of the danger that, although he subscribed to 'He travels the fastest . . .', Toby might be falling in love.

Mrs Neelie Drew, wearing a tight face, showed her up to the first-floor salon where the fire had just the right glowing life and the small round table was set for two before it. Although Neelie Drew was sometimes required to bring breakfast to the bedroom for both of them, they waited until the door closed behind her before embracing – gingerly, since the actress would not have time to repair her hair or ivory porcelain face before going down to the waiting cab.

Her mouth tasted of peppermints and the sea. She took off her gloves and furs and sat down at the table, where candles were lit and the cold food already set out. Toby took a bottle from the hearth and poured the wine.

Marie-May, though delicate as a dandelion puff, was always hungry. She began to eat at once, as they exchanged friendly gossip, Toby about patients, she about the theatre.

With the edge off her healthy appetite, she sat back and held her wine glass in both ringed hands. None of her rings was from Toby. Bracelets, brooches, pendants, but not rings. She was very definite about that.

'How is your family?' she asked.

'Very well, bless 'em.' Since he had no family, except his poor mother hidden in The Keep, Toby had begun to think of the Morleys as that. '*Peter Pan* was a huge success. Thank you, dearest Marie, for getting the seats. They couldn't have been better. The children especially were in heaven.'

'Never mind the children. What is there about this family for you?' She narrowed her pale blue eyes, the colour of flax flowers in an early morning mist. 'Are they potential lucrative patients?'

'I don't mix business with friendship. And anyway, there is nothing wrong with them.'

'Then what advantage are they to you?'

Toby leaned over the small table and filled her glass. 'None,' he said, with his face close to hers, 'if you will believe that.'

The lamps in the room were dim. The candle light made a halo of her fine flyaway hair. 'Then why are you so taken up with them?'

'I like them,' he said simply. 'They supply something I need.'

Marie-May raised her glass to his. 'Underneath the sophist-ication, the success, the wonderful-Mr-Taylor-he-cured-my-piles, the social *élan*, the glamorous actress . . . you are really an old Welsh bourgeois, Tobias Taylor.'

Chapter Ten

After the weekend of the Lord Lieutenant's ball, Bella had arranged to come home on Tuesday morning. On Monday she sent a telegram to Ladbroke Lodge to say she would return that afternoon. The Friday and Saturday and Sunday evenings had been bad enough. She could not endure another.

Two weeks before the ball, Gerald's mother had belatedly telephoned Bella's mother. 'Did that bad boy of mine never get in touch with your daughter? Please ask her to forgive him, Mrs Morley.'

Then Gerald, darling Gerald, had met her at the country station in the dog-cart. 'I say, Bella, you are a good sport to come.' Everything would be all right. On the high seat of the two-wheeled cart, bowling along in the wind, he did not talk much. Bella tied a scarf over her hat and kept looking at his manly profile, the weathered young skin, full lips red under the gold moustache, confident big hands on the reins, while he pointed out corking great ditches he had jumped and coverts where hounds had found.

At tea before the huge log fire in the reassuringly shabby hall, she met the other guests, who were not too threatening: married couples, Gerald's sister's fiancé, a dowdy cousin, two dull men of indeterminate age, one horsey, one balding with freckles on his head.

Disaster began when she came down in the green moiré

for dinner. A small witty girl with a deceptive cherub's face had arrived and boldly taken over Gerald. Worse, he was happy with this arrangement. Bella went upstairs and applied more Poudre d'Amour, and changed the coral necklace for tomorrow night's grander pearls; but Gerald and Babs joked and fooled about and threw bread at each other and danced to the gramophone after dinner in a quite sickening way that would not be countenanced at Ladbroke Lodge.

Babs and Gerald were a couple for the weekend. Bella hardly slept. When she forced herself downstairs for breakfast, it became clear that she was to be coupled to the man with freckles instead of hair on his head. Another of the failed, fortyish unmasculine bores who was invited here and there as an extra man. His shaven top lip was drawn in as narrowly as a flute player's. The bottom one was a pale worm. Bella knew almost nothing about men, or their kisses. She had never speculated on their mouths before Gerald had kissed her on the stairs at Hamilton House.

Freckles, in a frog-green hairy suit, helped her to porridge and kidneys and mushrooms and then put on an Inverness cape with a silly round collar and drove with her in the wagonette to the meet, whither Gerald and Babs had long since ridden off in scarlet coat and burgundy riding habit.

At the ball, Bella did dance with other men besides Freckles, but only once with Gerald, who fell over her large feet and made hunting noises. He disappeared before the end of the evening, and Bella heard from another Heckworth guest over late-night hot chocolate that he had been brought home drunk after running his car into a tree.

Early on Monday morning, Bella walked to the village and sent her telegram.

The chauffeur met her train. 'Changed your mind about your young man, Miss Bella?' He took her suitcase and looked at her inquisitively. She made some excuse. 'I was to have the half day off after fetching Mr and Mrs Morley from their luncheon engagement,' he remarked as they walked to the car. Ordinarily, Bella would have apologized, or at least felt guilty, but she felt nothing at all.

She was unpacking listlessly when the parlourmaid came up to her bedroom.

'Let me help you.' Sybil Crocker was out of uniform and inclined to be kind. 'I'm so sorry, dear,' she said.

'About what?'

'It went wrong, didn't it? Herbert said you seemed quite upset.'

'Herbert should mind his own business.' Not much chance of that when everybody below stairs knew everything. 'I had a lovely time.'

She kept her voice high and light, but it broke, and Crocker sat down on the bed and held out her arms and said, 'There now, come to Sybil, that's right, have a good cry, then.'

Bella did. She spilled out the pain of her thwarted love and hopes, and Crocker understood. She was a friend. It was safe to tell her, although from now on, Bella decided, as she blew her nose and caught sight of her hideous blubbery face in the dressing-table mirror, she would let it be known that Gerald Lazenby had been a passing fancy which she had now dropped.

When Sybil Crocker had gone away with the empty suitcase, Bella went out of the house and across Kensington Park Road and Portobello Road to see Madge at No. 72 Chepstow Villas.

'Hullo, Bella.' Flora Bolt opened the front door. 'How was your country weekend with the Great Lover?' It was not only the staff at Ladbroke Lodge who knew everything. It was the whole family.

'Very nice, thank you.'

'We thought you wasn't coming back till tomorrow, or they'd have made you go with them to the memorial dinner.'

'What memorial?'

'Come on, your own grandfather's birthday, the great wa-hoo himself, and your father to make a speech.'

'Oh yes, I forgot.' Bella had been so caught up with the weekend that she had not registered what else was going on.

'And I'm going to be there to applaud him.' Tobias Taylor came through the open drawing-room door, dazzlingly black and white with a ruched shirt front and swallow tails down his long slender legs. 'I'm sorry you won't be with us.' He looked at her closely. Bella turned her head away. 'What's wrong?'

'Nothing. It doesn't matter.'

'It does.' His manner was so completely different to Gerald's hearty indifference that Bella could have wept again.

'You must always think that everything about you matters,' Dr Taylor said seriously, and he stood in the doorway to watch her go up the stairs.

Madge was dressing for the dinner. As she and Bella talked, she moved about her bedroom, putting on one dress and taking it off and trying another, banging a brush at her short glistening hair, rifling through her jewellery box and holding different brooches up to her bodice and grimacing at them.

She tried to cheer Bella up briskly. 'I never did much like the sound of the Lazenby fellow. Everything in the saddle and nothing in the head.'

'No, Madge, there's nothing wrong with him. He still likes me. But my outlook is changing.' Coming miserably up in the slow Monday train, Bella had thought about this to cover failure. 'I'm drawn to these, what do they call them, New Women, who aren't satisfied with being just a wife and mother.' She stood fiddling with things on the mantelpiece. 'Even if I can never go to the University, I think I'd like to be independent.'

'Do you want a job?' Madge made a sceptical face at her. 'I'm sure Daddy would get you into Whiteley's, even if you had to start at the bottom.'

Bella looked at her incompetent hands. It was safe to say, 'I'm not afraid of work,' knowing that her parents would never allow it. 'I might give my life to serving others.'

Madge laughed at her pious tone. Bella sighed. No one ever took her seriously.

'I've not seen this.' She held out a miniature alabaster birdbath. 'Where did you get it?'

'Toby Taylor gave it to me. He knows I like birds. He brought it from Italy, or somewhere.'

So! Casual Madge. Bella could have smashed the little ornament into the grate. A really nice man comes into the family and Madge snares him. Unto her that hath . . .

A thunderous roar came from downstairs. 'Gwen! Madge! What the devil are you doing?'

'What's the matter with Uncle Leonard?' He was usually quite mild.

'Coming!' Madge opened the door and yelled down to the hall.

'We'll be late!'

Aunt Gwen opened her door wearing a peignoir, with her hair still down.

'What is all this silly shouting?'

Back at her own house, Bella found her parents also about to leave for the dinner.

Her father had fluffed out his greying side-whiskers and oiled his thinning hair across the dome of his head. His breast bore two medals awarded for some service to the Treasury. Her mother's bore impressive jewellery. We are the Morleys. We are going to be the stars of this occasion.

The butler opened the front door and Bella's father went out to the car, where Grandmother, who had been driven up from Goring, was waiting.

'I wish you were coming with us.' Her mother hesitated. 'If I'd known you would be back . . .'

'I wouldn't have cared to come anyway.'

'Of course you would,' Charlotte contradicted automatically. 'It's a pity – I'm sorry that – but you know,' she stumbled on, unfamiliar with maternal concern, 'it's not the end of the world to be disappointed in love.'

'What do you mean?'

'Well, dear, Crocker has told me. She was worried about you.'

What a friend. I'll murder her. Bella went down the tiled

hall and through a pair of pillars towards the back stairs, but Hurd had closed the front door and was on her heels.

'Something I can get you, Miss Bella?'

Yes, a new friend. Bella pretended that she was on her way to get a book from the study at the back of the house.

Leonard had been shouting in the hall at No. 72 because he was upset. Although always punctual at work, he did not really mind arriving a little late at his father's Memorial Banquet, organized by the E.A. Morley Admirers' Association. There would be less time to stand about drinking sweet sherry with the motley assortment of men and women for whom it was not enough to read the books of the People's Story-teller; they had to be keepers of the sacred flame.

However, there had been another note. It had been almost three months since the last dark message, and Leonard had begun to believe that the madman had been arrested, or swerved off into a different aberration.

But the note said:

He has forgotten me. I have not forgot and nor will you, arse-licker. Because if you don't make him send me the money, the disaster will be your fault.

The Assistant Manager was not going to risk the Chief's wrath with this. Mr Whiteley had put the earlier notes out of his mind, Leonard was sure. He was genially involved with the surge of business before Christmas, spending more time out on the floor, encouraging the staff, beaming at the clamouring children in the toy department, as if he were the spirit of Christmas itself. New staff had been taken on, there would be a New Year's bonus for everyone, if sales met his expectations. Customers were satisfied. William Whiteley was doing no harm to anybody. Why couldn't this evil lunatic leave him alone? Why couldn't he leave Leonard Morley alone?

Leonard's mother was already installed in the Waldorf Hotel Banqueting Suite, holding court. Leonard, feeling less agitated now that he was here and committed to this annual event, took Gwen and Madge over to her, and introduced Dr Toby Taylor, to whom she accorded the same suspicion with which she viewed the Morley Admirers and their proprietary attitude to her late husband.

But Toby would not have that. This man was becoming a good friend of the family, and he had been eager to meet its matriarch. Bending over her chair, he talked to her quietly in his pleasant voice, and the old lady seemed to be thawing. She was too stiff and stout to lean forward from the depths of the wide tapestried chair in which she had been installed, but the aigrette in her sequinned evening cap inclined a little.

'Is it true,' Leonard heard Toby say in his most liquid tones, 'that the captivating Mrs Davenport in *A Small Country Town* is based on yourself, Lady Morley?'

'Who says so?'

'I read that in a reprint of the *Illustrated London News Retrospective* about your husband.'

'Well, I dare say it's true.' Her beaded choker was too tight to allow her to nod, but she gave him one of her quite roguish smiles. 'I was not always this size, Dr Taylor.'

'Our bodies change all the time,' he said, 'just as our minds expand and develop. I like that idea.'

'You won't, young man, when you're my age, and have lost those scandalously good looks.'

'But then I shall possess qualities that you have now and I have not.'

'Ah yes, that's true.'

Dear old Mama, usually instinctively hostile, like dog meeting dog in the park, seemed to approve of Toby. She beckoned Leonard and told him he might bring his friend to Goring some Sunday.

Even Hugo thought better of him now, it seemed, since the 'bit of a bounder' was here to witness honour done to Hugo Morley as head of the family and spokesman for his famous father on this literary occasion.

The E.A. Morley Admirers, a very mixed collection, with the odder ones dressed as characters from the novels, insisted on some of the family being here, but at the same time rather resented them, since the Morleys' claim to the great man was only by accident of birth, whereas theirs was by choice of taste and appreciation. Hugo, who loved public speaking, was only allowed to introduce the real after-dinner speaker, a professor of literature who would expound on 'Ernest Austin Morley and the Late-Victorian Novel'.

Leonard observed Hugo as he got into his stride. Head back so that he was looking slightly down at his audience, white waistcoat convex as the side of a barrel, one hand on lapel, medals catching the light. A cruel man, Leonard knew, selfish, self-important, a snob with nothing to be snobbish about: my brother.

For tonight, and perhaps to steal some of the professor's thunder, Hugo had looked up some allusions to other writers contemporary with his father. He threw out famil-iarly such names as George Moore, du Maurier, Rider Haggard. But if he had read them, or read his father's books carefully enough to understand the soul of them, Leonard thought, he might be a more humane man. If E.A.M. were still alive, he would not countenance the victimization of poor Bella.

Hugo had already gone past his five minutes. The profes-sor was fidgeting. A man sitting opposite, dressed as the publican in *The Gambler*, had pulled out a watch from his canary waistcoat.

'It has been said that my revered father was the immedi-ate forerunner of H.G. Wells, George Bernard Shaw, George Gissing, in paving the way for the revolution of the common man.'

'What is he talking about?' Lady Morley was heard to in-quire.

'Fear not, brethren.' *That's* what Hugo should have been – a bishop! 'Fear not, for there will be no revolution. It is not needed. Equality, enlightenment, brotherhood, all are already here.'

Madge caught her father's eye, and choked into her wine glass. Bring in a Bolshevik with a bomb, Leonard thought.

'The revolution, you might say,' Hugo boomed on, 'was quietly effected by those men who, like my father, under-stood so well that emotional propaganda could gloriously succeed where violence would wretchedly fail.'

'That's enough,' Adelaide said very clearly. 'Sit down and be quiet, Hugo, for God's sake.'

It was the season of banquets. Before Christmas, Leonard

had to attend another kind of family affair: William Whiteley's annual staff dinner at the Cecil Hotel.

At noon that same day, one more squalid grey envelope came through the post for Leonard. He wanted to tear it up and throw it away unread, but knew that it would haunt him more disturbingly than if he faced it.

Tell him I shall be there. You are both in danger.

Guests and staff had cards of invitation to show at the door. Not very likely that a stranger could get in. However, as Leonard was crossing the pavement with Gwen to go up the steps of the hotel behind Mr Whiteley, shouts and scuffling made him whirl round quickly, his heart in his mouth. He clutched Gwen's arm, as he saw a man run across the street between the carriages and disappear into the small crowd in the shadows beyond the entrance lights.

'Leonard, don't grab me.' Gwen pulled away. 'What's the matter? You're as white as a sheet.'

When a shot comes at you out of nowhere, what does it feel like? The terror of pain may be worse than the actual impact.

'Come along, Leo, you're in people's way.'

'I thought I saw . . .'

'"He thought he saw a banker's clerk descending from the bus,"' Gwen quoted cheerfully, '"he looked again and found it *was* —"'

'"A hip-po-pot-a-mus!"' Leonard laughed with her, and relaxed.

But inside the hotel, he stayed nervously close to Mr Whiteley, scanning the lively, familiar crowd like a policeman.

'Don't nursemaid me, Morley,' W.W. said irritably. 'Give me some room. Why are you dogging me and looking so grim?'

Leonard told him. Behind a pillar, he showed him the frightening note.

'Same sender?'

'I suppose so, sir. I saw that there was a small disturbance in the street as you arrived. Did you see –'

'Some shouting, that was all. The usual crowd of hang-abouts with nothing better to do.'

Henry Beale was descending on them, already full of a greasy conviviality. Mr Whiteley pocketed the note. 'I'll see to it,' he said, but too vaguely.

'Shall you inform the police?'

The old man nodded and walked away, with his determined, plodding stride.

'A top-hole good evening, sir!' Henry Beale saluted his employer, and showed no surprise at being ignored. 'Having a good time, Morley?'

'Of course. Aren't you?'

'You don't look like it. Why do you have to pull the poor old guv'nor away to talk business even on a festive occasion – trying to gain kudos?'

'It wasn't business.'

The man was half drunk already. 'What, then, to make you look so anxious?'

Once again, it nagged at Leonard. Could it possibly be this invidious man who had been writing the notes? He was tempted to challenge him with, 'Isn't that how *you* want me to look?' and follow it up. Beale would deny it, but once the suspicion had been voiced, he would be impossible to work with, and the Christmas frenzy was still at its height, and the chaos of January sales to come.

William Whiteley's after-dinner speech was better than Hugo's, and more sincere. He stood up to prolonged applause. Admiring friends were there, and some politicians and notables whom he cultivated, but it was his staff who gave him the warmest welcome. He was still a Victorian, an employer of iron discipline, but he was also a patriarchal figure. Here he was at seventy-five, an upright man who had been forgiven long ago for separating himself from his wife and small children, a self-made gentleman, known all over the world. In nearly fifty years of hard work, he had forged ahead from one shop peddling ribbons and yard goods to a giant retailing empire which sold everything from a tap washer to a fleet of steamboats for an Indian prince.

He was silent for a moment, looking round over the hundreds of faces turned to him, his keen grey eyes smaller now as they had receded under the bushy white brows, his features broadened by the full white whiskers and squared-off beard. He stood firmly, solid and familiar as a civic statue.

He gave his audience a brief report on trading for 1906: turnover, one and a quarter million pounds sterling, ten per cent net profit. Six thousand employees, one hundred and sixty departments, including the new Lending Library, and nearly three hundred acres of land close to London, for farms, market gardens, warehouses and laundries.

'You know my motto,' his north country voice concluded. '"Add conscience to capital." Total that up and you can see that I have quite a nice little property to pass on to my sons.' Frank and William, on a dais with him at the high table, looked suitably amused and proud. 'But they will have to wait. Retirement? I don't know the word. *I* am still your Universal Provider for many more years!'

A storm of applause. Leonard's anxiety had subsided. He was proud of the Chief, and proud to be his right-hand man.

Next morning, he walked down Westbourne Grove in a chill driving rain from the east that cleared his head of claret fumes, and was busy from eight to eight, swamped with crowds and work.

Chapter Eleven

That young man of Madge's, Will Morrison, that she worked with at the East End Settlement, had gone off to Newcastle to see his family, so Flora Bolt was not surprised to open the front door on Christmas Eve to the deaf chimpanzee, Jack Haynes.

'I got here,' he told Flora with his gaping grin that made you want to shove a banana into it.

'So I see.'

'Don't be rude, Flora.' Madge came hurrying through the stained-glass door into the small outer hall.

'He can't hear me.' If he could, Flora would have asked him, 'What do you think the door mat's for?' She felt especially free and easy today. There was something about Christmas.

'Finding his own way here is part of his training to live a normal life,' Madge informed her. 'Well *done*, Jack!' She clapped her hands in applause, then took the sleeve of his lumpy jacket with the poacher's pockets – watch the ornaments, Madge! – and steered him in to the drawing room.

'Hullo, Jack!' 'Come in, come in!' Bella and Mrs Morley raised their voices exaggeratedly. Dicky rushed to greet him, gabbling away and moving his hands like a madman, his favourite trick since Madge had shown him some of the signs.

Next thing Flora knew when she came in with the teapot

and caddy and hot-water jug for Madam to brew, Bella was pounding out a carol on the piano and Jack was dragging his off-key bass roar after Dicky's choirboy voice.

When Flora came back with more crumpets, Jack was dwarfing a chair, holding his cup and saucer in his thick hands like a gentleman. When she came back with more hot water – up and down them stairs all day long, wouldn't it kill you – he was sitting on the floor by the decorated tree like a child, playing with the tin soldier who shot a penny into the darkie's mouth.

That evening, when Flora went up to put the stone hot-water bottles in the beds, she found Dicky still awake. Downstairs, some of Madge's young friends had come in for a small party, but the child was not allowed to stay up, because of tomorrow.

When Flora tucked Dicky up and turned to go, he said, to keep her there, 'Don't you want to have Christmas with your mother and Vi and your brother and Daddy Watts?'

'Save us.'

'What about Bill Bolt?'

'Save us with knobs on.'

'Are you still married to him?'

'I dunno, dearie.'

'You wouldn't leave us to go and live with Bull?' What made this sharp-witted nipper think it ever crossed her mind? 'If you bring me up a mince pie, Flo, I'll tell you something.'

'Tell me anyway.'

'My friend Noah saw a bad man hanging round this corner.'

'There's always bad men up and down the Lane. Bull don't know where I live.'

'Noah saw him twice.'

'He's a liar.'

'When will it be tomorrow?'

'Never, if you don't go to sleep.'

Flora was clearing up in the dining room when a piercing shriek came from upstairs. Dicky was out of bed and on the landing.

'He's here!' Flora ran up the first flight. 'I saw him.' Dicky stumbled passed her down the stairs. Doors opened. People were in the hall. 'I saw that man!'

Dicky cringed against his father as screams and commotion came from the basement.

'Don't go, Flora!' Gwen gasped, but Flora pushed among the guests, down the back stairs and panted along the passage through the disordered kitchen to the scullery in time to see Bill Bolt, with a twisted face of rage, struggling with Tat in the back doorway. The stumpy girl squared off and punched him in the stomach, and he knocked her over backwards, as Flora flew at him.

He grabbed both her hands in one of his great fists, as he had always been able to do, and laughed down at her with that old broken-tooth smile.

''Ullo, my love. I knew you was 'ere.'

'You get out, Bill Bolt.' She kicked him on the shin bone.

'Sod you, you bitch,' he said admiringly. 'I'm comin' in.'

'No, no, Bill, not here. They've gone for the Police.' They probably had. 'Don't get in no more trouble.'

'Meet me then.' Still holding her, he had moved back over the doorstep.

'I can't.' He twisted her wrists. 'Well, I might. If you go now. I'll – I don't know . . . Go quick.' She said anything, just to get him away.

He spat past her into the scullery and let go of her wrists. By the time Mr Leonard came muscling bravely through the scared women in the kitchen doorway, Bull had gone.

After Tatiana's head had been bandaged and Dicky was put back to bed, he sat up for a long time with the curtain drawn back, staring out of the window at the leafless arms and fingers of the plane trees, moving across the lamp light. If he had been asleep before, he would not have seen the shadowy bulk of the fearful man slip through the garden to the passage at the side of the house. He must stay awake to keep watch.

He yawned and yawned. Watering eyes blurred the windowpane. He did not hear the grown-ups come to bed.

The sky was grey and the street lamp out when he woke in a panic, suddenly bolt upright and screaming. 'He's here!'

'No, no, my darling. He's miles away. He'll never come back.' His parents took him into the big brass bed between them for what was left of the night.

On Christmas day, the family gathered in Chepstow Villas. There would have been more room at Ladbroke Lodge, but nobody wanted Christmas there, and Hugo and Charlotte had never offered it.

The grandmother Adelaide was to have been with them, but when Teddie went down to Goring to bring her up on the train, she refused to be budged: so Teddie travelled back alone, shoulders metaphorically hunched against possible family blame.

Friends and neighbours came in for milk punch. Leonard's police inspector friend Arthur French and his creamy-blonde wife walked up from farther down Chepstow Villas.

'Slops!' Tatiana saw him through the basement window. 'Top slops!' A constable on the beat, drinking stout in the kitchen with Mrs Roach, put on his helmet and left.

Arthur retailed a little crime gossip, which the women loved, even more than symptoms and remedies. Getting him alone, Leonard asked casually, 'Ever had any experience with – things like threatening notes?'

'Poison letters?' Arthur's creased face was drawn and tired. He had been up late last night, interrogating a suspected murderer.

'Yes, that's what they are. Poisonous.'

'You had any?' Arthur looked at him keenly.

Not knowing whether William Whiteley had contacted the police, Leonard said guardedly, 'I know of some.'

'Two a farthing, Morley, old man. We get dozens sent in, mostly harmless. "Sticks and stones may break my bones, but words can never hurt me."'

The family practitioner, Dr Buckmaster, always dropped in at Christmas. 'Little Bucky' had made a few convivial calls already and was inclined to be obnoxious. When Dr Taylor arrived, with a present for Laura, a football for Dicky and flowers for Gwen, Bucky, on his third glass of punch, challenged, 'Doctor, what kind of doctor?'

'I have a practice as a naturopathic physician,' Toby said, with Gwen's hand on his arm. She could almost smell the aromatic herbs and hear the wind across the meadow grass.

'Garlic and rhubarb pills,' Bucky sneered. 'New-fangled rubbish.'

'Herbalism is as old as the world,' Toby told him, and Gwen added, 'Dr Taylor has worked and studied abroad, haven't you, To-by?'

'Indeed?' Little Bucky sneered up at him with his bald, white-wreathed head tilted and his groggy eyes off the mark.

'I have spent some time abroad,' Toby said coolly, as if it were France or Germany, or even the United States of America. Well – Wales was abroad, a foreign country in many ways.

'Come, child.' Dr Buckmaster turned away to Teddie's daughter Sophie, pulling her up from the stool where she was reading *Little Folks' Album* to one of the children. 'You haven't put on any weight, I see.' Sophie crossed her arms over her chest. 'I hope you're not caught up in this ridiculous slimming craze?'

'It's such fun.' Sophie's Aunt Vera drew attention away from her. 'Everyone's talking about it. I want to try these new capsules. "Svelte", they call them. They advertise miracles.'

'No wonder,' Toby called across the room to her. 'Do you know what's in them? Tapeworm eggs.'

'Fella's a quack,' Bucky mumbled, but Toby and Vera, laughing, were off on their running joke about the man with the electric massage belt that had sent a tram off the rails, and his shocking wife who had electrocuted herself with a bottle of Dr Walford Brodie's Highly-Charged Liniment.

'Throw away your crutches and surgical boots!' Dicky crowed. He read the advertisements too. They were the best part of the magazines, because they sometimes showed ladies in their underwear.

After his terror of last night, Tatiana, whose father was rumoured to have been a Roman Catholic, had come upstairs this morning to give him her picture of the Madonna to hang over his bed.

Aunt Teddie, stuffily Anglican, disapproved. Such a crude, garish picture, too. A religion of peasants, and the girl had no business coming up from the kitchen with that bandage round her thick skull. They were all waiting now for the roast-goose dinner to be brought up. Teddie did not know how the women could keep up their idle chatter for so long. Her husband Ralph and some of the other men had gone off to the study. Left alone in an isolated chair, Teddie had nothing to say and nothing to do, except roll and unroll her neck ribbons and hope that Whiteley's goose would not be as fatty as last year.

Dr Taylor came over, and since there was no other chair, went on one knee in rather an absurd position to talk to her.

'I just wanted to say goodbye, Mrs Wynn, before I leave.'

'You're not staying for Christmas dinner?' The man seemed to have pushed his way far enough into the family, heaven knew.

'I wish I could, but I have another engagement.'

Oh, naturally. This humdrum family feast would not be entertaining enough for him.

'I wish you a merry Christmas,' he said.

'I don't care for Christmas very much, I'm afraid.'

'Only the children do, really.'

'Oh no, everyone else always seems to be enjoying themselves absurdly.'

'Perhaps they just put up a good show.'

That was a new idea for Teddie. She did not want to explore it, so turned it back to herself. 'And *I* don't.'

'Why should you, if you don't want to?'

That was also a new thought, among people who constantly exhorted her to 'Buck up, old girl!'

'It started all wrong anyway, this year.' The man was still on one knee, but apparently quite comfortable, so she told him about travelling all the way to Goring because no one else in the family would go, and her mother, who had bidden her to come, turning stubborn and refusing to leave the house.

'Was Lady Morley not well?' This Taylor person was listening to her. He did not get up and go.

'She pretends,' Teddie admitted. 'But I'm always afraid she will really have a heart attack one day, to make me feel guilty. I mean, I *would* be guilty.'

Confused, she looked down, her fingers making pleats in her brown skirt; but he said, quite unlike a man, 'That's difficult for you.' So she went on, 'It was impossible, I felt torn in two. My mother thought I should stay with her, but Ralph and the children wanted me here with them. At least, I think they did.'

'Mrs Ralph.' He did get up, then, and gave her a nod of farewell. 'Do you ever do what *you* want to do?'

Chapter Twelve

Aunt Teddie still felt very low and discouraged after Christmas. The start of 1907 promised her nothing, and she was not able to make a New Year resolution to 'Buck up, Teddie!'

She felt so tired all the time that she thought she must be ill. She sent for Dr Buckmaster. He charged two shillings a visit, but she did not have the energy to take herself to his surgery in Lansdowne Crescent, too far to walk from Campden Hill, too near to waste money on a cab.

When Little Bucky was shown into her bedroom, where Teddie wore a loose peignoir to show that she was ill, he strutted across to the window and opened the curtains.

'The sun is so bright.' She put up a hand. 'It hurts my eyes.'

'You don't want to mope in the half dark. Do you more good on this glorious day to get out and walk across Hampstead Heath.'

This was one of his stock remedies, but she took it seriously. 'I'm not up to that, Dr Buckmaster.'

'What's wrong?' He took her pulse, tapping a natty boot impatiently, and knocked a perfunctory knuckle on her hollow breastbone.

'I don't know. Everything. I'm always tired.' She raised her eyes to him in what Ralph called her bloodhound look. 'Sometimes I'm afraid I might have an incurable disease.'

'You shouldn't joke about things like that.'

'Oh no, I –'

'Nothing wrong with you, Mrs Wynn, that a little more gumption couldn't cure. If you could see some of my patients ...' He shook his bald, white-fringed head. 'I've just come from a poor dear lady ... eaten away with cancer.'

'Oh dear,' Teddie said dutifully. 'But sometimes I –'

'Never gives up. Spirit of a lion.'

Teddie felt worse. 'If I could just explain to you, Dr Buckmaster. Sometimes I think I –'

If he had sat down on the other boudoir chair and allowed her to talk, she might have told him, 'Sometimes I think I am losing my mind.' But he said briskly, 'My dear Mrs Wynn, I am a very busy general practitioner. I'm afraid I haven't got the time for a cosy chat. If you are really suffering from fatigue, I can give you some more iron tonic.'

'Iron constipates me.'

'Or the cocaine pills as a pick-me-up.'

'They make me feel funny.'

'Do you find comfort in your church?'

She shook her head. She hardly knew what he was talking about.

Dr Buckmaster took up his bag. Teddie rang the bell, and watched wretchedly as he went out with the maid.

'How was Dr B?' Ralph asked when he came home.

'*He* was all right, I suppose. I wasn't. He made me feel worse, really, because he wouldn't listen.'

'Doctors never do.' Ralph picked up *The Times* and took it into his study.

He was right. Doctors did not listen. They took you over and told you what was wrong or not wrong with you, but they did not let *you* tell *them*. No one listened to Teddie, because she was a bore. The only person who had listened to her lately had been that unusual man Dr Tobias Taylor, at Christmas.

'Do you ever do what *you* want to do?' she could hear him asking with that musical upward lift to his voice. She had thought quite a lot about his words in the last two weeks. Her whole upbringing, her marriage, her position as a woman, half Victorian, half Edwardian, had not prepared her for them.

Since she felt no better after Bucky's visit, she forced her flagging self to take action. She and Ralph had installed the telephone, but she hated using it, so she wrote a letter to Dr Taylor:

I would like to visit you professionally next week, if convenient.

He was not a conventional doctor, she knew. He dealt in treatments she did not know about. He was sophisticated, very involved in London life. He knew all kinds of people. He was from a different world. If he answered that he could not see her, or did not answer at all, that was that, and Edwina would have made a spectacle of herself once again.

He answered by return of post, giving her an appointment for the following Monday.

Teddie was very much afraid that he would tell the family about this, since he was so well in with them. If they teased her, she would not keep the appointment. She would say it had been a misunderstanding.

No one said anything, so after Ralph had left for the Temple she told the servant to call her a taxicab and travelled to Egerton Terrace, without telling anyone where she was going.

When the housekeeper, a full-lipped, knowing woman in a plain dress and long flowered apron, had shown her into the consulting room, and Tobias Taylor rose from a chair by the fire, Teddie said at once, 'No one knows I'm here.' It felt like an assignation. 'You didn't tell anyone about my letter?'

'Of course not.' Dr Taylor motioned her to another chair, but she was too nervous to sit down. 'Confidentiality is golden.'

'I was afraid the family would laugh at me.'

'For seeking help? They should praise you. Please sit here, Mrs Wynn. Try to relax. We have plenty of time.'

She sat on the edge of an armchair, her gloved hands clasped tightly. He sat near her, with his face half turned, not looking at her intently. There was no intimidating desk to keep doctor and patient apart, no fearsome examination couch, no apparatus, no charts, no amorphous things in jars on top of the bookcase. But Teddie was not going to be able to talk. She had got herself here, but she wasn't going to say anything.

He waited. Presently she ventured, 'You said I was seeking help. How did you know?'

'I could see you were in trouble.'

'I'm all right,' Teddie said flatly through half-closed lips. Then she said, without looking at him, 'I'm losing my mind.'

'No,' he said slowly. 'But you feel as if you were.'

Teddie stayed with him for more than an hour. The housekeeper brought hot chocolate and gingerbread, and made up the fire. When she looked back on that morning, Teddie could not remember a lot of what had been said. She knew that she had told him that Dr Buckmaster made her feel a fool.

'Perhaps there *is* nothing wrong with me. But there's something *wrong* with me. Vera thinks I'm going senile.'

He smiled. 'In your – what is it – early forties?'

'I shall be forty-seven this year.'

'Vera usu-ally likes to make jokes,' he said in that voice that was part question, part statement.

'They all do, but I'm afraid I have no sense of humour.'

She remembered that he had asked how she slept, and she had said, 'I mustn't complain,' and then told him about waking at three and not being able to sleep again. 'If I take laudanum, I can't wake in the morning.' She told him what she had told Bella: 'Sometimes getting up is like crawling out of my own grave.'

She was sitting back in the comfortable chair when he asked her, without emphasis, 'Are you still upset about what happened when you went to Goring at Christmas?'

Bother. She had told him about that at No. 72. Now she had to re-live it. Taking the station fly and keeping it waiting while she went into Heron's Nest and found her mother not packed, not even dressed. When she had finally slunk out, feeling like a punished child, and driven back to the station, she had had to pay the whole bill for the fly, which had waited nearly two hours in the cold.

'Upset?' Her voice had raised itself in Dr Taylor's quiet, softly lit room. 'I should be used to her torture after all these years.' She beat her fists on her knees, a child beating on her locked bedroom door, and almost shouted, 'I will never grow up until she's dead!'

She stood up, horrified. Somehow she got herself out of the room and down the stairs and into her elephant-grey coat, and would not wait for a cab to be called.

She might come back. She might not. Toby could not guess. Either way, when he met her again with the family, those flat bruised eyes of hers would glance at him fearfully, and he would reassure her, with one of his practised intimate smiles, that nobody would ever know. Meanwhile, he sent round to her Campden Hill house some ginseng capsules for the nerves, with dried hop flowers to infuse for an un-drugged sleep.

People had grown so conditioned to being given a bottle of this or that by the professional pill-pedlars – which is what so many doctors had become, with the advances in chemical remedies – that they did not believe that good could be done without a prescription.

Toby almost always prescribed something, even when it was obvious that the body's natural forces were going to restore health without extra help. It gave the clients confidence, and the herbal mixtures that Glyn made up for him could do no harm, even when they did not actually do any good.

He made a journey to the institution outside London to see his mother and talk to Dr Boone, the psychiatrist there who had helped him to develop some commonsense psychology.

His mother did not know him. She had shown no recognition for a long time now, but he sat by her poor wasted form, dying with the cruel slowness of a degenerative disease, and held her bird-claw hand and talked to her. He had brought her a present, a brightly coloured toy animal made of soft wool. She would not look at it or touch it. As always, he looked carefully into her eyes and flicked fingers in front of them to make sure she was not blind. He left the toy on the pillow of the bed to which she was confined, and hoped one of the nurses would not steal it.

As he walked down the long ward between the wretched wrecks of human beings, some of the women called out to him and beckoned, or made obscene gestures. In the corridors, inmates kept stopping him, wanting to talk, clamouring to tell him something that never got told, grabbing at his clothes, following him with entreaties.

He felt unravelled. 'I wouldn't do your job for anything,' he told Dr Boone in his circular room in one of the towers. 'How do you keep your sanity?'

'Well,' Dr Boone considered this, 'I'm not quite sure what sanity is. But there are rewards for me at The Keep. The new men are only interested in the acute pathologies, but some of the forgotten chronics do respond, you know, if you take the trouble.' He was busy with his pipe. 'And Mrs Boone and I do enjoy our house on the grounds.'

Toby usually brought him a case or two to discuss. He told Dr Boone about the dreamy, fair-skinned boy whose outdoor father did not want to believe he was normal ('Treat the father, not the lad, Taylor'), and something about sad, tired Edwina Wynn, and the tentative groping towards honest communication.

'I'm not sure yet what's wrong. I'll have to go carefully. I don't want to make a mistake, as I did with that neurotic, fainting woman who turned out to be diabetic.'

'No, that was unfortunate.' Dr Boone looked at him through fragrant smoke. 'You do send people for medical tests if necessary, don't you, Tobias?'

'Of course. I'm with the professionals, not against them. But so often clients come to me because of unsatisfactory medical or surgical treatment.'

'I know.' Dr Boone sighed. 'Me too. But by the time they are committed here, a colossal amount of damage has been done. This melancholic lady of yours – no doubt she has been a gift to the medical and pharmaceutical community since adolescence.'

'And nothing really wrong with her physically, beyond the expectable female complaints of the forties.'

'You might start with those.' Dr Boone, though not adventurous, had grasped the sexual content of Freud's new thought.

'It's difficult with these inhibited middle-aged women. They steer you away quite cleverly.'

'Give her time, Tobias. Melancholia builds up for years. It takes time to break down.'

'But I want instant miracle cures!' Toby admitted. 'Sometimes I think I should have been a faith healer. Arise and walk! That will be one guinea, thank you very much.'

Dr Boone smiled, tolerant of Toby as of any deranged person. 'As long as you do no harm . . .'

'I'd like to have that framed on the wall, but it might give the customers ideas.'

'Go slow. Have *that* framed. Be content with small results. And show the patients how to be, also.'

*

Towards the end of the January sales, Whiteley's staff was exhausted. Thousands of shoppers thronged the store every day, many of them rougher and cruder than the usual customer. Pockets were picked and merchandise stolen. If goods disposed of did not tally with cash receipts and account billings, it was the responsibility of the Department Buyer, who, if mean-natured, like Miss Maple in Gloves and Scarves, might pass the blame on to a harried assistant.

When the sales were over, Miss Maple, like some other buyers, would have to cut down the department staff. Two sisters, thin pale girls who looked underfed, and older than their years, ventured upstairs to the offices to appeal against the sack, or what Henry Beale called 'having their employment terminated'. Beale, as Chief Buyer, backed up Miss Maple. On January 23rd, the sisters came to Leonard Morley, washed out and tearful.

'We've been here longer than others in Gloves and Scarves, some that were only taken on before the Christmas rush.'

'What are Miss Maple's reasons for asking you to leave?' Leonard did not particularly like the Gloves Buyer, who had a straight mouth with negligible lips, but she was efficient, and apparently fair.

'She doesn't ask, Mr Morley sir, she tells. She's picked on us, consistent. She's blamed us for things gone missing from counters where we was not even serving. If we lose the job,' the elder sister said, 'we lose the dormitory room as well.' William Whiteley housed many of his unmarried female staff in nearby terrace houses that he had bought or built.

'What does Mr Beale say?'

'The decision st-stands, sir.'

'Then it must stand with me,' Leonard had to say. Beale backed up Maple, and he must back up Beale. That was how the management chain held together.

'Couldn't you ask Mr Whiteley for us, sir?' Two pairs of moist eyes clung to the edge of their last hope.

Leonard did not trouble the Chief with staff problems. In the old days, W.W. had been meticulous and too strict. Now that he was old and tired, he was distanced from individual causes, but the strictness was still there. All Leonard could say was, 'I'll look into it.'

The eyes did not brighten. He had let the sisters down. Sometimes he wished that he could exchange his demanding dominion for lowly service on the screws and nails counter. But then he himself would risk elimination by Mr Ludlow of Ironmongery.

When he came away from a fruitless visit to the office of Henry Beale – 'If you cannot rely on the integrity of our middle administration, the whole edifice crumbles. Surely you know our precepts, Morley?' 'Don't lecture me, Beale.' – a small grey envelope lay on his desk.

Last chance. He comes through or I kill myself. Damn you all.

If he does, there will be no more letters, Leonard thought with deliberate calm. He folded the scrawled paper, knelt to open the combination of the safe, and added the note to the other two that he had kept.

Edwina Wynn did return to The Clinique in Egerton Terrace, a week after Toby had seen her at a musical evening at Vera Pope's house, when she would hardly acknowledge him and seemed more than usually downcast

– 'Buck up, Teddie, they're going to play a cancan now. We might want you to dance.'

His housekeeper, Neelie Drew, took two telephone messages: one desperate from a consumptive lady whom Toby would not see because of the infection, and one hesitant from Mrs Ralph Wynn, making an appointment but qualifying it with, 'unless I'm unable to keep it'.

She sat on the edge of the chair, looking round the room, as if for spies. Toby wished that repressed women like this would take off their hats. It was difficult to get down to realities when they sat there with the neck rigidly supporting some overpowering creation like Mrs Wynn's wide brown matador headpiece, weighted with grosgrain rosettes.

'Would you prefer to remove your hat?' He sometimes tried this out, but it was no more welcome than if he had asked, 'Would you like to remove your bloomers?'

Edwina pretended that she had only come for some more of the hop-flower infusion, which she had found soothing. 'I keep a spirit lamp in my room to brew it up in the early hours, if I can't sleep.'

'That doesn't disturb your husband?' Toby took his opportunity to get a foot in the door of the marriage chamber.

'Oh no, he sleeps in his dressing room now, you know. It's a much more convenient arrangement.' She looked down, so that Toby could only see the ugly stiff rosettes erupting from the hat. 'It would not be dangerous for me to continue taking the tea?' She looked up anxiously, as if the hops were opium.

'No, of course not, Mrs Wynn. I'll put you up another

package.' Toby Taylor, humanist naturopath, knew better than to give it to her at once. 'May I ask,' he said, leaning back in his opposite chair, hoping to induce her to lean back too, 'whether you and Mr Wynn decided to occupy separate rooms *after* you seemed to lose energy, as you have told me, and joy in life?'

'Possibly.' She paused for a long time, drawing in her pale lips in a constricted way which tensed her jaw. 'Perhaps.' She frowned and shook her head. 'I don't know. It was a long time ago.'

'A happy marriage?' Toby ventured.

Edwina was surprised that he should ask. 'Oh no, Dr Taylor.' She looked at him without expression under the overpowering hat. 'People don't marry for happiness, do they? Ralph Wynn married me because I had a famous and successful father. He needed that status, you see, as a struggling young lawyer.' Pause for a sigh. 'I suppose I shouldn't have said that.'

'Everything we talk about is confidential, Mrs Wynn.'

'I don't mean that. Everyone knows about Ralph and me. Everyone knows everything in our family. The women gossip so.'

'You don't?'

'Whatever *I* say, it's usually the wrong thing.'

'Surely not?' Toby gave her an encouraging smile, but she had shut herself up inside herself again.

He went back to the marriage, to try to winkle her out, but when he inquired, 'Your parents were pleased?' she asked quite belligerently, 'Why should you want to know?' and he was afraid that she was going to demand the hop-flower tea and get up and leave.

'I *am* trying to help you, Mrs Wynn.'

'Why?'

'Because you asked me.'

'Did I?' She was back to her usual defeated drone. 'Well, it's no use.'

'Your parents . . . ?'

She shrugged her sloping shoulders, made even droopier by the double yoke of her heavy winter dress. 'My father didn't mind, I suppose. Mama didn't really expect me to marry anybody. She thought I would stay at home and be her Mother's Girl.' She put a wry expression on a face that had too many dry lines and fissures on it for her mid-forties.

'But you escaped.' Toby was proud of himself for keeping cynicism out of his voice.

'There is no escape.' Edwina sighed, determinedly negative.

He could see why her irritated family plagued her with, 'Buck up, old Teddie!' She must drive them mad with her pessimism. She would drive Ralph Wynn mad if he paid any attention to her. No wonder his life was mostly his showy work in the law courts and his well-known affairs with quite prominent ladies. But as Dr Taylor (sometimes he almost believed in his illicit title, since the Morleys clung to it), Toby's mission was not to be driven mad by this sad, dowdy woman with the face of a weary horse, but to try to find the key to her melancholia. Dr Boone had talked to him about this affliction, which weighed down many of the inmates of The Keep. 'They have imprisoned themselves,' he said. 'Once in a while, you may be lucky enough to discover in them the key to unlock the door.'

To discover the key to Edwina's melancholia, and –

dazzling thought – the cure for it. Why not? She was a hard nut to crack, but 'It's never too late' Dr Boone believed. If Tobias Taylor could find a way to lighten this poor lump of unrisen dough, what couldn't he do? He might get a specialist following in *la femme triste*.

He cleared his throat. 'Dr Freud believes . . .' He must go carefully to keep her in her seat. 'You have heard of the great Sigmund Freud?'

'I have heard Dr Buckmaster describe him as a sex maniac.'

He would. 'Dr Freud has propounded that none of us are aware how many of our psychological problems are rooted in childhood.'

Edwina nodded, her eyes on his. She could encompass that, knowing herself to be her mother's victim.

'And also,' Toby added looking delicately off to one side of the forbidding hat, 'in our sexual experience.'

Edwina dropped her head quickly. Her gloved hands clutched her skirt. Toby could see that she would never talk – perhaps not even think – about what she had probably experienced as the ghastly traumas of the marriage bed. He moved on to, 'And childbirth, too, can be an extension of that.'

Edwina said at once, 'I had a perfectly horrible time,' and called him 'doctor', to justify mentioning the subject. 'No one will ever know.'

'Tell me,' Toby said quietly. He had heard Dr Boone say this to distressed inmates who were still capable of communicating.

'Well, doctor.' Edwina looked up again at this invitation to talk about something that she had never been able to discuss. 'I was terrified out of my wits. The twins nearly killed me. When it turned out there was a second one coming after the first, I wanted them to kill me. The chloroform was useless. I begged the midwife to put a pillow over my head, so that I would be dead before Sophie was born. Isn't that despicable, Dr Taylor? I'm ashamed to have told you. I don't know why I did, because I expect it wasn't so bad after all. They said it wasn't. They said I was neurasthenic.'

'I expect you've told me the truth.' Toby spoke levelly, but excitement was growing within him. A clue, a clue – she's given me a clue!

'I cried and cried,' Edwina said quite proudly. 'For weeks, I cried. It was like living under water. I didn't – this is wicked – *I didn't like the babies*. The nurse was so shocked. "I shan't leave Madam alone with them," she said. I was thought to be an unnatural mother. You don't want to hear any more. I've told you what really happened, as you said. That is what happened to me.'

'It could explain many things.' Toby leaned forward, but she was leaning back now, limply, the hat pushed by the cushioned back of the chair even farther over her eyes.

'It happened because –' She paid no attention to him. 'Because I was not a good child. Not what my mother wanted. Not what God wanted either. I didn't say my prayers. When I die, I hope He will say to me, "I've already made you pay for your wickedness," and give me a ticket to come in.'

Edwina Wynn left The Clinique without her packet of dried hop flowers. She was too exhausted – almost sleep-walking – to remember, and Toby was too excited.

That evening, he went to the theatre to see Marie-May Lacoste in her dressing room before the play. He tried to tell her something of his exhilarated sense of achievement, but when she was making up, staring hypnotized at the mask of her face in the mirror, she was too preoccupied to listen.

She was not free to go out with him later for supper.

'The old viscount?'

'A new one. A duke. He owns half Staffordshire.'

It had to be accepted that she went out with a lot of other men, just as she accepted, more easily, Toby's other women.

He invited lecherous Leila, who shared the dressing room, but she had other plans, so Toby went to the Haymarket Rooms and played billiards restlessly, and then found two girls he knew in the bar-lounge of the Empire and spent the rest of the night with the younger one.

When he awoke, and walked home through the frosty, stirring streets, he still felt electric, like Vera's man with the vibrating corset. As soon as he could, he would go out to The Keep to find out from Dr Boone something about the pathology of women and childbirth.

Chapter Thirteen

On Thursday, January 24th, 1907, on his morning rounds, Leonard avoided the Gloves and Scarves department, in case two pairs of doleful eyes were raised to him in mute appeal. He would send for the sisters later in the day. If he had to convey bad news, it was only proper to do it himself.

This morning, he had something else on his mind. He had decided to tell W.W. about the last note, or at least try to find out from him whether he had received any recent communications from blackmailers.

If this person was really going to commit suicide ... Leonard had struggled with this question through a wakeful night. What was the right thing to do? What was correct in his position? Different considerations, but both important to him. The death of a stranger might not touch Leonard, but should he not at least inform the Chief, in case he knew him?

At about half past twelve, he took the note out of his safe. If William Whiteley rejected him contemptuously, as he had before, at least he would have given him a chance. In the corridor between the counting house and William Whiteley's office, he met Daniel Goodman, the Chief Cashier.

'Is Mr Whiteley busy?

'There is someone with him at the moment.'

'Who is it?'

'The gentleman told me he had come from Mr Whiteley's solicitor, Sir George Lewis. He is probably the managing clerk, come to pick up some papers.'

'I'll go in and see if they've finished.'

With the note in his hand, Leonard did not want to wait. He knocked and went into the office, where Mr Whiteley and the young solicitor's clerk, who wore a shabby suit and silk hat, were both standing up.

'Excuse me, sir. I'd like a word with you, if it's convenient.'

'I can't see you now.' The old man looked slightly rattled. Was he in some legal trouble? 'I'll see you presently.'

Leonard nodded to the visitor and went outside to talk to Goodman. From the counting house, he saw the office door open. Mr Whiteley came out, looking pale and agitated.

He called out breathlessly, 'Go and fetch me a policeman!'

'Yes, sir.' Daniel Goodman went off at once.

A policeman to get rid of the young man? What on earth –? As Leonard stepped into the corridor, he heard the visitor, behind the old man in the doorway, say loudly, 'Come back inside!'

'No, go away. I'm fetching a policeman.'

'Is that your final word?'

'Yes.'

'Then you are a dead man, Mr Whiteley.'

It was all said very quickly. As Leonard hesitated for a moment, paralysed with shock and surprise, there was the crack of a pistol shot, then another, and then fainter, from within the room, a third.

Everybody seemed to arrive at once, but nobody could save William Whiteley, the Chief, the grand old man. He lay dead on the floor, with blood welling up from a wound in his left cheek and another behind his ear. Inside the office, the young stranger sprawled, badly wounded, his mangy hat tumbled away into the corner by the wastepaper basket.

'Who is the man? Who is it?'

After the police had come, and two doctors, and the body of poor William Whiteley had been removed to the mortuary, and the wounded man taken to St Mary's Hospital in Praed Street, everyone kept asking each other uselessly, 'Who is he? Where did he come from? What did he want? Why did he do it?' All customers had been asked to leave, and the whole place was closed; but many of the staff still lingered in the buildings or in the street among the excited, curious crowd who had come to stare at the hastily printed notices in the shop windows: 'Owing to the death of Mr Whiteley, this establishment is closed for the remainder of the day.'

Apprentices, sales ladies, floorwalkers, clerks, window dressers, upholsterers, tailors, seamstresses, van drivers, butchers, confectioners – everyone was thrown out of orbit, confused, shocked and afraid, talking, arguing, crying, unable to make a move towards home.

What will happen? Will they hang him? I hope they do. Nothing will be the same now. It feels like the end of the world . . . What will happen to us?

The assassination of the Universal Provider was like the murder of God himself.

Leonard Morley stayed with the detectives who were searching the office for possible evidence. Later, Arthur French joined them. He said that the man with the Colt revolver, who was still alive and undergoing surgery to remove fragments of dumdum bullet from his head and face, had given his name as Whiteley, although that was established as not true, and that Sir George Lewis denied all knowledge of him. No clues about the fatal interview were found, no relevant papers. The suicide note, clutched in Leonard's hand as he ran to the scene of the shooting, was in the inside pocket of his coat.

After the office was locked and police posted inside and outside the building, Inspector French took his friend home. In the Scotland Yard motor car, with a glass screen between the back seat and the constable driver, Leonard said to Arthur, 'I have something I must show you.'

Two days later, Leonard, patrolling like an automaton through the ground-floor haberdashery sections, trying to restore the atmosphere of business as usual, remembered that he had not told the two sisters that their reprieve had not been granted. One of them was stretching a glove for a customer. He spoke to the other.

'About your notice . . .'

'I understand, sir, after what has happened. Don't trouble about us.'

'No, no, I think you can stay on. I'll explain to Miss Maple. Someone can be moved to another department. Don't thank me.' He held up a hand as she caught her breath. He could not face any emotion. Shocked and grieving, it was all he could do to get through the work of the day.

On the office floor, a sad place with all the women in black and the men with mourning armbands, and a laurel wreath on the Chief's locked door, he told Henry Beale what he had done. 'I'll square it with Miss Maple. Or you can,' he said curtly.

'You've gone against one of my buyers? Look here, Morley, I won't have this!' Henry's eyes were bloodshot and his skin flushed and sticky. He had been drinking since the tragedy. Any excuse would do. 'You shall not go against my authority,' he blustered.

'Authority,' Leonard said wearily. 'None of us knows what our positions are, until the new administration is sorted out with Mr William and Mr Frank and the Board.'

'*I* know what I'm doing. As Chief Buyer of this establishment, I must insist –'

'Oh, for God's sake.' Leonard left him.

'Shut the door behind you!'

'Shut it yourself, you pompous ass.'

With both of them on edge, and the whole store disordered – customers and staff alike – this was only one of many undignified skirmishes between them.

Four days after the tragedy, Leonard had to give evidence at Paddington coroners' court. As a witness, or a near-witness, of the murder, he had to recount what he had seen and overheard. 'Nothing about the notes yet,' Arthur French had instructed him. 'That will undoubtedly have to come up at the trial, but your duty today is simply to tell what happened.'

Leonard hated having to stand up before the coroner and the considerable crowd that had squeezed into the courtroom. He felt as if he were on trial. 'Take deep breaths,' Arthur had coached him, 'and don't fidget guiltily from foot to foot.'

'At about twelve-fifty, I entered Mr Whiteley's office on a matter of business.'

Dr Danford Thomas, the coroner, regarded him sternly. Rows of faces were turned to him. Reporters wrote in their notebooks. At the side, the widow, Mrs Harriet Whiteley, whom Leonard had never seen, sat between her two sons and a daughter, her ageing face expressionless behind the veil of her black velvet hat.

When Leonard had finished his recital, which was exact – he would never forget any of the details – he felt obliged to voice the thoughts that had been churning in his mind.

'I would like to add, Dr Thomas, with respect, that I am greatly troubled by guilt at having been so near to Mr – the late Mr Whiteley's office, but not able to prevent the tragedy.'

The courtroom was visited by a slight murmur, either of blame or sympathy.

'Thank you, Mr Morley. I see no reason for that last remark to go into the records. You could not be aware that the assailant had a revolver. When the office door was opened, you were near enough to hear, but not to interfere, and after the second shot was fired, the police surgeon has given evidence that death was instantaneous.'

'Thank you, sir.' Leonard felt no less guilty, as he returned to his seat next to his son Austin.

Gwen had not felt she could bear to attend the inquest, so Austin had been given the day off by his firm to be with his father. He was very serious and manly and responsible, but Leonard would rather have been with Gwen.

The coroner's verdict on the untimely death of Mr William Whiteley was: 'Wilful murder.' His assailant, having undergone intensive surgery, which included the removal of his right eye, would be charged when he was sufficiently recovered. 'In other words,' the *Daily Mail* quoted public opinion later in the week, 'he is being nursed back to health to be tried for murder.'

Two significant statements came from the inquest. A note scribbled on a page from a small notebook and found on the clothing of the man in hospital read,

To all whom it may concern. William Whiteley is my father, and has brought upon himself and me a double fatality by reason of his refusal of a request perfectly reasonable. R.I.P.

The identity of this man had by now been established as Horace George Rayner, of No. 32 Red Lion Street, Holborn. However, a statement had also been made by a man called George Rayner, who claimed to be this man's foster father, not his father. His mother, Emily Turner, had falsely registered her infant son as Horace Rayner, although his legal name was Turner. The police reported that he persistently claimed that William Whiteley was his father, and had said, 'I'm glad he is dead, because of the way he treated my mother.' This last was ordered by the coroner to be struck from the record, as irrelevant to the inquest.

Outside the court, Henry Beale accosted Austin and Leonard. 'Startling news, eh, about Saint William?'

'Shut your scurrilous mouth, Beale.'

'Told you I knew a secret about him, didn't I? I've known it for ages.'

'There's nothing to know. The killer is a madman. Everyone can see that.'

'Everyone but me.' Henry Beale winked, and put a finger to his florid nose.

Leonard had turned over the anonymous notes to the detective inspector in charge of the case, to whom Arthur French was careful to defer, with a statement about what had been written on the other two letters.

'Did you destroy those?'

'Mr Whiteley tore up the second one and asked me to destroy the first.'

Arthur told Leonard privately, 'I don't know whether the Crown Prosecutor will make the notes part of his case, as evidence of intent. If Horace Rayner denies writing them, and sticks to that, it may be difficult to prove that he did.'

'Before I knew he existed, I had an idea who might be responsible.'

'Who would that be?'

'In confidence, Arthur, Henry Beale, the Chief Buyer at Whiteley's. But that was an insane suspicion, festered out of my dislike of the man.'

'You should know that Mr Beale has already told the police, quite separately from you, that you received these notes and concealed them from Mr Whiteley.'

'Because the Chief did not want to hear about them! And he had suffered so much from blackmailers in the past, I was trying to protect him from distress, can't you see? Oh God, what a stupid shambles!'

'I know, I know -- calm down, Morley. But your colleague is making a black story against you. One might almost imagine that Mr Beale wanted to accuse you of being an accomplice to murder.'

'The swine. How does he know about the notes?'

'He says you told him.'

'Did I?' Leonard shook his head in confusion. 'I could swear I did not.'

'Mr Whiteley knew about two of the notes, at least. Could he have told Beale?'

'I doubt it. But –' Leonard was struck by a terrible thought. 'Is it possible that Henry Beale knew about Horace Rayner, as he hinted to me – that he actually knew the man?' How was Leonard going to face Beale in the store without knocking his ugly, sottish head off? 'What is he up to, Arthur?'

'Hoping to get your job, it looks like.'

When Teddie ventured again to The Clinique to see Dr Taylor, he asked her at once, 'How is your poor brother Leonard?'

'Leonard? Oh, you mean that dreadful murder. Yes, it is shocking, isn't it? We live in violent times, when no one has any respect for law and order. I shop at Whiteley's, but I don't know that I shall go there again. That poor old gentleman. What has he ever done to anybody?'

'Except take their money off them.' Dr Taylor, with his attentive brown eyes, had a way of saying droll things with a straight face. Teddie could not always tell whether he was joking or not. She had no sense of humour, she had been told.

'Everyone at Chepstow Villas is in a state of complete turmoil.' She was wearing her new sealskin hat, which

Bella had helped her to choose, since her daughter Sophie was so hopeless in shops. 'Leonard is to give evidence at the murder trial, you know. I went round there, in case Gwen needed me, but there was nothing I could do.'

'How is Leonard?' Dr Taylor asked again. 'I wrote my sympathies, but didn't like to intrude at a difficult time.'

'He's taking it very badly.' Teddie had broadcast this lugubriously, but when she had said it to an acquaintance in Bradleys, in Bella's hearing, her niece had surprised her by attacking her when they left the shop.

'Uncle Leonard is *brave*. You might at least support him, Aunt Teddie.'

'Don't speak to me like that, young woman.'

Bella stuck out her heavy jaw. 'You're gloating because No. 72 has had a bit of bad luck for a change.'

'How dare you!'

A hint of the truth hurts more than flagrant lies. Teddie was so upset that she had felt compelled to go to Egerton Terrace and talk to that nice Dr Taylor, who understood her. The visits were too expensive, but she had her own small legacy from her father, and Ralph was not interested in how she spent it.

They passed the first ten minutes discussing what she should be called: Mrs Wynn or Mrs Ralph – which was what Tobias Taylor usually called her within the family. Teddie pondered. At home, when she could not come up with an answer, someone would cut in and take the conversation away from her. Here, in the comfortable Clinique consulting room, she could spend her money on sitting in silence, if she wanted.

'Neither,' she decided at last. 'I come to see you by

myself, and for myself, Dr Taylor. It's nothing to do with my husband.'

'That's fair enough. You *are* yourself.' Sometimes he said things which sounded simple, but were really quite deep when you thought about them.

'Certainly not "Teddie", even though you are a friend as well as – as my doctor.' Teddie felt agitated with herself. 'My doctor' sounded too intimate, as though he had been mixed up in her confinements. 'I don't like "Teddie".' She was glad she had worn the dark glossy mushroom of a hat. She felt that it gave her some presence. 'Vera called me that years ago when she couldn't say "Edwina", and it stuck. But I've always hated it. It's like a man.'

'Why don't you ask the family to call you Edwina?'

'Because they wouldn't.'

'It's a beautiful name.'

'You may think so.' He need not think she would respond to flattery.

'I can't call you by that, however. It wouldn't be professional.'

They settled on 'Mrs Edwina'. No one had ever called her that.

This was all they did settle that afternoon. There were two men waiting to see Dr Taylor. (Two men! – what was he treating them for? Since Oscar Wilde, she saw something under every bush, without knowing what it was.) Mrs Edwina had only a short last-minute appointment, but she left feeling better.

After William Whiteley's grand funeral, with local flags at half mast and thousands of people in the streets to see the cortège pass by, Leonard was still heavy with loss, and with dread of the trial of Horace Rayner in March.

The family reacted in their various ways. Gwen was loving and tender. Leonard was surprised to find that they came together in sex more often than when he was happy and secure, and Gwen reminded him that it had been the same after his father had died, and she had unexpectedly conceived their second son Dicky when she was forty.

Dicky was jumpy. 'They're asking me about it at school.'

'Play deaf and dumb,' Flora said. She was sturdily sympathetic. 'I seen a murder done once,' she told Leonard. 'Down the Scrubs.'

'Did they make you give evidence?'

'No fear. They slung the body on the railway line so that the trains would run over it. You mind what you say at the Bailey, sir. Keep mum about the threats.'

'How do you know about them?'

'Everybody knows. I can't walk three steps down the Lane without they're bothering me for secrets.'

'What do you tell them?'

'"Shove off." The more you know, the less you tell. Remember that.'

Aunt Teddie had come hovering round at first, tongue-tied and wringing her hands, but after that she was not much in evidence. She seemed somewhat distrait and self-absorbed.

'Isn't it odd,' Madge remarked, 'that people who don't like themselves spend more time thinking about themselves than people who do? Sophie says she is even more wool-gathering at home than usual. If it was anyone but Aunt Teddie, one might suspect her of conducting an intrigue.'

'Madge!' At least she had made her father laugh.

Her aunt Vera got theatre tickets for *The Scarlet Pimpernel*, and also made Leonard come to dinner with some entertaining people. He did not like the play, and was dull in conversation at dinner, and too brusque with a guest who, insensitive to Vera's toe under the table, wanted to hear 'all about the Whiteley scandal'.

Adelaide Morley came up trumps, like a good shopkeeper's widow. 'This is bad for trade and bad for you,' she wrote to Leonard. 'I wish I was not a sick old lady, and could come to back you up, my son.'

Leonard should have gone to see her, but he had no time. Mr Whiteley's two sons were still too occupied with lawyers and accountants to take on their father's tasks. Henry Beale insinuated himself into some of the negotiations with W.W.'s personal contacts, and preened himself as if the obliteration of the Chief had promoted him above Leonard. He was obstructive and impossible, but Leonard was too busy to bother with him. Rather than being bad for trade, the tragedy had, ironically, increased business. There were more customers than ever. Whiteley's, for so long a magnet of excellence, now also had a ghoulish attraction. People even came up to the office floor, hoping to see the place where the dastardly deed was done, and a glimpse of a bloodstain. The gossip was horrible. There was no proof that Horace Rayner was William Whiteley's bastard son, but the public was delighted to think the worst. Leonard Morley, faithful Assistant Manager, so dedicated, like his leader, to what was fit and proper for Whiteley's, felt personally sullied.

Hugo was more worried about the Morley name being in

the papers again during the trial, as it had after the inquest. 'None of our family has ever been mixed up in anything like this.' Could Leonard give evidence under a pseudonym? Charlotte wondered. In 1903, when King Alexander of Serbia and Queen Draga had been assassinated, a prominent courtier had testified, wearing a hooded cloak.

Bella, although very loyal to her uncle Leonard, was muddle-headed about the villain. She followed the popular humane 'cause', which likened the recovering assassin to a pig fattened for slaughter. When she parroted at dinner, 'The death penalty is a crime worse than murder,' her father told the guests at his table, 'My daughter pretends to be so radical, but most of her ideas come from the yellow press.'

Leonard Morley did not agree with the anti-capital punishment brigade. To him, hanging was too good for the man who had cut down the Chief.

Chapter Fourteen

The issue at the start of the murder trial of Horace Rayner was the state of his mind at the time of the killing. Doctors in support of the defence talked of his mental instability and diminished self-control. His recent years of alcoholism, poverty and poor food had led, claimed his counsel, to impulsive insanity at a time of crisis.

Could he be held responsible for his actions?

The Times reported that the court had ruled him not medically or legally insane, but degenerate, through three generations of alcoholism – his mother, his grandmother and great-grandmother.

The young man looked shabby, but not degenerate. He was thin and ill and anxious, with a plaster on his face and a patch over his missing eye. From time to time, he put a shaking hand to his head, as though it hurt. It was two months since he had shot himself through the temple with the Colt revolver.

'He looks so hang-dog,' Gwen said tearfully to Leonard when they were back at home. 'I don't think I can bear to see him condemned.'

'I want you with me in court,' Leonard said. Soon, they would call him to give evidence. He needed her to be there. Gwen's apparent, and very feminine, dependence on him obscured his deep dependence on her.

'But if they are to judge him on intent, Leo, your story about the notes may be the final *doom*.'

'Don't use words like that, please. It's bad enough already.'

'You want Mr Whiteley avenged.'

'But not by me. I am not testifying about the notes for revenge. I'm obeying the law.'

'I don't want to have to hear you do it.'

'And I don't want to do it. Dearest, if you must be so sentimental, why not be sentimental about *me*?'

'Oh, I am.' Gwen dabbed a handkerchief at her eyes and the corners of her mouth. 'That's why I don't want to come to the Old Bailey any more. I'll be waiting here for you at home, with a good fire, and the tea things, and admire you for your strength, like a knight's lady when he returns from the jousts.'

Madge came to the Central Criminal Court, and Austin, joined by Teddie's barrister husband Ralph on the day it seemed that Leonard would be called to the witness box.

Mr Henry Curtis Bennett, for the defence, had reminded the jury that it was not his business, or anyone else's, whether the accused was actually William Whiteley's son. 'The point is that, rightly or wrongly, *obsessively*, he believed that.'

But the prosecution would not relinquish the question: who was Horace Rayner's father? The accused had stuck to his story of Mr Whiteley's long-ago friendship with his mother, Emily Turner, and of how his step-father, George Rayner, had told him, when he had been drinking, who his real father was.

'And then I did remember him visiting us as a child, powerful, domineering, and somehow – in some way connected with us. From that time, it preyed on my mind.'

The voice of the man in the high dock was not very strong, and his one eye had a way of roving round the courtroom, not staying on the face of Mr Muir, the prosecuting counsel, below him. When it rested for a moment on Leonard, he felt it, uncomfortably, as a plea for help.

Two men at the poor lodgings to which the accused had been reduced after his wife went back to her family had borne witness that they had heard him boast of a wealthy parent – 'the richest man in London'. The landlord of a hotel in Red Lion Street described him trying to evade rent on the promise of a thousand pounds expected to arrive from his father.

'Just before my mother died, she said –' Horace Rayner swallowed painfully, his Adam's apple darting in and out of his high collar. 'She told me, "If you ever need a friend, go to William Whiteley and mention my name."'

'And you did.' Mr Muir looked at him grimly over half spectacles.

Rayner then gave his account of the fateful interview in the office. 'Towards the end, Mr Whiteley said, "I can't recall the past." He was very cold. He told me to try the Salvation Army. I asked again, "Do you refuse to help me, with either money or a job?" He said that he did, and I said, "Then I have made up my mind to blow my brains out." I took out the gun. He said to me, "Don't talk so silly, put that thing down." I think I put the gun in my pocket. He started to leave the room. I asked him to come back, but he refused, and said something about a policeman. I don't remember any more, my lord.' His eye moved to the judge. 'I don't remember the shots.'

'Are you saying you did not fire them?'

'I say, I can't remember them.'

Mr Muir then read out the note that had been found in the man's pocket by police at the hospital: '. . . has brought upon himself and me a double fatality . . .' with its sorrowful ending, 'R.I.P.'

'You do remember writing that, Mr Rayner?'

'I think so. It must have been – impulsive insanity.' He quoted his counsel.

Leonard Morley was called to take the stand. He had watched other witnesses: Whiteley's staff, Rayner's landlord, and his aunt Louise Turner, who was awed and hesitant, and ordered to speak up. He determined on dignity. Inwardly he was the boy Leonard being forced to own up to a petty crime at Goring School. Outwardly, he was the dependable henchman and true friend of William Whiteley, head up, voice clear.

He gave the dates and contents of the five notes from the list the police had transcribed.

'And you kept some of these to yourself, Mr Morley?'

'Three of them. For the reasons I have already explained.'

'Please tell the court.'

Leonard told the court. 'Mr Whiteley was an old man, who had suffered greatly in the past from attacks by less successful traders. He was still working hard, and very happily. I did not want to upset him. When I did feel obliged to show him the second letter, he tore it up in a furious rage. It made me feel my first instinct had been right.'

'And what do you think now?'

'I beg your pardon?'

'In view of what has happened,' Mr Muir had the spectacles off and was using them for emphasis, 'do you still think you were right to keep the notes to yourself?'

'I couldn't let them see my doubt, Gwen,' he told his wife later, 'I had to say, very firmly, "Yes."'

'Of course you did, dearest. You had done what you believed was right.'

Leonard had seen Henry Beale in an extravagant black stock in the courtroom. He had seen young William and Frank Whiteley in their mourning bands. What did the brothers think about him? They had accepted his story, but had they been listening to Henry Beale's poison, and were they really thinking that he might have been able to save their father?

Mr Muir sat down with a dissatisfied grunt.

As at the inquest, Leonard felt as if he were on trial himself. Did all witnesses feel like this? In discussing criminal cases with Arthur French, Leonard had thought being involved would be exciting. Now he hoped that it would never happen to him again.

Slowly, keeping him awkwardly waiting, Mr Curtis Bennett rose to point out, with an assumed air of bored patience, that the defendant had consistently denied writing the notes and the police had not been able to produce a shred of evidence that he had. 'They are irrelevant to this trial, m'lud.'

Defending counsel nodded to Leonard, who stepped down and went back to his seat in what he hoped was a dignified way, his heart pounding as if he had bicycled three times round Hyde Park, trying to keep up with Madge.

'You stood up to it well, Leonard,' Ralph said afterwards. 'If I were prosecuting, I would have believed you as a witness.'

'Don't you believe everyone who swears on the Bible?'

'Only about one in ten.'

'Will they call me again?' Leonard wanted to go a long way away from London, from England, to an inn by the foothills of a small mountain, where he could watch sunsets with Gwen.

'Muir only called you today as a formality. The notes have nothing to do with the case. The jury has long ago made up their minds.'

'Which way?'

'They probably all shop at Whiteley's. Now let all of *us* go to the Waldorf Hotel and drink champagne. Austin? Madge?'

When Leonard got home, he felt unsuitably frivolous. He left it to Madge to tell her mother about the exemplary performance of the jousting knight.

Ralph Wynn was right. The next day the jury was only out of the courtroom for ten minutes before returning to deliver their unanimous verdict. Horace George Rayner was found guilty of murder, and sentenced by Lord Alverstone, the Lord Chief Justice, to death.

It surprised nobody. The surprise was that although William Whiteley had been an immense and popular figure of commercial legend, when Rayner's solicitor initiated a petition for a reprieve to the Home Secretary, thousands of people added their names to it. Ordinary citizens, clergymen, borough councillors, M.P.s, titled people – a hundred and eighty thousand letters flooded in within two days. Speeches were made. Sermons were preached. The cry rose again: 'Nursed back from death to Death!' An excited female offered herself to Herbert Gladstone, the Home Secretary, as a substitute customer for the hangman's noose.

No one at Whiteley's admitted to signing the petition except Henry Beale, who had the gall to ask Leonard whether he would add his name.

'Don't insult me, Beale. A life for a life. That's the least we can do for the Chief.'

But Madge had signed, and Bella had copied her. 'Don't look so injured, Daddy. It's not because we forgive Horace Rayner. It's our protest against the death penalty. Look.' Madge showed Leonard a copy of the letter they had sent in. 'A detested relic of a barbarous age.'

Mrs Roach and Tatiana had signed it, and some of the staff at Ladbroke Lodge. 'That creeping stain who calls hisself a butler,' Flora Bolt jeered. 'Trust him to take the side of a gaolbird.' She herself would need to think about it. 'If Bill Bolt had killed me when he come here Christmas Eve, wouldn't I want him to swing for it?'

'But you would be dead, Flo.' Dicky's logic was always good.

'Like poor Mr Whiteley. I've got to think about what *he* would want.' By the time she had made up her mind, the letter had been posted.

The outcry for the murderer's reprieve became an even greater public sensation than the murder or the trial. People were caught up in the drama of it, and swept after the banner of an easy humanitarian cause. On March 30th, Leonard and Gwen went again to the theatre with Vera and Charles Pope, who were great believers in the temporary replacement of real life by unreality.

None of them would ever forget the evening. Halfway through the second act of *What Every Woman Knows*, the play was halted. The actors stood in attitudes of suspense. The house manager came on stage to announce that His Majesty King Edward VII had commuted the sentence of Horace Rayner to penal servitude for life.

Sensation. Thunderous applause. Unparalleled drama. When the play resumed, to a house still buzzing with talk, it seemed very tame.

The populace was satisfied. No matter that Arthur Chapple, a lawyer, wrote to *The Times* denouncing the circus of maudlin hysteria by the irresponsible masses. 'Not trial by jury, but trial by the mob.'

Still less matter that Horace George Rayner had made a statement from Pentonville prison that he would rather die by hanging than live the rest of his life behind bars.

He was reprieved.

Chapter Fifteen

'Now I'll never know who wrote those accursed letters,' Leonard fretted to Gwen.

'What does it matter, Leo? They're finished, done with. Forget them.'

'I can't.'

Two months after his old employer's death, Leonard's mourning had reached the stage where sick regret had taken over from crisis, to delay the restoration of happier memories from the past. Whiteley's was recovering, business was buoyant, but that could not lighten Leonard's sombre mood. He had lost weight. He thought his sandy hair was thinning. He could not get rid of a chesty cough, which Little Bucky's mustard plaster did not dislodge. No. 72 was haunted by icy draughts. The high Georgian windows rattled, and you could hear the wind penetrating the gaps. The huge bathroom with the double basins and the eccentric geyser was freezing. The ventilation grilles on the Gents and the upstairs Place had to be stuffed with newspaper. Pipes in the servants' basement Place congealed. All the inmates of the house had colds or chilblains. Everyone smelled of camphor oil and eucalyptus.

Whiteley's was steam-heated. Customers' furs piled up in the cloakroom. No wonder Leonard could not shake off his cough, scolded Dr Buckmaster. The contrast between indoors and outdoors was too savage. Coughing, muffled in a scarf on perishing mornings, Leonard longed to be comfortably inside the store; but the old Chief's absence had left such a bitter void that coming to work was nothing like the joy it used to be. Leonard could not forget. Why did everyone else seem to have forgotten so quickly?

He liked it when a customer, seeing him patrolling the floors with his black silk cravat and wide armband, wanted to talk about William Whiteley, and to cluck about the sadness of it all.

'It must be hard for you, Mr Morley,' the elder Miss Moffat said perceptively, 'to see it all going on like this,' she nodded round the echoing tiled dairy hall, 'as though nothing had happened.'

'Thank you, madam. But we must remember' – he had formulated a pompous little public disguise for his gloom – 'that continued active trading is our best memorial.'

'It is what he would have wanted.' But Miss Moffat was not fooled. 'Oh *poor* Mr Whiteley. I knew him for more than twenty years.'

Her eyes were moist. Leonard coughed into a large handkerchief.

Day to day trade was thriving. The lure of spring round the corner stimulated shoppers to spend money. The fashion showrooms and ready-made departments were crowded with women anxious to cast off sombre winter clothing and try out the new textiles and lusciously named colours. Aertex ('It breathes!'), stockinet, loganberry pink, aubergine. The new 'health corsets' were sold out as soon as a fresh order came in. Engineered to thrust the padded bottom out and the broad triangular bosom forward like a fearsome stuffed bird, they were no healthier than last year's models, and probably even worse for the internal organs. But they were *the thing*!

That was important now. The old man's sons, with all respect, knew that they must look ahead, not back. The slogan of their Whiteley's advertisements was, 'Looking forward – it's The Thing!'

To which Leonard mentally added a second line of doggerel: 'The King is dead – long live the King!'

The new management structure was being developed. William and Frank, who were already on the Board as Directors, would become joint Chairmen in their father's place, with overall responsibility for the whole business. The General Manager's heart had kept him away for more than six months. The old Chief, ruthless with bad workers, but loyal to good ones, had kept the position open for him, but the brothers, who owed the man less, were considering an ultimatum. Come back to work, or resign.

Who would get the top job? Leonard Morley, Assistant Manager, thought, with all modesty, that he should be the man. Henry Beale, with all arrogance, thought that his exalted position as successful Chief Buyer made him ideal. The brothers Whiteley were rumoured to be considering top-flight London retailers to see who they might seduce away to Westbourne Grove. Leonard went soberly on with his work, taking responsibility, paying attention to staff, worrying about details; but he could not look far into the future.

'That bastard should have shot me too, Gwen.'

Most wives would have cried, 'Don't talk like that!' at the word 'bastard', if not at the death-wish. Leonard's wife, being Gwen, replied with comfortable amusement, 'Then you could have been buried at the old Chief's feet, like a crusader's dog.'

'Oh, you do me good, you really do.' Leonard hugged her: soft, fragrant, pliant. 'Because you won't let me take myself seriously.'

At the Loudon Street Settlement, the little deformed child Angel, who had hung on to life longer than anyone had expected, seemed at last to have reached the end of her struggle. Her mother had gone off with a spice pedlar and her brothers and sisters were dispersed into sweatshops and street gangs, so she was living at the Settlement all the time now, looked after by the come-and-go residents of the women's dormitory.

'Last time a doctor paid us a flying visit, he said, "All we can do is help her to die."' Madge was desolate. She loved the grimacing, indomitable child who fitted her convulsive limbs into her lap so contentedly, and watched her face for the chance of a joke.

'He should have taken her to the Great Ormond Street Hospital.' Bella was glad to show Toby Taylor that she knew the right thing to do.

The three of them were walking home through the bare trees and lifeless grass of Kensington Gardens after a visit to the Natural History Museum.

'He said it wasn't worth taking up a cot from a child who might be cured.'

'Is he the only doctor?' Toby asked, walking between the two cousins, tall and very 'toffee' in a long grey coat with a wide shawl collar and an insouciant tilt to his curly Homburg.

'It's hard to get them to come. At the beginning, when Arnold Toynbee made settlements a fashionable novelty, influential people wanted to help. Now that we're boringly well established, doctors and politicians don't bother.'

'*I* would bother,' Toby said, 'for what it's worth.'

'Would you? Would you really?' Madge stopped and looked into his face. 'Would you come and see Angel?'

'Of course. I don't know if I could help, but if her breathing's so bad . . . we could try thyme and pine oil. Did the doctor give her an inhalation?'

'He didn't think it was worth it. He looked at some of the new babies, and then he rushed off.'

'It's always worth it. I'll be there tomorrow.'

When Toby was talking, Bella thought, life seemed easier. He swept you along with his confidence.

'I wish I could come,' she said softly. 'I am so sorry for that poor little scrap.' She could feel her arms aching as she thought about holding this child they called Angel. Although she would like to prove to her mother that marriage was not the only worthwhile career for a woman, she sometimes did think about herself in a nursery with a baby, and even pushed a pillow under her loose nightgown to study how she would look, sideways in the mirror.

'Why *can't* you come?' Madge said impatiently, stooping to pick up a child's ball on the path and throw it back to him, while Bella was still thinking of doing that. 'I've asked you thousands of times.'

'Come with me, Bella.' When Toby looked down at her with that smile, she was glad she was a short woman. For Madge, the smile was more challenging, face to face. Tilted down towards Bella, it was protective, considerate.

But Angel looked so dreadful, dribbling and gasping, bundled up in her little wheeled box to protect her jerking limbs and her big unwieldy head, that Bella had no desire to pick her up and hold her.

Toby and Madge put the box on a table and made a tent over it for herbal steam. Taking the kettle to reboil it in the kitchen, Bella was afraid of the noisy competent women who were making soup in cauldrons and slamming pies in and out of the ovens and cutting long loaves of bread against their chests with knives like swords. She was glad to see Jack Haynes come in with a bucket of coal weighing down each arm. He tipped the coal into the bin and came over with the empty buckets to mouth, 'Bey-ya,' as he had learned to do when he was at Chepstow Villas.

Bella smiled and made the lifted hand sign, palm out, which Madge used for 'Hello'.

Jack put down his buckets to talk to her. She thought he said that he was glad to see her and that it was cold outside. Bella took a notebook out of the drawstring bag that hung from her belt, and by using signs and exaggerated lip movements and scribbling notes back and forth, she and Jack had some conversation.

''Ere, Jackie!' one of the women at the stove shouted. 'That coal bin's only half full. Deaf as a bleedin' post,' she said when he paid no attention, and all the women laughed.

Jack did not do so well with Toby. His grin faded, and he moved backwards with a closed face.

Will Morrison had come through from the classroom. 'He's a bit afraid of men,' he explained to Toby with his face turned away from Jack, in case he could read his lips. 'He seems to get on better with women.'

'I don't blame him, if he has the chance,' Toby said.

'He does. Too much.' Will threw a sideways glance at Madge, but she was bent over the child in the makeshift tent and did not notice.

'I must be off anyway,' Toby said. 'I'm meeting a man in the City. I should stop the inhalation now, Madge, and give her some water and honey. Try the steam again later.'

Toby had brought Bella here, but apparently she was to find her own way home. So when he remembered to ask her if that was all right, she said, 'I'm staying. Jack is going to show me some of his carpentry, aren't you?' She moved towards Jack possessively. A lot of the girls she knew would be afraid to be here among such coarse, unwashed people, and would not know how to make friends with this uncouth, wordless man. She was doing well. Perhaps she would come to the Settlement again.

'Jack has work to do,' Will said abruptly. He took Jack quite roughly by the arm and pointed to the coal buckets and then to the door where he had come in with them from the yard.

Madge rescued Bella by taking her into the long hall and telling her she could help to feed the cripples.

'I won't know how.'

'Don't always *say* that, Bella.' Madge hung an apron round her neck and pushed her towards a table where a woman was putting out bowls for the children. 'Just do it.'

'You were so rude to her,' Madge told Will. 'That wasn't necessary.'

'She was smarming round Jack like an idiot. Look, Maddy, don't you understand that poor man has feelings

185

and desires like the rest of us? Can't you see how he's teased by the attentions of women so far beyond his reach?'

'Oh, don't be silly,' Madge said in her brisk Physical Drill voice. 'Jack would never think of any of us in that way.'

'You are so naïve, all you good women.'

'And you're so sophisticated, I suppose.' Madge could always give a back answer.

'It *is* naïve of you to think he can go out into the world armed only with a hammer and chisel, and those wild hand signs you and he use.'

'They work,' Madge said.

'With you. But he ought to be learning a formal sign language.'

'Where?' Madge demanded. 'From whom?'

'Oh, I know.' They had left the clamour of the hall where food was being served to dozens of people, and Will leaned against the cracked wall of the passage. 'It's hopeless.'

'You never used to say that,' Madge said sadly.

Will was no longer the fierce young idealist who had drawn her into his own enthusiasm about what they were doing for those who had nothing, and what more could be done, for more and more unfortunates, until there would be no forgotten ones.

He did not live at the Settlement now. He was going to take up his law studies again. He had neatened his shaggy red beard. Aunt Teddie's husband, Ralph Wynn, had offered to take him into his chambers. He was not always there when Madge came to work at the Settlement. They no longer kissed when they could grab a moment alone.

She did not think now that she loved him, or that he had ever really loved her.

'Why do things always have to change?' Madge shivered in the cold stone passage and wrapped her arms round herself, since Will did not put his own round her.

'We lose some of our illusions,' he said.

'I haven't.'

'I suppose I'm defeated by the vastness of the problem, Maddy. These people have unfathomable needs, but all we are doing here is putting a very small bandage on a very large wound. You don't see it like that. You think you can save Angel if you love her enough, you and that quack friend of yours.'

'Toby is a doctor.'

'*Is* he? That's nice.' He threw the subject of Toby away. 'You think you can make poor Jack into a social creature. You'll break your heart. When he leaves here, how will he stay out of trouble? One day, Jack and I will be in court together.'

'Jack will never need defending.' Madge swung back her hair and put up her chin.

'Actually,' Will said, quite nastily, 'I'll be prosecuting.'

Bella was just beginning to get the hang of putting more soup into the child than over its clothes or hers when Madge took her away. 'Come on, we're going home.' Madge's colour was high and she seemed angry about something.

'Have you had a quarrel with Will?' Bella asked, as they walked to Mile End tube station.

'He's impossible.'

'Don't you love him any more?'

'I don't know why I ever did. When you're in love, men look better than they are. When you're not, they look worse.'

'Oh, I know.' But Gerald Lazenby still looked quite good to Bella. She had cut his photograph out of a society magazine. 'Have you and Will broken up then?' she asked, as they waited on the platform of the Central London line. Madge nodded. Sitting in the train, which was too noisy to talk, Bella found that she was, unworthily, rather glad. She had expected that Madge would marry Will, with her family's blessing, although he was not rich, and with Bella as an elderly bridesmaid of twenty-four.

The little girl Angel died early one morning in a choking agony. The women in the dormitory had swaddled her up and taken her away for their own burial rites by the time Madge came to work, and had put another child, a boy deformed by rickets, into the box cart.

Madge could not weep in front of their no-nonsense attitude of, 'Plenty more where that one came from.' She could not sorrow to Will, who had told her many times, 'You're too emotionally involved with the child.' So she wept to Toby Taylor, who, amazingly for such a busy man, turned up that day at the Loudon Street Settlement to see how Angel was.

'I kept – I kept on with the stea – the steam. But it didn't –' Madge felt quite natural crying in front of Toby in the big clothes cupboard, where she had gone to see if she could find something warm for the rickets boy. He did not panic, 'Don't cry, don't cry,' as most men did. He did not run his finger embarrassedly round his collar and say, 'I expect you'd rather be left alone.' He said, 'Get your coat, dearest bereaved Madge, and I'll take you out for a hot breakfast.'

After that, she went out with him two or three times, to a tea dance, and to *The Merry Widow*, with supper afterwards at the Trocadero, where Toby Taylor was greeted by quite a few smart people, including an actress with heavily mascaraed lashes and gossamer hair. He asked Madge to come up to his rooms over The Clinique in Egerton Terrace, but she would not.

How easy would it be to seduce this tall, forthright, golden girl? Toby wondered. Or rather, how difficult? A young woman brought up like Madge Morley in a bourgeois Bayswater family would need more than several glasses of wine, or an opportune weak moment, like the tears in the damp clothes cupboard, where there had been room for them to stand together with her silky head on his shoulder, but not for much else.

Nowadays, when many young women were growing up less inhibited, there were those who Did, or could be persuaded to Do, but still plenty of those who Did Not, for various reasons.

It was better to leave Madge with her reasons. His friendship with the family was too precious a thing, more valuable to his life than the flashier contacts he cultivated. It was warm and genuine on both sides and part of his increasingly respectable reputation as a naturopathic healer. He would do anything he was privileged to do for Leonard and Gwen in this painful, uncertain time after

William Whiteley's murder. He would not try (and perhaps fail) to seduce their daughter.

After supper with Madge at the Trocadero, he woke up his housekeeper, Neelie Drew, to come upstairs to his bedroom. Neelie was married to a club steward who lived in at his job, as she did in the basement of Egerton Terrace. They saw each other on Sundays. It was a good arrangement. Neelie, well paid, was a competent cook and housekeeper and a neat, polite receptionist, and a mistress only when needed. She had no claims on Toby and no jealousy, although she sometimes pouted her full lips at Marie-May Lacoste, just short of rudeness.

'Who was the Pear's soap virgin with the Dutch-doll bob at the Troc?' Marie-May was stagily jealous of other women of Toby's, although she herself had a husband and assorted short-term lovers. He told her.

'Oh, I see. Your respectable, salt-of-the-earth friends that you keep on about. Well, we needn't worry about *her*, need we, Bounce?'

They were sitting on the soft fur hearthrug with the shrill, tight-skinned little terrier she sometimes brought with her. She fed it choice scraps from the table, and wanted it up on the foot of the quilt when she and Toby were in bed together.

'You needn't worry about anyone, Marie.' She was 'between plays' at the moment, so he was seeing more of her. 'There is nobody like you, nobody.'

'That's true, Toby dear, and I love you for saying that.'

But her kind of love was different from what he had grown to feel for her, although he would not spoil their good times by voicing it.

*

Now that she and Will were no longer close, Madge was seeing other men, as well as Toby. With her father too tired and anxious to be his usual sociable self, the atmosphere at No. 72 was rather muted, so Madge bought one of the dashing 'American length' evening frocks in crêpe de Chine, and was out two or three times a week with Malcolm or Huntley or faithful Francis, childhood friend, who had never given up hope.

Her father always waited up for her, but one evening, when he had come home late from work, he looked so exhausted that she persuaded him to go to bed early and give her the key to the front door.

'But I'm always up for you, dear one. We have cocoa.'

'Not tonight. Don't bother with the Thermos, Flora.'

'No cocoa?' Leonard's face fell. 'You mean, you've only been drinking it for my sake?'

'Oh, Daddy, *please*.' If the situation at Whiteley's did not resolve itself soon, she might have to marry Francis, to get away from home. 'Give me the key, and I promise to have a gay time at Lucy's dance, knowing you're sound asleep.'

Lucy Vidler's engagement dance was not exciting. The pianist and the strings were not always in time with each other, and Madge had some dull partners. Francis was not as good a dancer as Toby, nor so witty. After the speeches and toasts to Lucy and her soldier, he became so sentimental that she had to laugh at him, which gave him an excuse to drink too much, which was one of the many reasons why Madge would never marry him.

He was handsome and amiable, with a good family name and money. Uncle Hugo and Aunt Charlotte approved of him enviously, but Madge had never managed to pass him on to her cousin. He had once taken Bella in a coach to the Derby, but she had been perversely silent and sulky.

'You are a hopeless person!' Madge had raged at her when she heard about it. 'How are you ever going to get a man?'

'Perhaps I don't want one.' Bella set her jaw. 'And certainly not your cast-offs.'

After the dance, Francis took Madge to the Kit-Kat Club, where they drank more champagne and kissed at the table in a dark alcove. They were good old friends, after all.

Francis was tipsily half asleep on the way home. Madge told the cabby to stop two doors down from her house, so the engine would not wake her father, and told him where to take her friend.

'Oh, but I say, Madge –' Francis grabbed for her, and she shut the door.

No. 72 waited peaceably, a light showing behind the glass panels on either side of the front door. Through the plane-tree branches, thickening with the promise of new leaves, the street lamp diffused a yellow glow on the front steps. In her mind, as she hunted for the key in her beaded bag, Madge projected herself into the familiar atmosphere of thick carpets, Ronuk polish, the savoury ghosts of dinner, dying fires, Gwen's lavender bowls, the crack of the stairs expanding, the slow beat of the grandfather clock.

The key was not in her bag. Standing on the top step, Madge shook everything out onto the seat at the side of the porch. She remembered that Francis had waggishly fumbled in the bag for her dance programme, to cross out names and write in his own. He must have pulled out the key and dropped it on the floor.

It was nearly two o'clock. If she rang the bell, it would wake everybody in the basement and probably her parents as well. Madge went back down the front steps and round the side of the house to the solid wooden gate that shut off the backyard. It was locked. Beside it, the high wall between No. 72 and No. 74 had broken glass set into the top.

She put her face to the back door and said quietly, 'Flora,' but the maid could not hear her from her room beyond the scullery. Madge had climbed over the yard gate as an agile child, but not in an expensive dress. She took off the amber crêpe de Chine, and with one foot on the scullery windowsill and the other on the gate latch, scrambled over in her petticoat and stays and bloomers. Like this, with the dress over her arm, she tapped at the window of Flora's half-basement room.

'Bleedin' Jesus!' She heard a gasp and a creaking commotion as Flora stood on the bed. The window opened at once.

Madge threw in her dress and crawled over the sill, dropping on to the pillow from the window high up in the wall.

'Anyone with you?' Flora stood on the bed to peer out into the dark, cat-smelling yard. 'Cor, Madge, I never thought of Mr Francis as an unbuttoner.' She brought her tousled head inside with a big laugh, clapping her hand over her mouth for fear of Mrs Roach.

'I lost the key.' Madge struggled into her dress. 'Good thing there are bars only on the front windows, not at the back.'

She tiptoed up the bare linoleum of the back stairs with the gold slippers in her hand and her dress undone. In the long dim hall, where the light from the outer lobby came through the coloured glass of the inside door in blurred blobs of blue and yellow, the massive clock ticked very solemn and loud, like a measured scolding.

A few days before Madge's late night escapade, Flora had seen her so-called husband Bill Bolt in the sooty gardens behind St Mary-of-the-Angels, where she had wheeled the baby she was minding for her sister Violet, who was supposed to be looking after it for her church work.

Oh God. Again that lurch of the soul and body towards him. Would she never be free? Bill was cleaner, better dressed, his eye was bright, the tilt of his cropped head cocky.

He told her that his wife had died. She did not believe him. 'Unless you killed her.'

'Ask no questions, you'll hear no lies. We're legal, Flo.' He put an arm round her waist, and bent to make a gruesome face into the pram. 'You can't go having other men's brats.'

'Get away! You know it's not mine.'

'I wish it was ours.' His hand moved up to her breast.

Don't let him make you go weak at the knees, she thought. But oh . . . Oh, Bill . . . 'Not here, you bastard!'

Flora's mother would not have him in her house. 'I'll come to Chepstow Villas,' he had whispered to Flora behind the sad laurel in the garden.

'After what you done to Tat? Mrs Roach would never let you in.'

'I'll come to the front door,' he swaggered.

'You dare and I'll have you arrested.'

But now ... Madge's words came back to her: 'Good thing there are bars only on the front windows.' Flora realized with a shiver that he could come to her back window, and no one would know.

Flora went down through the Portobello Road market to see if her stepbrother Ben knew where Bill Bolt was hanging out. She could not find him or his mate, and their curio stall was not pitched today. They must be at the races. She saw one of Dicky's street friends, quick-fingered Noah with the hair like sweepings under a bed. He saw her and dodged away from the sweet stall, but Flora caught hold of him.

'Turn out your pockets,' she growled.

'No, honest, I never.' He had chocolate round his mouth.

'I don't care what you done. You want a copper?' He held out a grubby hand. 'You know a man called Bill Bolt?'

'On the buses, innee? 'Im what they call Bull.'

'You know where to find him?'

'Might.'

'Tell me.' He shook his head, looking at his broken, oversize boots. 'Give him a message then, Noah. Tell him, "Sunday. St Mary Gardens."'

'Wossat mean?'

'He'll know.' Flora put the penny into Noah's waiting hand. 'And it's a secret, mind. Don't tell nobody.'

'I don't never tell nobody nothing.'

'Where are you going, Flo?' Dicky saw her bustling to clear the Sunday lunch.

'See my Mum.'

'And Daddy Watts?' Dicky was fascinated by the chesty old pirate with the red kerchief over one eye who was allowed to spit into a chamber-pot. 'I'm coming.'

'You're not. And don't follow me neither.'

'Noah and I are good at stalking. We're going to set up as private detectives.'

Flora put a coat over her black uniform dress, and slipped out while Dicky and the Master were fighting a battle with tin soldiers on the drawing room floor.

The comfortable safe haven of No 72 Chepstow Villas, solid and creamy in the pale spring sun, and the company of Madge and Dicky were Leonard's best comforts these days. He had bothered Gwen too much with his difficulties at work. She would cry gently at first when he came home unhappy, but after a while she seemed only to half listen to him, as if she were protecting her own sensitivity. Although she had been a Victorian girl, brought up without a father in a tear-washed family of women, Gwen did not like to cry. It gave her neuralgia. She had to send Madge or Flora upstairs for the salicylate.

With the news that the store's General Manager would definitely not return from his prolonged sick leave, Henry Beale was determined that he would beat Leonard for the job. He toadied up to William and Frank Whiteley, as he had to their father, and stepped on the Assistant Manager's toes whenever he could. Was it Leonard's anxious imagination that the brothers were cool to him? Henry had never let go of the subject of the anonymous notes. Were they listening to his poison? Did they still wonder whether Leonard could have saved their father? He could hear Arthur French saying, after the inquest, in his speculative Scotland Yard way, 'One might almost imagine that Mr Beale wanted to accuse you of being an accomplice to murder.'

Madge was often out these days, and Leonard did not burden Dicky with his grievances about the dastardly Beale, but the child seemed to sense when he was down. He would not sink down with him, like Gwen with her hurt tears, but would try to pull his father up with jokes and silly tricks and his own fresh young energy.

One of his favourite childish jests was to play about with the speaking tubes that connected the ground floor rooms with the basement. He blew the whistle in the mouthpiece of the tube in the kitchen, and when his father answered, put on a spectral voice or a comic foreign accent to make him laugh.

Leonard was indulgent, but he warned, 'Don't overdo it.' Dicky did it once too often. His father shouted back at him down the tube, 'You stop that, young Dicky, I mean it. I'm angry with you!'

Soon he heard the heavy front door slam. Going to look out of the window, he saw Dicky's tam-o'shanter bobbing along beyond the front wall.

'Where has the boy gone, Gwen?'

'Out with his friends.' She did not look up from the beautiful pheasant's tail she was embroidering on a cushion cover.

'You're too lax with him.'

'Don't be a bear.' She smiled up at his angry face. 'He never gets into trouble.'

*

197

Toby Taylor, walking from Notting Hill Gate to pay a call at No. 72, saw a fiercely moustachioed policeman with Dicky Morley outside the corner house, and crossed Chepstow Villas quickly.

'What's wrong, Constable?'

'Brought this young gent home, sir.' Dicky was dishevelled. He had no hat, and the reinforced knees of his black stockings were snagged and muddy.

'What has he done?'

'Nothing.' Dicky kept his head down, golden hair tangled over his eyes.

'An old person complained of being harassed, sir. Master Morley and his young mate – who I have my eye on – were following this person in the back streets in a sinister manner.' The policeman bit his lip so as not to return Toby's involuntary smile. 'I'm just going to have a word with his father.'

Poor Leonard. He had trouble enough without this. 'I'll take him in, Constable,' Toby said. 'I'm a good friend of the family.'

'You'll see that he gets a talking to, sir?'

'Oh, yes.'

When the policeman had turned away, Dicky looked up, and Toby winked at him.

'What will you tell my father?'

'Nothing.' They went up the front steps.

'Thanks, Uncle Toby. You're a topper.'

Chapter Sixteen

A good friend of the family, Toby was glad to be able to save Dicky's father from extra aggravation. Leonard was pleased to see him. Gwen was very welcoming. 'You're like Mercury shimmering into our dull lives, To-by!' Dicky was his friend for life. Only Edwina Wynn, also visiting No. 72, greeted him with more embarrassment than enthusiasm, and made an excuse to leave soon after he arrived.

Since Edwina had told him about the traumas of her confinement, Toby Taylor had shared the revelation with his friend Dr Boone at The Keep.

'She could not love the twins.' After the usual hopeless visit to his mother, he found the doctor sitting by the narrow railed bed of a catatonic woman who had moved and made a sound, and might awaken. 'And I think she still cannot care for them, not normally. Could this, just possibly . . .' He hesitated: he must not sound too facile with the meticulous psychiatrist. 'Do you suppose this could be a key to her persistent melancholia?'

'I have known of it, Tobias, although I've never treated a case. I have heard of women killing their babies, even when there was no reason for wanting to be rid of them.'

'If you were me,' Toby said diffidently, 'how would you proceed?'

'You can't undo what has happened.' Dr Boone leaned over the bed rails to pull down the lower lid of the catatonic woman. Her flat blue eye looked at him, startlingly, without apparent sight. 'You can only, as with any troubled patient, try to undo some of its effects.'

'Well look, she thinks she is helpless, you see?' When he was at The Keep, near his mother, Toby sometimes found himself slipping into a Welsh accent.

'Of course. And so your task, like my task here with many of the hysterics, is to open the eyes, very slowly, to the incredible truth of the body's own power. The nervous system has all the answers for itself, if only the perverse mind would listen. Lead your lady gently to listen to herself, Tobias.'

Toby was anxious to see Mrs Edwina again, but he had not heard from her. Was she afraid that she had revealed too much? If she would risk another visit, he would not urge her to go over the painful memories again. He would indicate as much, if he saw her with the family, but there were no gatherings at No. 72 while Leonard was still in a stew over Whiteley's. Should he telephone? Edwina had said, 'I hate the instrument,' although she and Ralph had had the telephone for a year. 'It's an intrusion. I never can think of what to say.'

One afternoon, when Toby was walking up pleasant Campden Hill on his way back from visiting a healthy hypochondriac in Holland Park Avenue whom he was dosing with flower essence placebos, which she thought were strong drugs, he crossed the end of Phillimore Place, where the Wynns lived. He had been to other Morley houses – Ladbroke Lodge, Vera and Charles's in Chelsea, Austin's noisy narrow house in Addison Road. He had lunched with Ralph Wynn at his club, but he had never been invited by Teddie, who entertained as little as possible.

It was a decent brown brick house with white windows, but the curtains behind them seemed to be impenetrable screens of muslin and lace. The maid who opened the door looked even glummer than her mistress.

'Mr Taylor? Madam's not expecting you,' she said negatively when Toby handed her his card.

'Ask Mrs Wynn if she's at home.' Toby smiled. The maid did not.

The hall in which he waited was panelled in dark wood. The carpets were rich, but sombre. The high window at the turn of the stair was thickly netted against daylight. The bulbs in the heavy wall fittings were too dim, and the electrolier in the hall ceiling still looked blackened from the days when it burned gas. The house looked like Edwina, not Ralph. It was obvious that he was not at home enough to bother about bringing in light and colour. Poor Sophie. No wonder her twin brother Greg had spent the Easter holidays on a school walking tour in Scotland.

When Toby followed the maid to the drawing room, he found Edwina standing by the mantelpiece mirror, fussing at her hair and dress. A chair was askew by the jigsaw table in the shrouded window, as if she had jumped up in a fluster.

'I was passing by, so I thought I would look in. I've not seen you for so long, Mrs Edwina.'

'I've been busy,' she said defensively. 'I've been caught up in the difficulties of poor Leonard and Gwen.'

'How are they?'

'All right, I suppose.'

Toby knew they were not all right, but Edwina's mind was not on them, so he went back to her. 'You like jigsaws?'

'They pass the time.'

'What *do* you like, Mrs Edwina?' He asked it lightly.

'Oh – the usual things, I suppose. Will you – er, will you sit down? Some tea?' She looked confusedly at the bell pull and then at him, moved towards a chair, but did not sit in it. She was obviously wondering whether this was a social call or a doctor's visit.

Toby was trying to make it easier for her when Sophie came in from her ladies' academy. When she saw Toby, she stayed by the door.

'Don't lurk, child. Come in and shake hands. What will Dr Taylor think?' Mother and daughter laid cheek against cheek.

'It's nice to see you.' Toby took the girl's thin, cool hand. 'How was school today?'

'The same.' She shrugged.

'You don't like it?'

'Not much.'

'Oh, *Sophie*,' her mother said in the exasperated voice her daughter seemed to provoke. 'After all the trouble your father and I took to find you the best finishing school. Music, art, theatre, outings, culture. Girls these days,' she told Toby, 'are quite too blasées. When I was at school in Henley –'

'Yes, Mother, we know.' Toby was glad to see the girl show some spirit.

'I'll have them send your tea up to the schoolroom,' her mother said.

'I didn't know you'd be here, Dr Taylor.' Sophie, innocent and disturbingly ravishing in her severe school blouse and tie, gave Toby one of her rare, transforming smiles. 'Or I would have –' She pushed at the sides of her plain grey skirt disdainfully.

'I just dropped in,' he said, his eyes enjoying her, 'to pay a brief social call.'

But when Sophie had left the room, he said at once, 'That was a white lie, Mrs Edwina. This is not a social call. It's a visit from your practitioner, but your family doesn't know about that, do they?'

'They mustn't know.'

'Why?'

'Well.' She wanted to say, 'It would spoil it,' but that would sound too intimate, and after she had made a fool of herself at The Clinique, she had not planned on there being any more of this association to spoil.

'Well,' she said again. She often began a sentence with 'Well'. She could hear herself doing it. It gave her time to think, or rather to put off giving the wrong answer. 'Well. I wouldn't want them to know what happened to me.'

'You mean about the difficult twin births?'

'That's ancient history. No, I mean about descending into hell and not being able to climb back up.'

'You talk about things "happening" to you, Mrs Edwina, as if you were passive and helpless against an outside punitive force. I believe that people are more in control of their lives than they think.'

This was upsetting. Teddie wished that the conversation was not taking place in her own drawing room. She wished that she were wearing a hat. You were more in command of the situation, in a hat.

'Control? That's only a word.' She must not accept everything this assured man said to her. 'Leonard is not in control of what is happening to him at Whiteley's.'

'But Leonard is not ill.' Dr Taylor looked very relaxéd, sitting there in her Heal's tapestry chair, but his deep brown eyes were watching her attentively. Teddie's heart began that fluttering trick it played on her.

'Am I ill?' She caught her breath.

Toby Taylor considered this, looking at the fan arrangement of ornamental paper and dried flowers which was in the grate, since Teddie always stopped fires on April 1st, whatever the weather.

'Yes,' he said, 'you are, to an extent, ill.' He looked at her with his eyebrows raised, to see how she would take this. It was a shock, true, but not a blow.

Ill. Her heart slowed down. 'Ill?' The word was familiar and reassuring, like not going to school and being in bed in the daytime with an eiderdown full of dolls, and Meggie, the long-ago maid at Goring, bringing milk and bread with the crusts off. 'If I am ill, then my, my . . .' What word was there for the weighted inertia that cut her off from human contact? 'My difficulties are not my fault, as you say they are.'

'I didn't say "fault". Let's forget that word. "Blame" and "fault" should be cut out of the dictionary. I said "control". If something is wrong, you know, it may be in your power to put it right.'

'Oh no, doctor.' That just showed how little he knew about her. It proved that nobody, not even he, understood her at all. I am a stranger on the earth, Teddie thought miserably.

'Mrs Edwina.' Oh heavens, he did what he had done that Christmas Eve at No. 72 Chepstow Villas. He crossed the space of burgundy hearthrug between them and was on one knee beside her chair. 'Believe me, my friend, and I think you are my friend, it is time to tell you this. I know that you suffer from melancholia a lot of the time, and feel tired and discouraged, but – no, don't get up.' He rested a hand lightly on her knee (how dare he?). 'Just listen. Your problems have not been imposed upon you by an implacable deity. You put them in, unknowingly, and now, with knowledge, you can take them out. Mrs Edwina, you have it in your power to stop feeling like this *any time you want*.'

'How dare you!' Teddie stood up, quivering. Her heart was at it again. With a hand on her chest, she reached for the fringed bell pull and summoned the maid.

Damn, Toby thought, hurrying away from Phillimore Place. That's done it. I thought the time was ripe to take a chance with her, but look here, Tobias Taylor, bull in a china shop, you didn't know what you were doing. He jammed his hat down on his head and strode down the hill towards Kensington High Street.

Looks as if I'd lost that game. Lost Mrs Edwina, just as I lost the Captain last month by offering him psychology when he wanted expensive miracle pills.

Oh, well. He got on a 49 omnibus which would take him to South Kensington. Plenty more patients where they came from, as long as I haven't lost the rest of the Morleys along with their weakest member. But if she squawks to them, they will be on my side. They're not fools. Nor is she, all evidence to the contrary. She is still the daughter of the great Ernest Morley.

At least I've given her something to think about. If she ever does think, the sad old sow. He had felt kindly towards Mrs Edwina when she was hanging on his words and making a little progress. Now that she had rejected him in outrage, he could contemplate, as he walked along Brompton Road, how much he disliked her.

Toby was thrown off balance when Edwina Wynn turned up meekly at The Clinique about a week later, and he had to start feeling kindly towards her again. She was wearing a spring hat, a starched straw that hid her eyes.

'You're angry with me, Dr Taylor.'

'No.'

'Yes you are, I know you are.'

Don't tell me how I feel! She *would* make him angry if she kept on. Talk about control. She had as keen a taste for it as the next woman.

He took a deep breath and said, 'You look better.' She would not normally want to hear that. She preferred to look as bad as she felt.

But she smiled. 'Thank you. I've been thinking,' she said, quietly, but not humbly. 'What you said about power and control. Perhaps it *is* time for me to do something for myself at last. Will you help me, Dr Taylor?'

By the end of May, Mrs Edwina was showing a little progress. A glimmering of self-esteem began to emerge from beneath the stones that had crushed it for so long. If she talked about her mother, it went under again, so they did not talk about her mother.

She was making a small effort. She kept slipping back

into the familiarity of gloom, but she did report a few actively happy moments.

'At Vera's the other evening, I drank wine and I said I had enjoyed a stroll in the park. They looked at me as if I had suddenly started swearing.'

Toby looked piercingly into her eyes, like Dr Mesmer, and said, 'Life is good, and so are you.'

'I wish you would tell my daughter Sophie that, Dr Taylor. She's so sulky and difficult, and she's still not eating enough to keep a sparrow alive.'

'I wish I could help.' Toby would like to have the pure young girl up here for a session. 'She's a lovely child.' Steady, Toby. She is also a Morley – forbidden fruit.

'I'm glad you think so,' Teddie said grimly.

'Can you get her to agree to see me?' Oh hell, I'll risk it.

'Dr Buckmaster's colleague threatened to put her into a hospital and feed her through her nose, like the Suffragettes. She'll do what I say.'

'But it would be better if she came of her own accord.'

'Dr Taylor.' She looked him in the eye. 'You have never been a parent. You are not equipped to judge things like that.'

'You show a good spirit, Mrs Edwina!'

'*Do* I?' She did not quite glow and beam, because her face was not made in that style, but she looked positively pleased with him, and with herself.

In bed in her room, her face turned towards the wall, Sophie Wynn lay curled in a ball, hugging her cold ankles, and went over and over what had happened in Dr Taylor's room at The Clinique. This was how she would tell it, when she told it, if she ever could tell it.

207

'How did it go with Dr Taylor, dear?' Sophie had been accompanied by the maid, having refused to go with her mother.

'It was all right, Mama.' Arms across chest, shoulders hunched.

'What did he say?'

'Nothing much.'

'Why are you blushing?'

'Let her blush,' Sophie's father said. 'It's very becoming. Probably the first time she's been alone in a room with a man.'

I suppose it was, ran the imaginary narration in Sophie's head. I mean, with a man who behaved like a man.

What was he like? her listener would ask, whoever her listener might be – Madge? Bella?

Well, he was quite nice at first. Asked me the usual questions – why was my appetite so poor, was I not hungry? Was I unhappy? I gave the usual answers. No answers really. I shrugged and pouted a bit, as he would expect of a 'difficult' young girl. He asked if I thought he could help me and when I said I didn't need any help, thank you very much, he said, in that soft sort of sing-song voice he uses sometimes on the grown-ups, and Aunt Gwen says, 'Oh To-by' and goes a bit swoony, he said, 'But I think you are not very happy.'

What did *you* say?

What was there to say? I don't know anyone of my age – except perhaps my brother Greg in his funny way – who is happy, and if Dr Taylor didn't know that, I was not going to make it easy for him. He talked about energy and he said he had a lot of it and I didn't have enough, and that the nerves must be stimulated to make my mind and body healthy and some more rubbish like that. We were sitting at opposite ends of the couch, and I was afraid he was going to move closer, but he didn't. He sat at the end of the couch and, and – I began to be afraid – *looked* at me.

'Don't be afraid,' he said. Isn't it awful when someone seems to somehow read your mind? 'You're trembling,' he said, in that voice. 'Don't be afraid. Listen, Miss Sophie, I'll tell you a story. Once upon a time,' he began, as if I was still in the nursery. 'Once upon a time, there was a man called Friedrich Anton Mesmer, who wanted to make people happy and to heal the sick. He would gather a lot of people together in a hall and this Dr Mesmer would make a dramatic entrance wearing a long lilac gown and carrying a magician's wand. He would glide about and wave the wand over certain people. If you had been there, he would have fixed you with his great burning eyes.' You know those eyes of Dr Taylor's? Like chocolate with little gold flecks in them when his face is up close.

'Then one of his handsome young assistants would come and gently massage your knees and your spine. Women were very strongly affected. They fell unconscious, laughed, cried, went into convulsions with it all. Then, for the special ones like you, Dr Mesmer would tell the young men to stimulate the magnetic flow by exerting a subtle pressure with his fingertips, like this, on your –'

I jumped up like a scalded cat. He had stood up too, in front of me, and his hands . . . I had to shout, 'Don't touch me there!'

And did he?

He said, 'Why not?'

'I hate it,' I said, because I do hate my – my bust, I try to hide it, but he said, 'It's beautiful' and I – I didn't know whether to cry or scream or faint or what.

And then?

He said, 'You see, you are like those women at the meetings of Dr Friedrich Anton Mesmer. The magnetic energy. Even you can't resist it, little Sophie.'

My God!

I know. I had to escape. I ran to the door. He didn't follow me downstairs. Our maid was waiting in the hall. She had my hat and I jammed it on and managed to get out to the carriage and get control of myself.

Did she see you were upset?

She never notices anything. Nobody knows. You're the first person I've told.

It's despicable! Your father will kill him.

I could never tell Papa.

You poor, poor girl. What will you do?

I think I shall become a nun.

You're a fool, Tobias. It's hands off the Morleys. But if the little ninny snivels, I shall explain that she's hysterical, which she is. I don't think she'll say anything, however. She's too craven. One day, she will thank me and Dr Mesmer for 'putting the finger', as it were, on what she needed. She will have to be led very gently to her awakening, but not by me, good friend of the family. I'm not going to risk losing that.

One evening, after Toby had taken Marie-May Lacoste to her rehearsal for the new operetta at Daly's, he met a girl he knew in Leicester Square, and she took him slumming to a few of her favourite haunts. In the taproom of a small hotel in Red Lion Street, off Theobald's Road, Pearl drank with some cronies, while Toby leaned against the small lopsided bar, its edge rubbed concave by years of elbows, and chatted to the landlord.

'This here is a very famous man.' A drinker in a checker-board cap prodded Toby in the ribs. 'Oh, yes, very famous. Been in the papers. At the Old Bailey, 'e was, and not in the dock, like some of his customers.'

'How so?' Toby asked, as he was evidently expected to.

'Give evidence, dinnee, few mumfs ago, about that feller what done in 'is rich old man.'

'Mr Whiteley's son?' Toby pricked up his ears.

'Mr Whiteley's bastard,' the landlord said. 'He was at my hotel for a while, a real hard-luck case. Desperate poor, bills up to here.' He pushed up his stubbled chin with the back of his hand. 'Wife left him, and cetera.'

'He rented one of your rooms?'

'He occupied one of my rooms,' the landlord corrected. 'I had to tell him, "If you don't cough up next week, you'll have to go back to the spike." That's Rowton House, the down-and-out crib in Hammersmith. "Now then, my good friend" – he liked to put it on a bit – "you know I'm expecting a draft of money. Any day now, my friend. My father is the richest man in London," he'd boast. Well, we didn't know who his father was at that time, though we knew he was to do with some big shop, because one of my occasionals let out that he himself worked for him there.'

'Who was that?'

'Big geezer with a red face. Name of Beale. Bit of a dipso, between you and me. Used to do some of his drinking here, where he wasn't known.'

Well, well. Toby had followed keenly the details of the murder trial of Horace Rayner. He remembered now that the hotel in Red Lion Street had been mentioned, and testimony of the defendant's boasts about his wealthy father.

Pearl wanted to go for a plate of oysters, and later he got rid of her and went to the stage door of the theatre to fetch Marie-May, furious because the director wanted to drop one of her songs, and hungry for an expensive supper at Romano's.

Chapter Seventeen

At Whiteley's, the conflicts and tensions came to a head at the end of May. Pianos and other musical instruments had been a big feature this spring. Advertisements, which depicted a man in tails swooned over by beauties with fans and jewelled snoods, promised: 'A piano from Whiteley's entitles you to a course of lessons from an internationally renowned teacher. You too can be the life and soul of the party!'

Leonard had arranged for a piano recital in the music department. Posters were up throughout the store and in every plate glass window. A variety of new and secondhand pianos were brought from the warehouse and polished by men in baize aprons. On the day of the concert, Whiteley's piano demonstrator played snatches of easy classic pieces downstairs to attract shoppers up to where a world-famous maestro would perform. Flowers were banked up, a carpet was laid, the catering department had provided claret cup and cake and rows of gilt chairs in a semi-circle.

Leonard was to be Master of Ceremonies. He had shaved well, and brilliantined his sandy hair to a darker shade. The maestro was late, but Leonard greeted the customers as they arrived. They sat on the gilt chairs, and waited. Mr William sat in the front row with Lady Porchester. The demonstrator obliged with some Chopin. Leonard stood where he could see the gate of the lift. The customers grew restless. The buzz of their talk was increasingly aggrieved.

Leonard went to his office and put through a telephone call to the agent through whom he had engaged the maestro.

'But Mr Morley, he cancelled a week ago, after he sprained his wrist. I came round to explain. You weren't there, but I talked to a Mr Beale. He said he would inform you at once.'

After Leonard had tied himself into apologetic knots trying to mollify the customers and Mr William, who was angry and embarrassed by the fiasco, he went in search of Henry Beale.

'Why did you not tell me the concert pianist had cancelled?'

'I did. I had to be in Birmingham the next day, so I left a note in your pigeonhole marked "Urgent".'

'You did not.'

'I did. Here's a copy. "Concert cancelled with regrets, etc., etc."'

'Am I going mad? I never saw it. It wasn't there.'

'You must have pulled it out with other papers and mislaid it before you read it.'

'Did you tell Mr Frank or Mr William?'

'They were in Paris at the Trade Fair. It was your responsibility anyway, Morley. I did the right thing. You can't accuse me of going against store protocol. I told you.'

'I accuse you of deliberately making a fool of me and trying to damage my reputation in the store.'

'Lower your voice, man. You don't want every ledger clerk to hear you.'

'I don't care if they do.' Leonard was furiously angry. He loathed and despised the beefy man who sat leaning back

214

arrogantly in his swivel chair, with a smirk of – yes, of triumph.

'You did this deliberately. I know that.'

'Really?' Beale raised his eyebrows and pursed his thick red lips.

'For months now, ever since the Chief was – ever since the Chief was taken from us, you've been scheming and manoeuvring. I know your game.' Leonard released some of the pent-up grievances he had been too discreet to voice. All the things that were true. 'And now you – your deliberate deceit, and lying to make me look a fool.' He was sweating and out of breath. He could hardly splutter out his words. 'I shall expose this!'

Henry Beale flicked spittle from his sleeve fastidiously. 'When all is said and done, Morley, it will be *your word against mine.*'

And who would the Whiteley brothers believe? Beale had ingratiated himself with them and praised their grasp of the business, had hampered Leonard whenever he could, had pulled off some showy purchases which might or might not make a profit, but which looked spectacular. Leonard Morley had stuck to his work, doggedly and devotedly supervising the staff and ministering to the customers. It was rumoured that the brothers planned to make changes, after a decent interval, to modernize some of their father's tried-and-true methods. Leonard had been William Whiteley's loyal henchman. Would they write him off as old-fashioned?

The agitated Assistant Manager was called away to attend to a shoplifting incident on the ground floor. Then he was waylaid by several customers who were upset about

215

the cancelled concert, by a mother who had lost her child, and by a cashier upstairs who needed signatures. When he was free to leave at last, he made his way along crowded Westbourne Grove and the peaceful pavement of Chepstow Villas, his tired strides pacing out the beat of Beale's voice, 'Your word against mine.'

Home, thank God. The one stable element. His own square beautiful benign house and private little plot of land. The dappled plane trees were crowned with bright new leaves. A cherry blossomed in the front garden of No. 72. Boxes fastened to the green-painted railings of the drawing room and dining room balconies had been filled with polyanthus by Gwen's little plantman from the Portobello Road market.

Mrs Salter and Flora and Tatiana had finished the spring cleaning in the hall. The wallpaper seemed lighter and brighter. Dust had fled the picture rails and the tops of ornate frames. Paint on the stairs and banisters was like thick soapy cream. The carpet glowed with its original colours.

In Leonard's study, the cover of his wide chair was loose and rumpled, and darker at the arms and headrest. The curtains comfortably remembered winter cigarettes and pipe smoke. This room would be cleaned last, when he was out of it during the July holiday.

He hung his coat on its own peg and, in his waistcoat and shirtsleeves, went into the drawing room to Gwen.

'I'm so glad to get home!' he said fervently as he came through the door.

'That's nice.' Gwen was at her desk. She took off her spectacles and turned round in the chair and held up her graceful bare arms. 'You always say that.'

'Yes, but today especially.' He kissed her warmly, then pulled away to look into her dear, untroubled face.

'You've just missed Austin,' she said. 'He came to fetch Elizabeth and the children. That baby is enormous. Austin says he'll be playing backyard cricket before you know it. When are you going to start the Sunday games?'

'Not yet.' Leonard had not the heart for it.

'Why not?'

'Because I – oh, Gwen, it's been such a bad day.'

'But it's all right now. Look, I've got good news for you.' She turned back to the papers on her desk. 'The information about the house near Chipping Norton came today. A tennis court, golf nearby for Vera and Charles, fishing, such lovely views. If we care to take the place, we can have it for the two weeks that we want in July.'

'Good.' Leonard sat down on the arm of the chair near her and hung his hands between his knees. 'A terrible thing happened at work today, Gwen.'

'What, my darling?'

'Henry Beale played a dastardly trick on me, the worst thing he's done yet.'

She listened while he told her the story, her grey eyes soft under the cobweb of drifting hair. 'There is a chance that William and Frank Whiteley may believe him. They may blame me for the disaster.'

'Oh, surely not. You're so pessimistic, Leo. You're taking the glummest view of it. Come, look at this picture of the holiday house I've found for you. It will raise your spirits.'

'Gwen, don't you understand? I'm in danger. I may lose my job!'

'Oh, fiddlesticks! But if that were really so' – she laughed and crinkled her eyes to the joke – 'we could take Norton Croft for *three* weeks.'

He stood up. 'Can't you take anything seriously? Don't you understand what's happened?'

'I'm only trying to cheer you up, dearest. You always make such a drama out of everything. Whiteley's isn't the centre of the universe. Why can't you be a lovable little H.G. Wells draper like Kipps?' She put her head on one side.

Leonard turned quickly and weaved through the furniture to the door.

'Leo, don't be angry –'

He shrugged into his coat and went out, with a slam of the front door and a clang of the garden gate.

Toby was paying a call on Hugo and Charlotte at Ladbroke Lodge, as he did once in a while because they were part of the family, and they knew some potentially useful people. Charlotte was entertaining a dim couple who had just returned from Europe, where they had met a decrepit Hanoverian count who had told them to visit his distant cousin, Carlotta Müller, now Frau Morley of Latbrück, a fine *Grundbesitz* in London.

Toby wandered to the other end of the drawing room, where Bella was sitting with the couple's tubby daughter, who had brought photographs. Beyond the back window, Ladbroke Square flaunted its full-dressed trees like a country park. Under the trees, a figure in a dark frock-coat walked away slowly, hands deep in pockets.

'Excuse me, Miss Bella.' Toby interrupted her boring exchanges with the fat girl. 'There's a man I do business with in the square. I've been trying to get hold of him. Would you lend me the key to go in?'

The subtly scornful manservant showed him down the outside steps at the end of the hall, and he went through the small back garden and into the square by the 'private gate' of which Hugo was so proud. He caught up with Leonard by the waterlily pool in the middle of the gardens.

'I saw you from the Lodge. What's the matter, friend?'

'Nothing.' Leonard looked down at the goldfish, then up at Toby. 'Everything.'

'Whiteley's?'

Leonard nodded. 'I thought I'd take a turn here to clear my head. My darling Gwen doesn't understand business problems.'

'Lovely women like that seldom do. May I ask what the problems are?'

'Nothing new. The odious Henry Beale is still trying to cheat his way to the top. Today he outdid even himself in perfidy.'

'Beale . . . the second time I've heard that name this week. Funny thing.' Toby told Leonard about the landlord of the Red Lion Street hotel.

'He may go there,' Leonard said glumly. 'He drinks all over town, I believe.'

'Yes, but he was in that hotel at the time when Horace Rayner was staying there. Odd, that. Leonard, don't you see?' Toby had only just seen it himself. 'This Beale has been hinting at collusion, because you kept quiet about those monstrous threatening letters. But do you suppose – is it possible – that he himself was somehow in league with William Whiteley's son?'

Toby went back to the hotel in Red Lion Street the next night. He went early, to avoid a crowd in the bar room, and found the landlord alone, leaning on the bar with the *Evening News* spread out under his elbows.

'This – er, this gentleman you talked to me about.' Toby lifted his face from the froth at the top of a pewter pint mug. 'The one who said he worked for William Whiteley. He was acquainted with Mr Whiteley's son then?'

'He met him here. Mr Rayner – God give peace to his bloodstained soul – he boasted to him of money expected, and what he would do if his old man didn't come through with it. Just dreams, you might say. Like asking my barmaid to marry him and emigrate. His mouth was bigger than his muscle, in my opinion. You could have knocked me down with a bent spoon when he turned assassin. Shows how wrong you can be, don't it? Fill you up, sir?'

'Thanks, no. I need a clear head.'

Toby walked part of the way home, getting off the bus at Hyde Park Corner and thinking very hard along Knightsbridge and Brompton Road. The next day, he was waiting for Leonard at No. 72 when he came home from work.

'Will you excuse us, Gwen? Leonard and I have some business to discuss.'

'Oh dear, I thought you came to see me, To-by.'

'No, he came to see *me*.' Dicky pushed between them.

'I did both.' Toby and Dicky were allies, sharing the secret of the policeman with the fierce moustache, and he was very fond of Gwen. If he ever married, which seemed doubtful, since he was getting along so well by himself, it might be someone like this gentle, scattered, light-hearted woman, rather than someone athletic and straightforward, like Madge, or more dazzling, like Marie-May. 'Talking business to Leonard is just a diversion.'

'You'll stay to dinner?'

'If I may.'

In the study, when Toby had told him the story he had woven out of facts and assumptions, Leonard protested, 'But I can't march in there and accuse the man of this. There is no definite proof.'

'There is very strong suspicion, though. My feeling is that if you lay this in front of Mr Beale, he'll crumble.'

Leonard looked distressed. 'It would be playing his game. Smear against smear. I can't do it.'

'But *I* can.' Toby had already thought of this.

'You?'

'Why not? I'm the one who has found him out.'

'But suppose there is nothing . . .'

'If there was nothing between them,' Toby was filled with a buoyant excitement, 'if it was only an innocent drinking acquaintance in a shabby hotel, then why did Henry Beale never tell anyone that he knew of the existence of Horace Rayner? Let me take a chance, Leonard, will you?'

'You won't say that I sent you?'

'Don't worry. It's my risk.' They shook hands. Leonard smiled at last.

Toby liked to take risks. His whole life was a risk, in a way, because, although he was genuinely helping people who had real or imaginary illnesses, he did not really know as much as they thought he did.

He decided to deliver his guesswork-as-fact to Henry Beale at the store. It was best to let loose his lethal charge in a place where Beale could not shout or attack him or make a noisy scene.

'Good day, sir. My clerk says you have a proposition to set before me.' Henry Beale, in an offensively high collar that kept his jowls propped up so that he could look down on the world, offered Toby a chair with a ceremonial gesture. 'Do I take it that you are an importer?'

'You may take anything you want.' Toby remained standing. 'If I am an importer, the commodity I bring to you is something that you already possess, something very large and very simple.'

'Don't speak in riddles, sir.' Beale ran his hands up and down his well-filled waistcoat. 'I am a busy man.'

'So am I. This is what I have to offer, Mr Beale.' The Chief Buyer prepared himself to disparage, as a preliminary to bargaining. Toby put his hands behind his back. 'Truth.'

'Truth?' Henry Beale scowled. 'What are you playing at?'

'The truth about the game that *you* played with one Mr Horace Rayner, illegitimate son of your employer, William Whiteley.'

To say that Henry Beale paled would only mean that he became a normal colour, instead of flushed. He looked at the door, and Toby stepped back to make sure it was closed.

'I have been to that little hotel in Red Lion Street,' he began. 'The one on the corner, with the bar room whose entrance gives on to the mews.' He stayed by the door, leaning against it with his arms folded and his ankles crossed, his brow lowered and his gaze directed at Leonard's enemy, who was now his enemy also.

'I don't know it.' Beale leaned a hand on the back of his chair. He looked as if he would like to sit down, but would not give Toby the advantage of height.

'Strange. They know you there, Mr Beale, and they know that, since about last July or August, you talked several times with Horace Rayner, unacknowledged son of Mr William Whiteley.'

'I have never met the man. Well – if I did, I didn't know who he was. Now look here, sir . . .' Henry Beale began to bluster and interrupt.

'Hear me out,' Toby said. 'It will be better for you if you do.' Watching Beale very closely, he told him the story that he had deduced.

'The first of the anonymous notes was received by Mr Leonard Morley, Assistant Manager of this store, in August, as he testified at the trial. I put it to you, Mr Beale –' Toby enjoyed sounding like a barrister – 'I put it to you that after you discovered who Horace Rayner was, you and he conspired to get money out of his father.'

'Oh, this is absurd.' Henry Beale sneered at him. 'I won't hear any more of this slanderous rubbish.' He sat down heavily at his desk and put his large oily head in his hands. 'Get out. I've got work I must do.'

'So have I,' Toby said pleasantly. 'It is to ask you to tell me this, if you will. In the event that Mr Whiteley had met any blackmail demands, what percentage of the money did you expect to receive?'

This was Toby's big risk, a pure guess, but he delivered it confidently. Had the shot hit home?

'How dare you?' Beale lumbered to his feet and pushed back the chair. 'Get out!' He moved towards Toby. 'Out of my office before I call the police and have you thrown out!'

Toby stood his ground, but he unfolded his arms. If the infuriated man struck out at him, he would let him have it back. He was lighter, but fitter and quicker of movement than Henry Beale, who was breathing like a bull, his face beginning to glisten with sweat.

'Are you going to get out?' Beale asked menacingly.

Toby shook his head.

'Then I shall send for the police.' The man stepped back towards the telephone on his desk.

'But do you really want the police here?' Toby teased him with a conversational tone. 'Do you want me to tell them how, by conspiring with Horace Rayner to write and deliver those criminally threatening notes, you also tried to ruin the career of your colleague, Leonard Morley?'

'God damn you, I don't know what you're talking about.' Henry Beale sat down again, his face half turned away, as if to collect himself. 'What has this got to do with Mr Morley?'

'His good friend, Inspector French, might answer that. I understand,' Toby lied, 'that fingerprints have been found on one of the notes that wasn't torn up.'

'The murderer's, of course.' Beale swung round, biting his fleshy lip.

'Or yours.'

'You're mad. You're – you're a liar and a lunatic, and a – and a –'

The gross, sweating man in the chair was beside himself, slobbering, stammering with rage, and what Toby triumphantly believed was guilt. He must go now, while he was on top. Keeping his eyes on Beale, he picked up his hat from the chair by the door and delivered his parting shot calmly.

'I shall leave you now to think this over, while *I* consider how best to break the news to William and Frank Whiteley, who, God knows, have endured enough already.'

'Now look here!' Henry Beale sprang up. 'Come back, sir, I haven't finished with you. Come back, you filthy liar, or I –'

Sweat it out, Beale, Toby told the door as he closed it behind him.

There were staff about in the corridors, and shoppers crowded him as he made his way downstairs. He had to contain his insane glee until he reached the street, where he could strut up Queen's Road to the park, swinging his stick and grinning with triumph and raising his hat in a gesture of goodwill to anyone who smiled at him.

Henry Beale did the gentlemanly thing, for once in his career. He resigned. The brothers William and Frank decided not to pursue the investigation and prosecute. Whiteley's had suffered too much notoriety already.

The Board of Directors would appoint Assistant Manager Leonard Morley to the post of Managing Director. A new Assistant would be hired, and the Head Buyer would move up to replace Henry Beale as Chief Buyer.

'So who did write them notes, then, when all's said and done?'

Madge said, 'We'll probably never know, Flora, and it doesn't matter.'

From overheard bits of conversation, filled in by Madge, Flora had the whole dramatic story to retail below stairs and to her mother and friends in Notting Dale. She tried to tell Bill Bolt how happy she was for the family, but Bull was not interested in them.

'You're happy,' he said, "cos you got me comin' in through that perishin' narrer window once in a while to give you what for.'

'You mustn't come no more.'

'Har, har.'

'I'm afraid.'

'They won't find out.'

'No, afraid of *you*. No, Bull, no – you're hurting me!'

Leonard started up stump cricket again in the backyard, with the big Sunday lunches: a welcome sign that everything was back to normal. Toby Taylor turned up almost every Sunday to score flashy boundaries by hitting the ball over the high back wall and the stable roofs into the mews.

'A tanner!'

He paid Dicky and Laura sixpence each to retrieve the ball.

He was the family hero.

So that when poor little Sophie, put out by his popularity, decided belatedly to reveal her terrible and humiliating experience at The Clinique, nobody believed her. Her mother, who formerly was always ready to believe the worst about anybody, would hear no word against her favourite physician. Dr Taylor himself dismissed Sophie's story as 'a common hysterical delusion of young female patients', and everyone believed him.

Gradually, after that, she began to eat food again in a slightly more normal manner.

'I knew you would come to your senses at last,' crowed her mother, who in some ways was even harder to stomach now that she seemed to be emerging from her gloom.

You know nothing, Sophie thought. I didn't have any of

the éclairs yesterday, and you didn't even notice. But if no one's going to believe me about Dr Taylor, or pay any attention to what happens to me, there's no point in starving, because obviously, no one cares.

Chapter Eighteen

The family decided to forget Sophie's aberration, but Bella remained intrigued. She agreed with everyone that the girl had made the whole thing up, but part of her mind furtively asked: Could it possibly be true? Everyone knew that Toby Taylor was a ladies' man, but Bella had not interpreted that in a physical sense. Now, after Sophie's story – 'He *did*, Bella!' 'Oh, he couldn't have.' 'No one believes me!' – she had to think of him in a new way. She could not help stealing glances at his hands and wondering guiltily: had those hands . . . ?

'How's Miss Sophie, then?' the butler leered, when Bella was visiting Sybil Crocker in the servants' sitting room.

When upstairs was unpleasant, which it was at the moment, because Bella's father had called her a hopeless disappointment, and her mother was sulking because the Lord Chamberlain had turned down her request for an invitation to the state visit of the King's nephew, Kaiser Wilhelm II, downstairs was a refuge. She did not think she was always welcome, but if you believed in democracy and a classless society, which Bella did in theory, you had to practise it.

'What do you mean, Mr Hurd?' Upstairs, the butler was Hurd, but in his own domain he was Mr. 'Why do you ask after her?'

He hooded his eye at Sybil like a snake. *They knew.* How?

Informers in Phillimore Place, or, God forbid, Chepstow Villas? Scandal ran from basement to basement like rats.

'She will come to no good, that one.' Sybil was mending a black stocking, with her little finger crooked above the needle. 'I always thought she had a common streak.'

'I don't know why,' Bella said. 'She's very quiet and lady-like.'

'Ha!' The butler enjoyed this. 'That don't signify. You ask my aunt in Pottery Lane. They come to her, you know, these high society girls, when they're in trouble.'

Bella did not want to hear any more, but was loath to leave, because she knew they would talk about her behind her back. She began to say, 'Thank you for the tea,' when a shrill clamour split the air in the passage outside.

'Oh, bells, bells, bells – she's at it again!' The parlourmaid put down her darning and got up. 'No offence, Miss Bella.' She went off with a hypocritical flounce.

Charlotte Morley had been excluded, not only from the Kaiser's reception, but from the Royal Academy Private View as well. Piqued, she would not go to the Summer Exhibition on an ordinary day, but she did eventually agree to go with Bella in June, when no one they knew would be there to witness their shame.

Someone was, however. When her mother was lingering over some particularly uninspiring portraits, Bella went back once more to try to decipher the 'problem picture', titled enigmatically, *Predicament*.

In a cluttered room, where you could see detailed orna-ments and every petal and tendril on the wallpaper, a young woman in outdoor clothes wept, head on table. An older man brooded by the mantelpiece, pipe in hand, small dog cowering on the hearthrug. A maid's head in cap and streamers looked anxiously round the door.

'What do you think, Bella?' A hand on her shoulder. She turned and found herself face to face with Toby Taylor.

'Oh – good afternoon. What do I think?'

'About the picture.'

'I really don't know.' She was not going to risk saying something he could think stupid.

'*Predicament.* You must have some opinion.'

'Well ... I think her father is forbidding her to see a certain man. But the maid might be coming in to say he's actually there in the hall?'

'No. She's his wife, not his daughter. She's *sinned*,' he said with glee. 'He's got to turn her out, dog and all, and he wonders if he's wrong, because she's been the light of his middle age. But too late! The maid is saying her taxicab is at the door. It's a dreadful picture anyway, with all that claustrophobic detail. I don't know why people waste time on it. What are your favourites this year?'

'I like the Sickert woman in the mirror, and the Colliers.' She played safe. 'His people are so very alive. You feel you – you feel you know them.' There were pictures at home, in which the people sometimes seemed more real and approachable than those with whom she lived.

'Yes, that's right,' he said. 'And you want to know them better, and to *be* in the places where they are. Come along and I'll show you some of the ones I especially like.'

They looked at a tall narrow painting of a busy London street. 'Listen.' He put his head on one side. 'You can hear the traffic, and the shouts of those men on the corner.' In the next gallery, they skirted the crowd looking dutifully at

Sargent's *Lady Sassoon*, Portrait of the Year, and were alone in a corner with an unpretentious landscape in which a low stone house stood at the edge of a field whose long grasses were threaded by a wandering path of trodden darker shades.

'I'm walking down that path,' Toby said dreamily.

'So am I. I can feel my hands brushing the tops of the grass.'

'That's what painting is for,' he said, 'to draw you powerfully in to be a living part of what the artist saw.' A woman in a hat like an iced cake had stopped to frown at his intense, persuasive voice, but he paid attention only to Bella. 'You understand that, don't you?'

She looked up at him with her head slightly lowered. She had seen women do this, to make their eyes look larger.

'Have you ever studied art, Bella?'

'With my governess, I did. She was very clever and original, but when I was sent away to school, it wasn't in the curriculum. However.' She raised her head, because it was tiring to keep looking up from under her brows. 'I would hope to make it one of my subjects, if I ever *could* go to a university.'

'That's your ambition, isn't it?'

She nodded. 'Somewhere like Leeds, where women can go to lectures, but not have to take a degree.'

'What is keeping you back then?'

'Well . . .' Somehow it seemed too trivially domestic to say: My parents. 'Well, I might not be accepted, for one thing.'

'Have you put yourself forward?'

'Not yet. One day I will, though.' He was much taller

231

than her. She looked up at him, as she hoped, fearlessly. 'I want to make something of my life!'

'Splendid,' he said. 'This country needs more educated women.'

'I think so too.' Bella basked in his approval. 'It's a time of freedom and opportunity for us, and I would like the chance to grasp it.'

'I have contacts in the academic world,' he murmured. 'Perhaps I can help.'

'*Could* you? Oh dear, there's my mother.' Charlotte had a stout arm up, beckoning over the hats. Bella turned away into the crowd. Toby Taylor did not follow her.

But a week later, he came up to her at a dance in Belgrave Square.

'Hal*lo*!' He seemed glad to see her, 'You look elegant in that dress.'

Bella knew she did not look elegant in anything, especially the expensive pale green overdecorated satin, but she repeated the trick of ducking her head and raising her eyes, which were her best feature.

'Are you having a good time?' he asked her.

'No,' she admitted. 'It was all right at first, but my partner went off to another ball to get a second supper.'

'The cad.'

'Oh, they all do that.' There were still dozens of men on the floor, but they were not dancing with Bella.

'Come on, then.' Toby Taylor pressed her gloved hand. 'Let's escape. I haven't a partner either. I was an extra man at a dinner party.'

'But your programme –'

'We'll throw it away. And yours.'

232

Bella slid the little white and gold programme off her wrist and stuffed it into the green satin bag that matched her dress, before he could see the empty spaces in it. She told her dinner party hostess, Mrs Gore-Brown, that her father's chauffeur had come for her – 'Oh, indeed? I wish I had known about these arrangements' – and went downstairs to get her cloak, half afraid that Toby would not wait for her, and she would have to grovel to Mrs Gore-Brown.

In the taxicab, she asked him, 'Where are we going?'

'Not to Ladbroke Lodge. They would want to know why you were back early. Come and see my home for a change.'

Oh, my God. Bella knew this was not right, not the right thing to do at all. In the light from a street lamp as they stopped at a corner, she saw his hands – those hands! – resting on the knees of his perfect evening trousers. He was so relaxed and casual, she could not protest, 'Oh no, I mustn't.' He would despise her as a silly, shrinking girl.

When he opened the door of his house, a woman came out of a ground floor room into the hall. 'Anything you need, Mr Taylor?'

Bella turned her head away inside the high collar of her dark-red cloak.

'No, you go to bed.'

'I've left your tray upstairs.'

In the comfortable salon, there was a plate of sandwiches and decanters of wine and whisky and a soda siphon.

'What does she think?' Bella asked nervously.

'My housekeeper? I often bring friends home. That doesn't make me a libertine.' Toby laughed. Bella took off her cloak in a desperate way, as if she had nothing on underneath.

*

Poor girl, she was so scared. She sat on the edge of her chair and pursed her lips to take tiny sips at her wine glass. Toby wanted to say: Relax, I'm not going to ravish you. But she might guess that he was laughing at her, and he did not want her to know that.

What did he want? Why had he brought Bella Morley back here? Sorry for her? Sorry for himself because Marie-May was being difficult and evasive about the Frenchman, who might be rich enough to tempt her to disentangle herself from Toby, who could not bear to lose her?

He sat down opposite Bella, leaning forward with his whisky glass in both hands, and told her that she had nice eyes. Under the heavy brows, her hazel eyes were large, though puzzled and a little unfocused. She looked down, and he said, 'Look at me, Belle. Do you mind me calling you that?'

'Nobody does.'

'Well, I shall, because you are *belle*.'

She had been unfortunate in her inheritance. Short thick figure, strong nose and lips from her Germanic mother, the family square chin which looked better on the male Morleys.

'Poor Belle,' Toby said, because she looked uncomfortable and nervous. 'At the Royal Academy, you told me, "I want to make something of my life," and I sensed in you –' Hang it, Tobias, this is a nubile young woman you have here, not a patient – but he went on, sounding like an imitation of himself imitating Dr Boone's gentle therapeutic manner. 'I sensed a sadness in you.'

'Why?' Bella whispered. She put down her glass with a hand that shook, and spilled a little wine.

'I don't know why. I just know it's there.' He waited.

'Well, I am sad,' she faltered, 'when I think that I – oh dear.'

She put her face in her hands. Her large feet, which had been neatly side by side in the green satin shoes, splayed sideways. 'Of course I'm sad,' she burst out through her hands in a creaking sob, 'because I can never – I'm never allowed to – I've tried all my life, but he . . .' She stopped, took down her hands and worked her face into control.

'Your father?' Toby had heard Hugo Morley sharpen his dull, cruel wits on his daughter.

'All I ever wanted,' Bella said, looking very plain and blotchy and not at all *belle*, 'was for him to be proud of me and to think I was worthy of my famous grandfather. I worked and worked with my dear governess, but then, instead of going to the clever school with Madge in Holland Park, I was sent away – my mother does everything *he* wants – and I hated it and it was cold and I got pneumonia and he used to sign his letters "Yours truly, H.W.W. Morley".'

She began to cry again, not covering her face, which might have been better. Toby made her drink her wine, and got up to pour her some more and to give her the clean handkerchief from his breast pocket. He laid a discreet hand on her disordered hair, and told her that he understood, was glad she had released some bad memories, and was honoured by her confidence, before he took her home.

His motor hansom drove away down Kensington Park Gardens as the half-asleep, grumbling housemaid opened the front door of Ladbroke Lodge.

'Bel-la!' Charlotte, with her head huge in a puffed frilled cap, was at the door of her front bedroom. 'That didn't look like Mrs Gore-Brown's carriage.'

'There were too many of us. They brought me in a cab.'

'And drove off without seeing you into the house? I'll have to have a word about that.'

Oh, please don't, Bella begged silently, as she dragged herself up the next flight of stairs, clutching Toby's handkerchief. 'My father made me suffer too,' he had confided. They were a pair.

When Toby had infiltrated himself into the solid, likeable Morley family, he had not anticipated their underside: pathological Edwina, Leonard in need of a knight-errant, and now Bella in the confessional. Be still, my Baptist ancestors. I might be called to the priesthood.

He was still seeing Edwina Wynn once in a while. Like the frog in the well, she slipped back from time to time, and had to be reminded who was in control of her life.

When she could not believe in herself, she tried God. 'I've been to church again,' she told Toby, watching from under a low, crinkled hat brim to see if he was angry, since perhaps *he* wanted to be God. 'I mean, not just to Matins on Sundays with Ralph and the twins, because everyone does that, but for a prayer. I couldn't pray before, because God had turned his face away, like everyone else. I pray for myself, and for poor Sophie not to be tempted to any more lies by Satan.' Since she had begun to believe in the deity again, she could also believe in the devil.

She had revealed to her relations how much that clever Dr Taylor had helped her, which was why she had sent naughty Sophie to him – 'And look, the child is eating again!' – and this added to Toby's popularity with the family. The old girl really did seem to have bucked up at last. She made her servants take down and clean the hall electrolier. She stood up to her mother, who had demanded that Teddie accompany her to Buxton Spa for a course of hydrotherapy.

'What shall I do?' she asked Dr Taylor. 'I don't want to go.'

'What shall you do? Simple, Mrs Edwina. He looked her full in the eye. 'Remember that no one else can tell you what you have to do.'

Chapter Nineteen

Adelaide was angry and 'hurt', which was why Aunt Teddie
did not go to Goring for the annual Morley Regatta in
June. This was no rival to the formal Goring-and-Streatley
Regatta, which attracted rowers from the Oxford and
Henley clubs, but a boating picnic downriver for a family
who liked to have days out together.

This year, they were in three punts and a small steam
launch hired by Vera's husband, Charles Pope. His daughter Henrietta brought her young man to drive the launch,
and Madge came with her faithful standby Francis. Her
new love interest, Guy, was an ex-officer who had suffered
severe leg wounds in a Boer ambush, and could not get in
and out of boats. Madge's latest lame dog. He played
backyard cricket from a wheeled chair and had replaced
Will Morrison at Sunday lunches.

Toby Taylor was invited to the river picnic as an honor-
ary member of the family. Bella was nervous, half abashed
because of her late-night tears, half excited to see him
again. She had carefully washed his handkerchief and dried
it stretched on the marble of her washstand, since she could
not let one of the maids iron it and see his initials. She
would return it after the picnic, when he and she would
take a stroll along the river bank. They never did, however,
because he brought an astonishing woman with him to the
Morley Regatta.

Toby had kept his two lives separate, but Marie-May had been nagging at him to introduce her to the Morleys. He wanted to please her, and it was a chance to dazzle the family. She was a fairly well-known actress. Bella had seen her on the stage, and so had· Leonard and Gwen and Madge. Dicky gave a whistle at sight of her, and got a smack from his brother Austin. 'This brat has spent too much time in the Portobello Road.' Francis cried, 'I say, how ripping!' when he found out who she was, and she smiled and purred at them all and was quite dauntingly decorative in a sailor blouse of radiant white muslin trimmed with peacock blue, and a tiny straw boater set on her amazing spun-sugar hair.

She brought along her shrill little dog Bounce, who wore a collar set with sparkly stones and barked at every mallard and coot on the water, and attacked the poor smelly old dog Maxwell, when he turned up with grandmother Adelaide in the wicker pony chaise. Women shrieked in various pitches, but young Helen Pope plunged fearlessly in to separate the snarling tangle. When she was shouted at: 'Never interfere in a dog fight!', she said, 'They won't bite *me*,' and handed the rubbery brown terrier back to Miss Lacoste, already displayed to best advantage against the cushions of a punt. 'He probably doesn't get enough exercise.'

'Probably.' The actress patted the cushions. 'Come and sit by me, my dear, and tell me all about your life.' Her way of defusing competition from fresh glowing youth.

'I'm a writer, you know,' Helen said before she had even sat down. 'That's going to be my life.'

'Delicious.' Miss Lacoste made her bewitching cat face. 'You shall write a play for me.'

239

From the wharf, Adelaide announced that she had only driven down from Heron's Nest because she knew they would not bother to come up and visit her, and she had no intention of setting foot in a boat.

'Nonsense, Mama.' Charles Pope, who was good with his mother-in-law, manoeuvred her with jokes and flattery out of the little carriage and into a seat under the awning of the launch.

With Leonard and Austin and Francis poling the punts, they all negotiated the Sunday traffic out into the stream, with instructions from Adelaide to both her family and the boatman. 'Push the *bow* out, Hadland. Austin, what are you doing? Keep your own water!'

The clouds moved away from the sun, and Austin allowed Dicky to punt under the railway bridge, where he and Laura hooted at their own echoes. Leonard's boat, with Gwen and Helen and Toby and the actress, pulled over to the left bank by Ferry Cottage to call the ferryman out to take Madge and Bella, who were riding their bicycles along the towpath, across to the other side of the river. Because of a wide right-hand bend downstream, the towpath had to change to the inside of the curve, so that barge horses would not trample away the outer bank, where the current scoured it on the turn. Horses were unhitched by Ferry Cottage and rowed over in the wide heavy boat, while the barge was poled across.

'Before the town bridge was built, was this the only connection between Goring and Streatley?' Toby Taylor asked.

'If you'd been a Roman, Uncle Toby,' Dicky called across from the other punt, of which, in his jaunty yachting cap, he was now Captain, 'you could have walked across where the Ridgeway meets the Icknield Way. The old causeway stones are still under the water.'

'Your son is adorable.' Marie-May turned to beam up at Leonard.

'We think he's precocious,' Helen told her.

Precocious or not, it was almost Dicky's eleventh birthday, so the picnic spot was his choice, in the water-meadows above Pangbourne where the multicolour Jacob's sheep grazed. Madge and Bella, who had had to wait for the slow ferryman, caught up on their bicycles as the boats were moored and everyone disembarked.

'Now tell me about *you*.' Marie-May invited Bella to sit by her on the tartan rug, but Bella said, 'There's nothing to tell,' and became busy helping to unpack food from the hampers.

Adelaide would not leave the launch. 'My rheumatics would kill me if I tried to step up on to that treacherous bank you've chosen. That daughter of mine doesn't know – or doesn't care – that I'm in pain,' she told Toby, when he brought her a plate of chicken and a glass of sparkling wine. 'She refuses to take me to Buxton Spa.'

'But you can go anyway, with Margaret Biddle,' Vera called from the meadow.

'I don't think I care to,' replied Mama in a martyred voice. Vera rolled her eyes exaggeratedly. Toby picked up their message: if her rheumatism gets worse, it will be Teddie's fault.

He could be heard saying smoothly to Adelaide, 'But if you don't take the cure, Lady Morley, it might make Edwina feel guilty, and I know that you, as a mother, wouldn't want that.'

Toby Taylor, where have you been all our lives? He did have a way with the matriarch. He took his own plate of food to the launch and told her about nux vomica for rheumatism, instead of the drastic quinine and mercury with which her doctor had assailed her.

'Dr Maitland – wicked old fool – says if I don't stop complaining, he will try blisters. As if I were a horse.' She pulled her mouth and chins wretchedly down into the stiffened lace collar that cut into the folds of her neck.

'If you were *my* patient, I would wrap you and the pain in warm blankets and leave you alone.' To this comforting suggestion, Toby added that he had recognized the heavily wooded hill above the curve of the river as the place where two of her late husband's characters had held tryst in *A Small Country Town*.

' "Where the trees," ' he quoted, ' "drop down to embrace their own reflections in the summer stream." '

Bella hoped that Marie-May Lacoste was put out because he was taking so much trouble to please her grandmother, but the actress was occupied with the other men. Francis showed off larkily, and Uncle Leonard, in his best white flannels that had shrunk a little (shame on Whiteley's famous steam laundries), was being very attentive and gallant in his 'Our Mr Morley' style.

Adelaide insisted that Toby should make the return trip with her in the steam launch, which gave Marie-May the chance to sit by the old lady and say, 'Please do tell me all about your life with your famous husband, Lady Morley,' and then talk about herself.

The punts were slow, working their way upstream, and the launch was quite far ahead when Henrietta's practical young man had some trouble with the engine. It spluttered and coughed and would make no speed. Toby went to help, and when the pressure-relief valve opened with a gush of steam, he jerked back his hand and knocked it against the exhaust pipe, which gave him a severe oily burn. The engine recovered, and since they were just downstream of Ferry Cottage, they stopped there to clean the hand. Marie-May, dramatically concerned, went into the little house with Toby and helped him to wash the dirt from the burn and bandage the hand with a strip of clean cloth.

The cottage was tiny, two small rooms on one floor, neat and clean, with a rainwater pump and primitive washroom at the back. The roof was one low wide gable, overhanging a white wooden arch with a set-back doorway. Decorated with two tall odd-shaped chimneys and a roof-ridge of dogtooth tiles, it was like a fairy-tale cottage, framed by thick bushes and briars, with geraniums in pots on the doorstep porch and only a narrow slope of grass between it and the river.

Marie-May was enchanted. 'Oh, how I envy you,' she gurgled to the monosyllabic ferryman. 'I would like to live here all the rest of my life!'

The man gave her an impenetrable look and went off to row his broad boat across the river, where Madge and Bella were ringing the bell that hung on a dead tree to summon the ferry.

And perhaps, dreamed Toby, if he could ever take Marie-May off somewhere in the country, away from the theatre and the artificial excitement of London, perhaps she would live contentedly there with him 'for the rest of her life'. But that was only an ephemeral fancy. She would never want to live away from the stimulation and bright lights of a city, and nor would he. That was not what he had left Wales for.

But she had been happy and lovely all day on the river, and those times with her had become increasingly rare. The French impresario was talking of a part for her in a Spectacular. There were more and more evenings when she was too busy to see Toby, or would cancel a supper engagement with him. She was making it obvious that she had bigger fish to fry. This was a new situation for Toby Taylor, who usually managed to be the big fish with other people, like the Morleys, and some minor social hostesses, and his patients, whom he did not discourage from dependence.

One of them, Mrs Marcus, declared that she had never digested a meal comfortably before she discovered The Clinique and Mr Taylor. He had not pointed out that she had possibly never eaten the right kind of meal. He put her on a sensible diet, and soothed her maltreated system with slippery elm and infusions of meadowsweet and fennel.

She came in almost every week to renew the herbs. When he had obtusely asked her, 'Shall I ask my herbalist to make you up larger packages so that you don't have to keep coming down from Hampstead?' she had said, 'Oh no, I need the excuse to be here.' Of course. After that, he learned to give some female patients their medicine in small packets and jars and bottles.

'So's you can get a fee every time they come,' Neelie Drew observed. But it was not only that. The attention was just as necessary for many people as the medicines.

But today, sitting near the open back window with Mrs

Marcus, the sky a washed blue above the Kensington roofs and his small flower garden sending up perfumed messages, Toby's mind was drifting away from the humourless account of meals consumed and flatulence resulting. Marie-May had been enraptured with Ferry Cottage on the river bank. Suppose he could offer her a night there, just the two of them, in that picturesque little romantic retreat . . .

'. . . and my husband doesn't really like rice pudding, you know, because it reminds him of a dreadful nanny he once had, but I insist on its being served two or three times a week, instead of those rich cream desserts.'

'Or perhaps you could have just a small rice pudding baked for yourself.' Toby came back to reality. 'To avoid fuss and aggravation.' Mr Marcus paid the fees. Might as well keep him happy too.

As soon as he had got rid of his last patient of the afternoon, a young man with chronic eczema on whom he was trying Paracelsus's 'Doctrine of Signatures', a paste made from analogous plants that were themselves scaly and resinous, the humanist herbalist took a motor hansom to Paddington and a train to Goring and walked along the towpath in soft evening light to Ferry Cottage.

The man, Todd, was still monosyllabic, but agreeable. His mother lived in a cottage at Gatehampton. He would be willing to spend an occasional night with her for a financial consideration.

'And if anyone wanted the ferry?'

'They can do what they do when I has the hump. Wait for me to feel like taking out that dratted boat.'

*

This year's annual staff outing was the first since the tragic death of William Whiteley. His sons Frank and William were there, but it was not the same. They were respected, but not feared like their phenomenal father, with his demanding discipline. Because he was feared, he had been loved.

Leonard, who had to organize the excursion, went with more than two hundred employees by special train from Fenchurch Street to Southend-on-Sea. It was the usual let-down-your-hair gathering. Some of the men broke out into striped bathing costumes and the women into short dresses and bloomers to frolic in the cold shallows. Beer was drunk, and easy laughter thrown back at the crude jokes of the concert party on their wobbly platform on stilts. The fat man always fell backwards off the edge and smashed a sandcastle, and it was just as big a scream every year.

'Not the same without Him though, is it?' One of the salesgirls saw that Leonard was not laughing. 'Remember how he used to call out, along of us, "Step back, step back!"? Like a boy.'

Leonard enjoyed seeing his well-drilled assistants cast off their obsequious restraint and become real people for the day. Even Mr Jenkins, who had walked the Whiteley's floors and answered the call of 'Jenkins, forward!' for twenty years and brushed beach sand off his hands with the same gesture with which he rubbed his hands at customers, unbent far enough to eat shrimps out of a paper bag.

'P-poor Mr Whiteley always loved these,' he stammered by way of excuse when he saw the General Manager's eye on him. On the way home, Leonard's carriage on the train sang 'For He's a Jolly Good Fellow'. They thought they were singing it for Mr Morley, but perhaps it was really for the old vanished Chief.

All the carriages sang all the way home. The outing was a rare release for everyone from the giant emporium that controlled their lives: from long working hours and fatigue and, for many of the young women, from the restrictions of living in the dormitory terraces of Moscow Road and Poplar Place. For Leonard, it was a relief from the constant anxieties of his passionate attention to detail and doing the Right Thing, from customer complaints about everything from unflattering hats to the price of fruit and vegetables, and from the increased scourge of shoplifting during the crowded July sales.

Not by the poor. It was usually a pair of middle-class ladies, one of whom would distract the assistant with fuss and questions, while the other shovelled small goods into voluminous clothes and bags. The Chief had always prosecuted, so Leonard nearly always called a policeman, who would stamp up the main stairs in uniform and treadmill boots and upset everyone.

But it was the Right Thing to do. Society was increasingly lawless. The more you pampered the public with the bounty of the world laid out for their delight, the more they took advantage.

How would the store manage without him when he took his two weeks' holiday? He wondered this every year, and every year, Whiteley's managed. The new Assistant Manager was working out very well. 'But if you would rather I delayed . . .' Leonard offered to Mr Frank.

'And have us prosecuted under the Shop Hours

Regulation Act? Mr Morley, please stop being indispensable, and go!'

Leonard went with his family to North Croft, the country house he had leased near Chipping Norton. There was golf nearby, a croquet lawn, rounders, bicycling, rambling, motoring along narrow dusty lanes in Vera and Charles Pope's green Renault.

Vera had learned to drive. When she unwrapped herself from her dustcoat and veil and goggles, she always pronounced it 'the thrill of my life!', even if she had only been down to the village to buy a newspaper.

'Why can't we have a motor, Leo?' Gwen pestered.

'Not yet.' Leonard would want to know a lot more about motor cars before he owned one.

'You said we couldn't afford it. Well, now your salary's increased and we can. I could learn to drive, if that's what you're afraid of.'

Austin guffawed. His mother was well known for being unable to operate even a gramophone or a clockwork toy, but to prove her point, she persuaded Vera to let her drive in the quiet lane that ran by the house. Almost immediately, she hit a bank on one side and a hedge on the other.

'You are foolhardy.' Leonard helped to push the car back on to the road before Charles could see it.

'It's because I'm so relaxed here.' Gwen leaned on his arm as they walked the few yards back to the house. 'And so happy.' The children were blissful. Elizabeth and Austin's fat baby rolled about on the lawn with his young nursemaid. Dicky strove to beat everyone at croquet and diabolo and was active from early morning until he collapsed, fighting sleep, after endless after-supper games with the indulgent grown-ups. He and Austin whistled about the place, which they were not permitted to do in the London streets. Little Laura followed Dicky everywhere, whistling bravely but breathlessly.

The grown-ups had become tiresomely keen on golf. One morning, Dicky had woken to the familiar feeling of exciting promise.

'Let's explore in the car!'

But Aunt Vera and Uncle Charles and Austin were dressed in their knickerbockers, and Dicky's mother and father and Elizabeth were going to walk round the nine-hole course. His mother liked to take one of Aunt Vera's clubs to 'have a shot', but, so far, she had never hit the ball.

Uncle Charles offered Dicky money to carry his clubs, but Dicky thought that too boring. When the Renault had conveyed its dust cloud down the lane, he mounted his bicycle and set off in the other direction, to pursue the exploration with which the new day had tempted him.

He was soon on roads where he had not been before. Turning towards the hills, he came to the level crossing where the North Croft maids said a train had hit a motor car last year and smashed its passengers to bits. Dicky dismounted and looked cautiously right and left before wheeling his bicycle across. 'A train was coming,' he would boast to Austin later, 'but I simply whizzed across.'

The road wound uphill, not steep, but hard-going. He stood on the pedals and ground them round, and could feel the muscles of his legs growing bigger. He would take the next side turning and then coast back downhill at speed. There were no side turnings. Dicky went on and on, pushing his bicycle now, sure that every bend was going to show him the top of the hill, plodding on when it showed him nothing but another bend ahead. He would not turn back. When he panted to the top at last, fields and hedges and neat villages were spread out below.

Where did you go, Dicky?

Up to the very top of the hill. It's miles and miles. You can see the whole of England. I could see our house like a white speck. I bet it's the highest hill in Oxfordshire.

It felt so glorious that he rode along the ridge for a while with the wind behind him and the world at his feet. On the left, a huge high stone stood by itself. A marker? Ancient sacrifices? A highwayman hanged here? Not liking the look of it, Dicky turned away down a short cart track which opened out to a different view, on the other side of the ridge of hills. There were more great stones here, a rough circle of them, odd-shaped, worn and pitted, not lying in the long grass, but standing crookedly upright like contorted gateposts. He did not like the look of them either. Stones should not stand about for no purpose, looking inscrutably over the valley.

But what sort of stones, Dicky old lad? You mean, you only gave them a look and ran away?

He dropped his bicycle on the ground and ventured into the circle of strange shapes, cautiously feeling the dry lichen, gaining courage to poke his fingers into crevices and holes which had been worn away like a honeycomb. I am exploring a secret place, he thought.

'This your bike?'

He jumped at the voice behind him. A small old man was on the cart track, stooping under a sack of wood on his shoulders.

'I'm sorry.' Dicky went quickly to pick up his bicycle. 'Shouldn't I be here?'

'Why not? Them stones don't mind. Been here a lot longer than you 'ave. Nor even me. Heh-heh.' Dicky laughed politely. 'Ar, you can laugh at it. But 'tis true.'

'What is?'

'The old king. Come to invade, he was. Didn't know about the witch. She turned him to stone, you see, on t'other side of the road, him and his soldiers here behind him. One day, young lad, them stones will come alive again.'

'Bosh.'

'They been seen to move down to drink from the stream at night.'

Dicky backed away from the nearest stone, a top-heavy monster that seemed to have a craggy nose and eye socket. 'Why doesn't someone knock them down?'

'Ar, you couldn't do that. Mustn't touch 'em. Might get turned to stone and all.' The bent old man moved on.

Golly! This was a much more exciting story than the recounting of golf strokes, which was what the grown-ups would be doing back at home. Dicky stuck his tongue out at the sinister stones and rode away fast. Downhill it was exhilarating, coasting between the ruts, back-pedalling frantically at the corners, putting his feet down where it was perilously steep, in the forbidden scraping that could ruin your boots. He would be late for lunch. The others must have been back for ages. At the level crossing, he did see an engine in the distance, and had to wait until its endless line of goods wagons rumbled by. Back at North Croft, he hurtled into the drive and dropped his bike, wheels spinning. Where was the Renault? His mind reeled into scenes of dreadful crashes, an express train bearing down, the motor exploding, falling off a cliff, his mother screaming.

'My word, you do look hot and dusty.' The nursemaid was sitting outside the french windows with Laura and the baby.

'Where is everybody? Have you had lunch?'

'Goodness no. They'll be back presently,' the nurse said placidly.

Dicky was bursting to tell his story, but not to this sluggish woman, and not in front of the baby. He pulled Laura away towards the shrubbery.

'Listen.' He backed her against a laurel bush. 'I found a terrible place, miles and miles away, up a mountain. There are all these beastly great stones, but they're not really stones, they're men turned to stone by a witch, and at night they come to life.' Laura's eyes were round with terror. Her hands were clapped over her mouth. 'I saw them, Laura. *I saw the stones move.* They were coming after me. My blood ran cold.'

Laura put her hands over her ears and squared her mouth down into a wailing cry.

'I rode back for my life.' Dicky fixed a stare on her. 'But it was too late, *I had touched the stones.*' She clutched her hair and stopped crying, stricken, open-mouthed.

'And now . . . and now . . .' he slowed his voice jerkily, 'the witch has turned . . . me . . . to stone.'

He stood like a statue with a blank face, and Laura tugged at him and beat him with her fists. 'No! No! Come back!' But he would not move. Her red face was flooded with tears. She shrieked and screamed, and was drowned by the engine of the car and Uncle Charles announcing their arrival on the horn.

Dicky came back to life, but Laura was running desperately across the lawn, stumbling and crying out and falling.

'How could you, Dicky? Stuffing the poor little thing up with all this rubbish about stones and witches!' The grown-ups were angry and did not want to hear his amazing story, which Laura had already sobbed out to them, all wrong.

'Why did you let him go off on his own, Gwen?'

'He didn't ask me.'

'Why not, Dicky? Why didn't you stay here as you were supposed to?'

His father was being stiff and stern, his eyes unloving.

'There was nothing to do here.' Dicky looked at him with the candid innocence that could usually soften him.

'Nothing to do? You don't know your luck, young man. When I was your age, I spent my holidays making up parcels in my father's shops.' The old story. Dicky looked down, and dragged the toe of his boot on the gravel.

'Don't be stuffy with him, Leo,' his mother said. 'He's quite all right going off on his own. He's sensible.'

'So sensible he makes up gruesome tales and frightens his little cousin half to death.'

'Well, he's inventive.' His mother put her arm round him. Dicky leaned into the safety of her perfumed tenderness.

'He's wilful,' his father said. 'I am quite angry.'

'My tummy hurts.' This was another softening device, but actually it did hurt, from all the pedalling and breathlessness and excitement.

'You shall have a good little Beecham's.' His mother took him indoors.

Bella usually went with the family on their holidays, but although she was invited to join them at North Croft, she had been vague, and it did not look as though she would come. Perhaps she had gone to Biarritz with Hugo and Charlotte after all.

'Or she might be mooning hopelessly about in London because of some man,' Austin said, 'like she did with that confounded Lazenby fellow. I hope it's someone halfway decent. Bella needs a man.'

'Every woman does, in your opinion.' Vera laughed at him.

They could not have guessed that the man who was keeping Bella mooning about in London when Ladbroke Lodge and No. 72 were under dust-sheets was Toby Taylor.

She had been to Egerton Terrace again, at his invitation, to talk about a friend of his who was a woman professor and might be able to advise her about her academic chances.

Bella's reaction was, 'I'm sure she would think I had nothing to offer.'

'Don't say that to Dr Mary Strong,' Toby snapped at her. 'If you put yourself down, so will she.'

'If I don't, she'll see through me.'

'And suppose she likes what she sees,' Toby said more gently, 'as I do?'

They had walked up Exhibition Road and taken a stroll in Hyde Park along the Serpentine, where Bella was proud to be seen with such a good-looking man, and wished that she had a fashionable white parasol to shelter this face which Toby pretended he liked. In the Dell below the bridge, they sat down on a patch of grass that was hidden from the path by bushes and flower beds, and Toby kissed her.

His mouth was nothing like Gerald Lazenby's, or any of the very few pecking or puckering or whiskered lips that she had briefly experienced. The kiss went on for a long time, and by the end of it, she was lying on the grass and allowing – wanting this suddenly rough man to undo the buttons on the front of her dress. She had never felt like this, even when she had a high fever and was delirious. When she opened her eyes, the sky was reeling round the tilted earth.

'That,' Toby said, sitting upright, 'was just the beginning.'

What did he mean? 'No, no, we mustn't.' Bella began to panic. 'Not in a public place. I must go anyway.'

She scrambled up, pulling down her skirt, and turned away from him while she did up the buttons of her bodice with hot, trembling fingers.

'I said, "That was just the beginning."' Toby looked up at her from where he still sat on the ground, chewing a blade of grass. 'And that's a promise, Belle.'

Oh, my God, oh, my *God*, what on earth was she to do? Thank heavens her parents were not at home. She would never have been able to behave normally in front of them, with her body and spirit on fire with exhilaration and shame because she had behaved like a common servant girl and sunk to the depths while scaling the heights of fearful joy.

She could not face the maids either, and certainly not the lynx-eyed butler. When she came out of the Underground station at Notting Hill Gate, she walked about the streets for a while to calm herself down and fade the flush on her face which she thought people had been staring at on the train. When she was more herself – who was she now? She could never be the same self as before – she went through Pembridge Crescent to Chepstow Villas, and walked up its leafy, shaded pavement to No. 72. If Madge was not there, Flora would give her a cool drink. If Flora noticed that a button was torn off the front of her dress, she would not be suspicious, she would sew another one on.

A familiar figure was standing aimlessly on the Portobello Road corner: trousers too short above big clumsy boots, patched jacket too thick for this weather, hair unevenly cropped. It was Jack Haynes, 'my deaf friend', as Bella spoke of him proudly.

She walked round to face him, so as not to take him by surprise. His heavy face lifted and split into its wide grin. His eyes searched Bella's eagerly, hoping for communication.

'Oh, Jack – hel-lo!' She stressed the sound and shape of the word. 'Are you looking for Madge?' She wrote out the letters with her forefinger in the air, which was the way he could understand the name of someone who was not there.

'Yah.' He nodded his head vigorously and raised his thick dark eyebrows in a question. 'Where she?'

'I don't know. Come inside,' she said, pointing, 'and Flora will give us some lemonade.'

'Come in, Bella.' Flora was always welcoming, but she said uncivilly to Jack, 'You still here?' when she opened the door. 'He come here earlier, wanting Madge. I thought he'd gone away.'

'I'll look after him,' Bella said. 'Could you bring us some lemonade and biscuits or something, and I'll talk to him for a bit.'

The chandelier in the drawing room had been taken down and was lying on a sheet on the floor in a hundred pieces. The carpet was rolled up to clean the parquetry floor, and most of the furniture was covered. Bella opened the bottom of the window and they sat on Aunt Gwen's deck-chairs on the balcony.

Bella had taken a notepad and pencil from the desk, and she and Jack had one of their almost satisfactory conversations, with signs and sounds and notes passed back and forth. She understood that he was only working now and then – hand turned over and over in a dismissive way, and helping with the boys at the Settlement.

'W-I-L-L.' He wrote in the air and made a sweeping outward gesture.

'Gone?'

This was news to Bella. She did not mind, unless Madge did. She did not mind much about anything just now, in the state she was in. She only had half her thoughts on the difficult, jerky conversation, but she had to keep going with Jack, who appeared ready to stay a long time, when what she wanted to do was to shout at him, 'Something marvellous has happened to me – I am in love!'

In the days that followed, she thought of telephoning Toby, but the phone at Ladbroke Lodge was in the hall, and when Bella made a call, one of the servants invariably found a reason to pass by her, or to start dusting or polishing, or rearranging the letters on the silver tray.

'This is just the beginning, Belle.' She would never get his voice out of her head. She had gone back to Hyde Park to walk nervously past the Dell the day after they had been there, feeling so electric that the eyes of passers-by must be on her, as if she were giving off sparks. This is where my life began, she thought. When a week had gone by without her hearing from Toby, she went to his house at a time of day when she did not think he would be seeing patients.

The housekeeper stood in the doorway and did not invite her in. 'Mr Taylor is away.'

'Oh – he's away?' Bella said stupidly.

'He's in the country with your aunt and uncle, didn't you know?'

'Well, yes, of course, that was what I came about. I wanted him to take something down for my aunt.'

'Oh yes?' Mrs Drew's manner was much less polite than when her employer was there.

'A book, as a matter of fact.' Bella patted the outside of her raffia bag. Just as well Mrs Drew showed no interest, since there was no book in the bag. 'Yes, well. Thank you.'

Feeling all hands and feet under the woman's unfriendly stare, Bella managed to start down the steps. The front door shut before she reached the pavement.

Toby Taylor went to Chipping Norton on the same train as Madge and her new friend Guy Davidson, who were also to spend a few days at North Croft. Guy had his wheeled chair in the guard's van, and Toby had Bounce, the little brown terrier, tied up there. Marie-May's operetta had been postponed, and she had gone to Paris. 'So she left the dog with me.'

'Bad luck.' Leaning on his stick, Guy pulled down his mouth, while Madge tried to keep the exuberant dog from jumping up at him.

'I like the little beggar,' Toby said. 'I would have a dog myself if I didn't live and work in London.'

'And Bounce is *her* dog,' Madge said perceptively.

Toby was glad he had come. The country air assailed them with sweet scents and breezes as they stood on the station platform, and he would enjoy distracting Madge from her preoccupation with the rather sullen ex-officer, who seemed as though he could easily be made jealous.

Steady with the manoeuvring, Toby warned himself. This is a pastoral weekend with your favourite family. London is the place for playing chess with people. They expect it.

Bella had not expected to become a pawn, and he had not planned it. What his next move would be he was not sure, but thank God she had not come down here with her cousin. He did not need to think about her.

Madge, it turned out, had taken this disabled man Guy to the Loudon Street Settlement to talk to the boys there about the war.

'Not particularly patriotic in the East End are they?' Toby said. 'They don't have much to thank England for.'

'Even less when I finished with them.' Tired and deathly pale at the end of the day, Guy had put aside the stick with which he gamely kept himself walking, and was in his chair with the others in the loggia.

'You should have been there to hear him, Daddy.' Madge was promoting this damaged man like a salesman with a new line of drugs. 'He was very fine. He told them that our glorious territorial victory left nothing behind but scorched earth.'

Leonard looked uncomfortable. He had inherited pride of Empire from William Whiteley, its marketer, and did not want it shaken.

'It was a Boer guerilla who did for me.' Guy held out his whisky glass for Austin to refill. 'But I still admire the way they kept on fighting. Give me a brilliant professional like De Wet any day, rather than that savage brute Kitchener.'

'Did you tell the boys that?' Toby asked.

'I did.' Guy could be moody and taciturn but, with some whisky inside him, he was pleased to shock the family. They looked uneasy. Toby glanced at Madge. She was enthralled.

'I told them not to let themselves be sucked into the great game. Why was I sent out there to be wounded? So that every last Boer farmer could be killed or taken prisoner and tortured, their women and children rounded up, their cattle slaughtered and their crops burned. Why should my life be ruined for that?'

Toby thought that fervent Madge, leaning forward with her hands clasped, was telling him soundlessly: Your life isn't ruined – I won't let it be!

'That young man sounds dangerously pro-Boer,' Leonard worried to Toby after dinner. 'What do you make of Madge being so taken up with him?'

'Don't worry,' Toby said. 'It won't last.'

'Infatuation?'

'Something like that.'

'I hope you're right. What can be done about it?'

'Nothing.' Toby laughed reassuringly.

Nothing that a parent can do, but Toby went to ask Madge to come for a walk with Bounce up towards the woods, to see if the owls were out tonight.

'No thanks.' Madge gave him a sweet smile. She was playing cribbage with Guy.

Next day, Charles Pope said that Toby could drive the Renault, and Madge wanted to go with him to see the stained glass in the church across the river, but Guy did not like churches, so Madge asked Toby to take Gwen and Elizabeth instead. All weekend, he could not get her alone. She was her usual friendly, funny self, but her time was taken up with Guy.

On Sunday, Dicky was desperate for his Uncle Toby to bicycle off with him to see the mysterious stones on the hill.

'Good idea. Come on, Madge, I know you want to see this spooky place.' Guy was having a bad day, and was in his room. A good chance to get Madge free.

'I don't know, Toby . . .'

'Do you good to have a bike ride. You're getting fat.'

'I know.' She laughed and slapped at her perfect, healthy figure. 'I'd love to, but suppose he needs something?'

'Let him ring for the maid. Damn it, Madge, what's happened to you? If you make yourself a slave, he'll get sick of you.'

'That's what you'd like, isn't it?' You could never deceive Madge.

'Come on, you two.' Dicky had his bicycle out of the shed already. 'If we're going, let's go!'

'Where?' His father came across the lawn.

'Up to the stone soldiers.'

'Sorry, old man.' Leonard was firm. 'Out of bounds. I'm not having any more of that hysteria.'

Dicky raged and argued, as he did when he was thwarted, which was not often, and then flung himself into an attitude and stood stock still. 'I'm bewitched! I'm turned to stone!' The dog jumped round him with shrill yelps. Laura screamed and howled and flung herself thrashing on to the grass. Guy called out of his upstairs window, 'For God's sake!' and Madge went indoors.

Dicky was angry and so was Toby. He went to look up trains back to London. Dicky continued to petrify himself at short intervals to set Laura off, until his brother Austin threatened to lock him in his room.

Nobody had ever locked Dicky in his room. There was no key, either at North Croft or at No. 72 Chepstow Villas.

Chapter Twenty

Not wishing to risk another snub from the housekeeper at Egerton Terrace, Bella went to No. 72 to find out when the family would be back, and therefore Toby.

'Tomorrow, if you please,' Mrs Salter the charwoman told her. 'What with the high dusting and the paintwork to finish upstairs, *I* don't know.'

'But they're not fussy people, are they?'

This had no relevance for Mrs Salter. Everything in the house was always cleaned in July. It was the pattern of life.

The charwoman did not want to risk her legs on the step-ladder, and Flora and Tatiana were very busy, so Bella tied a scarf round her hair and took off her shoes and climbed up with a feather duster to dislodge some of the year's dust and soot from the plaster fern decoration that joined the study walls to the ceiling. Working like this was freedom to her, whatever it was to those who did it year in, year out, and she was glad to be doing something for the house she loved. In the afternoon, she helped Tat to wash glassware in the pantry and had supper at the kitchen table, and played whist for pennies with the cook and Flora. Tatiana was not allowed to play cards for money. Mrs Roach's sister was said to have suffered from gamblers, including, perhaps, Tat's nameless father.

Bella did not want to go back to empty Ladbroke Lodge, whose high-ceilinged rooms and passages were full of silences and whispers, so Flora suggested she should stay the night in Madge's room. She woke after midnight to a terrible noise coming from somewhere below. Too late for Portobello Road drunkards. Robbery? Murder? The shouting and screaming came from the back of this house. Bella threw on a shawl and crept down the stairs, to meet Mrs Roach coming up from the basement with her hair like frayed grey rope and her hand on her heart.

'Oh, my Gawd, oh, my Gawd. 'E's done for her this time.'

'Who? What?' Bella took hold of the bundle of garments that was Mrs Roach in her nightwear, and shook her. 'Oh, my Gawd.' The bundle sank to the floor and sat there wobbling. Bella ran down the back stairs. Tat was in the scullery, growling. 'The bastard's gone.'

'Who? What bastard? Where's Flora?'

She was sitting slumped on the bed that filled the tiny back room, her hands clutching her neck, the nightgown sleeves stained with blood.

When the family arrived in two four-wheelers from Paddington, Bella was there watching for them. She opened the front door at once and came running down the steps to gabble out her story.

'He was here again! It was dreadful. I was here because . . . I heard all this noise, it was him, that terrible man!'

'He's here!' Dicky went white and clutched his father, his blue eyes frantic.

'No, he's gone, I don't know where, he got in somehow at the back and he –' Bella's face was breaking up into tears. 'I think he hurt Flora badly.'

264

'Where is she?' Madge was distraught.

'We don't know.' Bella wrung her hands.

'How can you not know? What happened?'

Bella shook her head dumbly. 'I don't know. They wouldn't tell me much. Madge, I tried to stop the bleeding and wrapped her up, but when I went back down with brandy, she – she was gone!'

'Where did she go? Oh, my poor Flora – Mrs Roach!' Madge ran down the back stairs, followed by her father. 'Where is she?'

'She run off.' Mrs Roach stood with her back to the dresser, her face like a mule's.

'All bleeding, she was.' Tatiana sucked in her breath. 'Blood all over.'

'Why didn't you go after her?'

Tat hunched her shoulders, looking frightened. The cook mumbled, 'Wouldn't let us.'

'Why?'

'Wouldn't involve this household.'

'Did you call the police?' Leonard asked.

'She said not to.'

'*Why?*'

'Wouldn't involve this household.'

'I'm going to call them now.' Leonard went upstairs.

'I'm going to find Flora.' Madge ran out of the back door and round to the front gate, pushing past the cab driver staggering in with a trunk.

She found her friend Flora where she thought she would be, where Mrs Roach and Tat must have known she would go, although they had been struck dumb. The door was locked at No. 7 Talbot Close, and when Madge banged, it opened a crack to show the sharp nose and crafty eye of Flora's sister Violet.

'We don't want strangers here,' she hissed.

'You know me, Vi, Madge Morley.' She pushed the door and squeezed past the girl into the narrow passage, which was smoky, as if something was burning on the kitchen stove. Flora was lying on the settee, barely conscious. The cloths round her neck were soaked with blood. When Madge loosened them a little to see the wound, fresh blood welled up. Flora groaned.

'It's all right, dear friend, it's Madge. It's all right, I'm here, I won't leave you.' Madge hardly knew what she said: words of comfort and of love.

She went to find Flora's mother, following the acrid smell of burning. In the kitchen, Daddy Watts had set fire to the bed, with himself in it. His wife was trying to drag off the smouldering blanket wrapped round him. Madge helped her to tip him out on to the floor, where he lay moving his legs feebly, like a dying beetle. The blanket was flung out into the alley. 'Fire!' Some children began to shout. 'Oi – oi – fire!'

'He don't want Flo here, Miss Madge,' Mrs Watts pulled her back into the kitchen, 'for fear that Bolt will come after her.'

'Get her out of here!' wheezed Daddy Watts from the floor.

'That's what I've come for, you stupid man.' Madge gritted her teeth to stop herself kicking him. She sent the petulant Violet out to find a cab.

'Won't find no cabs round here.' She swung her hair affectedly.

266

'Just get one!' Madge pushed her into the street, and went down on her knees by Flora, adding her own scarf to the sticky, clotted wrapping, holding her cold, worn hand, looking into her unseeing eyes, and promising her . . . promising her . . .

At the hospital, she still held Flora's hand while they administered chloroform and stitched up a deep gaping gash at the base of her neck. She stayed in the ward for two days before Madge was allowed to take her home. She and Bella and Winnie Stokes, who had come in to do Flora's work, carried her up the stairs and settled her in the spare room behind Madge's bedroom.

Madge hardly went out of the house. Even in sleep, she was on the edge of listening, like the mother of a baby, and she went in to Flora several times a night.

'What about your young man?' Flora whispered.

'Guy's all right. His man drives him over here if he wants to see me.'

'Why aren't you at the Settlement?'

'Someone is taking my place. My family comes first.'

Flora lay very still on her back, because the knife had damaged muscles and nerves and she could not move her head or one side of her face. 'I'm not family,' she said in her hoarse voice.

'You are to me.' Madge could feel Flora's pain in herself. They had always been close, but the love now was very strong. 'You are my sister.'

'You never had one of them,' Flora said, 'or you wouldn't set store by it.'

Violet had been sent up to visit, with acid drops, by Mrs Watts. She brushed her hair absorbedly at the dressing

267

table, and yawned a lot, and said perkily, 'Daddy says you had it coming to you,' before she was chased away by Dicky, who took her by her starched skirt and pulled her downstairs. After the door banged, he came up and ostentatiously washed his hands in the basin in Flora's room.

The rest of the family also felt very close to poor Flora, and responsible for her, and moved by the awareness of all the years of service given so cheerfully. When Gwen was reading to her the day's short story from the *Evening News*, Flora interrupted to ask, 'When can I get back to work?'

'Not yet. Winnie is managing all right.'

'She skimps.'

'Hush, you're still feverish, and your stitches aren't even out yet.' Gwen got up to rearrange the pillows carefully and give her some barley water. 'But it will be odd for you and me to be servant and mistress again.'

'Not to me, 'm.' Flora gave her new stiff, sideways smile.

One of the things she had said, when she could speak again in a whisper, was, 'Don't put the police on him.' But Leonard had already asked his friend Arthur French to see to the arrest of Bill Bolt.

The day after Dr Buckmaster came to take the stitches out of the long, healing wound – 'Who ever did this clumsy bit of needlework?' he fussed, fancying his own surgical skills – Arthur French came up the stairs to tell Flora that her husband was in a police cell and could be charged with assault with a dangerous weapon.

'No.' Flora whispered, shy of being in bed in front of the policeman. 'No, I don't want that.'

'You mean, you won't press charges?' The inspector frowned.

Flora shook her head miserably, and turned away.

'Why did I have to go and cry in front of him?' She twisted the bedclothes after he had gone.

'It's only because you're weak.' Madge had taken to wearing a white headscarf and a long white apron, to feel like a nursing Sister, which was what she would want to be if there was ever another war. 'But don't you want Bill out of your life, Flo?'

'I dunno.'

'Would you have minded having to give evidence? I would come to court with you.'

'It's not that, but ... well, no offence, Madge,' Flora said sadly, 'but you don't understand.'

'I *do*.'

'No.' Flora ran a hand under her nose. Her eyes were still bright with tears. 'There's things I can never tell you.'

'Sometimes I think I don't understand anything,' Madge said cheerfully. 'Even myself. Especially myself.'

'That makes two of us.'

It was a great pity that, after the careful arrangements Toby had made with the Goring ferryman, Marie-May had never enjoyed the romantic enchantments of the riverside hideaway. August had almost gone and it would be too cold, if she did not come back from Paris soon.

If she ever did come back. 'What shall I do about *you*?' Toby looked speculatively at the abandoned terrier, which jumped up at once, barking shrilly, ready for a strenuous game.

Deprived of its mistress, Toby might have tried to inveigle Madge to Ferry Cottage on some pretext or other. Although they had not been much more than what Madge called pals, he had nursed for some time a fantasy about her, as he did about many women in diversionary dreams, but after the rebuffs he had suffered at North Croft, he knew that pals was as far as she would go.

'That poor girl was here looking for you,' Neelie Drew told him, some time after his return from Oxfordshire.

'What poor girl? Why didn't you tell me at once? Did you make an appointment for her?'

'Oh, not a patient. That girl in the maroon cloak like settee upholstery.'

'Oh, *her*.' Poor Bella. It was true, some clothes did make her look like furniture.

'Yes, her. You want to know what I think, sir?'

'No.'

'What I think is this.' She dug the nails of each hand into the palm of the other to press up her bosom, elbows out. Usually discreet and docile, she enjoyed giving him a piece of her mind occasionally. 'I think you'll get yourself into trouble one of these days, messing about with silly young innocents. At your age.'

Toby was stung. 'You're older than me.'

'*And* I've got more sense.'

The front-door bell was rung by the first patient of the morning. Mrs Drew picked up the breakfast tray and went downstairs.

Messing about with silly young innocents? Not such a bad idea at that. Bella was crying out for it. It would help her to become the free woman she imagined herself to be, and she would never dare to tell the family.

When the day's work was finished, Toby went to No. 72

Chepstow Villas with some dried vegetable-broth mix for Flora Bolt, and then to Ladbroke Lodge to give Bella an invitation that brought the blood charging up her neck and face into her heavy cushion of hair.

On Friday, he went ahead of her to Goring and walked along the towpath with food and wine in a rucksack. The ferryman took his money and hung a sack over the bell on the mooning post, which everyone knew meant No Ferry, picked a cabbage for his mother and walked off across the fields.

Toby met Bella's train. She stepped down from the carriage quickly, looking furtively right and left as they went out of the station.

'What's up, Belle?' Toby laughed and put his arm round her, to put her at her ease. 'Afraid of me?'

'Oh no. Don't do that. I mean,' she glanced up at him with those puzzled round eyes, 'I'm afraid someone might see me – the stationmaster, or one of the servants at Grandmother's.'

Bella was delighted with the cottage. 'It takes my breath away,' she said. She had been breathing rather fast as they came from the station. 'Toby, it's so – so –'

'Romantic?'

She dropped her head and turned her eyes up to him in the way she had, which made her look like a cow.

'That's all right, Belle. That's why we're here.'

Oh Lord, this was going to be so pitifully easy. He opened the wine and they sat outside on the bank and watched a few late boats working upstream to Goring, or gliding swiftly down to Pangbourne. On the opposite bank, fat cattle stood motionless in the lush meadow, or knee-deep in the water at their trodden drinking place by the dead tree. Downstream, the lingering remains of sunset were a dying fire above the thick woods that marched down to the bend of the river.

Bella did not say much. She drank her wine in jerks and rearranged her skirt, which Toby then disarranged, to get her used to the feel of his hands on her legs. If she had been Marie-May, they would have been lying in the grass together, and be damned to passing boaters. Bella was nervous when a boat came by, convinced that it carried an acquaintance of her grandmother's. As twilight crept over the water and the cattle were only dim shapes, Toby lit the lamp on the windowsill in the front room so that a small square of light fell outside, and became bolder with the flustered girl until her protests grew faint and then ceased. By the time she was lying beneath him with her eyes screwed shut and her breath bursting its corsets, he knew he could do anything with her.

Crickets were shrilling a chorus all round them. Midges were attacking his bare arms under the rolled-up shirtsleeves. 'Let's go inside,' he said.

'It's so lovely out here.'

Toby had seen her glance fearfully through the open door of the little bedroom, and then quickly away.

'Lie down again,' she breathed, the part of her that was still sane thinking perhaps that all might yet be salvaged as long as she stayed away from the bed.

He pulled her to her feet. She left her shoes outside.

'Are we – are we going to have supper?'

'Don't be a silly child, Bella.' He shut the cottage door, because she would worry about that, as if the whole world passed by this deserted spot, and pushed her into the bedroom, where he had exchanged the ferryman's unappetizing blankets for a rug he had brought down.

After it was over, Toby rolled away from her off the bed without a word, and Bella thought that she passed into a kind of trance, or a blank sleep. When she came to her senses, naked under the soft rug, her body felt sore and battered, but at the same time floating, free and light.

Oh, my dear God – I've done it. Oh, what will become of me? She inspected her mind for guilt and found none.

She wrapped the rug round her and went into the lamplit room where Toby sat at the three-legged table with a glass of wine, eating cold pie.

'All right?' he asked. The intimacy of his questioning look! 'Come and have something to eat.'

'Oh, I couldn't.'

'It usually makes people hungry.' He threw a piece of food to the dog.

Bella went to the window and mooned out at the unseen river, which smelled of waterlogged ground and rotting leaves. 'I don't want anything.'

'Here.' He handed her a glass of wine. 'Drink this, Belle.'

Yes, I am *belle*. She took the glass in a hand that somehow seemed finer and more graceful. There was a small silvered mirror over the fireplace. She raised the wineglass to this new and beautiful creature who felt herself, like fallen heroines in books, radiantly transformed by love.

Her old Bella face looked back at her, hair everywhere, nose splodged, eyes puffy, one cheek red and creased. She turned away and put her glass on the table.

'No, drink that. Doctor's orders. Then I'm going to give you something with acacia in it, an ancient Egyptian nostrum which I have found quite useful for anxious female patients.'

'What are they anxious about?'

'Oh, heavens, Belle, how can you still be so innocent?'

I am not innocent now. I am an old, old soul, steeped in the knowledge of love.

He laughed at her. 'Do you even know how babies are made?'

Because Bella had been what Toby called 'a good girl', she was to go to Ferry Cottage again next week, just before her parents came home from France. Friday turned out to be wet and windy. Would they still go to the river? Bella had lived all week at such a pitch of excitement that disappointment now would break her heart.

The telephone rang at lunchtime. 'A gentleman for you, miss.' The butler raised his circumflex eyebrows at this rarity.

Bella was to go to Toby's rooms in Egerton Terrace.

'All right.' Her perilous heart leaped at the cadence of his voice. She might have exulted, 'I love you!' into the little telephone trumpet if Hurd had not been pacing the tiles with his hands behind his back, as if he were taking measurements.

Toby opened his front door himself and said, 'Come along, we're going out to dinner.' Bella hoped that they would get a horse-cab, which would give her longer alone with him, but Toby always managed to hail one with a motor. She remembered watching his hand on his knee, coming back from the dance, aeons ago in the mists of innocent time.

Because it was still light, they sat apart. Bella took off her glove and put her hand on the seat, and he put his over it.

'Afraid?' he asked, because the hand was trembling.

'Not of you.'

'Of what, then?'

'Nothing, when I'm with you.'

To make it possible to say that with some intensity, she did not look at him. When he did not react, she stole a glance and saw that he was gazing out of the window, his mouth pursed in a silent whistle.

It was not true, in any case. After dinner, they would come back to his rooms, and Bella *was* afraid. She both dreaded and longed to repeat the same shattering unravelling of soul and body which she had experienced in the ferryman's sagging bed. Should she jump out of the cab now, as it stopped for the crossing? Would she do 'it' well enough? Would Toby call her a silly child? Would she retch and throw up if he made her drink that horrible acacia stuff again?

She swallowed. 'Where are we going for dinner?'

'You'll see.'

She hoped there would be several courses, to delay what would come after; yet how would she be able to eat anything, because of longing for what would come after?

In her expensive petit-point bag, which her mother had bought last birthday when she wanted books, lurked like a loaded pistol a small but threatening cause of fear and embarrassment. She did know how babies were made, and when she knew that she was going to participate in a life of

275

sin again today, she had been moved, in the madness of unreasoning love, to confide in her friend the parlourmaid Sybil Crocker.

Sybil listened dispassionately while Bella babbled out her secret. 'You'll not tell anyone, will you?'

'Safe as the grave, dear. You can tell me who he is. Anyone I know?'

'Oh no, no, absolutely not. But the thing is, Sybil, suppose I – I mean, I never would, of course, but suppose it did happen that – because after all, things are different now, with people beginning to talk about Free Love and all that.'

'Are you talking about what I think you're talking about?' Sybil Crocker, Lady Domestic, used a surprisingly vulgar word. Bella blushed. '*Have* you, then?'

'No, of course not, but I wanted to know –'

'How not to get caught.' Sybil Crocker laughed, also crudely. 'Whoever could answer that a hundred per cent would make their blooming fortune.'

She got up and looked outside the door of Bella's bedroom. Spies were everywhere at Ladbroke Lodge, and she was one of them. She gave Bella some surprising tips, such as cocoa butter, and that if you did it standing up, you would be safe, because a man's gism could not travel uphill.

She later brought her this nasty little gadget which was now in the petit-point bag, provoking fear. How and when would Bella put it in? At Ferry Cottage, she would not have had time. Were you supposed to say, 'Stop a minute,' and fumble about with this ludicrous sponge on a string?

The cab drew up outside a small hotel in a Bloomsbury back street.

'Is this a restaurant?'

'We'll have something sent up to the room.'

'I thought we –'

'You think too much, Belle.' Toby jumped lightly out and gave her his hand. 'Just leave everything to me.'

Bella tied her scarf over her hat to hide part of her face, and hovered behind a flaking pillar while he talked to a severe woman with keys on a leather belt, like a gaoler.

'We're married,' Toby whispered as they followed the brutal belt up the stairs.

Married! Bella's foolish breast let out a great sigh that blew away university, career, independence, even Doing Good, that earnest Edwardian ideal.

Their room was dwarfed by an oversized bed, impossible not to look at, or bump into, or put things on. Impossible for one of them not to sit on it, since there was only one chair.

'You'll send up something later?' Toby had asked.

'Ring the bell, sir.'

After the door shut, Bella opened it again and went in search of the bathroom. That door was locked, so she squeezed into the tiny W.C., dabbed Sybil Crocker's magic ointment on the sponge and made a desperate shot at shoving it inside herself.

Toby drew the curtains and tenderly undressed her. It was lovely. Everything was lovely until he became more violent. When Bella gave an involuntary gasp, he said, 'Shut up.'

Were women supposed not to call out, 'No, no, you're hurting me!'? Toby swore. He tugged at the string and the wretched sponge plopped out with a sucking noise.

'What the hell?' He laughed, but harshly, not his amused To-by laugh. His face was sharp with bony planes and shadows and narrowed, glinting eyes. It was the face of a stranger. It was the body of a stranger, hard, impersonal, pitiless. As before, he hardly spoke.

Making an excuse not to see her home, he put her into a cab and paid the driver. Bella sank back on the squeaky leather seat, in a turmoil of astonished emotions.

I am a woman of the world, she decided. This is what they call Free Love. Perhaps I shall learn to enjoy it. Driving through Cavendish Square past a tall house where bright lights spilled from every window and well-dressed men and women came laughing down the front steps, Bella thought, rather grandly: I am a mistress.

But mistresses, in the novels of writers like E.A. Morley, gave their love in comfortable little houses with a carriage and two maids in sprigged cotton. Not in a shabby Bloomsbury hotel room with a bloated bed and an ill-disposed stain on the ceiling.

Chapter Twenty-one

Tobias Taylor . . . Toby sometimes let the mirror chide him, since he had no parents to do it, and he enjoyed his handsome, engaging reflection. *Will you never learn?*

Seduction of enlightened Edwardian women was all part of the game, the glorious game of life in your free and felicitous thirties; but bowling over an emotionally retarded and unawakened woman was never worth the clogging aftermath.

'Don't telephone me,' he had had to tell Bella quite sternly. 'Don't tell *anyone*. Don't call round, and please don't keep writing notes.'

'Because of Mrs Drew? Why should you care what your servant thinks?' Bella, deflowered, had taken to tossing her head in a clumsy attempt at insouciance, with an upward thrust of her square chin.

'I don't care, but you must think of your family. I wouldn't want you involved in any scandal, Belle.'

But he did care about Neelie Drew clenching her hands under her bosom and crowing, 'I told you so!'

He was still a frequent visitor at No. 72 Chepstow Villas, where none of that friendly conventional family would ever suspect him of being a despoiler of one of its virgins. Poor nervous little Sophie, whose life was improving as her mother's did, had long ago given up trying to describe Toby's Dr Mesmer demonstration, since nobody believed her. Dear old Leonard was always welcoming and glad to see him, saving up prime Whiteley's customer anecdotes to amaze him. Flora Bolt greeted him with a special lopsided smile at the front door, because he had been attentive to her when she was wounded, and he always paused in the outer hall to ask her how she was.

'All the better for seeing you, sir.' She had recovered her cheeky familiarity. 'And I don't say that to every man!'

'Especially not that brute with the knife?'

''E's out of me life.' Flora took Toby's hat and passed a fond forearm over the nap. 'I'm available, if anyone asks.'

Gwen still softly flirted, grey eyes skimming his as lightly as a dragon-fly. He and Vera joked and smoked together. Young Dicky gave him sauce just short of insolence, and put up his fists with a shout of delight when Toby squared off to discipline him.

Bella was often there when he was, or because he was, watching him slyly, laughing too much at his jokes, trapping him in a corner to breathe heavily, 'When, Toby, when?'

'Soon. I promise you. Soon.' He fobbed her off, but a girl like this, too dense to know she was being fobbed, could be deadeningly persistent.

Since the family could not help but notice Bella's flushed and moony air, Toby spread it about that she was 'in love', and hinted at a mysterious romance, which Bella took to be their secret code.

'*Ach*, I wish that were true.' Her mother retracted the shiny nostrils of her parrot nose in a sniff. 'But if it were, I should be the first to know.'

'More likely the last, I think, Mrs Hugo.' Toby had never attempted to call her Charlotte. 'But Bella and I tell each other things. We are like brother and sister.' Bella did not even notice the cruelty of this.

Ordinarily, Madge would have been quick to spot what was going on, or forced her cousin Bella to tell her; but Madge was not normal either, preoccupied with Guy, waiting for his summons on the telephone recently installed among the coats in the back hall, often over at his Brook Street rooms when she should have been at family occasions like Teddie's birthday dinner.

'Good health, old girl!' Leonard raised his glass to his sister. 'Life begins at forty-seven, doesn't it? A bit different from this time last year.'

He included Toby in the toast. It was open knowledge now that Dr Taylor, by some magical process, had helped Teddie out of her doldrums, although she herself had progressed to the stage where she maintained either that there had never been anything wrong with her, or if there had been, that she had effected the cure all by herself.

'To tell you the truth,' Toby admitted to Dr Boone on a visit to The Keep, 'I'm a bit huffed by her ingratitude.'

'Don't be so unprofessional, Taylor.' Dr Boone always treated him as a colleague. 'Isn't that what you've been working for all these months? The very climax of self-esteem: "There's nothing wrong with me that I can't put right all by myself!" The lady is a walking credential to your skills. It's a pity you can't use her in one of those before-and-after testimonials, like the truss advertisements.'

Today, Toby imagined that perhaps his mother knew him. She was sitting up in a high-backed rocking chair, tied in with a canvas restraint to stop her wandering. She could not walk now without support, but she had been known to crawl away on her hands and skinny knees, to be found under a bed, or in a cupboard.

With her grey hair pulled back into an untidy braid, she had one bare foot tucked under her and one on the floor, rocking, rocking, a perpetual pendulum. As she tipped forward, she stared at her son and he stared intensely back, trying to force recognition into those trapped, tormented eyes.

He spoke to her, as he always did, as if she could understand him, as if she would answer. Sometimes, for his own sake more than hers, he supplied her end of the conversation, as people do with their dogs.

. 'When I was a little boy,' he said to her, 'you sang to me when I was in bed, do you remember? "Yes, I sang sad Welsh songs that you liked. You never wanted jolly ones." And Dr Taylor,' he asked her, 'do you remember Dr Taylor?' She had always called his father that. 'With his square beard and the veins in his nose? "Of course I remember my own dear husband, you silly boy."'

'Talking to yourself?' One of the few attendants, a blowsy harridan with brutal eyebrows, passed by with an armful of fouled bedding. 'It's catching, ain't it? If you come here often enough, Mr T., we'll have to lock you up with the other loonies.'

'I'm determined to make her know me.'

'Pigs might fly!' She cackled as flatly and dottily as any of the inmates.

'Lock *her* up, won't we, Mother?' Toby leaned towards the rocking bag of bones when the nurse had gone. 'I'll strap her in your chair and take you away with me – fly away, escape, back to the river – cast out a line, paddle in the eddies – shall we, *shall we*?'

Staring into her face was like hurling yourself against nothing. The bones looked so brittle, the pale flesh frail as tissue paper, the eyes like a small animal at bay, and yet you could not penetrate to the real person.

Was there any real person left? Toby wondered, as he dejectedly went away. Perhaps the real Nora Taylor had quite cunningly departed from this body before it was locked up.

She will never know me. She will never give me any love. And I, thought Toby, walking outside the high wall of The Keep through the rain to the station, I shall go on collecting it from other women.

Good excuse, eh? He raised his head more jauntily, and rain fell off his hat down his neck. Not that I need an excuse for charitable causes like Bella, who got more out of it than I did. But she's had all she's going to get, poor Bella. I shall drop her gently but firmly, before she gets euphoric ideas about telling my beloved Morley family.

'If your mistress would only come back to me,' he said to the little dog trotting through the puddles, wet as a fat seal, 'I could stop collecting women. Marie-May, come back Marie-May . . .' 'Pigs might fly.' He answered for the impermeable dog, as he had invented replies for his insensate mother.

His patient, Mrs Marcus, loved him anyway. The sensible diet, the renunciation of brandy nips and the laudanum which was Hampstead Garden Village's idea of a harmless sedative, the powdered inner bark of slippery elm, laced into fennel tea, had made her a new woman. She was still a great bore – there were no herbal cures for that, but she sent several friends to the inestimable Mr Taylor, whether there was anything wrong with them or not. Toby prescribed for them. That was one of the many benefits of medicinal herbs. Even if they did you no good, they would not actually do you harm.

Dicky announced a mouse in his stomach when Gwen and Leonard were going out to dinner one chilly October night.

'Oh dear, I knew I shouldn't have let you go out after school. You must have caught cold. I'll get you a good little Beecham's.'

'Noah wanted to go and play at the Scrubs.'

'What did you eat?' his father asked. 'Were you buying those cheap sweets down the Lane?'

'It was Noah's birthday.'

'Then Noah has probably got a mouse in his stomach too.' Leonard laughed.

'Don't, Daddy. It hurts.' Dicky screwed up his face. 'I don't want you to go out.'

'Oh, I see. It's one of those "Don't go out to dinner" pains, isn't it, old son?'

Dicky snuggled his face into his mother's fur coat, being given its first outing of the winter. 'Ugh – camphor.'

'I used to love the camphor smell of my mother's coats,' Gwen told him. 'It made me feel safe and wintry and snug.'

'It was all right for you.' Dicky pouted. 'Grandmama never went out in the winter.'

'She *did*. My parents were always going to balls and banquets.'

'She was too old.'

'Only when you knew her, silly. When I first knew her, she was quite young.'

Dicky had lost interest. He never liked to hear about his mother or father as children. He wanted them always this age, existing only as the parents of an eleven-year-old boy.

'You are so spoiled,' Madge told him, 'that I might not even play draughts with you.'

'If you don't, I'll have a worse pain.'

'The boy takes after my mother,' Leonard said with some pride as they went down the steps of No. 72 to the waiting cab.

The dinner party was in Sussex Gardens, mostly couples they knew, with Dr Buckmaster, also the family physician here, as an extra man to balance the hostess's unmarried sister.

'My dear lady.' Gwen did not like the way he smarmed over her hand. She sometimes thought of changing their doctor, but did not know any others, and Leonard believed the old saw about the devil you know. Little Bucky was too familiar. Arrogant and sly, his manner suggested that he knew something about you that you would prefer not known. Gwen had a fear of contracting something which would enable him to see her without her clothes on. 'Radiant as ever. One could swear you were a young girl. And the captain of commerce himself! And your delightful family?'

'Very well, thank you.' She had to beam graciously at the insufferable little man, because guests were watching her.

Gwen knew that when she came into a room people looked at her, and other women smoothed their waists and touched up their hair. She liked to make her impression early, and then relax and enjoy the evening, putting herself out or not, as she chose. 'Dicky complains of abdominal pain, but you know *him*.'

'Yes, I know him.' Little Bucky had dropped the smarm in favour of his usual truculence. 'He's abominably spoiled.'

As the evening went on, Dr Buckmaster, attendant on many Bayswater families, became quite offensively drunk.

When a messenger arrived to call him out to a woman in labour, he laughed, wet-lipped. 'She's produced six already. She ought to know how to do it by now.' This was heard in the smoking room by Leonard, who retailed it to Gwen: 'But if he had gone staggering off to the poor woman, I would have forcibly restrained him.'

Dicky still seemed a little off colour when he came home from school next day.

'Have you been to The Place?' Gwen knew it was usually that with him.

'I got up too late and there wasn't time.'

'One tiny cascara tonight. Eno's in the morning. Your breath is not very sweet, dear.'

'Hah!' He huffed at her. 'My dragon breath can kill at twenty yards.'

'Oh, woe!' His mother obligingly keeled over backwards and Dicky fell on top of her on the sofa. She was always ready to drop a serious subject, even her pet nostrums, in favour of a giggle.

When Noah appeared at the back door – 'Come down World's End, Dick, see my uncle's monkey' – Dicky refused.

'Shan't ask you no more.'

'Don't, then.'

Dicky stuck his tongue out. Noah kicked an empty milk bottle and broke it. Flora grabbed for him, but he ran off:

not through the front gate, but over the wall into the next garden and over another wall, which was his and Dicky's favourite way of travelling. Flora shouted after him, her voice still slightly thickened from the damaged nerve that had left her with one corner of her mouth pulled down.

At dinner, Dicky banged his boots on the rung of his chair. 'You know I don't like liver and bacon.'

'I know you *do*.' Flora put the plate in front of him. 'With Mrs Roach's velvet gravy.'

'Ugh!' He pushed the plate away.

'That's enough.' Leonard would not tolerate food fads. 'Here, I'll cut up the meat for you and you'll eat it all.'

'Shan't.'

'You *will*.'

Gwen wished Leonard would not start these little contests, because he did not always win. When he forked a piece of liver into Dicky's mouth, the boy chewed it for a moment, his eyes watering, and then brought it back up.

'Wilful, you see, Gwen.' The child was quite skilled at making himself sick. 'Go to your room, sir.'

'I'll come up with you, dear,' Flora said.

'No, you won't,' Leonard snapped. 'You'll stay and clean up this mess.'

Dicky stamped up the stairs, kicking the carpet rods. Flora scooped up napkin and plate and banged out of the door. Gwen was sorry that Leonard had managed to upset both of them.

Dicky did not get up for school the next day.

'You've been eating sweets.' Gwen found the evidence in his room.

'I was hungry.'

'There you are, you see, because you didn't eat your dinner. Tatiana shall bring you a bowl of Benger's.'

When Leonard came back from Whiteley's, he told Gwen that she should get the doctor.

'Not Bucky, no,' she said quickly. 'After the other night, I don't want to see him ever again.'

'Then who? What about that new generalist Charlotte is so taken with? She says he's in line for a knighthood, but I think she invented that to make Hugo let him lance that boil. You'd better go round and get his name.'

On her way to the door, Gwen turned back and went to the telephone. In the precise, affected voice with which she spoke into this demanding new gadget, she asked the operator to put her through to Toby Taylor's number.

'I'm a little worried about Dicky, To-by.'

'What's the bad boy done now?'

'A bilious attack, I think.'

'Let me come and have a look at him. I'm having quite a success with digestions these days.'

'Oh, *would* you?' This was what she had hoped for, but they had never used Toby as a doctor, and she did not know if it was all right to ask.

Toby brought some laxative herbs. Dicky dribbled up a little of the infusion, but drank some more and lay still, his hand on his sore stomach. When Leonard came home, he found good Uncle Toby reading aloud one of the cowboy yarns that had replaced the Hugh Walpole school stories since Dicky had been to the American Bioscope shows at Notting Hill Gate.

'He'll be right as rain tomorrow. I've given some psyllium seeds to lubricate. Never fails.'

'You are so good.' Gwen and Leonard were lucky to have such a friend as this charming, clever man who sat so reassuringly by Dicky's bed in the little room over the front door.

The next day, when the herbs had not worked, Toby agreed that Gwen might try castor oil, 'when all else fails'. Dicky was pale and frightened, his blue eyes stricken, his fingers turning over and over the little tin car his uncle Charles had given him.

Mrs Roach squeezed two oranges, and they poured the incompatible mixture into the boy. The oil lay on top of the juice. It clung round his protesting mouth, and some of it came up in a compulsive heave. Toby was reassuring Gwen that enough had stayed down to be effective, when the tin model car was flung to the floor as Dicky was convulsed by an agonizing pain.

'It's all right, old fellow, it's all right.' Toby massaged him gently, and sat by him while he was shaken by chills and went in and out of a feverish sleep. Feverfew was given, and later that evening he woke in a drenching sweat.

'The fever is breaking,' Gwen and Leonard told each other. Dicky lay doubled up. He was still alternately flushed and chilled, his breathing shallow and sour-smelling, but the pain was better. Toby's hand on his troubled brow felt that his temperature was down.

'He'll be all right.' Toby got up.

Leonard, Gwen and Madge whispered to him on the landing. 'We can't thank you enough. Dr Buckmaster would never have given us all this time. You've done so much.'

'For friends? It can never be enough. And I love this boy, too, don't forget.'

289

A scream woke Gwen and Leonard in the middle of the night. Dicky was sitting up in bed, staring at the window. The street outside was quiet, but he could hear the men. 'They've come for me!' Shrinking back against the pillow, he made the coughing, retching sound that he had heard the drunks make, reeling down from the Sun in Splendour on Saturday nights.

He was like a mad creature. He did not know his parents or Madge. He croaked for water through dry, cracking lips, but could not swallow.

Gwen sat on the bed and held him while he fought her feebly. 'Ring up Toby. Tell him to come round here.' But Leonard went down Chepstow Villas and woke up his policeman friend Arthur French, who knew what to do.

Mr Vernon Brett was assistant to Sir Frederick Treves, who had operated on King Edward for appendicitis. He saw that there was no time to get the child to the hospital. The kitchen table was scrubbed. Quantities of water were boiled, and walls and dresser and range were hung with carbolic-soaked sheets. Vernon Brett took off his coat and tied a long apron over his waistcoat and trousers. Rubber bands held back his rolled shirtsleeves. He chewed on his moustache. His eye had a fierce glint.

Leonard and Austin were allowed to be in the kitchen. Gwen and Madge and Flora clung together in the scullery. Mrs Roach and Tatiana trembled, praying and bewailing in the basement passage. Leonard was standing by his half-conscious son on the big table, talking to him, stroking his arm through the sheet in which he had been wrapped.

'Hold him for me, please.' Mr Brett's assistant poured chloroform on to a pad and held it over Dicky's face. Dicky twitched, jerked convulsively and then was limp and still, his strong boy's body suddenly tiny and insignificant under the white kitchen light pulled down low on its pulley over the table.

Leonard stepped back away from the sickly sweet smell. He stood in a corner by the window and would not look. From outside, light was showing through the curtains. A few early horses went by, a motor. Birds began to sing. Austin made himself look. What else could he do for his little brother except not be afraid and sickened?

The surgeon's clean pink hand pressed gently on the knife, through the delicate skin, through whatever was beneath, until Dicky's secret insides yielded up a gush of blood and putrid pus. The assistant dripped more chloroform on to the pad. Austin turned his head away, dizzy and faint, but made himself look back ('I watched, I didn't shrink from it,' he would tell Elizabeth, to whom he told everything, in a way he had never been able to do with his parents).

Mr Brett, his eyes flinty, showed Austin a small handful of inflamed intestine and then, worst of all nightmares, the ruptured appendix snipped off and lying in his palm, blackly oozing.

Austin had fainted backwards against his father, so he did not see the quick stitching and bandaging. He was in the study with his parents and Madge and Mr Vernon Brett, who was standing on the hearthrug with a small glass of brandy, while the rest of them were sitting, weak and blank. 'The vermiform appendix ruptured, probably yesterday.'

Austin knew that he could not tell Elizabeth what he

had seen in the kitchen. Would he ever be able to eat another meal in this house, cooked down there?

'Thus, the abdominal cavity is inflamed. What we call peritonitis.' They looked at him like a kindergarten class. 'The situation is very grave.' Mr Brett finished the brandy and then sucked it off his moustache with his bottom teeth.

It was Madge who asked courageously, 'He might die?'

The surgeon nodded.

'He *will* die?'

He turned his hand over, this way, that way, and shrugged. 'Why did you not send for a doctor sooner?'

'A friend of ours,' Gwen whispered, 'who *is* a doctor, he was here, treating the bilious attack. Psyllium seeds to – to lubricate?' She looked up hopefully.

'When did he last see the boy?'

'Yesterday. He said Dicky would be all right.'

The surgeon growled, and moved towards the door, so as not to have to look at them. 'I think he may have killed your son.'

All day, No. 72 was full of people, sitting about, waiting, talking in safe clichés, picking up magazines and putting them down, moving from room to room. The house seemed transitory, like a railway station. Bella came, Vera, Teddie, Charlotte and Hugo, wanting to have coffee made. Austin and Elizabeth and Laura, who whined to see Dicky, Arthur French's wife, Mr Frank Whiteley from the store, come to lay an arm round Leonard's shoulders and tell him to take as much time off as he liked. Nurses, messengers, Mr Vernon Brett again, newly shaved, coming down from Dicky's room to drink a cup of tea in the drawing room and turn the glint of his eye on the family, and then turn it away. Quite soon after he had left, in a big polished car with two chauffeurs that impressed Hugo, Dicky died.

Bella slipped away and ran up Kensington Park Road to Notting Hill Gate. There were no cabs, so she took an Underground train to South Kensington and walked, dry-eyed and staring, not seeing where she was going, only avoiding people on the pavement because they got out of her way. She did not look at Mrs Drew, but pushed past her and went straight upstairs and into Toby's consulting room.

'Bella – what on earth?' He got up from the desk. 'I might have been with a patient. What do you want? How's Dicky? I'm going over to 72 as soon as I've finished these letters.'

'Don't go.' Bella stood by the door, clutching her coat round her as if she were in a winter storm. 'Oh, Toby.' Tears suddenly poured down her face into her shuddering mouth. She had not cried yet, not when everybody burst out weeping, and Flora could be heard on the back stairs, bawling and blaspheming, not when she was on the train, staring at her muddled reflection in the opposite window.

Toby got up and came over to her. Oh, Toby, put your arms round me! She implored silently. He gave her his handkerchief. 'Stop that snivelling and tell me what's happened.'

Bella took a gasping breath and told him that Dicky had died after an operation for acute appendicitis.

'He can't have – what are you saying, Bella?' Toby's shock and distress flared into anger. 'I saw him yesterday. He was better – I swear he was better!'

Bella looked at him in agony. 'The surgeon blames you for not seeing what was wrong.'

'He would.' Toby gave a harsh laugh. 'To cover his butchery. Bella,' he said emotionally, 'Bella, tell me. How is your poor, poor family taking it?'

'They blame you too.' Bella saw him through a curtain of tears. 'That's why I came. They are very angry.'

She went back to his house two days later. She had to. Poor Toby, she was his only friend.

'He's gone.' Mrs Drew began to shut the door.

'Gone – where?'

'Don't ask me. Abroad, he said.'

'How long for?'

'How should I know? Rent's paid up in advance, and my salary, in case you're worried.'

She stood and stared boldly from the open door, which was worse than if she had slammed it, forcing Bella to retreat under the fire of her gaze.

Chapter Twenty-two

For some reason, Austin wanted his little daughter to see the body. Dicky looked very beautiful, with his golden curls so alive round his head and his face of an angel pausing in flight; it would give Laura reassurance and strength. Austin himself had never been allowed to see anyone dead, not his famous grandfather, not his mother's parents. He had been absurdly sheltered, he argued wildly, not making any sense.

Laura stared in terror. She put out a finger and touched the cold still hand. Instantly she began to scream, as she had screamed when Dicky had told her at North Croft that he would be turned to stone.

'The witch!' she shrieked. 'She's done it! He said she would. How could you let her, Daddy, Daddy, Daddy!' She beat against her father's legs. 'She's turned him to stone!' She ran like a hunted rabbit and bolted herself in the upstairs Place. She was hysterical for days. No amount of gentle insistence that Dicky had gone to be with God could prevent her from suddenly staring into corners and shouting, 'The stones have got him! He's stone!' Passing the old graves in the cemetery at the end of Kensington Park Gardens, she cried out, 'All those stones are *people*!' She was not brought to the funeral.

Outside No. 72 Chepstow Villas, a small crowd had gathered in the heavy rain to see Whiteley's hearse and the carriages drawn away by Flemish Blacks. Noah and his friend Tiger had come up the Lane with wet hair plastered over their peaked, frightened faces and fistfuls of limp flowers that had fallen from a market stall. When they saw that the procession was leaving, they dropped the flowers and ran after the hearse. The top-hatted driver looked behind him, then reached round with his long whip to lash the boys away.

The mourning clothes of grey and black were quite becoming to Gwen, but she did not care how she looked. She only glanced in the mirror to remind herself that her ravaged face was a just punishment.

She and Leonard were not usually given to guilt and to analysing their mistakes, but now, in the days and nights of their insane grieving, the guilt was the hardest torture to bear.

Toby Taylor was not here to be blamed, so they blamed themselves for trusting him. 'You told me to get Charlotte's doctor, Leo,' Gwen wept. 'But I – I was the one who called for Toby instead.' Her drowned eyes looked out of deep shadowed caves.

Leonard could remember all the times when he had lost patience, not through the boy's fault, but through his own absurdity. 'I can hear myself saying on the lawn, that lovely day at North Croft, "I am quite angry".'

'You only meant "somewhat angry",' Madge said.

'But he could have taken it to mean "*completely* angry".' Leonard dropped into a pew at the side altar of St Peter's and prayed dementedly, 'Grant me five minutes with him – just five minutes.'

His safe, comfortable home in Chepstow Villas had turned into a morgue. People crept about in soft shoes. No one raised their voices. Visitors came and went, in a drift of murmurs and whispers. No one wanted to eat, but meals kept coming up from below stairs. Behind every closed door, someone was crying.

Leonard could not cry. He had been turned to stone too, he thought. 'Stay at home, my dear man,' Frank Whiteley urged, but Leonard went back to work very soon, because he could not bear it at home. He remembered that when the old Chief was killed and everything had gone wrong at the store, his home had been his escape and refuge. Now Whiteley's was his escape. He rose, washed, dressed and shaved like a machine, kissed Gwen, who stayed late in bed now, ate eggs and toast in silence, and hurried down the Villas and across Chepstow Road and along Westbourne Grove like a silly little frock-coated mannikin, drawn forward on a string.

Good morning, good morning. Oh, Mr Morley, sir, how *are* you? Good morning. Yes, I've a lot of work to do. Thank you.

He pushed the door of his office shut behind him just in time before he fell into the chair and dissolved on to the unwelcoming ridges of the rolltop desk, in an ocean of tears.

After a while, he was able to pull himself together. He raised his head and wiped his face with a handkerchief, and made himself look at the framed family group above the desk, from which Dicky, perched on the arm of the back-yard bench, laughed back at him.

Leonard straightened out his clothes, brushed his nonde-script hair, checked his tie and collar wings in the small hand glass he kept for that purpose, and went out on to the floor.

This was where he belonged. Not as a king roving in power through his dominion, like William Whiteley, but as the regulator of the whole fabulous display of merchandise and its acolytes, the sellers and the buyers, moving in his own element, eyes everywhere, ready with a smile or a frown of concern, oiling the huge machine with attentiveness and goodwill.

He missed nothing. 'Excuse me, madam, please don't touch the Chinese porcelain.' 'Mrs Betts, I think the chrysanthemums are just a little tired . . .' 'Made up your mind, then, have you, sir?' A click of the fingers. 'Mr Hoiles, forward!'

Hugo said that Leonard had the soul of a shopwalker, and Hugo was right. There was plenty of office work to be done upstairs, but this was safer, out among the people in his familiar role, allowing himself a brief pause in which he did not think about Dicky.

He stood on the main stairs, a few steps up from the ground floor, his favourite vantage point to get the whole detailed bustling picture of crowds moving in and out between shop and street, threading along the counters, clustering by a special display. A tall man brushed past him going up the stairs, and apologized, and the past rushed into the present with the memory of that pleasant genial voice: 'I say, I'm most desperately sorry.' This was where Toby Taylor had first come into his life.

Leonard moved quickly down to the floor. 'Good morning, madam.' 'Yes, can I help you?' 'Good day to you, Lady Walker. How is Sir Alistair?' 'No, I'm sorry, lacquerware has moved upstairs, madam, while we redecorate.' Shoppers smiled and nodded and appreciated him. From behind counters, the assistants, men and women, watched him covertly. They knew. The customers could see the black armband, but it might have been for a distant relative.

'*Mr* Leonard Morley.' A beautiful woman whose name he did not know stood in front of him. 'I heard about your – your son.' She dropped her voice. Leonard bent his head. 'I'm so very sorry.'

He looked up at her. Behind the veil, such compassion was in her eyes and in her soft pink mouth. He bit his lips.

'I remember a few years ago, seeing him here with you – Dicky, wasn't it? I gave him my box of peppermints – parading about with you so confidently. Forgive me. Are you all right, Mr Morley?'

Leonard nodded, gave his infinitesimal bow and moved off along the crowded aisle.

Toby had decided quickly to go to Paris. He would hide there, lie low, perhaps find Marie-May Lacoste, perhaps move on into Germany or Italy, and return to his practice when the fuss had died down and there was no risk to his good name.

It was ironic that in a major crisis of life, some very small detail could hold you up. The dog Bounce. Neelie Drew despised it. He could not leave it with her.

The ferryman at Goring would take it. Todd liked dogs and he might be pleased to have this energetic little barker staying with him at the lonely towpath cottage. Toby left his bags in the cloakroom at Victoria, where he would collect them for the boat train tomorrow, and went with the dog to Paddington. It was a cold, windy day at the end of October. Toby, raw from Dicky's death and his own searing guilt, did not want to be recognized. He had wrapped himself in his old dark-green serge cloak, acquired in one of his medical student winters to keep him alive on the freezing run across the courtyards from his lodgings, when he was called to the wards or the operating theatre at night. He put a muffler round his neck and jammed his old broad felt fishing hat low on his head. The dog still wore its collar studded with fake glittery gems, which he had bought to amuse Marie-May. They must look a bizarre pair.

When they walked from Goring station, under the railway bridge and round the first bend of the river's double curve, Toby saw the big ferryboat on the other bank, where a barge horse was being loaded. The barge, taking felled trees upstream, had been poled across the river and was tied up to piling outside the low red-brick cottage, which squatted like a mushroom on the soggy bank.

The dog, a real opportunist Londoner, ran about excitedly exploring all the new seductive smells, and then stood by Toby at the landing stage, defying the approaching rowboat and the floating horse with short shrill barks. Bringing the boat round parallel with the bank, the ferryman looked over his shoulder.

'It's me, Todd. Mr Taylor,' Toby called to him. 'Come to ask you another favour.'

'Ah?' There had been good money in it before.

'I'll pay you well,' Toby got to the point at once, 'If you'll look after my dog for me while I go abroad.'

'Ah.'

'That's settled, then. Good.' Toby reached down for the boat's bow rope and looped it over the post at the landing.

There was no bargeman holding the horse, which was obviously an old hand at the ferry. It was shifting its huge shod feet, adjusting its balance to step placidly up on to the bank, when the damned dog, the rotten, arrogant terrier, made a dash at it, jumping into the boat and nipping at its legs.

With a lot of clatter and splashing, the horse kicked out and the stern of the boat swung out into the stream. The horse was half in and half out of the river, floundering up the bank with a great churning of mud.

The two men on the barge were shouting and cursing. The starboard oar was in the water, and the ferryman was slumped in a heap, his hands clutching his head.

A burly bargeman took the horse by the bridle and kicked the dog into the river, where it swam neatly back to shore and ran off among the bushes. 'All right, Toddy?'

The ferryman groaned. Toby knelt on the landing boards and pulled the man's hand away from his head. The temple was smashed, and pulpy with blood. They lifted him out on to the grass, and Toby padded a rag from the bottom of the boat and tied it to the wounded head with his muffler.

They carried him, unconscious now, and laid him in the cabin of the timber barge. The horse was hitched up and shouted at. He leaned into his collar and plodded off on the slow haul to the station to get Toddy on a train to the cottage hospital in Wallingford.

Toby watched them out of sight round the bend. He went into the cottage and made up the fire to boil the kettle for some tea. He was suddenly very tired. Stricken and shocked from the tragedy of Dicky, he had scrambled together his hasty plans, and was in a suspended state, halfway between England and France, the future just as unreal as the immediate past.

Now he had caused another tragedy by bringing the wretched dog here. The ferryman might die. If he lived, he would not come back for a long time, to row his heavy boat back and forth across the river. His livelihood would go, perhaps the house, too, and the boat, if they did not belong to him. So here was another life ruined by Tobias Taylor, great humanistic healer, to add to the shattered lives of the beloved family, whom he might never see again. He drank his tea out of a grubby mug, and because he could not yet bear to think about the Morleys, he thought about the ferryman, laid out along the carriage seat on his way to find a doctor. A doctor! If anyone in Paris calls me 'doctor', they will get my fist in their face. All doctors are useless parasites.

In his mind, he damped down the fire, threw away leftover food for the ducks, made the boat secure bow and stern, brought in the oars, locked up the little house and set off up the towpath for the station. If the dog did not return, he would leave it here to be found, or to find someone. It was a self-reliant little pig. His thoughts performed these necessary tasks, but his body still sat slumped by the fire.

The ferry service did not cease because poor Todd was badly hurt. Toby stayed on at Ferry Cottage with the dog. He let his beard grow, and wore his shapeless hat and kept the cloak wrapped round him, inside out, the black lining soaked and muddy, as he rowed across the river for the barge horses and few November passengers, and his gentleman's hands grew hard calluses. Bounce barked for him when the ferry bell rang on the dead tree. The dog rode in the bow of the boat, balanced four-square with his front legs on the thwart, and yelped stridently at any other boats that came by. He had lost his jewelled collar. Toby thought that one of the men on the barge had stolen it.

Arthur French came up the road to No. 72. He or his wife dropped in on the family almost every day, anxiously, as if they were children who should not be left alone.

'I have a bit of news for you, Leonard.' Arthur cleared his throat. 'I didn't want to tell you, because it has nothing whatsoever to do with your – situation, but you would read it in the paper anyway.'

Horace Rayner, who had murdered William Whiteley almost a year ago, had attempted to take his own life in Pentonville prison. 'He cut his wrist very deeply, I heard. If the officers had not found him when they did, he would have bled to death.'

'He should have,' Leonard said dully. 'Do you remember, after the death sentence was commuted to penal servitude for life, he said that he would rather die than spend the rest of his life behind bars. Why didn't they let him die?'

'Why didn't *he* die, instead of Dicky?' Gwen said irrationally, and began to cry again. She still cried every day, three or four outbursts at different times, and when she was taken away to lie down, she fell asleep.

She went out shopping, to Whiteley's or Arthur's Stores, but not any more down the Lane, and not by herself. She went with Madge or Bella or one of her sisters-in-law, because she was too uncertain. She saw her grandchildren, but not for very long, and muddled through some of her usual jobs: counted the laundry wrong, mislaid bills, or paid them twice, washed china ornaments in the pantry with Tatiana, and did not mind when she broke something.

Formally in mourning, the family did nothing social and saw only each other. Leonard had been to Goring to talk to his mother. She wanted him to stay at Heron's Nest with her, and when he would not, insisted that he take her back with him to Chepstow Villas. She was quite a nuisance there, selfish in her grief and critical – as if they needed to be told that Dicky had died because of their stupidity, and it was a relief when her companion Margaret Biddle came in a hired car and fetched her back.

'You can say this for Her Ladyship.' Flora stood on the top step with Madge to see her leave. 'Her departure has given us all something to be glad about.'

Aunt Teddie's grief was mostly centred on herself, since the changes in her had not been fundamental. Dicky's death was a personal affront: 'Just when I was beginning to feel life was worth living,' which she made worse by adding, 'and no Dr Taylor to cheer me up.' Austin was in a terrible state. Six-year-old Laura, who had always been an easy child, had suddenly become rude and difficult, demanding attention, resenting time spent by her mother and the nurse with her small brother, and her father's time spent at Chepstow Villas, where nobody wanted to play games with her any more. She threw tantrums and sulks and invented unspecific ailments. 'My ankles won't bend. My hair hurts.' She would not go upstairs at No. 72, where she had seen Dicky turned to stone. She never spoke of him, but sometimes she tried, in an ineffective way, to be tomboyish. Austin had to scold her for whistling in the street.

By the end of November, Madge had gone back in a haphazard way to help at the Loudon Street Settlement. She hoped to be able to do something for Jack Haynes, because she felt guilty about having taken him up in such a big way last year, and then neglected him; but Jack was not staying at the Settlement any more, and the cabinet-maker who was training him had not seen him for a long time. Madge was once more seeing a lot of Guy Davidson, and was torn between his demands and the needs of her parents, who often seemed more like her children now. Guy sometimes seemed like a stern, domineering father. He was only four years older, but he thought himself more experienced and sophisticated than Madge, who had always been so confident in her energy and intelligence. When they went out together, she sometimes pushing his chair if he was not up to standing or walking, he wanted her to be the best-looking woman; yet he did not like it if men admired her.

'I'm not your slave,' Madge had told him, when he had clicked his fingers across the room for her.

'Bitch,' he muttered. She had never heard a man say that about any woman. His powerful hand was tense and trembling on the arm of his chair. When he was angry, his eyes were flat and frightening. When he was in a good mood, he could be exciting company, laughing and joking outrageously, with the air about him of reckless adventure that Madge had seen in his boyish pictures when he took her to visit his parents. When he was low-spirited, or in pain, he told her that he would die if she ever left him.

Madge did think about breaking free. But then I'd have nothing, she cried to herself, as the grandfather clock soberly greeted her late at night in the shadowed hall. I must have something!

Going upstairs without her shoes was a weary climb. Dicky used to leave his door ajar when she was out. He was always insensibly asleep, but she would creep in and leave on the bed whatever she had brought home: a chocolate or a party favour, or a gardenia buttonhole, or a theatre programme, or a rosette from a protest meeting.

Charlotte did not notice that Bella was tired and off colour. After the blow that had felled the family, nobody could be said to be on colour. Bella got up earlier than her mother, so that Charlotte did not know that she started her day by being sick in the bathroom.

Bella thought the vomiting and dry heaving were symptoms of her turmoil of emotions: mourning the lost family angel at the same time as secretly mourning the family villain. Toby, Toby, when will you come back?

Am I going into a decline? She was not getting any thinner. After being sick in the blue and gilt heavily patterned basin which her mother had ordered from an expensive firm who supplied sanitary ware to the German royal family, she could always eat a good breakfast.

One cold morning when Hurd the butler was in the hall with her father, primping up the astrakhan collar of his full-skirted coat, Bella found herself alone in the dining room with the parlourmaid.

'Sure you've got enough? Don't mind us downstairs.' Sybil pointed her nose at the loaded plate Bella was bringing away from the chafing dishes. 'Eating for two, aren't you, dear?'

'What? What do you mean?' Bella stopped between the sideboard and the table.

'I hear from the washerwoman that she has not seen any monthly towels from you for quite some time.' Sybil Crocker was above giving the lowly creature a name, but not above listening to her gossip.

'That's because I'm upset. It happens to a lot of women.'

'You're right there.' The parlourmaid gave a mirthless laugh, jerking her sharp face forward like a bird of prey. 'But it's not usually called being upset.'

The tall door opened and the butler slithered round it. Bella put her plate down on the starched white tablecloth and began to eat her breakfast.

Later, discussing symptoms, interrogating Bella, who was frightened and confused, it was generally agreed in the servants' hall that the poor ignorant girl had fallen pregnant. 'Bit of a shock for your ma and pa.'

'You'd never tell them?'

'Like the grave.' Sybil made a cross sign on her stiff aproned bosom.

Having no one to talk to, Bella was driven to discuss her crisis with these interested parties downstairs.

'Find the man. Make him do right by you,' was Cook's opinion.

'I don't know where he is.'

'Anyone we know, dear?' They wheedled Bella for information, giving her slices of Victoria sandwich, but she would not tell them.

'I must say.' The butler leaned back in his chair, assessing Bella narrowly from under the disconcertingly dark eyebrows that did not match his pale oiled hair. 'I never would have thought it of you.'

'It was only once.' Bella blushed.

'That's all it takes.' The housemaid went off into one of her raucous laughs, clapping her hand over her mouth and letting down the front legs of her chair with a bang at the butler's frown.

'Well – twice, as a matter of fact,' Bella admitted.

'There's a bad girl.' Sybil put on a shocked face, but they were none of them shocked. They seemed almost to admire Bella for what she had dared to do, as if it was an entry into their club.

'What shall I do?' she asked them.

'Well, there's mustard baths and gin.' The parlourmaid counted off on her fingers. 'Or so I hear, not ever having had what you might call personal knowledge. There's Epsom salts or Towle's pills, though it's a bit late for that. There's falling downstairs or jumping off a table. There's driving down Exhibition Road in a growler without springs.'

'There is also my auntie,' Hurd put in. 'Don't let's be forgetting her. She has a reputation second to none.'

'For what?' Bella asked innocently, and they told her.

'Oh no, I couldn't possibly.' Bella put her hands over her stomach in fear.

'You know what happens to young girls who fall pregnant?' Sybil's eye was like cold bacon. 'They get put away. They're labelled moral imbeciles and locked in an institution.'

Bella rode her bicycle to the house where Hurd's aunt practised her witchcraft. She pedalled down Lansdowne Hill across the curving streets that followed the lines of the old Hippodrome racecourse, and turned up Clarendon Road towards Pottery Lane.

She and Madge had ventured down there once or twice when they were foolhardy children, and it did not seem to be any more salubrious now. The gutterless streets were filthy with mud and refuse. Some of the dwellings were almost derelict. Hobgoblin boys ran after her, jeering at her divided serge skirt. There was a miasmic smell all about, of pigsties and something worse. She had read in the Kensington paper about 'the ocean', the lake of slime and poisonous gases that was held to be responsible for the deaths of twenty per cent of local babies and children. And here came Bella Morley, to add another to their number.

The house of the butler's aunt was round the corner from a grim beleaguered church and was, as he had said, a cut above the rest. It stood in a little yard with a few bedraggled bushes. Its plaster walls had once been painted pink, and the doorstep was decently whitened.

Bella stood with her bicycle at the arched entrance to the yard, and saw a light grow in one of the two windows as someone carried a lamp into the room. She saw the shape of a woman with a shawl over her head, waiting for her beyond the low latticed panes.

Go forward, Bella Morley. But the small scene was horribly reminiscent of the fatal cottage in *Hansel and Gretel*. Bella pushed her bicycle back under the arch, staggered a little as she tried to mount it under the gleeful eyes of the hobgoblins, and rode away as fast as she could up the hill to Kensington Park Gardens.

"Ow did you get on with 'er?' The butler did not bother to mind his aitches below stairs.

'She wasn't at home.'

''Ave to go back, then.'

'Yes.' Bella had left her bicycle in the shed and come in through the back door. 'I will, but don't bother me about it, none of you. No one is to breathe a word to anyone, or I'll get you all sacked.'

'You and 'oo else?'

'No one is to mention it to me. *Please.*'

She knew now what she would do. She would have this baby. Toby's baby – what a marvel it would be! Somehow, somewhere, she would find Toby and tell him, and he would be pleased and they would marry and the family would forgive him, for Bella's sake.

Chapter Twenty-three

Hiding at Ferry Cottage, Toby was in a limbo in which he did not have to think. He explored the river banks, collected firewood, walked to the farm at Gatehampton for milk and bread, and bought a few supplies from an itinerant trader on the road. He dug worms from the muddy backwater where the boat was pulled in at night, and with the ferryman's rod he managed to catch a few dace and perch. One red-letter day, he caught a chub that must have weighed three pounds.

Toby's beard grew in dark and bushy between the low brim of his hat and the high collar of his enveloping cloak. He liked to sit on the bank in the ferryman's Sunday boots, far sturdier than his London ones that were already wrecked and leaking, and watch the slow winter life of the river go by. The ducks at first seemed like throngs passing. Then, as he watched them more closely, he saw that there were actually only quite a few ducks going up and down the same stretch of the river, like a stage army. When the water surface was still, coots and water rats crossing from bank to bank made tiny arrowhead tracks, which Toby watched until the last tremor at the edge of the wake died in the sunk reeds.

On a clear night, the moon was brighter in the oily water than in the sky. Toby had never been so alone before. There were not many ferry passengers, but he kept the money for Todd in a pot on the mantelpiece: twopence for a horse, a penny each for pigs that were driven over from the farm to be sold on the other side, sixpence a wheel for a handcart, two penny coins for a passenger, the same fare that the Romans used to put on the tongues of the dead to pay Charon to ferry them across the river Styx.

'Two coins to cross the Styx,' Toby joked to a cheery young stranger. 'No one returns.'

'Oi will,' the young man said. 'Come about sunset. Where's old Todd, then?'

'He was hurt. I'm helping out.' No one had questioned Toby running the ferry, any more than they would question it when he was no longer there.

The irrepressible brown dog, which was a cunning hunter, lived on rats and mice and the occasional waterfowl. Toby started to call it Cerberus.

Bella knew from discreetly prurient gossip that some women 'showed' earlier than others. Although the tall bathroom scales with the heavy weights that dropped on your foot showed a gain of only a few pounds, there was a definite swelling of her stomach, and she did not know whether it was all right to tighten her corset. It was lucky that although the S-shaped look, with pouter chest and tucked back waist was still fashionable, the Empire line was coming in again. At a shop where she was not known, Bella bought herself a soft heavy dress that flowed out loosely below the bosom.

'That's quite passable,' her mother conceded, 'even though you wouldn't let me choose it with you. I hope it doesn't mean she is planning to go without stays, like some of these brazen young women, don't you, Hugo?'

'Please, Charlotte.' This occasional coarseness in his wife was unpleasantly Germanic. 'Spare me the grisly details.'

In her mauve Empire dress, with the beaver-trimmed raglan that she had always liked, although Madge said it made her look like a walking tent, Bella went once more to Egerton Terrace and rang the bell.

'Yes?' The housekeeper, not in uniform now, looked formidably at ease.

'I just wondered if you could give me Dr Taylor's address. I have an unpaid bill,' Bella invented desperately, as the woman's insolent silence forced her to say something, 'I'd like it settled.'

'So would he, no doubt, if I knew where he was.'

'You don't know?' The woman was obviously lying.

'I've told you, haven't I? Now, if you'll excuse me . . .'

Bella went away in her brown beaver tent, and sat for a while in an A.B.C. teashop at South Kensington, where she ate an éclair and a *mille-feuille* to satisfy the craving for sweet things that she had always had, and which was justified now. When dusk began to settle, she walked back to Egerton Terrace. She did not completely believe that Toby was not there.

As well as the lower floor where the housekeeper lived, two of the upper front rooms were lighted behind drawn curtains. If she waited long enough, she would surely see the front door open and Toby come jauntily out to start his evening's entertainment. After the lamp-lighter came by, Bella stepped just out of range of the street light and stood for a long while in the shadow, watching the upstairs windows.

*

As December dragged on, with its inescapable promise of winter, and the dread of how they would all get through Christmas without Dicky, there were a few unseasonably warm days that made you feel worse when you could not enjoy them.

There was something that had been on Leonard's mind, and he decided to do it now. He would hire a motor launch at Goring and make a small pilgrimage to cast a wreath for Dicky on the river he had loved so much. Gwen could not face it, but Austin and Madge would go, and Bella said she wanted to go, too, although she was slowly growing frantic about the future.

She had thought Uncle Leonard would hire the boat above the flashlock and take it upstream, as he usually did, because it was easier to punt back with the flow of the current, but he wanted to go downstream to the water-meadows above Pangbourne where Dicky had had his last picnic. They made the journey in silence, Austin piloting the boat, each busy with their own thoughts. Beyond the railway bridge, Bella turned her head away so as not to look at Ferry Cottage.

Opposite the meadow where the Jacob's sheep had grazed and Bella had run races with Dicky and Laura to make it look as if she was having a good time while Toby's actress flirted with the other men and Toby quoted E.A. Morley's *A Small Country Town* to Grandmother, Leonard stood up and cast the big wreath of evergreens and chrysanthemums out upon the water. They all said a prayer as the wreath floated away. It spun into an eddy, caught on a waterlogged branch, and broke free to dwindle out of sight.

They were more talkative on the way home. Madge

brought out the Thermos flask and sandwiches from her basket. There was a feeling of relief that the little ceremony had been performed. Something had been done for Dicky, and they could talk about him more easily. 'Do you remember . . . ?' 'He always had to be Captain. I can see him with that jaunty little yachting cap on the back of his head.'

Passing Ferry Cottage, where a spiral of smoke hung in the still air above the crooked chimney, Bella's stomach suddenly bubbled up like molten lead, and she thought she was going to be sick. A dog was barking. Not just any dog. It was the unmistakable high shrill yelp of Toby's brown terrier.

Next morning, Bella took the train back to Goring and walked along the towpath. The ferry boat was crossing the river towards her, the dog standing alertly in the bow. There were no passengers, only the ferryman, rowing steadily with his back to her. He was muffled up in a dark cloak with a shapeless hat pulled low on his head.

The dog sprang across the gap between the boat and the bank and ran towards her, yelping and jumping about. Bella stood still in the wet grass and watched the rower throw a rope over a post and step out on to the landing stage. He had a full dark beard, and his cloak and hat were stiff with weather and water stains.

He stared at Bella, but did not smile until she said breathlessly, 'Toby.'

His dark eyes gleamed and his teeth showed very white through the moustache and beard. He turned back to look at three ducks going past on the river.

Bella went towards him. 'Toby, I've come to tell you –'

'Look, look, Bella, the eternal triangle. The drake swims

ahead of the female. The second drake, he's always just behind, hoping and clucking. Sometimes they fly to the bank to shake him off. He can't fly, I think.'

'Never mind about the ducks.'

'I do. I spend a lot of time watching them.' Apart from the disguise, this was a different Toby.

'Can we go into the house?' Bella asked.

'Of course. I'm sorry. I spend so much time out here. Come in, Bella, and tell me why you're here.'

Inside, Toby took off his hat and cloak and dropped them on the floor. Bella would not sit down.

'Can you guess what I've come to tell you?'

He shook his shaggy head. The skin of his face was browner, and not very clean.

'I'm going to have a baby.'

'You can't be.' He laughed, as he had laughed at her when he pulled out the sponge and string.

'It's true.' She smoothed down the mauve wool dress over the slight swell of her belly. 'I'm – I'm pleased about it. Are you?'

'Why should I be?'

'Because we could be married.'

'Married! To the family murderer? You're mad, girl. They'd cut you off without a bean.'

'I wouldn't mind.' Bella moved closer to him. 'I'd be with you. We'd be the three of us against the world.'

Toby laughed again and sat down in the old chair and leaned forward to poke at the fire. 'Sounds wonderfully romantic. Only –' He paused, looking at the fire, then threw down the poker and said, 'Look here, I'll have to tell you this. I've got a wife already.'

'We've never seen her. You're lying.'

'Hush. She – well, she's in an institution. It's very sad. She'll never be well enough to come out, but she'll always be my –' He stopped, and gave Bella the disarming, candid look that she had seen before when she knew he was not telling the truth. 'Always be my wife.'

Jack Haynes had come back to the Loudon Street Settlement one day when Madge was there, and she had told him about Dicky's death.

'Deh?' His troubled eyes searched her face. He could not seem to understand it.

Madge spelled out Dicky's name, then spread her hands out, palms down: *Finished*. She rubbed her fingers in her eyes to signify crying, and Jack did that, too. There were real tears on his thick lashes.

He told her, 'I come see your mother.' He was very fond of Gwen.

'Yes.' Madge nodded. It might be helpful to her mother. When you were talking to Jack, you had to concentrate on him and what he was getting from it, not on yourself. 'You come to 72.' She wrote the number on the air.

Flora was alone at No. 72 Chepstow Villas. Mrs Roach and Tatiana had the half day off, and Gwen Morley had gone to Addison Road to see her grandchildren.

Flora had her shoes off and her feet up on the kitchen stool. The infernal telephone could ring its head off. Anyone at the front door could go away . . . Someone at the *back* door? Who the hell? Tradesmen always came in the morning, and there were no deliveries expected.

The back-door bell jangled again as if it had come off its spring.

'All right, all right.' Flora padded into the scullery in her stockinged feet. 'Keep your wool on!' She pulled open the door with a scowl.

'Thanks for the loving welcome.' Bull Bolt stood there, cocky, corduroy-çoated, smelling of beer through his broken-toothed grin.

Flora stepped back, speechless. Her hand automatically went to her neck, where he had cut her.

'Don't worry, love. I didn't bring me blade.' With a hand on each side of the door frame, he leaned towards her, peering through into the kitchen. 'Coast clear, eh? I seen the old cow go out, with the little vixen.'

'You can't come in, Bull.' Flora was trembling with shock. She was conscious of the weakness at the side of her mouth.

'I'm in.' He stepped into the scullery. He had new boots, and a check waistcoat. He looked more prosperous. 'Get me a drink.'

Flora shut the door into the kitchen and stood against it. She did not want him to come close to her and put his hands on her. She did not want anything to shake her determination never to have anything to do with him again.

'Been too long, Flo,' he said huskily, those rogue's eyes teasing her.

'Not long enough, Bill.'

'I been up north, see. Got meself a good job, on the trains, and turned respectable.'

'That'll be the day. It hasn't stopped your afternoon boozing, I see.'

'Why wouldn't I fortify meself before coming to ask my girl to come up north and throw in her luck with me?'

'You must be mad, Bill Bolt. I'm not leaving here. It's my home.'

'Got meself a little place, see, and enough money coming in to take care of you. You and me, Flo, we could –'

'Bill, don't, for God's sake.' Flora could not bear it. 'Don't ask me to –'

In the basement passage, the front-door bell whirred across her distress. 'I've got to answer it. You go away.'

'I'll wait. That's what you want, isn't it?'

'Flora, are you all right?' Bella asked. The maid was flushed, shoes off, and breathing fast.

'I can't run up them back stairs like I used to.'

Bella was already beginning to find herself a little breathless if she hurried upstairs. That would get worse, as the baby grew. She would have to spend time off her feet. Why couldn't Toby look after her?

She knew he had lied about being married. Taken off his guard. She should not have sprung it on him out of the blue. Worried and unhappy, she had just written him a desperate letter, begging him to change his mind.

He might not answer. She would send it anyway.

'Is Mrs Morley at home?' Bella had brought Aunt Gwen a light romantic novel that she hoped would cheer her up.

'I'm sorry, she's out.'

Flora did not ask Bella if she would like to come in. She seemed preoccupied, as if she was busy, so Bella gave her the book and went down the steps, taking the letter to

Toby out of her pocket to post in the pillar box on the corner of Denbigh Road.

At the gate, she saw the deaf man, Jack Haynes, wandering up the street towards her, broad shoulders hunched, hands deep in the pockets of a patched and sagging coat.

'I'm glad to see you.' Bella pointed to herself, then to him, and clapped her hands. He looked over her shoulder at the house.

'Are you going to see Madge?' Jack did not know the concept of a question, so she made it a statement. 'See Madge.' He shook his shaggy head. 'See Madge mother.'

'Yah.'

'She's not there.' Poor fellow, he must have come here to show sympathy for the family.

'Dicky dead,' Jack was saying.

Bella nodded, her eyes filling with tears.

'Why? Someone kill him?'

Bella drew him into the gateway. 'They say it was Toby. T-O-B-Y T-A-Y-L-O-R.' She wrote the name with her finger, in the air. 'Doctor you met at Settlement.' He nodded. He understood that. 'Toby's fault.'

Bella began to cry. Tears had come too readily since Dicky had died. Jack clenched his fists and frowned.

'Toby killed Dicky,' Bella sobbed.

'Bey-ya.' He had always seemed attuned to her, this man who was so cut off from most of the world. He patted her arm and pulled his mouth down like a clown.

Because she was crying, Bella was going to bring Jack away from the street into the garden, but suddenly she heard violent shouting and curses from the direction of the back door, and a wild-looking man charged up the passage and out through the gate, pushing Bella and Jack aside, and disappeared round the corner of the Portobello Road.

Was this the terrible 'Bull' who had attacked Flora before? He had knocked the letter out of Bella's hand. Jack bent to pick it up.

'I'm going to post it.' Anxious to get to Flora, Bella pointed at the pillar box down the street, and held out her hand. She did not want Jack to see the address on the envelope: Toby Taylor, Ferry Cottage, Goring-on-Thames.

But Jack held on to the letter. 'I do it,' and went off towards the pillar box, as Bella ran to the back door to see if Flora was all right.

Jack had not posted Bella's letter. He had put it in his pocket. He knew what he must do. A large part of his life was spent not knowing what he was going to do, and when he had a determined goal, like this one, he felt happy and strong.

He was familiar with the railways, and dodging the ticket collector. At Goring station, his eye quickly picked out a place at the end of the platform where he could duck behind goods wagons in a siding and cross the lines without going over the bridge. Although he was large, he had had plenty of practice at becoming invisible in his old days as a look-out for the East End gangs.

A boy dangling bare feet in the high river was fishing from the boat wharf below the bridge.

Jack showed him the envelope.

'Ferry cottage?' The boy jerked his head to the left, and Jack started off on the path that ran alongside the river. Such a different river from the one he knew that idled its broad way through London, black and greasy and foul with sewage and rubbish and the bloated bodies of dead cats and dogs, and sometimes people. Here, ducks and even a pair of swans cruised on the sweet clear water between bushes and trees that trailed wet branches along the stream. There were no houses. He came at length to a solitary cottage, outside which a man was sitting in a boat, baling water out of it with a tin bowl. He was heavily bearded, but when he looked up, Jack saw that it was the doctor who had been at the Loudon Street Settlement giving steam treatment to the child called Angel. She had died too.

He got out of the boat, this man who had killed the Morleys' boy, who had killed laughing Dicky and made Madge and Bella so sad. He was saying something. Red lips moved within the beard.

Jack stood on the grass bank above him, holding a heavy piece of wood that he had picked up on the path. The man Bella called Toby threw down the bowl and stepped up towards him. He was not expecting to be hit, so when Jack swung the piece of wood it caught him on the side of the head and knocked him down. Before he could get up, Jack was on him. After a struggle, he got his hands under the man's thick cloak and, kneeling on top of him, was able to strangle him until his astonished face turned blue and purple and he stopped breathing.

Jack got up and looked around. The broad-bottomed ferryboat rocked heavily on the swollen river. Two or three ducks hurried by downstream, their feathers ruffled forward by the wind. Jack dragged the man Toby to the bank, where he pulled him upright, bent him double and threw him into the river after the ducks.

322

Toby kill Dicky. Jack kill Toby.

Sybil Crocker had been biding her time. She was waiting to see what Miss Bella would do before unloosing her powerful ammunition to best effect. When she saw that Bella was going to do nothing except drift about in a feeble kind of panic, whispering, 'Promise you won't tell!', as if the addition to the population of Bayswater would go away if it wasn't mentioned, Sybil made her move. The effect was gratifying.

'You promised not to tell!' Bella was dissolved in tears, her hair tumbling down and her big nose red as a strawberry. 'My mother is beside herself and my father is going to kill me! You promised you wouldn't ever tell.'

'I always keep my promises,' Sybil intoned high in her nose, righteous in the knowledge that Mrs Hugo Morley would not give her daughter the satisfaction of knowing that she listened to servants' gossip.

'Then how –'

'Listen, dear, your mother's got eyes, same as the rest of us. How long did you think you could hide your little secret?'

Hugo was so disturbed with rage that his wife was afraid he was going to have a stroke. Dr Foley, who was in line for a knighthood, had warned him about arterial tension. The things he said to Bella were so savagely cruel that Charlotte, in her muddled way, wanted to take Bella's side, but she was terrified to do that for fear of sending Hugo over the edge.

When he screamed at Bella, 'Out! Out! Out of my house. I wish you had never come into it!', Charlotte's first instinct was to put her arms round her daughter and lead her away. But when she moved towards Bella, Hugo shouted, 'Charlotte!' and she stopped and turned away and could not respond when Bella sobbed despairingly, 'Help me, Mother!'

Everybody in the family very quickly knew that Bella was going to have a baby. Everybody's servants knew. Hugo had forbidden it to be talked about, but that was not possible in this family.

The Morleys fancied that they were unfolding admirably into the new liberalism of the twentieth century. The patriarch, E.A.M., had pushed aside some of the Victorian taboos to create prostitutes and criminals and the riff-raff of the canals as fascinatingly human as his middle-class characters with their dark secrets and yearning aspirations. The People's Story-teller had said, 'This is how life is,' but never, 'It ought not to be like this.' His descendants, however, to whom he had given the lead, fell down at the first real challenge. They were scandalized by Bella. Even Vera and her husband, who told *risqué* jokes, could not laugh this one off.

Bella stayed away from her Uncle Leonard and Aunt Gwen because she was ashamed. Madge was the only person with whom she felt safe, because Madge treated her as if she was the same person as before, whereas everyone else, even those who tried to be charitable, behaved as if she were someone different.

'I'm afraid of my father. He would like to kill me,' Bella moaned up in Madge's room.

Instead of saying, 'No, no, of course he wouldn't,' Madge said thoughtfully, 'Yes, I expect he would. What good does

324

he think it could do to be so brutal and vicious now? It's hard to believe he is my father's brother. You couldn't find two men more different.'

'He has threatened to beat me until I tell him who the –' Bella had difficulty with the word 'baby'. 'Who its father is.'

'And you won't.'

'He can beat me insensible. I'll never tell.'

'Never tell anyone? Even your best friend? Even me?' Madge was as curious as everyone else. 'I suppose it's someone I don't know.'

Bella shook her head. 'You know him.' She longed to tell. Even though Toby was the villain now to all this family, Bella was still proud that it was she and no one else whom he had chosen for a love affair.

When she did whisper, turning her face up out of Madge's pillow, 'It's Toby,' Madge's eyes opened wide and she coloured up and drew a great breath to be angry, so Bella said quickly, 'He'll marry me, I know he will.'

'Where is he, then?'

'Abroad. He's abroad, doing medical research.'

'He'll never come back,' Madge said.

'He *will*.' Bella sat up and pleaded. 'He will come back and marry me.'

In late December, Toby's body was found farther down the river, trapped by the sodden cloak in the posts and chains of Pangbourne weir. The landlord of the Swan Inn at the side of the weir recognized him as the temporary ferryman, and he was identified as Tobias Taylor by papers found at Ferry Cottage, where a prowling, hoarse-throated brown terrier attacked the men who went into the house.

325

Jack Haynes saw the story in a news sheet by the flare of a coffee-stall lamp. He did not want to wait until the police came for him. He turned himself in with a fair degree of pride – 'Toby kill Dicky. Jack kill Toby.' – He had done the right thing. The police had some difficulty understanding him and getting him to understand them. Asked whether someone could speak for him, he wrote down Madge Morley's name and address.

When she came to the police cell and stood on the other side of the barred gate with her golden head bare and her eyes brimming, she did not ask him why he had killed the man. She said, 'Because of Dicky,' and wrote the name in the air.

Jack gave her his good grin. 'I,' he said, thumping his chest, 'did it for *you*.' He pointed at Madge through the bars and there was just room for her to take his hand.

Bella's father sent her away to a home in the country which secreted the fallen daughters of gentlefolk, at some expense, through the waiting time and confinement.

Bella did not put up any resistance. Hugo's hatred had battered her almost into a sleep-walking state. Madge came to say goodbye to her and to tell her about her visit to Jack in the police cell.

'He is not trying to hide anything, because he's quite proud of what he did, poor Jack, the only way he knew to do something for us. He did it for Dicky.'

'And because I was so unhappy,' Bella said self-centredly. 'When I met him at the house, he couldn't bear to see me so unhappy.'

Chapter Twenty-four

On New Year's Eve 1907, Madge decided to marry Guy Davidson. They were at a party together, and Madge made him stay until midnight so that they could be a part of the singing and embracing and foolish sentimental mixture of tears and laughter. They drank champagne and Guy asked her, 'What's in store for you this year, Madge?'

'I don't know.' Madge could not look far ahead. Jack's trial would be coming up in a few months. One day he and I will be in court together, Will had said, although he could not possibly have foreseen that innocent, confused Jack would be the third victim of the stupidity of Madge and her family.

'I do know,' Guy told her seriously, under the New Year noises. 'You're going to marry me.'

'I can't.'

'Why not? What else are you planning?'

'I don't know.'

'All right, then.'

It was to be a small quiet wedding. Leonard and Gwen tried very hard to be pleased about it, although Guy with his halting walk and his pale, ironic face and offhand manner was very far from the noble, chivalrous bridegroom Leonard had liked to imagine at Madge's side at a splendid reception at the Piccadilly Hotel, catered by Whiteley's.

When Madge went down to Surrey to tell Bella the

news, her cousin, self-centred as ever, said at once, 'I won't be able to be there.'

Madge showed her the unusual antique ring on her left hand. That was what you did when you were engaged. 'Are you glad for me?' she asked.

Bella answered in her unenthusiastic voice, 'You wouldn't have done it if Toby were still here.'

'What do you mean? Toby and I were never anything more than friends.'

'You would have liked to be.' Bella looked out of the window at the sad winter garden where a few girls walked with a tall, chilly-faced custodian. Then she put on a small self-satisfied smile and said, 'But he chose me, didn't he?'

Poor Bella, in this hideously furnished house, scrubbed and polished within an inch of its cheerless life, carrying a baby she seemed not to imagine ever being a separate physical reality, and deluding herself that Toby had loved her.

In one way, Madge thought drearily, as she walked down the drive to get the station bus, Bella was better off with Toby dead, and only the stuff of dreams.

After Madge had married and gone to live with Guy at his rooms in Brook Street until the house that was being decorated for them was ready, Leonard and Gwen both felt older than they were.

During the critical time after William Whiteley's murder last year, when Leonard did not know whether his job was secure, they had enjoyed a resurgence of their love life. Since Dicky's death, they had only held each other in bed for comfort and courage. They had never in their married lives talked about sex; they had only enjoyed it and exchanged secret glances the next morning. Does sex peter out in your fifties? Leonard wanted to ask Gwen. Is it like that for everyone?

One night, they had been to dinner with Austin and Elizabeth, and Madge had been there with Guy. Elizabeth was a charming little hostess and quietly funny. Austin was noisy and cheerful, and Guy had been so friendly and agreeable that his parents-in-law sat down with the wine decanter when they got home and stayed up late to talk contentedly about Austin's good marriage, and Madge's honest, refreshing influence which might after all transform the war-embittered soldier.

Daydreaming thus, hungry for happiness again, they drank more wine than usual, and finished up rediscovering each other in the big soft bed.

Sex did not peter out in your fifties, thank God. Leonard felt younger, walking briskly down Westbourne Grove the next morning, with a muffler over his chin against the east wind.

William and Frank Whiteley, who, although in their thirties, were always known as Young Mr William and Young Mr Frank, had acquired a good grasp of the business during the last year. They were making active plans to redesign the whole complex of connecting departments into one mammoth emporium with an imposing entrance in Queen's Road. They showed Leonard some architect's designs. Pillars, massive white stone facing, broad plate-glass windows, galleried levels round the sweeping curves of a pearly marble staircase such as had never been seen in a public building in London. Over all, a high glass dome would spread light on to the splendid marble staircase and ground-floor halls where customers would move in space and radiance.

'We'd like to be ready to open about 1911. The old order changeth, eh?' Mr William watched Leonard's face.

'To something a bit too pretentious for me,' Leonard admitted. 'Perhaps it will be my cue to retire.'

This would relieve the minds of the young gentlemen, if they were wondering how they would ever get rid of 'Our Mr Morley'. But they said at once, 'Don't you dare!', which pleased him, whether they meant it or not.

The cold weeks of chests and chilblains crawled on with the perennial slowness of February and March. In the servants' hall at Ladbroke Lodge and the kitchen at No. 72 Chepstow Villas, they continued to talk about Bella and her condition. It was not worth letting the subject drop, because before you knew it, that poor baby would get itself born, with the subsequent to-do of what would be done with it. Bella had talked wildly about keeping it, but the general opinion was that it would be discreetly adopted and never seen again.

'Shocking, innit, poor little mite,' Mrs Roach droned in the wicker chair during the dark afternoons before it was time to start dinner. 'I'm quite shocked.'

'You must be,' Flora answered, although she privately knew that the death of the cook's sister in childbirth was a fiction, like the sister herself. It was Mrs Roach who had once read Russian romances, and Tatiana was actually her daughter. She had kept it dark in order to ensure a roof over their heads.

Flora was glad when Madge came back to Chepstow

Villas to visit, and they could talk freely as they used to, although Madge was now supposed to have the dignity of a married woman. She could not see her parents as often as she would like, because Guy had not been well and she was busy, but Flora guessed that, poorly or not, that dot-and-carry husband of hers would be the type to be jealous of her family attachments.

'I have to do more nursing than I expected,' Madge said when she and Flora met at the Express Dairies teashop in Notting Hill Gate, because Flora wanted to get out of the house on her afternoon off. 'One of his old leg wounds has gone septic again. I haven't been able to go to the Settlement for a while.'

'If ever.' Flora wiped cream off her chin. They were working their way through a plate of gateaux.

'I'll have to see how he is. Do you know what his mother told me, Flora? At the wedding, she said it. She said the doctors didn't expect him to live very long.'

'What wicked rubbish!'

'I know. But he's not very sensible about his health. Sometimes he'll stay in bed for nothing and want me to wait on him hand and foot. Sometimes he insists on going out with his cane when he's weak and exhausted and can hardly stand up, and shouts at me for trying to "baby" him.'

Ah, men! It did not need saying.

'I do love him, Flo.' Madge leaned forward anxiously. 'You know that, don't you? But when he's feeling rotten and being difficult, he – well, he drinks too much, you know.'

'Oh lor',' Flora said. 'What's wrong with these men of ours? What's wrong with us, Madge, that makes us pick

331

'em?' The words 'sacrifice ourselves' were in Flora's head, but she would not use them to Madge, although she did think that was what Madge had done, as she had herself, barmily, for Bull Bolt.

The waitress brought more hot water and Flora poured them another cup and said in a low voice, because there were domestic spies in Notting Hill Gate as well as everywhere else, 'Shall I tell you something disgusting?'

'Of course.' Madge tilted her head into her hand to listen. Her short gold hair had lost some of its brilliance. Her eyes were lightly shadowed now, in a thinner face.

'Well, you know when Bill come in through my window and cut me up?' Madge nodded. 'I'd invited him.' There, it was said. What a relief. And Madge had not changed her expression. 'He'd been sneaking in a bit regular. Remember that night when you lost your key? That give me the idea. But Tat had said she thought she'd heard a noise, and then you was all coming back from the country, so I said to him not to visit no more. That was why he cut me. He always carried a knife, you see.'

'Poor Flo.'

'Stupid Flo.'

'Would you ever go back to him?' Madge asked. She knew about the kind of perverse, wayward love that didn't get you anything much but trouble.

'I'm daft enough. Good thing, I suppose, that I don't know where he is.'

In May, at the home for wayward girls, Bella gave birth to a small, neat baby boy with thin dark hair and eyes like boot buttons.

Would she keep him or let him go? 'Life is very difficult for the upper classes,' Flora observed. 'If it was our Violet now – and I wouldn't put it past her, the way she's carrying on – my mother would bring up the poor little fellow like her own. But Madam Muck – can you see her!'

Charlotte had no intention of even going to Surrey to see her new grandson. Gwen and Madge went down when he was about a week old, with Helen Pope, who was fond of Bella, and anxious for any new experience.

They found Bella alone with her son in a small room kept for mothers with babies. It was sparsely furnished with a bed, an undraped bassinet, a wash-stand and slop bucket and a nursing chair and footstool. An improving print hung over the small stingy grate. 'The coal scuttle is rather small,' Gwen said.

'At least it's there.' Bella held the baby awkwardly against her shoulder. 'Before your baby is born, you don't get a fire in your bedroom unless you're ill.'

They all took turns to hold the small, passive baby, who turned his beady eyes from one to the other, as if he could already focus. Who did he look like? Bella had insisted that the father was nobody the family knew, but Gwen and Helen could not help speculating on the straight black hair (not sandy Gerald Lazenby, obviously), the bright round eyes. Madge thought to herself that she caught something of Toby in him, but that was only because she knew.

'What was it like,' Helen asked, avid with curiosity, 'him being born?'

'Dreadful.' Bella took the baby from her quickly and rocked him in her arms, with a softer, more comfortable expression on her face than any of them had ever seen.

'Oh, Bella.' Madge felt very touched. 'How can you bear to part with him?'

'I'm going to keep him.'

'But your parents –' Gwen began uncertainly.

'He's not their baby. He's mine.'

'Good for you.' Madge kissed her. They all showed that they were glad, and promised her help and support. Bella was pleased to have done something right.

She gave them a tour of the austere mid-Victorian house, carrying the child wrapped up in the soft blue shawl Gwen had brought from Whiteley's Babywear. A custodian with keys on a thong round her neck stopped her in the corridor.

'Come, come, Mrs Morley.' You were called 'Mrs' after your baby was born; before that, your pregnancy was disregarded, except by the issue of roomier smocks. 'You know baby is supposed to be down in his cradle at this time.'

'I can't leave him in the room alone.'

'Why not? He's got to learn.'

'He's asleep anyway,' Helen told the woman, 'so what is the difference?'

'That shawl will have to be washed before it is used.' The woman trod away in heavy black shoes like a nun.

They saw the sewing room and the dining hall and the sitting room where a small group of young women in identical smocks quickly gathered up cards as the door opened.

'Oh, it's only you.' They clamoured round Bella's baby, who woke up and let himself be petted. Their own would be taken away and put to a wet nurse as soon as they were born.

'Why?' Madge asked outside the room.

'They are told it's for the child's own good,' Bella said, 'and most of them are such ninnies, they believe it.'

'Baby farming.' Helen looked fiercely at an aproned custodian who crossed the hall with a tight grip on the arm of a weeping girl. 'This place is loathsome. I'm going to write about it and expose it.'

Helen had recently written a newspaper piece about the scandal of worn-out old horses shipped live to Belgium for slaughter. A newspaper had printed it, and she was now hell-bent on saving the world through journalism.

She was still giving off puffs of outrage as they left Bella and went out to where the Popes' chauffeur waited with the car.

'I didn't think the place was so very bad,' Gwen said placatingly.

'Not very bad! It's a disgrace.'

'Well.' Gwen leaned forward to shut the sliding glass between them and the driver. 'Those girls did get themselves into trouble, after all.'

'The men did nothing?' Madge and Helen rounded on her. 'Why should they get away with it?'

'Now, Madge,' Gwen said, 'that's not the kind of talk for a married woman.'

'It's married women who *do* talk like that,' Madge said, and Helen added, 'The last protest meeting I went to, where a woman was lashing about with a whip, I felt pathetically young. Most of the suffragist women now are married, Aunt Gwen.'

'Then they should have something better to do.' Gwen Morley had never cared for the Suffragettes.

335

'The only reason my mother would like to have the vote,' Madge told Helen, 'would be so that she could refuse to use it.'

The few babies who were not farmed out by the home were christened as soon as possible, in case their feckless mothers neglected this duty later. Bella had caused her child to be christened Hugo, in a last hopeless attempt to please her father.

'He'll not allow it,' Charlotte said.

'It's the child's legal name, Mother.'

'Well, call him something else with the same initial. Why not Howard? Quite a respectable name.'

Bella shrugged. She did not tell her mother, or anyone, that she had given her son the middle name of Tobias.

Charlotte, disguised by a heavy veil, had visited the new little family in Maida Vale, where she had set Bella up in an inconspicuous house, with a cook-general and a nurse-maid. She came once more, without telling her husband, but not again after that.

Bella was barred from Ladbroke Lodge, with or without little Howard, but they were both always welcome at No. 72 Chepstow Villas. Sometimes she would leave the nurse-maid there with the baby while she went shopping or paid a visit to Madge. Flora heard her say to her aunt Gwen, 'It's nice for you to have a little one about,' and was furious that any member of this family, even gormless Bella, could be so stupid.

In the summer, Bella took up with the kind of man with whom she would never have made friends, hardly even spoken to, in the old days. Dominick Owles, several years older, was a master builder, a man who had done well in his profession and thought himself the equal of Bella Morley, so-called widow of an unspecified victim of tuberculosis. He and his men were working on a house three doors down from Bella's. He had always lived at home, and never seriously courted. He fell genuinely in love with Bella. That was the important point that people overlooked when they were offended by her being involved with someone so common. In her twenty-sixth year, Dominick Owles was the first man who had ever loved Bella.

Dominick had been brought up in a narrowly religious style. His attachment to Bella Morley could just about condone her past – although he sometimes saw her as a charity case and admired his own nobility – but could not extend to the baby. He would not dandle, smile or coo. If he looked at Howard, it was with a serious face, and Howard stared back at him. On the nurse's half day when Bella looked after the child, Owles did not like taking second place. He sometimes spoke rather pompously to Bella about becoming her husband, but not of becoming the stepfather of Howard, to whom he referred righteously as 'another man's child'. The nursemaid began to find herself robbed of some of her time off. Since her young man was, in his impetuous way, also rather demanding, the occasional coin palmed to her by Dominick Owles did not quite compensate.

Chapter Twenty-five

There was no Morley Regatta on the river Thames this year, but Leonard's summer holiday from Whiteley's came round as usual, and he and Gwen took a house in the country for three weeks, because that was what they had always done.

'Life must go on,' people told each other, and Gwen tried not to answer, 'Why?' Eight months after Dicky's death, the family was out of mourning, and she was supposed, by those who did not know her well, to be 'all right' again.

Austin brought his family to Sussex. Madge and Guy were too busy moving into their new house.

'Or is that his excuse?' Teddie wondered.

She came with Greg and Sophie, who had grown into such a normal young girl that it seemed a waste of time to have got so worked up about her short flirtation with neurasthenia. She was already informally engaged to a very suitable young man of good family and substance, which allowed Aunt Teddie to queen it a bit over her sister and sister-in-law, whose daughters were less satisfactory.

Madge . . . oh well, Madge had made her bed and must lie in it, although it was questionable, Aunt Teddie hinted, with the prurience of the unsexual, whether the poor crippled man could actually . . . as it were . . . 'Excuse me.' A clearing of the throat like sandpaper on rust.

Teddie might be quite disappointed when she learned that Madge was adding on a nursery to the new house at the top of Putney Hill. It was a modern stucco bungalow with the rooms all on one floor for Guy's convenience, and a garden that led on to the Heath. Guy was working with a fund for disabled servicemen, helping to raise money, and goad the Government. The office was not far from the new house, in a nursing home for ex-officers, where he himself could get treatment if he needed it.

By September, Bella had become quite rattled by the demands of a four-month-old baby with a chronic rash and the unreasonable attitude of her 'Dommie' Owles, and decided that she could no longer be expected to cope with a life that seemed to her unfairly irksome. She closed up the Maida Vale house and moved into No. 72 Chepstow Villas with the baby.

Hugo stayed away from his brother's house. Charlotte walked down from Ladbroke Lodge in one of her best hats. She was embarrassed with Gwen and Leonard, not knowing whether to be disapproving or grateful. She criticized the nursemaid, and the baby for persisting with his rash, and started a terrible quarrel with Bella, which shook the house.

When the nursemaid failed to come back after a Sunday off, Gwen cajoled out of retirement the old nanny who had looked after Austin and Madge and then Dicky, until he grew too old for her.

Nanny Morley talked incessantly about Dicky, which released in Gwen a secondary state of weeping that frightened Leonard. He thought Gwen must have cried enough, until he saw that these tears, with comfortable old Nanny to cluck, 'There, there, don't take on so,' were a natural washing away of some more of the pent-up grief.

Gwen became drier and brisker. There was more for her to do, with Bella and Howard and Nanny in the house. She began to take Laura down the Portobello Road on Saturdays and to stroll with Bella and the perambulator along Westbourne Grove to Whiteley's food halls, instead of letting Mrs Roach give the orders at the back door.

She was on the telephone again to Vera every morning at nine-thirty, leaning against the coats in the hall, absorbedly chatting back and forth about nothing.

How had women filled their mornings before Alexander Graham Bell empowered them? Leonard had been unsure whether the craze would last, but more and more business was done over the wires, and Whiteley's were selling domestic phones from America in curious and ornate designs as fast as they could be shipped across the Atlantic.

In early October, Bella took off. She told Uncle Leonard and Aunt Gwen that she was going back to Dominick Owles to make her life with him. They said, 'No, no, you can't do that, Bella, you have a child now. You're not a free agent.' But she went anyway, leaving Howard behind.

Charlotte told Gwen, on Hugo's orders, 'You can't possibly keep that child.'

'Will you take him, then?' Gwen asked pertly.

Charlotte did her imitation of a cock pheasant surprised out of a hedge.

'Calm down,' Leonard said. 'We'll do what we think best.'

'But you *can't*!' Charlotte stamped her foot. She obviously did not want to go back to Ladbroke Lodge and tell Hugo, 'They're holding on to that baby.'

'Bella will be back soon, I'm sure,' Gwen said. 'We're just looking after Howard until then.'

The little boy was thriving. Bella had become tired of breast-feeding him after the first few weeks, and Nanny was now varying the Mellin's Food with broth and groats and coddled eggs. He grizzled less as his stubborn rash at last began to fade. Nanny had accused it of being 'Maida Vale rash, bound to clear up when you get him out of that damp valley', although most of Maida Vale was on the side of a hill. And Vera had brought in a jar of chamomile cream that Toby had given her last summer for the painful sunburn with which Henrietta had returned from an ill-advised trip to the Italian lakes.

'Did Toby Taylor give you this?' Gwen asked suspiciously.

Vera hedged, but the label on the jar bore the name of the man in Wales who had supplied The Clinique.

'Take it away.'

'No, it might work. Why deprive poor little Howard?'

Gwen bit her lip, her knuckles clenched white on her skirt.

'It's not the baby's fault,' Vera said gently, and she took the cream up to the nursery.

Soon, there would be another addition to the family. Austin's wife Elizabeth was expecting her third child in another few weeks.

Laura had resented her brother John, but she was not bothered this time by the idea of another baby. She had become too settled in her new independent, boyish ways. After she was able to come to No. 72 again without hanging back and shivering and being sick, she played different games there. No more lead soldier shooting the penny into the blackamoor's mouth. No more dancing to the piano, or cut-out paper dolls with her grandmother. She wanted to play with Dicky's trains and puff billiards game. But when she came down with an armful of rails and began to fit them together on the floor by the drawing-room window, Gwen dropped her book and took off her spectacles, and Laura saw that she was crying again.

'What's the matter, Grandma?'

'Dicky's trains . . . Oh, Laura, I can't bear it!'

'Will it always be like this?' Laura asked Austin. 'Will I always have to live in the shadow of my cousin's death?'

Shocked by the dramatic maturity of this, Austin took refuge in a diversion. 'Dicky wasn't your cousin, you know. He was your uncle.'

'Wasn't! He was only a bit older than me.'

'Yes, and soon you'll be the same age as Dicky was when he left us. You could – look, Laura, you could, in a way, live his life for him.'

Austin knew he did not always say the right thing, but this was inspired. It gave Laura leave to be boyish when she wanted, and Austin began to do more things with her that he would do with a son. He helped her to dig her own plot in their narrow back garden, he took her to the races, and arranged with Madge for riding lessons on Putney Heath. Leonard had been persuaded to start stump cricket again in the backyard of No. 72 and Austin was working on his father to let Laura be the first girl to be allowed to play.

Since the ceremony of throwing the wreath on the river, Leonard, who was drawn to symbolic expression, had thought a lot about some more permanent token of remembrance. When the acute pain of grief began to recede, he was frightened of losing the memory of his young son.

Photographs, which were all over the house, were necessary, but they had been taken when Dicky was alive, at various ages. The same urge to do something for him *now* that had sent Leonard out in a boat to the water-meadows last November sent him to talk to a stonemason who worked for Whiteley's funeral department.

The mason had carved a beautifully simple memorial plaque, a wreath of laurel surrounding the relief of a young boy's head above Dicky's name and dates. Leonard had hung the plaque on the brown brick wall that was the back of the mews houses at the end of the yard.

Gwen came back from the Portobello Road market one Saturday with one of Dicky's ruffianly friends, the hedgehog-haired urchin called Noah, who had accosted her perkily when she was buying bananas. She gave him one, and took him home to see his friend's memorial.

Noah stood in front of it, frowning and biting his thumb. He looked at Gwen's corner flower beds and asked Leonard hoarsely, 'Is 'e buried 'ere, then?'

At one of the season's last cricket games, young Mr Frank Whiteley, who was in the habit of walking up from Porchester Terrace on Sunday mornings, swung his bat and hit the tennis ball against the plaque. He was horrified. He apologized embarrassedly, but Austin said, 'No, it's all right, sir. It's quite difficult to hit, so my father and I decided that it scores a six.'

The symbol of loss had been suitably incorporated into the mythology of No. 72 Chepstow Villas.

In the afternoon, Madge and Guy made the long train journey from Putney Bridge and turned up unexpectedly. Leonard and Gwen and Austin and Elizabeth and the children were finishing a late lunch. Flora brought up extra cheese and fruit plates, and Madge and Guy sat down, looking a little tense. They had obviously come to say something serious.

When Flora went out with her loaded tray, Madge said rather nervously to her father, 'I've got to tell you something.'

'What? What?' Laura clamoured, sensing drama.

'Come along.' Elizabeth raised her eyebrows at Madge, who nodded, so she lifted John from the high chair that had been every child's from Leonard on down, and took the children up to the nursery. Laura could be heard protesting and kicking the stair rods. Austin shut the dining-room door.

Madge was silent for a moment, her gaze resting on the faces of her mother and father.

'Go on, then,' Guy said in his abrupt voice, which he did not realize still bore traces of his enemy, the military. 'Say what you've come to say.'

'I have had a letter from Bella.'

'Oh – where is she?' Gwen asked.

'She seems to be somewhere in Hertfordshire, where Owles is working on extensions to the Garden City. No, wait, Mother.' She saw that Gwen was full of questions. 'Let me tell you this. I'm afraid it may be' – she looked at Guy – 'rather difficult for you.'

Her father reached across the corner of the table and took Gwen's hand.

'She sent me some papers,' Madge went on, 'about the baby. His baptismal certificate, some notes from a doctor and the matron of the home, that sort of thing.'

'But why?' Gwen frowned. 'You mean, she's not coming back?'

'I don't know. She said I was to give the papers to you, not to her parents.'

'Hugo would burn 'em,' Leonard said.

'There is a birth certificate, which will be a shock.' Madge watched their faces. 'I did know, about the father. Bella had told me before he was born; but I wasn't going to tell you.'

Gwen put her hand to her mouth. Leonard said, 'Oh my God.'

Madge nodded, and Guy cut in, 'She registered the baby as Hugo Tobias Taylor.'

Later, Austin sent his wife and children home in a cab, but stayed to talk with the family at No. 72.

'And suppose Bella never does come back,' he asked his mother, 'would you still want to keep the baby?'

'I don't know. Would we, Leo?' Gwen turned to him, as she still did, from the habit of making him feel he had all the answers. 'Today, after Madge had told us, I tried to see if I could recognize the devil in him. He looked the same. Placid. Adorable. But suppose he grew up to look like . . . ? I would never be able to forget. And I try so hard to remember not to let myself remember that moment in the study. Mr Brett, the surgeon, was halfway out of the door. I don't want to have to go back and back and always hear him saying, "I think he may have killed your son."'

Flora had not taken her afternoon off, because she knew that something was up. When she brought the tray with the hot-water kettle for Madam to make tea in the drawing room, her heart ached for the sadness there. She could have cut it like butter.

345

Surprisingly, it was Guy who dared to say, when he and Madge got up to leave, 'Last year, you could have killed that Taylor fellow yourselves, if poor Jack Haynes hadn't done it for you. Am I right?' When he threw out those brusque challenges, it was a statement, not a question. 'None of my business, I know, but Madge has told me how much you all did love him.'

'That makes it worse,' Leonard said, 'doesn't it, Gwen? We feel guilty that we did. But I still can't hate him.'

'Good,' Guy said cheerfully, resting on his cane, leaning a hip against the sofa back, 'because that wouldn't do you any good.'

'The man was an impostor and a quack,' Austin said bitterly.

'But he did help quite a lot of people, didn't he? What is a quack, after all? A dedicated amateur? A faith healer?'

The family watched him cautiously. Was it perhaps all right, then, to let themselves remember that Toby had, after all, believed in what he did?

'I hate the domineering medical profession – with good reason.' Guy gave his sardonic smile. 'I don't like quacks much either, but they do at least recognize the right of an Englishman to go to hell in his own way.' With Guy, you did not always know if he was making a joke, and if he was, you could not always see it. 'Come on, Madge, it's getting dark.'

'No.' Gwen reached out a hand. 'What else?' she asked softly.

'I've said too much.' Guy left the room, abruptly, as he often did, without saying goodbye.

After the immemorial Sunday supper of sardines, cold

346

meat and beetroot salad, Austin stayed late talking to his father.

'That cranky fellow is right, damn him,' Leonard said. 'I did love Toby. He was one of us. I –' His face crumpled. 'I miss him. Oh, Austin, son, forgive me. Oh, God, I wish he hadn't died! So horrible . . . so horrible . . .'

Because his father wept, and groaned as if he were in pain, Austin could not go home. He stayed in Dicky's little front bedroom that had once been his own. Unable to sleep, he lay awake, disturbed by the old unchanged experiences of the boy he had been. Creaks from the landing, as it relaxed its sinews, his parents' low voices in the next room. Running water and the clank and rumble from the cistern overhead. His father throwing open the bathroom window to let the steam out and the cold air in for the next comer. The gas lamp outside the window, hatched by plane-tree branches. The public houses were closed on Sundays, but after St Peter's clock struck midnight, a few desultory drunks from somewhere came bawling down the Portobello Road.

In the morning, his father was dressed and brisk, impeccable for Whiteley's, no emotion, no trace of the agonizing tears. Austin still felt heavy-hearted from the night before. He could actually feel the weight of his heart in his chest.

Outside the front door, he and his father shook hands politely.

'Dad.' Austin wanted to reach again the vulnerable man within the 'Our Mr Morley' exterior, already prepared for the street and the Monday morning store. 'What will –' He fumbled for the right words, and came out with a childish, 'What will ever make it all right?'

347

'This family,' his father said. 'This house.'

Then he settled his top hat and went down the hearth-stoned steps, clanged the front gate and turned briskly left down Chepstow Villas.